## DATE DUE

| | | | |
|---|---|---|---|
| MR 2 0 '08 | | | |
| AP 2 | | | |
| AP - 8 | | | |
| MY 7 2 '08 | | | |
| | | | |
| 03/20/10 | | | |
| 4/28/10 | | | |
| | | | |
| | | | |
| | | | |
| | | | |
| | | | |
| | | | |
| | | | |
| | | | |
| | | | |
| | | | |

DEMCO 38-297

# CONSPIRACY GAME

This Large Print Book carries the
Seal of Approval of N.A.V.H.

# CONSPIRACY GAME

## CHRISTINE FEEHAN

**THORNDIKE PRESS**

*An imprint of Thomson Gale, a part of The Thomson Corporation*

Detroit • New York • San Francisco • New Haven, Conn. • Waterville, Maine • London

# THOMSON
## GALE
™

Thorndike Press® Large Print Core.

The text of this Large Print edition is unabridged.

Other aspects of the book may vary from the original edition.

Set in 16 pt. Plantin.

**LIBRARY OF CONGRESS CATALOGING-IN-PUBLICATION DATA**

Feehan, Christine.
    Conspiracy game / by Christine Feehan.
      p. cm.
    ISBN-13: 978-0-7862-9447-3 (hardcover : alk. paper)
    ISBN-10: 0-7862-9447-7 (hardcover : alk. paper)
    1. Women circus performers — Fiction. 2. Psychic ability — Fiction.
  3. Telepathy — Fiction. 4. Africa — Fiction. 5. Large type books. I. Title.
  PS3606.E36C66 2007
  813'.54—dc22                                      2006103025

Published in 2007 by arrangement with The Berkley Publishing Group, a member of Penguin Group (USA) Inc.

Printed in the United States of America on permanent paper
10 9 8 7 6 5 4 3 2 1

nox noctis est nostri

# The GhostWalker Symbol Details

**SIGNIFIES**
shadow

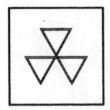

**SIGNIFIES**
protection against
evil forces

**SIGNIFIES**
the Greek letter *psi*, which
is used by parapsychology
researchers to signify ESP or
other psychic abilities

**SIGNIFIES**
qualities of a knight—
loyalty, generosity,
courage, and honor

**SIGNIFIES**
shadow knights who protect
against evil forces using
psychic powers, courage,
and honor

For Cindy Hwang and Steve Axelrod, who believed in me enough to take a chance on the Game books — thank you.

# FOR MY READERS

Be sure to write to Christine at Christine@christinefeehan.com to get a FREE exclusive screen saver and join the PRIVATE e-mail list to receive an announcement when Christine's books are released.

# ACKNOWLEDGMENTS

I want to thank Domini Stottsberry for her help in the tremendous amount of research necessary to make this book possible. Brian Feehan and Morey Sparks deserve much gratitude for sitting up nights discussing military tactics, and I'd be remiss in not mentioning my husband, Richard, who must sit with endless patience as I describe action scenes and insist on his input! As always, Cheryl, you are incredible!

# THE GHOSTWALKER CREED

We are the GhostWalkers, we live in the
    shadows
The sea, the earth, and the air are our
    domain
No fallen comrade will be left behind
We are loyalty and honor bound
We are invisible to our enemies and we
    destroy them where we find them
We believe in justice and we protect our
    country and those unable to protect
    themselves
What goes unseen, unheard, and unknown
    are GhostWalkers
There is honor in the shadows and it is us
We move in complete silence whether in
    jungle or desert
We walk among our enemy unseen and
    unheard
Striking without sound and scatter to the
    winds before they have knowledge of

our existence
We gather information and wait with endless patience for that perfect moment to
deliver swift justice
We are both merciful and merciless
We are relentless and implacable in our
resolve
We are the GhostWalkers and the night is
ours

# CHAPTER 1

Night fell fast in the jungle. Sitting in the middle of the enemy camp, surrounded by rebels, Jack Norton kept his head down, eyes closed, listening to the sounds coming out of the rain forest as he took stock of his situation. With his enhanced senses he could smell the enemy close to him, and even farther away, hidden in the dense, lush vegetation. He was fairly certain this was a satellite camp, one of many deep in the jungles of the Democratic Republic of the Congo, somewhere west of Kinshasa.

He opened his eyes to narrow slits to look around him, to plan out each step of his escape, but even that tiny movement sent pain shooting through his skull. The agony from the last beating was nearly shattering, but he didn't dare lose consciousness. They would kill him next time, and next time was coming much quicker than he had antici-pated. If he didn't find a way out soon, all the physical and psychic enhancements in the world wouldn't save him.

The rebels had every right to be angry with him. Jack's twin brother, Ken, and his paramilitary GhostWalker team had successfully extracted the rebels' first truly valuable American political prisoners. A United States senator had been captured while traveling with a scientist and his aides. The GhostWalkers had come in with deadly precision, rescued the senator, the scientist, and his two aides along with the pilot, and left the camp in shambles. Ken had been captured and the rebels had had a field day torturing him. Jack had no choice but to go in after his brother.

The rebels weren't any happier with Jack for depriving them of their prisoner then they had been with Ken. Jack had laid down the covering fire as the GhostWalkers were extracting Ken and had taken a hit. The wound wasn't critical — he'd been testing his leg and it wasn't broken — but the bullet had driven his leg out from under him on impact. He'd waved his team off and resigned himself to the same torture his brother had endured — one more thing they shared as they had in their younger days.

The first beating hadn't been so bad — before Major Biyoya showed up. They'd kicked and punched him, stomping on his wounded leg a couple of times, but for the most part, they'd refrained from torturing him, waiting to find out what General Ekabela had in mind. The general had sent Biyoya.

The majority of the rebels were military trained, and many had at one time been of high rank in the government or military, until one of the many coups, and now they were growing marijuana and wreaking havoc, raiding smaller towns and killing everyone who dared to oppose them or had the farms or land the rebels wanted. No one dared cross into their territory without permission. They were skilled with weapons and in guerrilla warfare — and they liked to torture and kill. They had a taste for it now, and the power drove them to continue. Even the UN avoided the area — if they did try to bring medicine and supplies to the villages, the rebels robbed them.

Jack opened his eyes enough to look down at his bare chest where Major Keon Biyoya had carved his name. Blood dripped, and flies and other biting insects congregated for the feast. It wasn't the worst of the tortures by any means, or the most humiliating. He had endured it stoically, removing himself from the pain as he had all of his life, but the fire of retribution burned in his belly.

Rage ran cold and deep, like a turbulent river hidden beneath the calm surface of his expressionless face. The dangerous emotion poured through his body and flooded his veins, building his adrenaline and strength. He deliberately fed it, recounting every detail of the last interrogation session with Biyoya. The cigarette burns, small circles marring his chest and shoulders. The whip marks that had peeled the skin from his back. Biyoya had taken his time carving his name deep, and when Jack made no sound, he'd hooked up battery cables to shock him — and that had been only the beginning of several hours at the hands of a twisted madman. The precise, almost surgical, two-inch cuts covering nearly every inch of his body were identical to what this man had done to his brother — and with each slice, Jack felt his brother's pain, when he could push away his own.

Jack tasted the rage in his mouth. With infinite slowness, he eased his hands to the seam of his camouflage pants, fingertips seeking the minute end of the thin wire sewn there. He began to draw it out with a smooth, practiced motion, his brain working all the while with icy precision, calculating distances to weapons, planning each step to get him into the foliage of the jungle. Once there, he was certain of his ability to elude his captors, but he first had to cover bare ground and get through a dozen trained soldiers. The one and only thing he knew, without a shadow of a doubt, was that Major Keon Biyoya was a walking dead man.

Two soldiers tramped through the camp toward him. Jack felt the coil inside of him winding tighter and tighter. It was now or never. His hands were tied in front of him, but his captors had been careless, leaving his feet free after the last torture session, believing him incapacitated. Biyoya had smashed the butt of a rifle into the wound on his leg several times, angry that Jack had given no response. Jack had learned at a very young age never to make a sound, to go somewhere far away in his head and separate mind from body, but men like Biyoya couldn't conceive of that possibility. Some men didn't, *couldn't* break, even with drugs in their system and pain wracking their bodies.

A hand bunched in Jack's hair and yanked hard to bring his head up. Ice-cold water splashed in his face, ran down his chest into the wounds. The second soldier rubbed a paste of salt and burning leaves into the wounds as both laughed.

"Major wants his name to show up nice and pretty," one said tauntingly in his native tongue. He leaned down to peer into Jack's eyes.

He must have seen death there — the cold rage and icy determination. He gasped, but was a heartbeat too slow in trying to jerk away. Jack moved fast, a speeding blur of his hands as he looped thin wire around the rebel's neck, dragging him backward off balance, using him as a shield as the other soldier jerked up his gun and fired. The bullet slammed into the first rebel and drove Jack back.

Chaos erupted in the camp, men scattering for cover and firing toward the jungle, confused as to where the shooting was coming from. Jack had only seconds to make his way to cover. Pulling a knife from the waistband of the rebel, he stabbed the dying soldier in the lung and turned the blade to the ropes binding him, still holding the soldier as a shield. Jack threw the knife with deadly accuracy, drilling the rebel with the gun through the throat. Dropping the dead body, Jack ran.

He zigzagged his way across the open ground, kicking logs out of the fire pit, sending them scattering in all directions, deliberately running through the soldiers so that anyone firing at him would chance hitting one of their own. He ran at one soldier, slamming his fist into the man's throat with one hand and relieving him of his weapon with the other. He leapt over the body and kept running, ducking into a group of five men scrambling to their feet. Jack kicked one in the knee, dropping him hard, wrenching the machete from his hand and delivering a killing blow before whirling through the other four, slicing with an expertise born of long experience and sheer desperation.

Shouts and bullets rang through the jungle so that birds rose from the treetops, screeching into the air. Screams of the wounded mingled with the desperate sounds of angry leaders shouting to establish order. A soldier rose up in front of Jack, sweeping the area with an assault rifle. Jack hit the ground and somersaulted, lashing out with his foot, taking the man to the ground, ripping the rifle out of his hands, and using his enhanced strength, delivering a killing blow with the butt of the gun. He slung the weapons around his neck to leave his hands free and snagged a long knife and another rifle as he raced toward the cover of the jungle. The soldier had inadvertently provided him with covering fire, shooting several of his fellow rebels.

Jack dove for the thickest foliage nearest him, somersaulting into the leafy ferns, and ran at a low crouch along the narrow trail made by some small animal. Bullets rained around him, one or two coming too close for comfort. He kept moving fast into deeper jungle where the light barely penetrated the thick canopy. He was a Ghost-Walker and the shadows welcomed him.

The rain forest was made up of several layers. At the emergent level, trees grew as high as two hundred and seventy feet. The canopy was about sixty to ninety feet above him, where most of the birds and wildlife resided. Mosses, lichen, and orchids covered the trunks and branches. Snakelike vines dropped like tentacles. Palms, philodendrons, and ferns reached out with large leaves to provide even more cover. The understory saw very little sunlight and was dark and humid — perfect for what he needed.

Once into the darker areas, he blended into the foliage, the stripes and patterns of the jungle covering his skin, from his face down his neck, his chest, and arms. His specially designed camouflage pants picked up the colors surrounding him and reflected them back so he virtually disappeared into the vegetation, as if the jungle had eaten him.

Jack leapt into the trees, using low-lying branches, climbing swiftly up to the crotch of a tall evergreen tree that was particularly heavy with foliage. From his view, he could easily see the forest floor. It looked bare, but he knew it was teeming with insects, like a living carpet over the poor soil. He waited, knowing the rebels would come swarming through the jungle. Major Biyoya would be furious that Jack had escaped. Biyoya would have to answer to the general, and General Ekabela wasn't known to treat kindly anyone failing him.

Shouted curses and orders, anger and fear in the voices, drifted with the smoke through the trees. Jack hoped one of the burning logs he'd kicked out of the fire pit had set on fire the small leaf-covered hut the major liked to use.

Jack took stock of his weapons. He had two assault rifles with limited ammunition, a machete, and two knives, and sewn into his pants were several garrotes. More than guns and knives, Jack had his psychic and physical enhancements, products of experimentation enabling him to become a member of the covert GhostWalker team.

Around him, the heavy foliage kept him hidden and the vines enabled fast travel up and down the trees should he need it. The sound of the rain was a steady companion, but the heavy drops barely penetrated the thick canopy above him. The moisture that did touch him helped to ease the oppressive heat.

The soldiers entered the jungle in a standard search pattern, the men spaced no more than four feet apart, but spread out to cover a wide area. That told him the major was on scene and directing his men, establishing order in the midst of chaos. Jack hunkered down, rifle in his arms, and watched the rebels emerging through the broad, leafy plants and giant ferns. They thought they were quiet, but he heard the steady gasp of breath as air moved through their lungs. Even without that, he would still have spotted them easily. To his GhostWalker-enhanced vision, the yellow and red heat waves of their bodies glowed neon bright against the cooler jungle foliage. He smelled the excitement oozing from their pores. It should have been fear. They knew they were going into the jungle after a wounded predator and that he would be hunting them, but they had no way of knowing what kind of man he was.

Jack had moved fast across the bare ground of the camp, but once under cover of the shadows, he was certain he'd hidden his tracks. He'd been careful not to disturb the plants on the trees as he'd gone up, leaping most of the way, landing lightly on the balls of his feet so as not to smear moss or lichen to give away his presence. They expected him to run toward Kinshasa, to get away as quickly as possible. None of them looked up, certainly not into the high canopy, and he sat quietly while the first wave of about thirty soldiers passed him by.

He examined the weapons thoroughly, familiarizing himself with the feel of each one. He took his time weaving a sheath for the machete, using a vine for the sling. All the while he watched and listened, hunting in his mind, picking his trails from his vantage point, listening to the whispers of the men as they passed directly under his tree. Thirst was a problem, and as soon as the last of the stragglers had passed, he stashed one of the rifles in the crotch of the tree branch and made his way back toward the edge of the camp in silence. Using the vines to spider across the treetops, he cut a succulent vine containing replenishing liquid and held it to his mouth, careful to keep from spilling a drop.

A chimpanzee screamed a warning a few hundreds yards to his left, and he froze, gradually allowing the hollow vine to slide back into the tangle with the rest. Inverting his body with slow precision, he moved like a wraith, headfirst, down the vine toward the forest floor. Dangling a few feet above ground, he made a graceful turn to set his feet carefully on the damp surface, landing in a crouching position, weapon up and ready. He froze when the two perimeter guards looked directly at him but didn't see him, his body blending in with the trees and foliage around him. The two lone soldiers looked around themselves warily, and exchanged heated comments culminating in one handing the other a joint.

Smoke billowed from one of the huts, and Jack caught glimpses of small flames still flickering in the remains. Two soldiers worked to stack the bodies of the dead while a third and fourth helped the injured. Jack skirted around the clearing, keeping to the heavier foliage as he closed in on the armory. He knew the weapons cache was enormous. The supplies had belonged to the former government and had come from the United States. When the general and his soldiers abandoned their jobs in the military and scattered, they had raided a number of the government armories. As an army they were well stocked, well trained, and completely mobile, a good five thousand troops strong. The general ruled the area with a ruthless and bloody hand, keeping people in line with swift violence whenever he deemed lessons necessary. The main encampment was at least a hundred miles into the interior, and the smaller, satellite camps spread out from there like a spider's web.

Near the armory, Jack dropped to his knees and elbows, crawling through the layers of rotting vegetation. Ants, beetles, and termites poured through the leaves and branches, over and around him. He ignored them as he kept moving forward at a snail's pace, staying to the shadows as much as possible. One guard walked over to another and gestured toward the wounded men, talking animatedly.

Jack moved forward inch by inch, until he was out in plain sight, his skin and clothing now reflecting the deeper colors of the ground. Night had fallen, and the sounds emerging from the interior of the forest had changed subtly. A cheetah coughed in the distance. Birds called to one another as they settled in the higher canopy. The chimpanzees quieted as the larger predators emerged. The insects grew louder, a continual sound that never ceased. Fog rolled in over the mountains and drifted into the forest and along the floor.

Jack kept moving steadily across the ground, heading for the area where the guards were heaviest, his goal the circle of vehicles with the cargo inside. The main armory would be a bunker at the central camp, but all the outlying camps had to carry supplies with them — and they would keep those supplies under heavy guard and as mobile as possible. That meant in the vehicles. The jeeps and trucks were parked a short distance away from the camp for safety.

The guards were set six feet apart. Most were smoking or talking, or watching the surrounding jungle. The two closest were taking bets on what the major would do to the prisoner when they got him back. Jack slithered through the grass to the first jeep parked in the tight circle. He rolled beneath it and examined the area with a cautious lift of his head. The arms were in crates in the truck to the center of the circle, right where he'd guessed they would be. He made his way to the back of the covered truck and once again waited in the grass while the beetles crawled over his body. When the closest guard looked away, Jack went up the bumper and leapt in like a human spider.

They were well supplied with guns. He helped himself to several clips for the M16s as well as for a nine-millimeter handgun he took. The boxes contained assault rifles, belts and cans of ammunition, as well as crates of clips. Boxes of grenades were toward the front, and claymore mines with detonators and wire were at the back.

Jack had shifted back toward the tailgate, needing to stash his supplies, when a bloody barrel caught his eye. His heart jumped in his chest as he reached down to clear debris from the weapon. The sniper rifle had been carelessly thrown in with a crate of AK47s. It was a Remington, covered in his brother's blood, even bearing a few smudged prints. He recognized it immediately; it had never been treated with other than the utmost respect. He picked it up and cradled it to him, running his hand over the barrel as if he could wipe away what had been done.

Jack's fingers tightened on the rifle as memories poured over him. Sweat broke out on his body and he shook his head, driving away the sound of childish screams and the feel of pain and humiliation, the sight of his brother staring at him, tears streaming down his face. That face changed to that of a man's, and Ken was looking at him with that same despair, that same pain and humiliation. When Jack lifted him, he had been horrified to see that the skin had been peeled from Ken's back, leaving a raw mass of muscle and tissue covered in flies and insects. He heard the screaming in his own head and looked down at his hands and saw blood. There was no washing it away and there never would be. He breathed deeply, forcing his mind away from the madness of his constant — and all too real — nightmares.

Major Biyoya had a lot to answer for — and torturing Ken was first on the list. Jack wasn't walking away quietly. He'd never just walked away in his life. It wasn't in him and never would be. Biyoya was going to be brought to justice — his justice — one way or another — because that was what Jack did.

He slung the rifle around his neck, tucking the scope and shells into an ammo belt. As fast and efficiently as possible, he gathered his weapons, using a pack from the back of the truck. The nine-millimeter handgun was a must. He took as many grenades, blocks of C4, and claymore mines as he could carry. Loaded down, he crept to the tailgate of the truck and peered out. The guards were watching the cleanup of the mess he'd made of the camp. Jack went out of the truck headfirst, going down to the ground and sliding beneath the truck for added cover.

It was a much more difficult challenge to move his supplies from the circle of vehicles back to the jungle. He inched his way, feeling the numerous bites from insects, the oppressive heat, the ground and grasses tearing up his body, and the mind-numbing fatigue. He could no longer block the fiery pain of his various wounds. In spite of the darkness, it took longer than he'd anticipated crossing the open circle and making his way through the guards.

He was nearly away from the vehicles when one of the guards turned abruptly and walked straight toward him. Jack froze, sliding his cache of weapons under the broadleaf plant closest to his hand. He had no choice but to lie prone in the darkness, relying on the camouflage of his body. The guard called to a second one and the man ambled over, shifting his rifle across his body. They spoke in Congolese, a language Jack was somewhat familiar with, but they were speaking rapidly, making it difficult to make out everything they were saying.

The Fespam Music Festival in Kinshasa was supposed to be larger and even better with the performances that had been brought over from Europe this time, and the guard desperately wanted to go because the Flying Five were performing. The general had promised them they could go, but unless they found the prisoner, no one would be going anywhere. The other guard agreed and dropped a cigarette almost on Jack's head, crushing it with the toe of his boot before adding his own complaints.

Jack's breath stilled. The Flying Five. What kind of a coincidence could that be? Or was it sheer luck. Jebediah Jenkins was a member of the Flying Five and he had served with Jack in the SEALs. If Jack could make his way to Kinshasa and find Jebediah, he could get the hell out of Dodge — or would he be walking into another trap?

The moment the guards moved on, he began to inch toward the forest again. Once into the heavier foliage, he went up into the trees, stashing his supplies and taking the time for another satisfying drink. He repeated the trip into the circle of vehicles, making his way back through the guards to the supply truck. This time, he went for more claymore mines, wires, and detonators. Patience and discipline went hand in hand with his profession, and he had both in abundance. He took his time, thorough in his setup, never once allowing his mind to freeze under the pressure, not even when soldiers nearly stepped on him.

He wired the beaten path leading into the jungle — tents, the outhouse, and every remaining vehicle. Minutes turned into hours. It was a long time to be in the enemy camp, and he felt the strain. Sweat dripped into his eyes and stung. His chest and especially his back were on fire, and his leg throbbed with pain. Infection in the jungle was dangerous, and he'd been stripped of his gear and all medical supplies.

Somewhere in the distance Jack caught the cry of the chimpanzees and immediately sorted through the sounds in the rain forest until he caught the one he was waiting for — the sound of movement through brush. Biyoya was bringing his soldiers home, wanting to wait until they could examine the damp ground for tracks. Jack knew Biyoya would have confidence in regaining his prisoner. Rebel camps were spread throughout the region, and few villagers would risk death and retribution by hiding a foreigner. Major Biyoya believed in torturing as well as ethnic cleansing. His reputation for brutality was widespread, and few would be willing to oppose him.

Jack finished his last task without haste,

before beginning to crawl backward toward the jungle. He angled his entry away from the well-used trail and into the thicker foliage. The smell of the returning soldiers hit him hard. They were sweating from the suffocating heat in the interior. He forced himself to maintain his slow pace, making certain not to draw the eyes of a sentry to him as he slipped under the creeper vines and broadleaf plants surrounding the camp.

He lay for a moment, his face in the muck, and let himself breathe before pushing to his feet and running in a crouch back toward the taller trees. He could hear the soldiers' breath blasting out of their lungs as they hurried back to their camp, their angry leader berating them every step of the way.

Jack stood for a moment under the chosen tree, breathing his way through the pain, gathering his strength before crouching and leaping up to the nearest broad branch. He worked his way from branch to branch until he was in the thickest of them, sitting comfortably, his brother's rifle cradled in his arms while he waited. The night was comforting, the familiar shadows home.

The first group of rebels came into sight, in a semiloose formation, eyes wary as they tried to pierce the veil of darkness for any enemies. Two jeeps had gone out with the group, taking the muddy, torn-up road that curved away from the forest and then looped back for miles into the interior. The jeeps were coming toward camp, motors whining and mud splattering around them. The main body of soldiers came through the trees, still spread out, guns at ready, nervous as hell.

Jack fitted the scope to his brother's rifle and calmly loaded the shells in.

The blast was loud in the quiet of the night, sending a fireball into the sky. It rained metal and shrapnel, sending debris slamming into the camp and embedding metal into trees. The screams of dying men mingled with the cries of birds and chimpanzees as the world around them exploded into orange red flames. The lead jeep had hit the wire right at the entrance to the camp, tripping the claymore and blowing everything around it into pieces. The soldiers hit the ground, covering their heads as fragments rained from the sky.

Jack kept his eye to the scope. Biyoya was in the second jeep, and the driver instantly veered away from the fireball, nearly spilling the passengers as the vehicle careened wildly through the trees. Biyoya leapt out, ducking into the foliage, screaming at the soldiers to fan out and look for Jack.

Using the chaos of explosions and screaming men as cover, Jack squeezed the trigger, taking out one of the soldiers on the edge of the forest. Switching targets, he rapidly fired three more times. Four shots — four kills. Not wanting the soldiers to spot where he was firing from, Jack immediately caught hold of a vine and went down headfirst on the opposite side of the tree from the soldiers, crawling hand over hand, until he could flip to the ground. He landed softly on the balls of his feet, fading into the overgrown ferns and dropping to his belly. Through the brush, he could slither along the almost invisible game trail that brought him up behind Biyoya's personal guard.

Jack rose up, a silent phantom, blade in hand. He went in fast and hard, careful to make certain the guard couldn't give away his presence with a single sound. Jack slipped back into the foliage, his skin and clothes blending with his surroundings.

Biyoya turned to say something to his guard and let out a shocked yell, leaping back away from the dead man and ducking around his jeep. He shouted to his soldiers and they sprayed the jungle with bullets, lighting up the night with the flashing muzzles. Leaves and branches fell like hail, raining from above, and several soldiers went down, caught in the cross fire. Biyoya had to shout several times again to establish control. He ordered another sweep through the surrounding forest.

The soldiers looked at one another, obviously not happy with the command, but they obeyed with reluctance, once again shoulder to shoulder, walking through the trees. Jack was already back in his tree, leaning his weary body against the thick trunk.

He slumped down, but kept his eye to the scope in hopes of getting a clear shot at Biyoya. He tried to keep any thought of home and his brother from his mind, but it was impossible. Ken's body — so bloody — so raw. There hadn't been a place on him that wasn't bleeding. Had Jack been too late? No way. He'd know if his brother was dead — and if it was at all possible, Ken would come for him. Even now, might be close. Intellectually Jack knew better — knew Ken's wounds were too severe and that he was safe in a hospital thousands of miles away — but he couldn't stop himself. Jack reached out along their telepathic path, the way he'd been doing since they were toddlers, and called his brother. *Ken. I'm in a fucking mess. You there, bro?*

Silence greeted his call. For one terrible

moment, his resolve wavered. His gut churned and fear swamped him. Fear for his own situation and something nearly amounting to terror for his brother. He held out his hand, saw it shake, and shook his head, forcing his mind away from destructive thoughts. That way lay his own destruction. His job was to escape, to survive, to make his way to Kinshasa.

The soldiers tramped through the forest, using bayonets to thrust into the thick shrubs and ferns. They stabbed the vegetation on the floor and walked along the banks of the stream feeding into the river, blades pounding the damp embankment. The jeep slowly began to move, only the driver and soldiers surrounding it vulnerable as they made their way past the wreckage of the first vehicle into camp.

Jack lowered the rifle. It was going to be a long night for the soldiers. In the meantime, he had to plan his way to freedom. He was west of Kinshasa. Once in the city, he could find Jebediah and hide until they found a way to call for extraction. It sounded simple enough, but he had to work his way through the rebel encampments between Kinshasa and his present position. He wasn't going to kid himself; he was in bad shape. With so many open wounds, infection was a certainty rather than a possibility.

Weariness stole over him. Loneliness. He had chosen this life many years ago, the only choice he had at the time. Most of the time he never regretted it. But sometimes, when he sat thirty feet up in a tree with a rifle in his hands and death surrounding him, he wondered what it would be like to have a home and family. A woman. Laughter. He couldn't remember laughter, not even with Ken, and Ken could be amusing at the most inopportune times.

It was too late for him. He was rough and cold and any gentleness he might have been born with had been beat out of him long before he was a teenager. He looked at the people and the world around him stripped of beauty, seeing only the ugliness. It was kill or be killed in his world, and he was a survivor. He settled back and closed his eyes, needing to sleep for a few minutes.

He woke to the sounds of screams. The sound often haunted him in his nightmares, screams and gunfire, and the sight of blood running in dark pools. His hands curled around the rifle, finger stroking the trigger even before his eyes snapped open. Jack took a long, deep breath and looked around him. Flash fires came from the direction of the camp. Several of his traps had been sprung, and once again chaos reigned in the rebel encampment. Bullets spat into the jungle, zipped through leaves and tore bark from trees. The ghost in the rain forest had struck again and again, and fear had the rebels by the throats.

On and off over the next few hours, some hapless soldier tripped a trap, probably trying to get rid of it, and the camp would erupt into pandemonium, confusion, and panic nearly leading to rebellion. The soldiers wanted to head for the base camp and Biyoya refused, adamant that they would recover the prisoner. It was a tribute to his leadership — or cruelty — that he was able to rally them after each attack. There was no sleep for anyone, and the fog crept into the forest, blanketing the trees and mixing with the smoke from the continual fires.

Through the haze, Jack saw the camp on the move, abandoning their position. Biyoya screamed at his men and shook his fist at the camp, the first real indication that the long night had taken its toll on him. He'd lost more than half of his soldiers, and they were forced to group in a tight knot around him to protect him. They didn't look very happy, but they marched stoically through the forest on the muddy, torn road.

The rain began again, a steady drizzle that added to the stirring life of the jungle. Chimpanzees resumed their eating and birds flitted from tree to tree. Jack caught a glimpse of a boar moving through the brush. An hour went by, soaking his clothes and his skin. He never moved, waiting with the patience born of a lifetime of survival. Biyoya would have his best trackers and sharpshooters concealed, and they would wait for him to make a move. Major Biyoya didn't want to go back to General Ekabela and admit he'd lost skilled soldiers to his prisoner. His *escaped* prisoner. That kind of thing would lose the major his hard-earned reputation as a ruthless interrogator.

Jack's eyes were different, had always been different, and after Whitney had genetically enhanced him, his sight had become amazing. He didn't understand the workings, but he had the vision of an eagle. He didn't care how it was done, but he could see distances few others could conceive of. Out of the corner of his eye, movement to the left of his position caught his attention, the colors in bands of yellow and red. The sniper moved cautiously, keeping to the heavier foliage, so that Jack only caught glimpses of him. His spotter kept to the left, covering every step the sniper took as he examined the ground and surrounding trees.

Jack began a slow move into a better position, but halted when he heard a feminine scream in the distance followed closely by a child's frightened cry. Jack jerked his head up, his body stiffening, sweat breaking out on his brow and trickling down into his eyes. Did Biyoya know his trigger? His one weakness? That was impossible. His mouth went dry and his heart slammed in his chest. *What did Biyoya know about him?* Ken had been brutally tortured. There wasn't a square inch on his twin's body that hadn't been cut with tiny slices or stripped of skin. Could the interrogation have broken Ken?

Jack shook his head, denying the thought, and wiped the sweat from his face, the movement slow and careful. *Ken would never betray him, tortured or not.* The knowledge was certain, as much a part of him as breathing. However he'd gotten his information, Biyoya had set the perfect trap. Jack had to respond. His past, buried deep where he never looked, wouldn't let him walk away. Trap or not, he had to react, take countermeasures. His gut knotted up and his lungs burned for air. He swore under his breath and put his eye to the scope again, determined to take out Biyoya's backup.

The woman screamed again, this time the

sound painful in the early morning dawn. The knots in his belly hardened into something scary. Yeah. Biyoya knew, had information on him. He was classified, and the information Biyoya possessed was in a classified file with a million red flags. *So who the hell sold me out?* Jack rubbed his eyes again to clear the sweat from them. Someone close to them set the brothers up. There was no other explanation.

The screams increased in strength and duration. The child sobbed, begging for mercy. Jack cursed and jerked his head up, furious with himself, with his inability to ignore it. "You're going to die here, Jack," he whispered aloud. "Because you're a damned fool." It didn't matter. He couldn't let it go. The past was bile in his throat, the door in his mind creaking open, the screams growing louder in his head.

He leapt from the safety of his tree to another one, using the canopy to travel, relying on his skin and clothing to camouflage him. He moved fast, following Biyoya's trail into the darkened interior. The ribbon of road flowed below him, hacked out of the thick vegetation, pitted, mined, and trampled. It looked more like a strip of mud than an actual road. He followed it, using the trees and vines, moving fast to catch up with the main body of soldiers.

He slipped into a tall tree right above the heads of the soldiers, settling in the foliage, lying flat along a branch. Somewhere behind him the sniper was coming, but Jack hadn't left a trail on the ground, and he would be difficult to spot blending in as he did with the leaves and bark. A woman lay on the ground, clothes torn, a soldier bending over her, kicking at her as she cried helplessly. A small boy of about ten struggled against the men shoving him back and forth between them. There was terror in the child's eyes.

There was no doubt in Jack's mind that Biyoya had constructed a trap, but the woman and the child were innocent victims. No one could fake that kind of terror. He swore over and over in his mind, trying to force himself to walk away. His first duty was to escape, but this — he couldn't leave the woman and child in the hands of a master torturer. He forced his mind to slow down to block out the cries and pleas.

Biyoya was the target and Jack had to find his place of concealment. Jack inhaled sharply, relying on his enhanced sense of smell. If his nose was right — and it nearly always was — the major crouched behind the jeep just to the left of the woman and boy, behind a wall of soldiers. Jack circled around and lifted his rifle, taking the bead on Biyoya, knowing the soldiers would be able to pinpoint his trajectory.

The bullet took Biyoya behind the neck. Even as he fell, Jack switched his target to the man kicking the woman and fired a second round. Calmly, he let go of the sniper rifle and took up the assault weapon, laying down a covering fire to give the woman and child a chance to escape. The soldiers fired back, bullets smacking into the trees around him. Jack knew they couldn't see him, but the muzzle flash and smoke were a dead giveaway. The woman caught her child to her and took off into the rain forest. Jack gave them as long a lead as he dared before moving, sliding back into heavier foliage and leaping up through the branches to use the canopy as a highway.

Ekabela was not going to let this go. Jack would have every rebel in the Congo chasing him all the way to Kinshasa.

# CHAPTER 2

Briony Jenkins huddled in the darkest corner of the room, hands over her ears, eyes tightly closed, desperate to shut out the assault of thousands of people and their suffering. It had been such a mistake to take the job. She'd tried to tell Jebediah she couldn't do it, but it meant so much to the family — so much money the circus needed to stay solvent. How in the world was she ever going to perform? She could barely see with the pain shattering her head and with spots dancing in front of her eyes. There was no medicine she could take, no relief from the suffering and violence in this place.

"Briony?" Jebediah crouched beside her.

She shook her head, pressing her hands tighter over her ears, as if that would keep the thoughts and emotions from flooding her mind. "I told you I couldn't come to a place like this. I'm going to be sick again." She couldn't look at him, didn't dare open her eyes and see light. Her body shook uncontrollably, and tiny beads of sweat trickled down her face. "I'm getting another nosebleed."

Jebediah ran cold water on a cloth and handed it to his younger sister. "I had no idea it would be this bad. I thought you were doing all those exercises to help shield you from whatever it is that causes this."

Briony bit back her retort, clamping down hard on her temper. She was on psychic overload and it wouldn't help to get angry with Jebediah. Sure, her brothers and the other members of the circus had pressured her to come, but she could have refused. She should have refused. And she had told him it would be this bad. Jebediah and the others had simply chosen not to listen, because it wasn't in their best interests. She pressed her lips together and tried to breathe away the pain. Jebediah might as well have been stabbing ice picks through her head, but it wasn't his fault. He had no idea what psychic overload actually was — or felt like.

She remembered the many times her parents had tried in vain to comfort her when she huddled in a ball in a corner of a dark room and rocked herself back and forth, trying to ease the pain in her head. At times she could hear them discussing

49

whether or not she had some form of autism. She *needed* to be alone. She didn't like close physical contact. They were so hurt by her behavior. *Shattered.* She still woke up with her mother's sobs ringing in her ears, and her voice asking why didn't Briony love them? Briony *adored* them; she just couldn't get too close without terrible repercussions, and there was no way to make them understand that the pain was real, not psychological.

She knew exactly how this scenario would play out. She'd gone through it a million times. "This is Africa, Jeb," she reminded him, "a country rampant with suffering. There's AIDS and death and rape and loss and it's swamping me."

His mouth tightened. He didn't like her to bring up anything even hinting of psychic overload. He didn't believe in it and, like her parents, thought it was a form of autism. He wanted her to fight through it and succeed in being "normal." "Can you stop the nosebleed?" He glanced at his watch. "I need you to be able to perform, Briony."

She wanted to throw something at him. "You say that before every performance and I always manage to make it. Go away, Jebediah. I need to be alone."

Her other brothers pressed closer. Tyrel,

as always, looked sympathetic, Seth angry, and Ruben disgusted. Ruben always chose to bully her, thinking that would somehow make her shape up. Seth yelled at her, and Tyrel eventually would get annoyed with both of them and run them off. The ritual had been going on as long as she could remember, and not once had any of them understood that she couldn't help what was happening to her and that their presence, with their intense emotions, only made it worse.

"There's a rumor going around that the rebel leader's troops have been pouring into the city looking for someone," Tyrel said. "That's not a good sign, Jeb. You know they're going to look at all foreigners."

Jebediah swore. "If the rebel troops are coming into the city, the soldiers are going to be very nervous and trigger-happy. Why would they come into the city armed and ready for trouble?"

"Hell, I don't understand any of the politics here," Seth replied. "Everyone hates everyone and they want everyone else dead."

No one had to tell that to Briony. The heightened tension in the streets increased her inability to function. There was poverty and sickness and so many tragedies she wanted to crawl into a hole and muffle out all emotion, sound, and thought.

"Your skin is changing color again, Briony," Ruben said impatiently. "I told you to watch that around people."

"We aren't people; we're her family," Tyrel pointed out. "Leave her alone."

Ruben persisted. "Well, how can she do that? Like some lizard or something."

Briony sighed, pushing her pounding head into her hand. It felt like someone was hammering nails into her skull, but there was no pointing that out to anyone. The show had to go on — and Briony always, *always,* came through. It was a matter of pride with her. She was a Jenkins and whatever they did, she could do — and would do.

"Anyone could walk in here," Ruben defended.

"I locked the door," Seth said. "Snap out of it, Bri. I'm not kidding around with you. You're too old for panic attacks."

Briony had had enough. They had ten minutes until they were on, and if her brothers didn't leave, she wouldn't be able to pull herself together. "Get out." She bit the words out between her teeth, glaring at them.

Her four brothers looked startled. It was the first time she had ever interrupted the ritual. They were big men, muscular and well built with dark hair and piercing blue eyes. She had wheat and platinum hair, dark, chocolate brown eyes, and was about five foot two. She looked nothing like them, and certainly didn't have their adventurous personalities — although she wished she did. She never really sassed them, although she considered herself pushed around a bit by them. At once all their faces dropped.

Ruben crouched down beside her. "I didn't mean to upset you, Briony. We can work it without you if you can't make it this time. It won't be easy, and you know the crowd isn't going to like it, but if you can't pull yourself together this time . . ."

Seth sucked in his breath. "Yeah, I could maybe take your spot, honey. Why don't you try to go to bed? Maybe you'll feel better in the morning."

"We can call for a doctor," Tyrel offered. "Your doctor has always flown out within an hour of a call."

Briony would have laughed if her head wasn't splitting apart. "I've never missed a performance. Just give me a little alone time and I'll be fine."

Jebediah waved the others out of the room and sank down beside her, reaching out a hand to push back her thick mop of blond hair. "We need you, honey, I won't lie to you, but I'll call the doc if you think you're going to need him. We have several performances to do, and if the rebels are really sneaking into the city, the emotions are only going to get worse."

It was such a concession for Jebediah to admit that anything would make her condition worse. "I don't like the doctor." Briony rubbed her hand over her face. "He stares at me like I'm an insect under a microscope. There's something not right about him."

Jebediah sighed and sank back on his heels. "You're being paranoid again."

"Am I? Why is it the rest of you can go to any doctor you choose, but I have to have a specific doctor, one that flies halfway around the world to treat me?"

"Because you're special and Mom and Dad promised. I keep their promises and so should you."

"I'm all grown up." When he didn't respond, she let her breath out slowly. "I'm serious, Jeb, just give me some space. I can beat this." She wasn't certain this time. It was the worst she'd ever been, other than when she was a child, unable to cope with or understand what was happening to her. Feeling desperate, Briony closed her eyes and began to breathe slowly and evenly, looking for that calm, tranquil spot inside of herself.

She was barely aware of her oldest brother leaving, concentrating instead on putting away the emotions of the people in the city, of the soldiers and their guns and dark deeds, of the hatred and fear battering at her mind. Once she was calm enough, she dealt with the ever-present fear of high places. If there was one person in the world who shouldn't be doing trapeze or high-wire acts, it was Briony.

"Let's do it," Seth called from outside the door.

Briony stood, looked in the mirror to make certain there was no blood on her face and that she could manage a high-wattage smile, and then ran out to join her brothers. The audience had swelled to immense proportions. She didn't look at them, concentrating on the beat of the music. They used a blend of popular African and Cuban music to do their performance, a dangerous trapeze act.

Briony completed a quadruple somersault; Jebediah caught her and sent her flying out toward the taut high wire, where she was caught by Tyrel and swung up onto the wire. Seth and Ruben continued the flying act while she ran across the wire without a pole, and as Ruben flew back toward Seth, she crossed him in the air, diving to Jebediah through a ring of fire Tyrel held. It was a wild, frightening act, done with exact precision and timing, and at least two of them flying in the air at all times.

No one knew why Briony had such incredible balance or strength, but to the act, it was a huge boon, drawing thousands to their performances. It helped that her brothers were handsome and incredible athletes. No one had an act like theirs, as daring and complicated and showy. Briony thought the hip-hop beat and the drums only added to the excitement of the show. Adrenaline poured through her body as she flew through the sky, concentrating on her mark, listening for her brother's command. He caught her and sent her spinning back through the air. She tucked and jackknifed, turning as she came out of it, to reach with her hands and connect with Tyrel.

The applause was accompanied by a roar of approval. The audience stomped their feet and called for more. Briony waved and smiled when Tyrel squeezed her arm, and she dove from the wire, arms outstretched as if she could really fly, doing a slow-motion, graceful somersault, coming under Ruben. He was doing the exact same sequence over the top of her as they exchanged places. Briony and Ruben waved again to the roaring crowd and caught a rope to slide down, coming together, hand in hand, to bow. They waited for their brothers to join them, all of them taking a final bow together.

The wild music and adrenaline rush had helped to keep the crushing emotions at bay, but as she stood in the spotlight, she felt the impact like a physical blow. She stumbled, forcing her smile to remain in place as the pain crushed her head in a vise and twisted hard knots in her stomach. Thousands of people were around her, all giving off waves of emotions. Everything from elation to the deepest despair. She could feel the tension, see the men moving through the crowd with guns, occasionally shoving a hapless individual, faces grim, no caring in their eyes. Her eyesight had always been phenomenal. She had the ability to see a mouse moving on the forest floor, and she could easily see and feel the fear of the women as they gathered closer, trying not to be noticed by the soldiers.

As soon as she left the center ring, Briony raced for the bathroom and threw up what little she'd managed to get down earlier. She changed quickly from her skimpy, sparkly costume into a dark pair of jeans and a top. She could hear her brothers, laughing, excited, heading to the clubs to check out the nightlife. Kinshasa was reputed to have numerous nightclubs, and many people, in spite of the turbulent problems in the outlying areas, chose to travel there for the clubs.

"You okay, Bri?" Tyrel called out. "You want me to stay with you?"

"No, of course not, I'm fine," she called back. "You have a good time, but be careful."

"Lock the doors after us," Jebediah instructed.

"Will do." She wasn't going to stay in the room and suffocate. She knew the Congo River was close. The rain forest would be still and quiet, at least away from people. She would be able to breathe again, but she knew better than to let her brothers know she was heading out. They'd lose their minds.

Briony had utter faith in her ability to blend into the night. She could do extraordinary things — things even her brothers didn't know about. She'd had rigorous training only her parents — and perhaps Jebediah — were aware of. She just had to make it through the city without being detected and get into the sanctuary of the rain forest.

She tied a scarf around her neck and added a hat to cover the mop of blond hair. She could change her skin color, something her brothers found repulsive. It had started sometime around her sixteenth birthday, right after she'd been hospitalized for some strange thing the doctors said she had. It had taken awhile to learn to control it. The shading sometimes happened when she was upset or angry, but she could bring it on at will, matching her surroundings so she seemed to disappear.

She hesitated just inside the door. She was afraid to face the onslaught of raw emotions. Walking through the streets, knowing she would be subjected to the intense emotions of the people, was a nightmare, but if she didn't go and find a refuge, she wouldn't make it through the next few days, and her brothers needed her to perform.

Briony squared her shoulders and stepped out. She had studied the map of the streets and knew exactly where she was going. She was also certain she could fight off or outrun any attacker, so she strode with purpose, all senses alert to trouble, but walking briskly through the streets back toward the Congo River and the rain forest.

Why was she so different? Why was she able to read thoughts and emotions if she were touching someone and feel them if she was near? Her parents had insisted on a rigorous, almost military training, very physical, for as long as she could remember, yet when her mother held her, she felt fear mixed with love. Did her mother fear her strange abilities? And if so, why had she insisted Briony develop them, yet keep them secret? Secrets kept her apart from her brothers and the other performers around her. Secrets and her extraordinary differences. She detested those differences.

The streets were crowded, people everywhere, still late at night, many already preying on the night population, easy marks with too much drink and drugs. The smell of marijuana hit her hard. She was very sensitive to scents, had always been able to identify people and animals in near proximity to her before anyone else, and now the unwashed mingling with the overperfumed made her queasy.

She made it through the streets without incident and followed the river into the rain forest, where she picked up her pace, jogging easily along a winding path that led to a deep stream feeding the river. She kept going along the stream, seeking a refuge, a place where she could curl up and just breathe in peace.

It was hot and humid in the forest. She stopped to wade into the water and stood there listening to the sounds of insects, the flutter of wings, and the movement of creatures through the trees. For the first time in days, she felt the tension ebbing away.

Briony dipped the scarf in the cold water and pressed it to the nape of her neck. Desperate for relief, she waded deeper into the small stream. Her brothers were going to kill her for disappearing, but she wasn't going to survive the next few days if she didn't find somewhere to get away from the suffering. Whatever she'd learned about shields didn't work in Africa. There were too many people, too close, and far too much suffering.

How many performances had they agreed to? And did it make sense? Why would the festival pay them so much money to come up with an acrobatic performance to African music? The act was spectacular, but the offer came *before* they'd come up with the idea. Why didn't that bother anyone in the circus? Where would the festival get that kind of money? And if they had that much money, when the festival was all about music, why would they want a circus act? Briony glanced around her, once again feeling unseen eyes on her. Was she the only one who wondered why her family was in Kinshasa? And why did she always feel as if someone was observing her?

The music festival was a tribute to African artists and their music. It made no sense to invite a circus act. Jebediah, Tyrel, Ruben, and Seth just shrugged their shoulders and said not to look a gift horse in the mouth, but Briony felt something was off. Everything felt a little off-kilter to her. Her bizarre education, her abilities, even the fact that she had a special doctor, flying in the moment she got a sniffle — and even that was strange — the fact that she rarely had viruses. Usually she was ill from the constant bombardment of emotions battering at her daily. Her brothers told her she was paranoid, but, as she was now, she was often uneasy, certain someone was watching her. She looked around, seeing with her enhanced vision, looking for heat images, anything that would tell her she was in danger, but there was nothing, not even a change in the constant hum of insects.

Briony rubbed her pounding temples and waded downstream, farther away from the hustle and bustle of the city. Soldiers on every corner with guns, the underbelly teeming with hidden violence, the nightlife seemed a glitzy cover for the desperate and the criminal to do their worst. She wanted to go home.

For a moment she went very still. Home. What did that even mean? She loved her family. She loved the circus, but it was killing her to stay with them. She didn't know any other way of life and there was nowhere for her to go. At least her brothers knew she was different, and although they didn't understand, they did their best to hide her peculiarities from others.

Briony smelled unwashed men, heard voices, and immediately shrank closer to the bank, changing her skin color, relying on her darkened clothing to help blend. As three armed soldiers approached, she looked around to ensure she was alone, crouched, and leapt effortlessly into the branches of a tree, some thirty feet up. She remained very still as they passed beneath her, searching for tracks along the forest floor. They were definitely hunting someone, and she realized it was stupid to be so far away from the protection of her brothers. These had to be the rebels everyone was so afraid of. She watched them as they made their way very stealthily through the trees toward the city.

Briony waited until she could no longer hear them before jumping back to the ground. With a little regretful sigh, she waded out into the water again. Even here, on the edge of the wild, she wasn't really alone. Once more she bent down to soak her scarf in the cooling stream. She didn't want to go back; her mouth was already dry just thinking of it. As she began to turn, the water around her rippled, her only warning. An arm, much like a band of iron, whipped around her throat and the tip of a knife pressed against her side.

"Don't scream." The voice was pitched low, but held such a threat she stiffened. Her captor's body felt like an oak tree with no give in it, and the way he held her gave her no real chance at escape without sustaining a major injury.

She counted her heartbeats to slow her breathing. "I wasn't planning on it."

He spoke English with an American accent. "You're a GhostWalker. What the hell are you doing here?"

The voice was more of a whisper in her mind than in her ear. She knew she was a strong telepath, but this was something more. *And she didn't feel his emotions.* The realization stunned her. In her entire life, even with her own family, she'd been burdened with the overwhelming feelings of others. For a moment, she was so shocked her brain refused to process the information. She stayed very still, trying to reason it out, ignoring the persistent whisper in her ear.

The tip of the knife touched her skin and Briony jumped. "You do that again and I'm not going to be so nice," she hissed. Could she take him? He was stronger than any man she'd ever trained with. She felt the power running through him, felt the difference in him — the same difference she'd always known was in her. Again she forced herself to relax. No one was like her — not even her family. How did she know he was?

"Who are you?" she asked, knowing he wasn't going to answer. Military for certain. Maybe a mercenary.

"What the hell is a GhostWalker doing here? You don't answer me in five seconds, I'm going to start slicing off body parts."

"I don't know what a GhostWalker is. I'm performing at the music festival. I do aerial stunts with my brothers, the Flying Five. I'm one of the five."

There was a small silence. "Why the hell would a circus performer be at a music festival?"

"You tell me," Briony said. "I haven't

figured it out yet, but they paid my brothers and me big bucks to come here." He hadn't relaxed his guard even for a moment.

Her captor swore, the words viciously ugly. "I saw you go up that tree and change your skin color to blend into your surroundings. Don't lie again. No one can do that but a GhostWalker. No one."

Briony wanted to know everything he knew about the GhostWalkers. If they could do the things she could do, was she related in some way? She felt him stiffen, arms tightening. His lips pressed against her ear. "Don't make a sound."

She inhaled and at once knew the soldiers were doubling back. Fear shot through her. She knew what happened to women caught out on their own.

"Can you hold your breath? Are you trained?"

She knew what he meant and she nodded.

"How long?" He demanded tersely.

"Twenty minutes if I'm careful." She didn't lie, and wanted to see if he was shocked. As a child she'd been forced to stay under longer and longer periods of time. She'd thought everyone did it, until once, at the dinner table, when she was bragging to her brothers and they were making fun of her for lying, she saw her mother's mouth tighten with disapproval and she'd never mentioned it again — to anyone.

"You're going under with me."

It wasn't a question, and he was already exerting pressure on her, taking her into the water, not making a sound as they slowly submerged, as if he took it for granted that anyone could stay under that long without breathing equipment. The knife never wavered and neither did the arm locked around her neck. He gave her plenty of time to take a breath, and she did so, drawing air into her lungs as they crouched down in a small section of the stream covered with reeds.

Briony dug her fingers into his arm, holding on, trying to conquer fear. She felt sometimes that she'd spent most of her life trying to hide that she was frightened. She had always been afraid, and after a while, it was simply a way of life. She was afraid of everything, and sometimes it disgusted her that she could never quite overcome those shadows dwelling so deep inside of her. She forced herself to be still, not wanting her captor to be aware of how very frightened of him she really was.

Part of her was excited, wondering, in spite of the danger, whether he could do the things she could do. And if he could —

what did that mean?

Jack could feel the small tremor continually running through the body of the young woman he held so tight against him. She was small, hardly more than a girl, but she felt like a woman — had smelled like a woman, all soft curves and fresh scent. She was terrified, but hiding it well and that made no sense if she were a GhostWalker. She would be highly skilled in martial arts, in hand-to-hand combat, in weapons of every kind. She should have complete confidence in her abilities. She was without a doubt physically enhanced and, he suspected, psychically as well. She breathed under water the way they'd all been taught, one small release of air at a time.

Jack found himself all too aware of the woman in his arms. He had been from the moment he touched her. Every single detail seemed imprinted in his mind. On his body. The shape and texture of her. The brush of her silky hair against his face when he'd first locked his arm around her throat. The pads of her fingers pressing deep into his arm as they crouched together beneath the water. Nothing like that had ever happened to him before. It never mattered whether his opposition was a man or a woman; it was a job. He did whatever it took to complete the job. She was no object; she was a woman. He couldn't get the feel or scent of her out of his mind, even now, under water, as if somehow her body had melted into his skin and imprinted on his bones.

The soldiers spent time beneath the tree, talking in whispers. Jack knew they were hunting him. A minute. Two. Three turned into five. Five into ten. The soldiers remained, crouching by the stream, drawing a map in the damp earth. Fifteen minutes went by. Jack slowed his breath even more.

The woman's fingers dug deeper into his arm. The tension went up noticeably, and he felt her rising terror of drowning, but remarkably, she held still. The minutes continued and he expected panic, was prepared for it, but she held her ground, forcing the slow release of air to allow her to stay beneath the water. She'd been trained, all right, but she was losing air and needed to surface. Her terror was in his mind — swamping him — tasting bitter in his mouth.

Jack tried to ignore her fears, but the empathy between them was too strong and gave him no choice. He caught her head in his hand and turned her face to his, leaning forward until his lips feathered over hers. It was a mistake. He felt that feather light touch all the way through his body, a wild slam of his heart, a tightening of his groin, something deeper shifting and moving inside of him. He breathed into her mouth, so that he was literally the air she breathed, so that she took him deep into her body where he belonged.

*Where the hell had that thought come from?* He swore he not only felt an electric current sizzling through his veins, he felt possessive — and he was a man who never had strong sexual or emotional reactions in a relationship with a woman — he never allowed it. He avoided attachments, yet every cell in his body — in his brain — urged him to pull her closer, to take possession of her. He stared directly into her eyes, enormous with fear but determined not to give them away. How could anyone have so much fear and yet remain so utterly still, so aware of the danger surrounding her? It took courage and discipline to be able to breathe under water when self-preservation urged you to surface.

He curled his arm around her waist, anchoring her, trying to give her some reassurance that they wouldn't drown or be attacked. *It's all right, baby.* He whispered the words in his mind, trying to think of something to do that would indicate he wouldn't force her to stay under if they ran out of air. He could fight if he had to, although he was in bad shape and he didn't want to risk gunfire. The sound would carry in the night. He didn't want to bring the general's army down on them. *I'm not going to let you die here.* What did men say to women to ease their fears? Hell, he didn't know. He was way out of his field of expertise.

Jack became aware of her utter stillness. Her eyes had widened and she stared at him as if he'd grown two heads. There was no faking the shock on her face. Whatever this woman was, she was not a member of the psychic teams he'd trained with. She heard him. She was every bit as strong a telepath as he was. *You can hear me.* He made it a statement.

One of the soldiers waded into the stream, turning Jack's attention back to the danger. The situation was critical. Breathing for both of them, he was running out of air, and the soldier was almost on top of the woman. *Don't move.* He put as much force into his voice as he could, the command absolute. This time he framed her face with his hands and leaned down to take her mouth, pushing the air into her lungs. *You understand?*

Damn. He couldn't control his accelerated heartbeat or the strange flutter in his belly — but it had nothing to do with fear of the soldiers and everything to do with the peculiar woman. She nodded slightly.

*Keep your eyes closed until I come back for you.*

Her fear nearly took her into panic, he could see it in her eyes, but her mouth firmed and she nodded again, the long lashes coming down, eyes squeezing closed tight. Jack didn't wait, couldn't wait. The second soldier was in the water and the first was about to trip over the woman's leg. He caught both ankles and yanked hard, dragging the man under, burying the knife in his throat, and rising almost at the second soldier's feet, cutting thighs, belly, jugular, and throat so that he too dropped away, leaving Jack to face the third man. He reversed the knife and threw hard, burying the blade to the hilt in the rebel's throat.

It took only seconds to retrieve his knife and wipe the blade clean. He left the soldiers' weapons exactly where they fell and went back for the woman. They couldn't leave anything for the general's trackers to find.

*Come up but keep your eyes closed. I'm getting you out of here. What the hell is your*

72

*name? I'm Jack.*

There was a brief hesitation, but she was desperate for air. She rose, visibly shaking. Jack caught her around the waist, one hand covering her eyes. "Let's go, but step light, we don't want any evidence of you being here."

"My scarf," she said, "I dropped it. And my name's Briony Jenkins."

He knew that name. And he knew of the Flying Five — and this was more of a coincidence than he could swallow. He looked around quickly. The scarf was floating a short distance from them. She'd taken it under water with them, but released it when he brought her up. The fact that she remembered it under the traumatic conditions increased his growing respect for her. *Keep your eyes closed.* He let go of her and turned to retrieve the scarf.

Briony took off running. All she had to do was get into heavier brush and she could disappear. The soldiers were definitely hunting her captor, and she wasn't going to lead them — or him — back to her brothers. She heard her heart pounding frantically and the sound of her breath rushing out of her lungs. Her eyes remained on her goal; she didn't dare turn to see if he was behind her. Every step counted.

He struck from behind, a hard tackle that knocked her to the ground, facedown, trapping her arms before she had a chance to get them out from under her. The wind exploded out of her, and his knee drove hard into the small of her back, one hand fisted tightly in her hair and the other pressing the tip of his knife against her jugular. "Don't you fucking move," he hissed. "Are you trying to get yourself killed?"

"Do it then," she spat back, her mouth full of dirt and leaves. "I'm not leading you back to my family so get over it."

"You think this is some kind of game?"

"I don't care if it is." She didn't bother to try to control the violent trembling. What the hell did she care if he knew she was afraid? Let him kill her. He wasn't going to get what he wanted. And why did his presence disturb her so much?

"Get up." He dragged her up by her hair, the knife never leaving her neck.

She couldn't fight him, she realized with a sinking feeling. She had four strong brothers, and, in spite of her diminutive size, she was stronger and faster than all four of them. She was trained in hand-to-hand combat and several forms of marital arts, but he didn't give her an opening. Not one.

"You're hurting me."

"Then stop struggling."

She hadn't realized she had been. She forced her body back under control. "What do you want?"

"I was in the SEALs with a Jebediah Jenkins. The last I heard, he was the catcher for his family's act in the circus. He had a sister, Briony, and three brothers."

"Let go of me." *She wasn't feeling anything.* It didn't make sense. He had killed the three soldiers, she was certain of it. Violence made her particularly ill; in fact, most of the time, she had nosebleeds, migraines, vomited, and even once, when she'd found her parents dead, she'd gone into convulsions. She no longer had her former headache, not even with being so afraid and him pulling her hair.

"Are you going to run?"

"I don't particularly want to get slammed to the ground again, thanks," Briony answered.

Okay. It wasn't true that she wasn't feeling anything. Her entire body was in some kind of weird meltdown that had never happened before. She first noticed it in the water, sitting so close to him, looking into his eyes. *When his lips touched hers.* She jerked her thoughts away from how hard his body was, how strong he was. She had to be sick to even have a reaction to him when he was viciously yanking her head back. "And let go of my hair, you're hurting me."

Jack instantly relaxed his hold on the wet strands and then scowled, shocked that he'd done so. What in the hell was wrong with him? She was a potential enemy. There was no doubt in his mind that someone had set him up, and it had to be a conspiracy among several people to place him in the hornet's nest — and that meant they had used his feelings for his brother against him. Ken had been lured in — captured and tortured for one purpose, and that was to bring Jack to Africa. Someone knew Jack's triggers and they were using them ruthlessly against him. Briony Jenkins was definitely a GhostWalker, no matter what she said. And how big a coincidence was it that a friend — a fellow SEAL — was in Kinshasa at the same precise time? "Damn it, I don't believe in coincidences."

Briony turned her head to look at him, startled that he was thinking the exact same thing she was thinking. Had someone maneuvered her brother into Kinshasa for some purpose other than to play the music festival? "Neither do I." She studied his ravaged body, horror and compassion creeping in despite her resolve not to be swayed by him.

Jack had been tortured. Deep cuts and burns marred his chest, shoulders, and belly. His eyes were flat and cold and hard as stone, yet no one could have suffered such abuse and not be in terrible pain. *And she wasn't feeling it.* She always felt human and even animal suffering if she was in close proximity to it. It was almost a relief to her to be near him. He seemed to provide the necessary filters she didn't have in order to function around people.

"My God. How can you be walking around? Did the rebels do that?" Her voice came out a hoarse whisper. Before she could stop herself, she stepped forward and reached out to touch his muscle just above where the skin was shredded. "You need a doctor. You're already infected."

A tremor ran through his body at her touch. So light. A mere drift of the pad of her fingers, but he felt it through his entire body. "We have to keep moving. I pissed off their general." He watched her face for a reaction, but she was staring in horror at his wounds.

"I can't feel your pain." Her dark gaze rose to meet his. "Why is that? You know, don't you? You know why I'm different, why

77

I can't function like everyone else. No one else would have known I could stay under water like that, not even my brothers. Why? What am I? What are you?"

# CHAPTER 3

Jack's gaze moved restlessly through the forest. "We have to keep moving. The rebels are searching for me and they aren't going to stop."

"Answer me," Briony insisted. He was swaying on his feet and didn't even know it. The man was going to collapse, and there was no way she could leave him to die.

"GhostWalkers are enhanced both physically and psychically."

Her heart began to pound. "How did they get that way?"

Jack took a step and his legs went out from under him. Briony caught him before he hit the ground. He tried to push her away. "Go. Keep moving. Circle back through the forest until you're on the edge of town. They'll be watching, so use the trees if you have to, but get out of here."

"Oh, shut up."

Amusement crept into his eyes. "I don't

think anyone's ever told me to shut up before." His arm slid around her shoulders, one finger pushing the wet strands of hair behind her ear.

"I have a lot of brothers, so don't let it go to your head. Why are men such idiots, anyway?" Like she could leave him now. Her brothers would have told her the exact same thing. She blew her hair out of her eyes and looked around her. Jack was a heavy man. He'd lost too much blood and his skin was fiery hot, indicating fever. "Okay, tough guy, you're going to lean on me and we're going to start back toward the city. And don't waste energy arguing. Just do it."

Her mind was racing with the possibilities. Could she have been enhanced physically and psychically? It made more sense than being born so different. She could run faster, jump higher, stay under water longer, do things no one else she'd ever met could do. How? When? All the visits to her special doctor, the one she detested, the one her parents insisted she go to, were beginning to make sense.

She slipped her arm around Jack's waist and took most of his weight. If she wasn't enhanced, how could she practically carry a man of his size? He was twice her weight. "How were we enhanced?"

"Dr. Whitney."

Her mouth went dry. She knew that name. Knew he was the one who had put her up for adoption, who had designed her education and provided medical care for her and her family her entire life. Her birth father? Had he even been her father? What was she? Some kind of freak experiment?

Her mind began racing with the possibilities. *Why were they both there in Kinshasa?* Was it a coincidence that Jack and her brother Jebediah were in the service together? What were the odds that they would all end up in Africa together, especially since someone had paid an exorbitant amount of money to get them there?

Briony risked a brief glance at Jack's face. Even ravaged by pain and suffering, he was handsome in a masculine, chiseled sort of way. His features seemed carved out of stone, not real, but hard and weathered while remaining good-looking. He kept his gaze focused ahead, walking steadily, but more and more his weight was on her. The slow blood loss, coupled with exhaustion and his terrible wounds, was taking its toll. "Keep walking. One foot in front of the other." The closer she got him to the city, the less distance she'd have to carry him — and it looked like carrying was going to be involved.

They struggled for about a mile, following the stream. Briony had paused to get a better grip on him, when he suddenly pushed her to the ground, covering her body with his. His skin changed color to match the darker vegetation on the forest floor, and she immediately did her best to match his stripes. Jack had been nearly unconscious, but suddenly he was alert, pulling a handgun and signaling her to silence.

*What is it?*

*Sniper. He's been tracking me since I escaped the rebel camp. He's damned dangerous. You should have left when I told you to go.*

Briony's heart tripped into overtime and she tasted the familiar dryness of fear. She took a deep breath to combat the adrenaline and forced her mind away from panic as she lay listening. *He's behind us and to our right.*

*That would be him. Hopefully he didn't spot us while I was being careless.*

Briony squeezed her eyes closed tight and tried not to breathe. She hoped not, as well. She couldn't let this man suffer any more. No matter who he was or what he'd done, no one deserved to be tortured like he had been. She took a deep breath. *Are you a good shot?*

Jack looked at her. *You aren't going to do anything stupid.*

*You're going to pass out, tough guy. I know the signs. We don't have all that much time and we can't afford him behind us. I'm a good shot — but . . .* She hesitated.

Jack's hand tightened on the nape of her neck. *Whatever you're thinking — don't.*

Briony knew they couldn't outwait the sniper. Jack was going to pass out. How he'd rallied enough to know what was going on was beyond her. *I'm thinking I'm scared.*

*Don't be. I'll get you out of this. See those trees to our right? I'm going to cover you. You do a slow crawl to the trees and get into the branches. Use the branches to make it to the river. Keep your skin camouflaged and don't draw attention to yourself.* Jack slipped her the handgun. *You know how to use this thing?*

Briony hesitated then put her hand over the gun. There was no way to explain to him what the aftermath of violence could do to her. Feeling someone's emotions, feeling them die would bring a total meltdown. On the other hand, she was well trained, an expert marksman, and she believed in self-defense. *I know how to use it.*

He turned toward the region of forest

where he was certain the sniper followed them. On his belly, eye to the scope, he waved her forward. *Go. Get out of here. Don't stop moving until you're safe in your room.*

Briony inched her way through the ferns and rotting leaves, her heart pounding overly loud. She detested being a coward, wondering why, with all her special skills, she was always so afraid. She made it to the trees and crouched in the deepest shadows, studying the branches and vines for the best shelter, for the best position. With her extraordinary night vision, she was able to see some twenty-five feet up and over two trees, to a particularly large tree trunk with an umbrella of branches spreading in every direction, perfect for her needs.

Briony leapt to the lowest branch of the nearest tree and began to climb swiftly. She was slight, her body made for the aerial acts she'd practiced since she was a toddler. It was easy to use the vines to pull herself through the trees until she reached the tree beside the one with the larger, thicker trunk. She had taken care to stay hidden within the foliage when she climbed, but now she deliberately reached out and shook a branch, not too hard, just enough to give away her position.

*What the hell are you doing?*

*Drawing his fire to give you a target.*

*You do that again and I swear I'll beat you within an inch of your life.*

She could hear the menace prowling through his declaration — but felt it was an empty threat. Jack was a scary man, but he wasn't a man who would ever beat a woman — just the opposite in fact — unless she was the enemy. She'd caught that information in his mind. *Well, I'm not leaving you behind. Get ready to shoot something because I'm going to let him see me.*

*Damn it. Just damn it.*

Helpless male rage filled her mind, but she didn't wait — couldn't wait. Her courage was going to fail if she didn't act right then. Briony allowed the branch of the tree to sway just a little more, as if something heavy had stepped onto it. There was no wind in the forest, and the movement would draw the eye of the sniper instantly. Briony leapt to the next tree, sheltering behind the wide trunk, just as the bullet sent splinters of bark showering over her. Several pieces embedded in her arm and one in her chin. On the heels of the first shot came the second.

*Tell me you're all right.*

Briony clung to the tree, forcing her knees to be stiff when her legs had turned to rubber. The bullet had hit only inches from her head. The sniper had fired a lot faster than she'd anticipated. She sagged against the trunk and waited for her body to stop shaking. Blood trickled from the stinging wounds, but the splinters were mere scratches when it could have been so much worse. *Did you get him?*

*Stay still. There were two of them. I took out the sniper, but his spotter is just as capable. You aren't hit.* Jack made it a statement as he kept his eye to the scope, waiting for a shot at the spotter. He detested the fact that he was distracted by worry. He was *worried* about her. *Answer me now or I'm coming to you.* He would too. He'd risk getting shot just to make certain there wasn't a scratch on her body — at least not one he hadn't put there. His fingers itched to shake her for taking such a chance.

*I'm fine. Those shots are going to be heard by someone. They've got friends.*

*Get the hell out of here. Back to your room. Take a shower and get rid of those clothes. Ditch the gun in the forest. If anyone does any searches, you were asleep the entire time.* Jack rested his head on his rifle for a moment and then put his eye back to the scope. The lens blurred. He was weak and running out of time. In another few minutes he wouldn't be able to protect her — and that made him feel the edge of desperation.

Briony stood for a long while in the tree, too shaken to move. She'd always had incredible night vision, and now, staring into the area where the sniper had been, she spotted the broad leaves of a philodendron plant swaying slightly. The spotter was making his way toward Jack.

*Do you see him?*

There was no response — not even awareness. Briony's breath left her lungs in a rush. Jack was unconscious, or nearly so, and the enemy was creeping up on him. Before she had time to think, she leapt down to a tree branch that swept the ground. The forest floor was thickly carpeted with vegetation and cushioned her footsteps as she stealthily made her way through the underbrush back toward Jack. She had no real idea of what she was going to do, but she couldn't let him die.

She didn't examine too closely the need to keep Jack alive. There was no time for introspection, only to know she couldn't leave him. She shoved her way through the tangle of vines and bushes, dropping flat to crawl along a narrow animal trail. She pushed through a particularly thick mass of ferns into damp earth. A noise to her left had her dropping flat. She lay still for a moment, her heart pounding.

Briony inhaled. She had an amazing sense of smell and she could tell exactly where Jack was, and how close the spotter was to him. Jack lay on his belly, the rifle cradled in his arms, but his head was down. She willed him to move.

*Jack! Wake up. He's almost on top of you. You've got to defend yourself.*

Jack heard the urgent command, the fear and anxiety in Briony's voice. It drove him to find the strength to focus, to scent the spotter. The man was already on top of him. Jack turned to face him, knowing in that split second, that heartbeat of time, that he was too late — that he was a dead man. *Get out of here.* It was the only warning he could give Briony. He didn't have the strength to bring up his rifle, let alone the time.

The spotter stepped out of the brush and lifted his gun. Four shots rang out in rapid succession. Jack waited for the bullets to strike his body, but the spotter jerked and half spun to face away from him. His knees buckled and he went down hard, face into the ground. Jack forced his head up. Briony stood a few feet away, the gun in her hand, tears running down her face. She was shaking, her arm still outstretched, her gaze locked on the dead man.

Jack reached inside himself for one last burst of strength, struggled to his feet, and staggered over to her, his hand over hers. "Give me the gun, Briony."

She didn't release it — didn't look at him. She was shaking so much he was afraid she might accidentally pull the trigger again. He clamped his fingers over hers and, with his other hand, caught her face and forced her head to turn away from the body as he searched for a gentle tone. "Just let go, baby. I've got it now. Look at me. Only at me."

Her gaze met his, eyes swimming with tears. "I killed him." She turned away from him, retching, over and over.

Jack took a step closer and saw her eyes begin to roll back in her head. *Briony!* Deliberately he filled her mind with calm strength. He knew what violence could do to a psychic, and he wasn't about to allow her to fall. He caught her face in his hands. "Look at me. Stay with me."

Briony heard his voice as if from a great distance. She didn't want to go back, there was too much pain there, but his voice refused to let her retreat. With tremendous effort, she stared into his deep gray eyes.

"You're okay. Everything is going to be fine," he assured her. "I'm an anchor. Just let me do my work." He'd been too close to passing out and he hadn't provided barriers for her, but he focused on drawing the energy away from her.

He'd never expected to be so moved by the sight of a woman's tears — or by the fact that killing a man had made her physically ill. Worse, he could see splinters in her chin and along her arm. He didn't even have a medical kit to help her. "We have to get out of here. The rebels are going to be swarming all over this place." He roughened his voice, hoping to snap her out of it. "Come on. *Now*, Briony."

She wiped her mouth with the back of her hand, nodding her head. "I'm sorry, it's just that . . ." She trailed off and looked back toward the body on the ground.

Swaying unsteadily, Jack reached out and caught her to him. "Stop looking at him. He would have killed both of us. Move *now*." His thumb slid over her chin, wiping at the trickle of blood.

Briony blinked up at him and then firmed her mouth. Her arm slipped around his waist. "I'm all right now." She began walking with him toward the city, once again taking some of his weight. He had taken the stabbing pain away, but he couldn't take away the horror squeezing her heart.

"You should have left when I told you to go. You could have been killed."

"Just walk."

"I'm not going to make it, you know. I'm burning up, lost too much blood, in fact I can't see very well. The rebels looking for me had to have heard the shots . . ."

Briony sighed. "Save your strength. Just keep walking. I'll get you to the city, and my brother can figure out a way to get you out of Kinshasa."

Jack kept putting one foot in front of the other, determined not to pass out. He'd be damned if a female was going to carry his butt, and damned if she wouldn't do it if he couldn't walk. There was something about her that just plain got under his skin. He'd long ago chosen his path, and it didn't include a woman of his own or a family. Briony Jenkins was a woman made to belong to a man — heart and soul. She was the kind of woman that a man married and knew with a certainty she'd stick it out through good or bad, right beside her partner. Worse, she was the kind of woman a man might kill over, and he certainly was more than good at that. It made for a bad combination.

Briony glanced up at the man leaning more and more of his weight on her. He was swearing over and over under his breath. Sheer will kept him on his feet. "Do you need to rest?"

He didn't answer, but kept walking. They made it back to the stream, and Briony stopped him, sitting him on a fallen tree trunk. It was a measure of how far gone he was that he didn't protest when she helped him to sit. Her bizarre childhood training was suddenly an asset. Somewhere close by she sensed several men. She waited as long as she could, giving Jack a chance to rest before dragging him up again and setting off toward Kinshasa. She had to skirt around groups of soldiers hunting in the forest. Each time, their scent gave them away before she ever came close to them.

Once inside the city itself, she hoped they looked as if they'd been drinking. It was difficult to hide the sniper rifle and he wouldn't release it to leave behind, so she kept it locked between them, hoping their bodies hid it from anyone who might spot them. She chose the deserted streets and alleyways as she made her way with him back to her room.

"A few more steps, Jack," she said encouragingly. The man must have a will of absolute iron to keep going. He never faltered, stoically walking in spite of the raging fever.

His body was hot and dry, desperate for something to drink.

She kept to the shadows, skirting around the pockets of people they encountered. She avoided all contact with the soldiers on the corners, careful not to draw their attention. Once they were in the alley beneath the window of her room, she leaned Jack against the wall.

"I'm going up to open the window. Do you think you can make the jump?"

Jack slid down the wall to sit on the ground. He nodded, but didn't look at her. Briony wasn't so certain. She crouched and made the leap, catching the windowsill by her fingers. She drew herself up onto the narrow ledge and pushed open the window.

*Jack.* She was afraid to call out to him, all too aware of the soldiers and the possibility that the rebels had followed them into the city. *Can you make it?*

He didn't answer. Briony put one hand on the sill and leapt back down to the ground, landing lightly on her feet beside him. She put her hand on his shoulder. "I'll take the rifle." She reached for it.

Jack came alive, jerking back, his movement graceful and smooth, practiced, sliding away from her, coming to his feet, the rifle coming up. He shook his head. "Sorry.

I'll keep it. It belongs to my brother." He sagged back against the wall. "Where the hell are we?"

"My room is right up there, Jack. Can you make the jump? I don't want to bring you through the hall where someone might see you. This is safer for both of us." Safer for her brothers as well. She still had lingering fears that Jack might be in Kinshasa for reasons to do with her oldest brother.

Jack wiped sweat from his face. "I think so." But he didn't move. He closed his eyes, allowing the rifle to hang by the sling around his neck, his hands dropping to his sides as if his arms were too heavy.

Briony heard a slight noise and turned to see a soldier entering the alleyway. She clenched her teeth. This had to be the night from hell. They were never going to get into the safety of her room at this rate, and how could she possibly keep the soldier from seeing Jack's tortured body or the gun slung around his neck?

Desperate, Briony shoved Jack against the wall, her arms sliding around his neck. She leaned her body into his and lifted her mouth. The darkness surrounded them, enfolded them, so they became a shadowy silhouette the soldier could barely make out. She heard his footsteps approaching. If he saw the rifle now hidden between them, or saw the condition Jack was in, they were both in terrible trouble.

*Jack.* She whispered his name intimately, needing to rouse him, to make him more aware of the danger they were in. His name came out soft in her mind. An ache. Her lips feathered over his, tiny kisses along his bottom lip.

Jack's heart seemed to drop away. He felt her rising fear, but she stuck it out, stood with him, in front of him, protecting him, just as she had in the forest. Somewhere deep inside, that small spark of humanity he had left yawned wider, stretched, and the longing he rarely allowed himself to think about now had a name. *Briony.*

He breathed her into his mind, inhaled her into his lungs. One arm came up around her, drew her even closer, hand sliding down her spine, although he never opened his eyes. The other hand went between them to the knife at his waist. There was nothing sexual in the way he touched her, he wanted only to comfort her, but somehow the shape and texture of her body still managed to find its way through his fingertips and imprint the memory on his brain.

His hand settled in the wet strands of her hair and he pushed her face against his shoulder, wincing as she came into contact with his wounds. *Don't look. Just stay still.* He slowly withdrew the knife from his belt.

*Wait.* Her fingers curled around his neck. *Please, just another moment. He might walk away.* She willed the soldier to walk away. A lone guard curious in the middle of the night, not knowing death was only a breath away. There was no doubt in her mind that Jack, as ill as he was, would kill the man. Weak, his body ravaged by fever, he acted on instinct, on his extensive training. He was a killing machine, and anyone in his way was going to die. It had to be such a terrible way to live.

She closed her eyes tight, praying the soldier would shift directions. *Please, please, please don't let Jack have to kill him.* For the first time in her life, she deliberately tried to implant a suggestion in another's brain. She "pushed" at the soldier to return to the street.

She forgot that Jack could read her thoughts until his fingers bunched in her hair. She looked up at him. *I'm sorry. I don't want you to have to feel like that, taking a life.*

He opened his eyes to meet her gaze. She had the biggest, softest, most compassionate eyes he'd ever encountered. His expression hardened. He *didn't* feel anything anymore. That was the trouble. Not until now. This moment. Looking down at her too-innocent face.

He was a rough, hard man, capable of great cruelty and unrelenting, swift retaliation. He could shoot a man a mile or more away. He could rise up out of a stream and cut someone down without them ever having known he was near. He was a ghost in the forest or the desert. Some called him death and most avoided him. Here she was, looking up at him with compassion and even caring on her transparent face. He wanted to crush her sinfully sweet mouth under his, and yet, all the while, a part of his brain knew exactly where the soldier was, planned his every move, the step to take him away from Briony and the smooth throw that would end a life.

The soldier abruptly turned and walked back down the narrow alley, leaving them alone in the shadows. For a moment she sagged against him, the relief making her legs rubbery. "That was so close. Thank God."

He didn't tell her that God had left him a long time ago; instead he buried his face in the softness of her neck and inhaled her scent, wishing he could keep her. She fit in his arms and in his mind, but she would never fit into his life. He would hold on too tight, keep her too close, so close she wouldn't be able to breathe. She couldn't possibly understand a man like him, his sins so black there was no redemption, his rules his own, and his code one beyond civilization.

"Jack?"

Her voice pulled him out of his semi-stupor — or maybe it was a dream; he honestly couldn't tell anymore. He put her away from him and looked up at the window. "I can make it, and I'll cover you."

Briony didn't protest. He'd be lucky to make the leap, let alone try to protect her, but pointing out his rapidly deteriorating condition wouldn't get him into the room faster. She simply nodded and sent up a silent prayer that he make it on the first try. She wasn't altogether certain she was strong enough to jump the distance with him on her shoulder. Briony stood back to give him room, all the while keeping an eye on the entrance to the alley. "Go now," she encouraged, afraid the soldier might return.

Jack leapt, catching the windowsill and pulling himself into the room. Briony let out the breath she'd been holding and followed him up, sliding through the window and crouching on the floor, wanting to cry with relief. Now that she had the man in her room, she wasn't sure what she was going to do with him, but she calmly closed the window and hurried to get a bottle of cold water before turning on the light.

"Drink. You're dehydrated and burning up with fever. I'm going to clean your wounds and give you a shot of antibiotics. We carry medical supplies with us and I'm not bad at stitching when I have to do it."

"You give me the supplies and I can handle it," he assured her, sitting on the edge of the bed. The room was small and the bed looked inviting. "Nothing ever tastes quite so good as water." He trickled the fluid down his throat, resisting the urge to gulp it. "Thanks."

"You're welcome." Briony dipped a cloth in cool water and held it to the back of his neck. "You've got a really bad infection, Jack. I know you could sew the wounds yourself, but why don't you rest and just let me take care of you for now."

Jack took another, longer drink, his parched body greedy for the cool liquid. He took the cool cloth and bathed his face while he watched her mix up a solution in a bowl. "Get me tweezers."

"What?" She looked startled.

"I'm going to take care of your face and

arm. You'll get an infection if we leave it. I won't be in any shape to do it after, so get me the tweezers now."

"You've got to be joking."

"I don't joke." His voice was grim and he swayed, reaching for the wall to steady himself. "I mean it. You're not touching me until I fix you up. And if I pass out and someone comes, you get the hell out of here. Go through the window, up to the rooftops, not the alley, they'll trap you in the alley. Use the rooftops as long as you can and head back to the forest. You can hide out there."

"Do you boss everyone around?" She pulled the tweezers from her medical kit and handed them to him. "I feel like an idiot having you get splinters out of me when you're sliced to pieces."

He caught her chin and began to pull the largest splinters from her skin. "You saved my life. Thanks. I don't owe very many people, but I'd be dead if it weren't for you." He cleaned her chin with the antiseptic and held out his hand for the antibiotic ointment.

"I don't want to talk about that." Her stomach lurched uncomfortably. She closed her eyes against the memory of the man lying dead in the forest.

"He would have killed me."

"I know. Are you finished?"

"I don't like the way your arm looks. It was fairly deep. Keep putting the cream on it." He handed her the tweezers. "Yes, I boss everyone. It works better for me that way."

"I see. And does everyone do what you say?"

"The smart ones."

She couldn't help but look at his ravaged body, sliced into pieces. His obviously muscled belly, his thick chest and broad shoulders and arms had taken the brunt of the torture. He had two odd tattoos. She realized she wasn't seeing them with her normal vision, but rather with enhanced vision, as if seeing them under a UV light. She touched one. "These aren't normal. The ink is different."

"No one can see them other than one of us."

She wanted to know more, but instead of questioning him, she knelt down on the floor in front of him. Cleaning his wounds was imperative if he was going to survive. "This is going to hurt."

"Just get it done."

"You want to put down the rifle?"

Jack blinked down at her, surprised that he still had the rifle slung around his neck.

He placed it beside his hand on the mattress and added the handgun and two knives alongside of it before taking another drink. He leaned back until his head was resting against the wall. "Go ahead."

Briony braced herself. She didn't like hurting anyone, and washing the wounds with antiseptic was going to torture Jack all over again, but it couldn't be helped. "I could get one of my brothers if you'd be more comfortable."

"Briony." He said her name with a slight note of exasperation.

She just heard the weariness. His eyes were glazed with fever and he desperately needed to lie down. Pressing her lips together, she began the arduous task of cleaning him up. The knife wounds in his chest were hideous, blackened and crusted with bugs and infection. His body shuddered and broke out into a sweat, as she washed and applied topical antibiotics, but he stoically took it, occasionally drinking from the bottle of water.

"Ken. My brother."

Startled, she looked up. His body continually shook, but his expression didn't change, no matter how many times she had to wash the various cuts. "What about your brother?" Someone had rubbed a mixture of salt, leaves, and a paste into the open wounds, and getting it out wasn't easy.

"I boss him, but he doesn't always listen."

She flashed him a tight smile. "Good for him."

He swallowed several times as she scrubbed the deepest cuts, the ones so infected she wasn't sure even the potent antibiotics she had would help.

"Jack." Briony took the empty bottle of water from him and gently applied pressure to his shoulder. "Lie down for a while. You're safe for the moment. Go to sleep if you can while I do this. It's going to take some time."

In spite of his desire to remain alert, Jack found his body stretching out on his side without his permission. "I'm just going to rest for a minute."

Briony noted that his fingertips touched the handgun, as if he needed the reassurance that it was there, but his eyes closed. He didn't look softer or boyish in repose. He still looked as hard and dangerous as when he watched her with his restless gaze. She continued washing his chest, taking her time, wanting to do a thorough job the first time. The wounds were deep and ugly, a name carved into his chest. There were burns and tiny slices as if someone had taken a razor-sharp knife and made cuts every inch in perfect symmetry up and down his body, in long rows of ugly wounds.

She had no idea that she was crying as she began the job of sewing the wounds closed. On some she could use butterfly bandages, but most were deep enough to require stitching. She gave him a shot of antibiotics before coaxing him to turn over. His back was terrible, with long strips of flesh missing. It was no wonder the man was running a raging fever. Insects had swarmed to the feast. Sweat beaded on his body and the shaking continued, but he never uttered a single sound.

It took her long into the night to clean him up, eventually managing to get him to help her remove his boots and the filthy pants he wore. There were more signs of torture, the tiny slices cut into his legs and buttocks, even around his groin, as if they'd teased him with the idea of what would come later. Under other circumstances, she might have been too shy to clean a man in such intimate places, but the damage was so severe and, although at times she knew he was aware, he didn't open his eyes. Briony tried to be impersonal, but she felt sick at the idea that one human could do such things to another. By the time she finished, she felt protective and maybe a little possessive over him.

She pulled a light sheet over his body and brought him more water with antibiotic pills, bullying him enough awake to take them as well. Briony slipped her arm around his head to support his neck while he drank.

He hesitated before taking the pills, his eyes boring into her with suspicion. "Nothing to knock me out. I heal fast and I can take the pain."

"No, of course not, although now that you say that, it wouldn't be a bad idea." She pushed her fingers through the close-cropped hair, raking leaves and twigs from it. "Just antibiotics. We have to hit the infection hard. You need a doctor."

"You did a good enough job," he said gruffly, taking the pills with half the bottle of water. "Thanks."

"You're welcome. Go to sleep." Briony's arms ached, and although she still wasn't experiencing the psychic overload of too many emotions bombarding her, she had a killer headache from using telepathy, and she was shaking from the night's events. The thought that she'd killed a man, the sight and sound of it, sickened her.

She took a long shower, rinsing her hair and her body over and over as if that could remove the memories of the evening. Nothing seemed to help and the headache persisted. She brushed her teeth and once again scrubbed her hands before entering the room to check on Jack. His skin was hot to the touch, but he appeared to be sleeping. Turning off the light, she sank down onto the floor beneath the window and drew up her knees, hugging herself tightly.

Her brothers were going to lose their minds when they found out what she'd done. Jebediah might just kill her and put her out of her misery. She wasn't looking forward to the morning and his inevitable lecture on her safety and the safety of the family. The entire night had been too overwhelming. The man lying only a few feet from her had been mercilessly tortured, and now, even in his sleep, his body shuddered as if still feeling every abuse.

Life didn't make sense to her most of the time. And she never felt safe, or as if she belonged. Everyone around her tried; it wasn't her family or friends — it was her. She rocked herself slightly, trying to bring some comfort when the images of blood and death rose up to flood her mind. Jack stirred, and pain rippled across his face. She looked up, alert to see if he needed anything, but he appeared to be dreaming. When he settled back into a deeper sleep, she laid her head on her knees, feeling the burning wash of tears she couldn't prevent.

Blood and death surrounded him. Jack was drowning in it, helpless to get to the woman floating down the river. He reached for her, but missed her outstretched hand and knew he'd lost her forever. She didn't call out to him, but cried softly, tears pouring down her face. He heard the sound, muffled, heart-wrenching, and his eyes snapped open, gun tracking around the room.

Briony huddled on the floor, knees drawn up to her chest, head down. Her silver-gold hair spilled around her face, and the sight of her like that made his heart begin to pound in his chest. He swore silently between clenched teeth, his body too tired and too beat up to move, to get to her. Slowly he lowered the gun, resting it back on the bed.

"Briony."

Her head snapped up, one hand wiping at her eyes, a swift movement that she tried to hide. "Are you in pain? You must be. We've probably got something for pain in the kit." There was a small tremor in her voice, but she rallied, covering her distress.

"Come here."

She stilled, her eyes too large and drowning in tears, long lashes spiky and wet. Jack could hardly bear the sight of her like that. She should have been somewhere where she was safe and protected — not in Kinshasa where anything could happen to her.

"I said come here."

The hard note of command stopped her weeping. "I heard you." He looked so determined, as if he might get up and come over to her in spite of his injuries. Briony got to her feet and crossed to his side, laying her palm on his forehead to assess his fever. "Do you want more water?"

He nodded, his gaze never leaving her face, his eyes still glazed with fever. She took out another bottle and removed the cap before handing it to him.

"You washed your hair." Jack let the liquid slide down his throat, savoring the taste of it. "Whatever you use smells good." He caught her wrist when she turned away. Tugging, he indicated the bed. "Don't sit on the floor. I'm not in any shape to do anything and it's more comfortable." Mostly he wanted to comfort her. It wasn't something he'd ever thought he'd be doing, but he'd give it a shot just so she wouldn't cry anymore. When she didn't respond either way, he pulled her down to the mattress.

"I could jar you."

"I doubt it." He let his fingers slide over her tear-wet face. "Don't be doing this."

"What? Crying? Every time I close my eyes I see that man dead. Or I see someone cutting you into little pieces." She pressed her fingertips to her temple. "I'm afraid to go to sleep."

"You have a headache. Did you take anything for it?"

"My headache is rather insignificant next to what the rebels did to you. I can't believe you were running around the forest. You should be dead."

"I wasn't going to die and give them the satisfaction." He took another sip of water, his fingers tangling in her hair. It was softer than he'd first imagined. "They would have done better just to put a bullet in my head."

"Why didn't they?"

Jack set the bottle of water on the small nightstand beside the bed and used both hands to massage her temples. Her body felt small and soft next to his, and he actually had a reaction to her, disconcerting when he was trying to be comforting. She was too innocent for a man like him to ever have sex with her. He'd shock the holy hell out of her, be too rough, too demanding, too everything. His body hardened even more and he shut the door on that line of thinking. There was no way he was going to allow it to happen. *How could his body react when he was beat up all to hell?* Nothing about the situation made sense to him and that made him leery. He was always distrustful, but his reactions to Briony were completely out of character.

"The general wants people to be afraid of him. The crueler he is, the more everyone fears him and he gets what he wants. Torture and genocide and rape are good ways to intimidate people."

Briony was silent for a long time. She sighed. "My brothers won't listen to me. They think I'm paranoid, but the music festival offered us an enormous sum of money to perform here. It didn't make sense to me then and even less since I've been here. The festival doesn't have that kind of money and we weren't going to be that big of a draw. You served with my brother and we're both enhanced psychically and physically. I've never met anyone like me before. In fact, this is the first time in my life I've ever been able to be near another human being without feeling their emotions and being sick. Don't you think it's all too much of a coincidence?"

"If you're paranoid, Briony, I am too."

"Tyrel told me there's a rumor that rebel soldiers are sneaking into town. If they aren't here for the music festival, my guess is they're looking for you."

"I'd have to say when they find the bodies on the outskirts of the city, they'll definitely come looking."

"Jebediah's going to be really, really angry with me."

"Don't worry about your brother. He knows me." Jebediah knew him all right, and he sure as hell wouldn't want Jack Norton lying in the same bed with his sister. Jack lay staring up at the cracked ceiling, one hand in her hair, the other over the gun, listening to her soft, even breathing and wondering why he already felt like she belonged to him.

# CHAPTER 4

Pounding on the door jarred Jack and Briony from their sleep. The gun was already in Jack's fist and he waved her to the safety of the bathroom.

"Open the door, Bri!" Jebediah yelled. "I'm standing out here with coffee and you're still asleep. Get a move on."

"It's my brother," Briony said unnecessarily, but she wanted Jack to put the gun away. She deliberately moved in front of him, blocking his sight to the door, pressing her hand to his head to check for fever. She raised her voice. "Just a minute, Jebediah. Have a little patience."

Jack swept her out of the way with his arm. "Stay to the side of the door when you let him in. Someone could be standing behind him with a gun to his head."

"He would have warned me," Briony objected. "Don't shoot my brother."

"Stand to the side of the door." When she

remained frowning at him, he clenched his teeth. "Damn it, do what I tell you."

Briony huffed out a breath just to show him he annoyed her, although it didn't seem to faze him. She told herself she obeyed to keep Jack from getting upset as she unlocked and opened the door, not because he was downright scary at times.

"Here." Jebediah handed her a cup of coffee as he leaned in to kiss her cheek. As he did, his gaze jumped beyond her to the bed where Jack lay on his side beneath the sheet, the gun steady in his hand, aimed straight at Jebediah's heart. "What the hell are you doing here, Norton?" Jebediah jumped to place his body between the gun and Briony.

"I'm so glad you remember Jack, Jeb," Briony said, trying to be cheerful. "He needs to get out of the country and I thought you might be able to help."

"Lock the door." Jack slowly lowered the gun and put his head on the pillow, draping one arm over his eyes.

Briony turned the lock and leaned against the door, blowing on the coffee to keep from having to look at her brother.

"Just how did you meet up with Jack Norton, Briony?" Jebediah demanded.

"I went to the forest on the edge of the city," she admitted.

"Damn it, Briony." Jebediah advanced on her threateningly, looming over her shorter figure. "What were you thinking to take a risk like that? Going out into the forest when I told you to stay put."

"Jebediah." Jack's voice cut in, his tone very low, almost purring. "You talk to her like that again around me and I'm going to rip out your heart. We clear on that?"

Briony's heart jumped at the threat. Coming from anyone else, it would have been melodramatic, but Jack sounded like he meant it. His tone was mild, he hadn't raised his voice; in fact he hadn't even sat up, one arm was still slung over his eyes, but something in his ultrarelaxed posture seemed deceptive — as if inside he was coiled like a snake, ready to strike at any moment. She had never in her life met anyone so casual about violence.

Jebediah backed up. "She's my sister and my responsibility, Jack. She could have been killed." He almost sounded conciliatory.

"I already raked her over the coals. Once is enough for anyone." Jack's tone said to drop it.

Briony sank down onto the edge of the bed and looked up at her brother. "I'm sorry. I needed to breathe. I couldn't stay here surrounded by all the people . . ."

Jack's arm snaked out fast, his fingers settling around her wrist. "Don't apologize. You're not an anchor. You can't be around so many people and not feel their misery. Your brother ought to know that about you by now."

"What the hell are you talking about, Jack?" Jebediah demanded. "My sister isn't any of your business."

Jack sat up slowly, the sheet falling away to reveal the masses of cuts and burns and carvings on his chest and shoulders.

"God, Jack." Jebediah swallowed hard, his gaze jumping to Briony's. "Who got ahold of you? You need a doctor."

"Briony took care of me."

Jebediah's expression hardened. "*Briony?* What's going on between you two?"

"Wild sex, Jebediah," Briony snapped, sarcasm dripping from her voice. "I'm not sixteen, you know, and you're totally embarrassing me." She handed the coffee to Jack. "Does he look in shape to perform?"

Jack looked at her over the top of the cup, his eyes meeting hers, a sudden raw intensity turning the deep gray of his eyes to a liquid silver. "I would have accommodated you had you asked."

A ghost of a smile curved her mouth, but inside her stomach did a funny little flip.

He didn't look as if he was joking. Her womb did an unexpected clench and she had to look away from him.

"That's not funny, Jack," Jebediah snapped. "Don't even think about my sister that way."

"I'm heading to the bathroom and don't have much on," Jack pointed out. "So if you're on the shy side, you might not want to look."

She'd already looked. Briony turned toward the window, not wanting either of them to see the color stealing up her neck to her face. "I washed your clothes," she said, "and hung them up on the shower, but I doubt if they're dry. Jebediah, would you get him jeans and a shirt?"

Her brother waited until Jack disappeared into the bathroom before crouching down in front of her. "Are you crazy?" he hissed. "Do you have any idea who that man is? Or what he's capable of doing?"

Even with Jack out of the room, his close proximity kept the anger, shock, and alarm her brother was exuding from hitting her quite as hard as it usually did. "As far as I can see, Jeb, he's been tortured and needs help. Can you get him out of here?"

"The soldiers in the city are all stirred up. That's why I brought you coffee rather than have you go out this morning. A few dead bodies were found early this morning, reportedly rebels. The fear is that they're infiltrating the city, and that's why the army is on alert. They were searching bars last night."

"The rebels are looking for Jack. He escaped from their camp."

"And they want him bad enough to come into Kinshasa, with soldiers on every street corner?" Jebediah scratched his head. "You're right, we'll have to get him out of here. They'll look closely at us because we're foreigners. I'll get clothes for him and you keep him out of sight. Is he strong enough to travel?"

"Yes, but I don't have any idea how. He needs a doctor, though. If you have antibiotics in your travel kit or any of the others do, bring them to me."

Jebediah nodded. "Are you sure you're all right, Briony? He didn't hurt you?"

She shook her head. "He protected me, Jebediah." She wanted to share with her brother the things Jack had revealed about the "GhostWalkers," but the fact that she felt no pain around Jack and did with her brothers would bother Jebediah. He'd be hurt by the revelation, and she'd made up her mind a long time ago that she was done hurting her family. They weren't ever going to know how much she really suffered in their presence.

Jebediah cast a quick glance at the bathroom door. "He must have contacts as well. Has he said anything about what he was doing here? Whether he was supposed to reach an extraction point?"

"He hasn't said much of anything."

"That would be Jack. He plays it pretty close to his chest. I'll get him clothes, keep the door locked."

Briony followed him and locked the door, setting the coffee aside for Jack when he came out of the shower. She was going to give him another shot of antibiotics the moment he came out, feed him and get more fluids down him. He had to get strong fast and that meant he needed to kick the infection.

The water shut off, and a few minutes later Jack emerged, towel wrapped around his narrow hips. His dark hair was still wet and the raw knife wounds were red and angry-looking scattered over his body. With stitches everywhere, he looked a little like Frankenstein. He had broad shoulders and powerful arms, and was well built, with massive upper body strength and defined muscle. His face was all masculine, tough and weathered with several scars. Other older scars, both from knives and bullets, marred his skin in several places over his body.

"You look a little worse for wear," Briony observed as she handed him another bottle of water. "Drink this, take another pill, and you can have the entire cup of coffee. I won't even ask for a sip."

She looked beautiful to Jack. Sunshine and flowers in a meadow. He tried not to stare at her, taking the water and downing the pill she gave him without question. It hurt just to look at her, and her scent was plain driving him crazy. He turned his back on her and walked to the window to check the alley below them. He heard her sharp inhale and knew she was staring at the mess of his back. The front looked worse, but he was alive so he wasn't complaining.

"I don't mind sharing the coffee with you." His voice was gruff — or maybe rusty. He hadn't really used it in a while. When talking was necessary, Ken had done most of it. Jack hadn't meant for his statement to come out intimate, but it sounded that way, an invitation. Just being close to her stirred up his body, and his blood pounded in his veins. It was disconcerting to have such a strong reaction to a woman.

"Jack you're prowling around the room like a caged tiger. Sit down and let me look at your wounds."

He glanced at her, and his heart did a peculiar somersault, his pulse raced. He pressed one hand to his chest, shocked at the way he couldn't control his response to her. He sat down because it was easier than trying to walk when it was becoming painful. He realized at once that that was a terrible mistake. She bent over him, her body so close to his he felt her through his skin. Her scent enveloped him until he couldn't do anything but breathe her in. He was acutely aware of every detail of her body — the curve of her cheek, the length of her lashes, the steady beat of her heart. Every stroke of her fingers, as she applied topical antibiotics, felt like a caress designed to heighten his need of her.

His erection grew thicker and harder, blood pounding, centering in his groin. Her breasts brushed against his arm as she leaned across him to get to a wound on his chest that was particularly inflamed. If his body had hurt before, he couldn't remember it, with the throbbing ache between his legs. He couldn't think with the roaring in his head and the taste and feel of her imprinted in him.

Jack gritted his teeth and tried to use his brain. He was a loner, a solitary man who needed no one and kept it that way. Every woman had been someone he could take or leave, and he liked it that way. This woman wasn't the leaving kind and he knew better than to want her. He had discipline. Control. He heard a noise escape, a growl of need he couldn't prevent. The sound was as primitive as the way she was making his body feel. Worse, she had somehow gotten under his skin.

His fingers settled around her wrist, and he tugged at her until Briony turned her head and looked at him. Their eyes met and an electrical charge of spine-tingling awareness shot down his spine.

"Did I hurt you?" Her voice caressed his skin, her breath warm and inviting, fingertips stroking back his wet hair. "I'm trying to be gentle, but you have so many deep cuts."

"Sit on the end of the bed." He sounded rough even to his own ears, but it didn't matter. She had to get a distance away from him or he was going to roll her body under his and do all the things playing out in his mind that would shock the hell out of her.

Briony smiled at him. "Do you order everyone around?"

Her smile lit up her face. It did something special to her eyes, turning the deep brown to a melting chocolate. Another growl escaped, and he tried to look away, but she seemed to mesmerize him. "Yes," he bit out between clenched teeth. "Just do what I say when I say and we'll be fine, Briony."

She laughed. The sound sent a shudder of pleasure rippling through his body. He was suddenly very afraid for both of them — for his honor and her innocence. "Have you ever heard of self-preservation? Because I don't think you have much in that department."

Briony seated herself on the edge of the bed. "I have plenty, thank you. It's just that you really do expect everyone to do what you say whenever you command them. You can't control other people, if they won't allow it."

His gaze drifted over her face possessively. "You aren't one of those other people. I'm trying to do the right thing here and keep my hands off of you."

Briony's heart jumped. Her pulse pounded. His scent had been driving her crazy, like some aphrodisiac she couldn't resist. She'd tried not to let him know, but she'd needed to touch him, needed to be close to him. She tried to tell herself it was because for the first time in her life she could be in the close confines of a room with another human being and not feel the pain of his thoughts and emotions. She moistened her suddenly dry lips and was instantly aware of his burning gaze following the sweep of her tongue along her bottom lip, turning her gesture into something sexual.

"At least you have the sense to be nervous."

The sound of a fist against the door made her jump. Jack swept out his arm to block her with his body, gun coming up so smoothly she knew it was an automatic gesture.

"Briony!" Jebediah bellowed. "Open up."

Jack didn't know whether to be relieved or to curse. "The man has never been quiet," he said. "Remember to stand to the side of the door."

"No, he hasn't," Briony agreed as she unlocked the door, doing it the way Jack insisted.

Jebediah handed jeans and a shirt to Jack and a syringe to Briony. "Seth also has antibiotics in his medical kit." He reached into the hall and dragged a tray in. "I brought food as well, figured you hadn't eaten in a while."

Jack nodded to him and took the tray.

"You look like shit, Jack," Jebediah observed. "The rebels weren't fooling around with you. If they cut you up any more, you'd be in pieces."

"They skinned Ken." There was a hard note in Jack's voice, one of deadly purpose. "They cut up him up from his feet to his head. They'd just gotten started on me. I was lucky."

Jebediah swore under his breath, and glanced at Briony and caught her blinking back tears. "You're too soft, Bri," he snapped. "You always have been. In the real world, shit happens and you have to be tough."

Jack raised his head, gray eyes glittering with more than menace, with promise of retaliation. "Leave her the hell alone. She's fine just the way she is."

Jebediah bit back a retort as he shrugged. "I can call a few people, Jack, see what we can do to get you out of here; otherwise I'll think of a way to smuggle you out."

"I can call for an extraction, but I need to call people I trust."

Jebediah's jaw tightened. "You think someone set you up?"

"I know I was set up." The cold gray eyes never left Jebediah's face, watching with that same deadly intent. "Nice that you happened to be here." The comment was casual enough, but nothing Jack Norton said was ever that casual.

"Look, Jack, I'm not in the military anymore. I work my family business and I have nothing to do with anyone. I have no ties to the CIA or any other organization. Whatever is going on here, I had nothing to do with. You should know me better than that. I have no reason to turn against my country or my friends." Deliberately he reminded Jack of their past together.

"Money is a powerful motivator."

"Don't accuse my brother of such a terrible thing. We're risking our lives to help you," Briony snapped. She swiped his arm with antiseptic and waved the syringe at him.

Jack caught her wrist. "Are you going to stab me with that thing?" For one moment amusement flared in his eyes, and then receded just as quickly.

"Absolutely. Don't be such a baby. I'll bet you were all tough when they were cutting you into pieces."

*They didn't have big brown eyes and look at me like they're going to cry for me.*

There was an intimacy talking telepathically that she couldn't deny, and his voice held such a caress it sent a shiver through her body. Briony shook her head and gave him the injection. *You certainly have a way with women.*

He didn't reply, merely ran his finger down her arm, a soft, light touch with the pad of his finger. Heat surged through her, breasts aching, the throbbing between her legs increasing with sudden urgent need. Her response was so intense she couldn't move for a moment. She just stood there like a deer caught in the headlights, staring down at him, afraid naked longing would be transparent on her face.

His fingers tangled with hers, as if he was removing the needle from her hand, but he didn't let go. "I'll need a way to contact my people, Jebediah. In the meantime, this place isn't the best defensive position. I don't have a lot of room to maneuver if they come for me, and they'll know Briony helped me. I don't want any trails leading back to you or your family."

"Bri, take him to the practice arena. It's about a block from here, Jack. Dressed in my clothes and walking with Bri, you should be fine. I'll find a way to make the contact."

"Thank you, Jeb. I appreciate whatever you can do," Jack acknowledged.

"We'll get you home safe," Jebediah promised, raising a hand as he left.

"Eat," Briony instructed. Jack's thumb slid back and forth absently over the back of her hand. She wasn't certain if he was aware of it, but she was. Every feathering caress sent a shiver through her body. She pulled her hand away and backed up a few steps to try to get some breathing room. Every breath she drew into her lungs brought his masculine scent swirling through her veins. "How can you be so broken and yet not even give a single sign you're in pain?"

His gaze brushed her face, dropped to her mouth, and drifted over her body. He took a bite of toast and chewed thoughtfully. "You perform in front of thousands of people. You're here, in Kinshasa where people are killed and raped and even tortured. You feel everything they feel. So you tell me, how do you do it?"

"It's different." Briony was a little shaken, that he knew — that he could see her life, her sacrifices for her family, so clearly.

"How is it different?"

"I choose to do it for my family. To fit in. To be a part of something."

"So they'll love you?"

Her head whipped around, eyes darkening with temper. "Why do you do that? You sound so utterly calm and mild and yet you're deliberately trying to provoke me."

"I'm just asking a question."

"You don't think my family would love me if I didn't perform with them?"

"I think they'd love you no matter what, but I don't think you do."

Briony turned away from him. "You don't know anything about me or my life."

"I'm inside your head. You think I can't feel your emotions?"

She spun around again, a shocked look on her face. "You can? I can't feel yours. You said you were an anchor. What does that mean *exactly*?"

"I draw emotion and energy away from you, act as the filter you don't have. And yes, you could feel my emotions if I allowed it, and no, I can't really feel yours unless your guard is down. Sometimes you let me in and other times you don't. Like now. The door is nailed closed. You don't want me to know anything about your family."

"I don't know you."

He finished off the food in silence and drank the rest of the bottle of water. Pushing aside the tray, he stood up. Nearly every inch of his body was covered in wounds yet he didn't even wince.

Briony winced for him. "I have a pain-killer. It isn't very strong, but maybe it would take the edge off."

"I don't need it. Try to get my pants to dry. I'll need those when I leave." He crossed to the bathroom, but didn't shut the door, standing just out of sight as he tossed the towel to one side. "If I was going to harm your family, Briony, they'd be dead already." He opened the door wider as he buttoned up the jeans. Her face had gone pale. "Was that your first dead body?"

Briony clenched her fist. He sounded so casual she wanted to throw something at him. There was nothing casual about taking a life. "No. I found my parents — murdered." She could barely get the word out.

He drew in his breath. He was feeling her emotions now. Raw pain. A flood of sorrow mixed with guilt and fear. "That's never going to go away, and I'm telling you that from experience. I found my mother dead. I was nine years old. I can still see every detail. All the blood. The way her face was smashed in. There was so much blood." He shook his head. "A hell of a thing for either of us to carry around for the rest of our lives, isn't it?"

His voice hadn't changed at all, still mild. Low. But she heard a vibration of menace running through her head. He didn't show emotion at all, but he *felt,* and the intensity was like a volcano waiting to erupt.

"I think someone killed them because of me." She told him because he seemed to believe her when no one else took her seriously.

He stopped in the act of pulling the T-shirt over his head. "Why?"

"I don't know. I heard them arguing with someone out in the stable with the horses. I heard my father say very distinctly they wouldn't allow Briony to try such a thing, it was too dangerous. I heard shots. Just two shots. I ran as fast as I could, and I'm fast, but when I got there, they were both dead and whoever did it was already gone. Each had one bullet in the head, right here." She pressed her finger between her eyes. "I never saw who did it, and the murderer had to be close, but I couldn't find him." She looked at him. "I couldn't even smell him."

"What did they want you to do?"

"I have no idea. I told my brothers, and they went through the messages and paperwork in the trailer, but couldn't find anything. The police didn't find their killer." She looked at him. "How did your mother die?"

Jack pulled the shirt over his head. He'd never told anyone. Never opened that particular wound. He'd had no intention of telling her either. Damn it. There was no stitching that injury closed, and he *was* going to tell her, but he had no idea why. "She was beat to death. He used his fists and then a baseball bat."

"Jack." She wanted to put her arms around him. She felt his emotions now — black rage — ice cold. "I'm so sorry. What a terrible thing. Who would do such a thing?"

"Her husband." He glanced around the room. "You have a hat in here? Maybe a backpack?"

Why had she thought he didn't have emotions? The room was shaking, the walls undulating. "Jack." She reached out to touch him.

Jack knocked her hand away, clearly a reflex action. He was strong, and she felt the impact right through her body. Their eyes met. Held. A muscle jumped in his jaw.

"I'm sorry. Did I hurt you?" He stepped close to her, almost protectively. "I don't know why I did that."

"I'm fine." She pulled a backpack out of the tiny closet to avoid looking at him. She had to blink back tears — not because he'd hurt her, but because his pain was so raw and his rage so deep, she needed to weep for him, because he hadn't — wouldn't.

"Damn it. I don't usually talk this much."

She handed him the backpack and rummaged through the drawers for a hat.

"You actually put your clothes in the closet?"

She glanced at him, knowing he needed to change the subject. He would never be comfortable with personal revelations. "Of course. What do you do with your clothes?"

He looked around the small room. "I don't actually stay in hotels much. I'm usually outdoors. But maybe a duffel bag."

Briony pushed a hat into his hands. "That should do it. Let's go." The close confines of the room were really getting to her. Jack seemed to be everywhere. She'd never been so aware of a man.

Jack stopped her before she could open the door. "Wait. Always check. *Always.*" He set her to one side and stood to the other, his gun in his hand, held flat across his body. "Open it slowly, just a crack." He crouched low, sweeping the hallway before signaling to her. "You have to think security at all times, Briony. You're a GhostWalker whether you like it or not, and you've got the training."

"I'm not going to be hunting people in the jungle," she objected. "I perform in a circus. I fly."

"Walk on my left side. Stay up with me. If

we run into trouble, drop behind me and take off, using my body as a shield while I cover you. Stay away from my gun hand and walk in step."

She sighed. "Do you have any more rules?"

Again that very faint trace of amusement touched his mouth and faded just as quickly. "You have no idea."

"I can only imagine."

"Soldier at seven o'clock. Don't look at him, look up at me. Stay under my shoulder and put one hand on my waist. Just rest it there. Keep walking and talk to me, smile and laugh the way you would with one of your brothers."

"I'd be kicking my brother for ordering me around," Briony said, flashing him a quick smile. "You do know what century you're living in, don't you?"

"Doesn't matter. I know how to stay alive, and when you're with me, I'm going to make certain you do too."

"That's so comforting; thank you, Jack." She slowed and nodded toward a warehouse. "They set us up to use this building because it's so tall. Hot as hell, but definitely roomy."

Jack held open the door and glanced back to see the soldier walking around the corner.

He followed Briony inside and stopped, looking up at the trapeze and high wire. "You perform up there?"

She nodded. "I dive through rings of fire and run across the wire without a balance pole. It's a unique act. I can do a quadruple somersault because I can generate a lot of speed when I fly. Quads just aren't done."

He studied her face. "Do you like it?"

She blinked up at him and then kicked the toe of her shoe against the rigging as if testing it. "My family's been in the circus for generations."

Jack continued to look at her averted face. "That's interesting information, but not what I asked. You don't like it, do you?"

She shrugged. "I have trouble being in a space with so many people. It can be difficult, but I'm used to it." She sent him a small smile. "It's actually pretty amazing to be with you. I don't feel sick or in pain at all."

"Why do you keep doing it?"

She stretched to catch a dangling rope. "Because it's my life. It's what we do." She went up the rope, her body fluid and graceful, pulling herself up hand over hand, not even using her feet.

Jack caught the rope next to the one she went up and began his ascent, traveling faster to catch up with her. She increased her speed, forcing him to increase his. He heard her soft laughter, a challenge to him, and he passed her, reaching out to catch her rope with one hand, halting her progress.

She wrapped her foot in the rope and grinned at him. "You have such an ego."

Her mouth was only inches from his, and her tantalizing feminine scent seemed to fill his lungs, until he was breathing her through his entire body. He loved the shape of her mouth and the way her smile lit her eyes.

"You don't even know." He leaned into her, dragging her rope even closer. If he was any kind of a man, it had to be said. "You shouldn't be alone with me." He didn't release her. She could drop away from him, but she couldn't climb any higher.

They stared at each other for what seemed an eternity. "Close your eyes."

Her eyes widened. She blinked twice, almost as if mesmerized, but then her lashes fluttered and she pulled back, shaking her head. "You can't kiss me."

"I'm going to kiss you."

"I don't kiss anyone."

His eyebrow shot up. *"Ever?"*

"I can't touch people. I mean, I do my family, but it has — repercussions."

"You kissed me."

"That wasn't a kiss."

Jack allowed the rope to slip out of his hand, but kept pace with her as she climbed above the highest platform. He watched her swing upside down, perform a slow somersault in the air, and set her feet onto the platform. "You don't have repercussions when you touch me." He did the same controlled maneuver so that he stood beside her. He caught her by the shoulders and dragged her close to him, his grip unbreakable.

Without another word he lowered his head to hers. There was no point in arguing — he *had* to kiss her. He couldn't think of anything but the shape of her mouth, the soft texture of her lips — and he wanted to taste her. Almost from the first time he'd caught her feminine scent, she'd filled his mind, until he could think of little else.

The moment his lips touched hers, time seemed to stop, to stand still. There was only Briony in his world. Not his shattered body, wracked with pain, not his firm resolve to keep her at an emotional distance — everything that had come before was gone, until there was only this one woman. She tasted of hot spice and honey, an addicting rush that sped through his veins with the speed of a fireball and settled deep inside of him. He would never get her out. He could spend the rest of his life kissing her and it would never be enough.

He caught her face in his hands, holding her still while his mouth moved over hers and his tongue probed deep, wanting more, claiming more. He started with the best of intentions, a light, feathering kiss, tongue tracing her soft lips and teasing until she opened for him, but the moment he sank into the magic of her mouth, soft and warm and so inviting, he couldn't prevent the groan of hunger, the ravenous need that broke free so that he took complete control of the kiss, using every bit of experience and expertise he had. He didn't want to give her time to think — only to feel — to want him the way he wanted her.

Something struck the metal frame of the building, and Briony pulled away, swinging her head around, her breath coming in a ragged gasp. "Soldiers?"

"Maybe," he replied grimly.

"They're at the door," she warned. "Quick. Lie down in the exact center. You're in the shadows up here."

Jack obeyed, expecting her to lie beside him. Instead, she hurried to the rope, pausing with one hand on it.

"Stay prone. You're too high; they won't be able to spot you," Briony hissed. She eluded his outstretched hand as she caught the rope more firmly and slipped halfway down to the floor. She was still dangling a good fifteen feet in the air as she began to perform a series of slow moves, changing positions with flowing precision, each move requiring tremendous strength and skill.

*What the hell do you think you're doing? You're driving me out of my mind, woman.*

*We don't want them searching the place, and my brothers and I come in to practice all the time. Just stay still. If they find you, they'll kill me and my brothers.* She broke off abruptly, praying he wouldn't go psycho on her.

Jack bit back any retort. There was no use arguing with her; she was already out in the open. He could kill the rebels, was fully prepared, but it would bring down a hellstorm on them. Damn her. She had no right to take chances with her life — not to protect him or her brothers.

Three men entered the building. Their movements were furtive, as if they were afraid of being seen. They weren't dressed in uniforms, but they carried themselves like the soldiers she'd seen on every street corner. They stared up at her for a long moment, and something in the way they looked at her made her shiver. She stopped in mid-somersault and sat up, looping her foot through the rope to peer down at them.

*Rebels,* he warned.

*You think?* Her mouth was dry, heart pounding. "I'm sorry, you're not supposed to be in here while we practice."

"Come down now," one called to her and pointed to the floor. He let her see the gun inside his jacket.

Briony allowed fear to show on her face. It wasn't very hard — she *was* afraid. "I'm telling you, security will be here any minute, you'd better leave."

He drew the gun and aimed it at her. "Get down here."

Even with the heavy accent, Briony understood. She slowly made her way down the rope. "I'm with the circus act performing at the music festival. My brothers will be here any minute. I have no money . . ."

Jack's heart pounded with fear for her. He slid the gun out of the backpack and laid it on the platform, his finger on the trigger. Sweat beaded on his brow. The rebels made artwork out of raping women as brutally as possible. When he killed them, it would bring not only the rebels down on him, but the soldiers as well.

"Close your mouth," the rebel snapped, stepping toward Briony. He deliberately loomed over her to intimidate her.

*They're used to everyone being afraid of them.*

Briony swallowed hard, stopping herself from nodding in acknowledgment of the information as she watched the shortest of the three shut the door.

"We're looking for an escaped prisoner."

Briony put her hand on her hip. "You aren't soldiers or security, and take a look around, does it look like I'm hanging out with prisoners?"

The leader slapped her hard, knocking her backward. Briony staggered, but kept on her feet. For a moment her ears rang, and then she felt the blast of rage, so deep, so intense it snapped her to attention. *Don't you dare go berserk and shoot him.* She breathed deeply to try to calm Jack, knowing he was a heartbeat from killing the man.

Briony put her hand to her stinging face. The big man advanced on her, deliberately aggressive, shoving his gun at one of his partners. He said something in his language she shouldn't have understood, but it was all too clear. He thought she needed a man to show her who was in charge. Knowing Jack was close by was oddly comforting.

The man caught the front of Briony's shirt and she caught his wrist, locking on, exerting pressure, staring straight into his eyes. At the same time she pushed hard into his brain, forcing her mind into his. *If you touch me, you will die. Leave now. Take these men and go before it's too late.*

He let go of her as if she had burned him, muttering the local word for "witch." He grabbed his gun from his companion and spun away from her, hurrying out, snapping a command to the others. They followed him out, slamming the door hard.

Briony sagged with relief, covering her face with shaking hands. Jack slid down the rope and strode toward her, his features hard and set, eyes glittering dangerously.

# CHAPTER 5

Jack locked the deadbolt on the door with a resounding thud and just kept coming, walking right up to her, hands gripping her arms hard. He gave her a little shake. "What the hell were you trying to do? He was going to rape you. If I felt it, you had to be swamped with his intentions. What's wrong with you?"

"Everyone underestimates me because I'm so small. I knew I was stronger than he was. I wouldn't have let him touch me."

"He *did* touch you. He fucking hit you, while I hid like a dog up on that platform. He *wanted* to hurt you. He reeked of it. You had to have smelled him. He was excited by the idea of hurting a woman like you." His palm covered her red cheek.

"And I handled it," Briony snapped, her own temper beginning to rise and mix with the nearly mind-numbing fear. She jerked her head away from him because his touch affected her way too much. "I *handled* it. I'm capable of taking care of myself. I wouldn't just let a man rape me."

"Hence the word *rape.*" His eyes narrowed. "You weren't safe, Briony. Not then and you aren't now either. You should be screaming your head off."

"I wouldn't bring the soldiers in here. They're trigger happy. And I'm not afraid of you. You want me to be, but I'm not."

"You should be. Do you have any idea what I want to do right now?" His hand slid back up to her face, cupping her cheek and pressing his palm to her burning skin as if he could take the sting away.

"Yes. You aren't even trying to keep me out." The intensity of his emotions swamped her and robbed her of her anger and fear. He *needed* to touch her — to feel her close to him. He couldn't think with wanting her. Briony had never had anyone look at her the way he did, or be so fierce in his protection of her.

"I want you to see me for what I am, Briony. I'm hard and can be cruel and I don't have those gentle feelings you deserve in a man." All the while he spoke, his hands belied what he said, thumbs sweeping soothing caresses over her swollen cheek.

"I can't touch you. You have too many

stitches, Jack. We can't possibly . . ."

She broke off when he caught her hands, fingers weaving through hers, pushing her against the wall and pinning her arms there while he leaned in to continue kissing her. Hot, needy kisses. Urgent and hungry. Each kiss deepened, roughened, became more demanding than the last.

On some level he knew he was too experienced and rough for an innocent, but he couldn't stop. Every bit of discipline and control seemed far away, out of reach, no matter how hard he tried to find it. The roaring in his head drowned out all sense of honor and became a pounding desire so intense he couldn't think beyond burying his body into hers.

It was her scent, the soft skin, the heat of her mouth, and the taste of her. She offered herself up to him and he wasn't strong enough to resist. The offer had been there in the dark chocolate of her eyes. Shy maybe, hesitant even, but he recognized the hunger growing in her. The moment he slid his hands under her shirt and absorbed the feel of satin and silk, knew the lure of her scent was on every square inch of her body, he had to have more.

"Jack." Briony whispered his name, fear rising in direct proportion to her need of him. She'd never felt so edgy, so desperate for relief. She wanted his hands on her, wanted his body in hers, yet she knew little of what to expect between a man and a woman. He was too big — too strong — and in his present state she doubted if she could control the situation. She wanted the rush to slow down, to give her time to think.

Jack felt a tremor run through Briony, and he tilted her face to force her to look up at him. "I'll be careful with you, baby. Trust me." He hoped he was telling the truth. He'd never felt such an overwhelming desire to be with a woman. He trailed kisses from her temple to her cheek, down to the corner of her mouth. All the while his hands moved over her skin, tracing her ribs, the small, tucked-in waist, gliding up to cup the soft weight of her breasts, thumbs teasing her nipples into hard peaks right through her lace bra.

A soft sound escaped her throat, a breathy, urgent plea that made him nearly crazy with wanting to strip the clothes from her body. It wouldn't be enough to take her like that, fast and hard and without thought. He *felt*. It was unexpected and even unsettling, but he needed to savor the feel of her skin, the sound of her soft, breathy moan, the dark richness of desire building in her eyes for him. Her body fit his, every curve, the flare of her hips and soft swelling breasts.

Jack had never expected to want her the way he did, or to feel her inside of him the way he did, but he wasn't going to waste his opportunity. He didn't give a damn that his body was a mess. He had never experienced belonging. She belonged with him — and he with her. She didn't look at him the way the rest of the world did. She didn't see his sins. She didn't know his heart had died a long time ago. She looked at him and saw a man — not a monster. He couldn't even look in the mirror and do that, but he could through her eyes.

He leaned in to kiss her again, hands tunneling deep in her thick, silky hair. Her mouth opened for him, responded with hot passion. He took his time this time, refusing to be rough, savoring her taste, the feel of her. He slowed his wandering hands, dwelling on her curves and soft valleys, mapping her body in his mind — storing the images there. This would have to last him a lifetime, and he wasn't going to rush it.

Briony couldn't believe how gentle he was — how tender. His mind was a haze of need — of hunger — desire so intense he could barely think or breathe, but instead of stripping the clothes from her body, he unwrapped her as if she were priceless and fragile — with a tender care bordering on reverence. Her breath caught in her throat when he removed his clothes, tossing them aside carelessly, revealing the terrible cuts and burns on his body.

"Jack," she whispered his name in an agony of need. "We can't. We should wait until you're healed."

"I won't feel anything but you," he answered, knowing it was true. He lifted her to set her bottom on the edge of the railing and stood between her legs to give him better access to her body without further damaging his own. He couldn't afford to pull the stitches loose and risk more infection, but damn it all, he wasn't about to lose this opportunity.

He kissed her again, long, slow, drugging kisses until her eyes were glazed and her body trembled beneath his touch. He trailed kisses down her neck, over the curve of her breasts to her nipples. He felt ravaged with hunger for her, his mouth suckling a little too wildly, teeth teasing and tugging and dragging her into a much more experienced foreplay than her innocent eyes told him she should have, but he couldn't stop from taking the gift she was giving him.

"I've never felt like this, Briony." He

couldn't wait, couldn't make love to her as he wanted, and it was frustrating to him. He needed a bed and about twenty-four hours instead of a practice room where someone might attempt to come in at any time.

He pressed a finger into her tight channel. She made a soft sound of need, her slick cream making it easy to stretch her a bit with two fingers. He couldn't wait. Her scent was teasing him, his body swelling to painful proportions. She was hot and wet and so tempting — looking part sexy temptress and part innocent.

He caught her hips and held her to him, pressing into her slick, welcoming entrance. She was too tight, too hot, too everything, the feeling so intense his body shook with the need to slam into her and bury himself to the hilt. Her dark eyes widened and she shook her head. Before she could protest, he pushed deeper. "Relax, let me do the work, baby. It's uncomfortable the first time, but once we're past that, I'll make it good for you."

Briony couldn't touch him. She needed to hold on to him, but there wasn't a place on his body without cuts. The urgent need to have him inside her was slipping away, to be replaced by fear. He was too big. It was that simple. Her body couldn't possibly be designed for a man his size. Briony moistened her lips and edged backward away from the stretched, burning feeling.

Jack tightened his grip on her. "You have to relax, Briony. You're tensing up on me." He leaned forward, a little frantic, unable to prevent himself from kissing her, again and again, coaxing her passion, cupping one breast and teasing her nipple until she was flooding him with her need and gasping for breath.

He slipped farther in, pushing through her tight folds until he felt her resistance. "Look at me, baby. Look only at me." He wasn't a man to be with a virgin. He was rough and dominant and didn't know the first thing about innocents. Hell, he couldn't remember a time in his life when he had been innocent.

Jack reached deep to find gentleness, to be patient. He wanted her first time to be something more than a man sweating and heaving, taking her fast and without care. He wanted to hold her close and make her feel the beautiful, extraordinary woman she was. "Tell me this is what you want, Briony. Tell me you want me." She had to want him. He wasn't certain he was enough of a man to pull back if she was too afraid, but he'd try — for her — he'd try. Sweat beaded his brow. Her scent drove him insane. Her body, so hot and tight, a perfect haven for him, tested the limits of his control. "Son of a bitch, baby, I'm not going to be able to hold back much longer. Tell me. Say it so I know I'm not a complete bastard and you want this too."

Her fingers slid in a caress over his face. "I want you more than anything, Jack. I'm absolutely sure."

In spite of the fact that there was fear in her eyes, and in her mind, he caught her hands, tipping her back, as he leaned over her, his fingers tight around hers to give her an anchor, pressing her wrists into the wood by her head. One hard thrust and he was through the barrier, burying his rock-hard flesh deep into her. She gave a strangled cry, and he made the supreme effort to stop moving, to let her adjust to his size. It was difficult when his body wanted to rage out of control. He gritted his teeth, feeling his pulse pound and his cock jerk with the strain of waiting.

Briony caught her breath. He still felt too big, stretching her to a burning point, but somehow the feeling faded and the urgent need to feel him moving deep inside took over. Careful of his torn body, she couldn't participate other than to lift her hips to meet his thrust, but she wanted to touch his skin, to take him in through her pores, to hold him close to her. He thrust deeper and lightning zigzagged through her body, sizzling and crackling and spreading heat to every cell.

A single sound escaped her throat. He held her down, his hands on her wrists like shackles, holding her in place while his body began a pulse-pounding rhythm. *Restraint. Restraint. Restraint.* The chant was a desperate refrain in his head. She was so tight it was nearly painful, and her scent was ripe, calling to the male in him, thundering in his head and heart and hammering in his groin until he could barely think with wanting to bury himself deeper and deeper, harder and harder.

He breathed deep to maintain control, when he felt like a man long starved for this one woman, this perfect body, a perfect fit. The taste of her — the feel of her — was almost more than he could bear. In his wildest, most erotic fantasy, he had never had a partner he wanted the way he wanted Briony — and she had to be a virgin.

There wasn't a square inch of his skin that wasn't sliced to pieces; he couldn't hold her against him, couldn't make contact the way he wanted. He needed to hold her close, crush her body beneath his, yet he breathed. *Restraint. Restraint. Restraint.* He was not going to scare her by demanding too much, by taking too much. So okay, there was something deep and primitive and satisfying about knowing he was the only man who had ever touched her this way. He was a selfish bastard — a groan escaped, his mind hazing over. He couldn't think anymore, the pleasure wiping out every coherent thought.

Piercing pleasure washed over Briony, rushing through her body with far more force than she'd ever imagined. Every stroke sent streaks of lightning racing over her skin, sizzling through her veins, and contracting her womb. Her muscles tightened and tightened, an unrelenting pressure that continued to build past any expectation she'd ever had. It was frightening to be held down, to look up at his face, the savage lines cut deep, the intensity in his turbulent eyes, yet at the same time it heightened her sexual pleasure, pushing her beyond any limits she might have had.

He surged into her again and again, stretching her impossibly, filling her so full she wanted to scream with pleasure, yet it was almost too much. The scent of him nearly drove her crazy, the building inferno she couldn't stop. She needed to catch her breath, to pause, just for a second. Her muscles shuddered, clamped down as he slammed the full length of his shaft deep into her, driving into her over and over like a man possessed.

There was pleasure and pain, fear and joy. Sweat broke out on his body, several of his stitches across his buttocks and hips burst as he surged deeper, harder, the friction from her velvet, tight sheath nearly spiraling him out of control. She began to struggle for freedom the moment she realized cuts were opening on his body, but he couldn't stop. *No, baby, don't. Don't fight me. We're there. I need this. You need this. Let yourself go. Come with me.*

The words brushed intimately against her mind. Perhaps if he'd spoken them aloud she would have found the strength to stop him for his own sake, but his plea was too caressing, too needy. She lifted her hips to meet his invasion, rising with every stroke, tightening her muscles around him to heighten their pleasure, feeling it crash over her — through her — building to such an intensity she could barely keep from screaming. Her inner muscles spasmed, and Jack's body jerked as she clamped down. His voice, a hoarse whisper, sounded sexy, even erotic, as he emptied himself deep inside of her. She felt the thick hot jets filling her, mixing with her own cream, their combined musky scent triggering another wild spasm.

Jack's hands slowly slid away from her wrists, down her arms to tunnel in her hair. He closed his eyes, just feeling her, savoring her hot body tight around his, her skin unbelievably soft, her hair thick and beautiful through the pads of his fingers. He kissed her again, needing the taste of her in his mouth. Pain began to creep into his sensitized nerve endings, but he held it at bay just a few moments longer, giving him enough time to trail kisses down her throat to her breast, just to feel her skin. He opened his eyes to take in the sight of her stretched out like a sacrifice — a gift.

"You're the most beautiful thing I've ever seen in my life."

Briony reached up to touch his face, her touch so gentle it nearly was his undoing. He pulled away from her, feeling the burn of tears. Hell. He hadn't cried since he was a toddler. The woman was killing him.

"Get dressed," he said gruffly, looking around for his clothes. He dressed in silence, a small part of him ashamed of himself that he'd taken her offering, but the bigger part wanting her again and again.

"Jack, I have to go," Briony said. "We don't have much time. If my brothers come and the door is locked . . ."

"Jeb knows I'm with you; he'll assume you were trying to protect me." He wished to hell he hadn't used that particular word. He should have been protecting her. He held her close, stroking caresses through her hair. "I should have waited until we were in your bedroom. Tonight, after you do your thing, I promise to do a better job."

"It was my first time, Jack. For a first time, with me not knowing what I was doing, rockets went off." She lifted her face so he could kiss her. "I have to go to the dressing room. We'll have my brothers looking for me soon if we wait much longer, and you need to get out of sight."

"Sometimes out of sight is in plain sight. I'm watching you tonight."

She kissed him again, suddenly hungry for him. "Stay safe." She hurried off, turning to wave twice, her smile melting the hard knots in his belly.

From his position in the shadows near the entrance for performers, Jack found his heart in his throat, watching her body flying through the air, her sequined costume glittering like a star speeding across the sky. The stunts were fast-paced and dangerous, a blend of fire, rope, and swing, with everyone in constant motion. Jack watched Briony, hardly noticing her brothers. Mostly he felt her.

The stunts required her full attention and there was no way for her to hide the pain wracking her body. He was a trained soldier, had extensive combat experience, and knew torture on a much more intimate basis than he would like. He knew how to separate his body and mind and block pain. She didn't block it exactly. She felt it, but refused to acknowledge it. She endured.

He felt every hammer blow as if someone was driving a sharp stake through her skull. The blows fell with rhythmic force as the anxiety level in the audience grew with each succeeding stunt. He pressed a hand to his cramping stomach. Bile rose, but he fought it down. He willed himself not to get a nosebleed, felt the blood trickle to the corner of his mouth, and narrowed his eyes when he saw her hand move with blurring speed to wipe her face.

He *detested* watching the performance, his fingers curling into fists at the certain knowledge that she was suffering — *and she did this several times a day — nearly every day.* He turned away, swearing under his breath. Why would her family allow such a thing? What the hell was wrong with them? And what was wrong with her that she deliberately tortured her body every single day?

He wanted to snatch her up and run, take her somewhere he could protect her and keep her safe from the constant bombardment of everyday emotions. If he stayed there a moment longer, he was going to climb the rope and pull her out of there right in front of all of the soldiers and whatever rebels were scattered in the audience.

Briony completed a full twist and felt the satisfying smack as Jebediah caught her wrists and sent her flying back toward Tyrel. The high wire under her feet, she ran across, counting the beats of music to get to her cue. As she did so, she saw Jack slip out. At once pain flooded her body, so hard, so fast she nearly missed as she dove through the ring of fire. Jebediah's alarm at her missed timing felt like a blow to her brain.

She took a breath and forced her body under control for the rest of the show. Jebediah waited until they were alone in the makeshift dressing room, silently handing her a cloth to wipe the blood from her nose and mouth. "You almost missed, Briony. There isn't a safety net."

Ruben, Tyrel, and Seth fell silent, their laughter fading as they turned to her. Their concern only heightened the pain stabbing through her.

"I know. It was worse this time. It won't happen again. I'll be prepared."

Jebediah frowned as he watched her wipe at the blood. "Get some sleep tonight. It's almost over, a couple more days." Jebediah waved his brothers out and waited until they closed the door. "Give this to Jack. I was able to get a message to his brother at the hospital and Ken's arranged transport. There's a ship that will be waiting off the coast. A helicopter will extract him." He slipped a satellite phone into her hand. "He shouldn't leave the room until necessary. We're going to act like we always do every night and hit the clubs. You stay in your room with that door locked, and I mean it this time, Bri. This is dangerous. If someone betrayed Jack and delivered him to the rebels, they might intercept what we're doing and we'll all be in serious trouble."

"I'll stay in, Jeb," Briony promised. *He was leaving.* She knew he had to go and he would at least have medical care, but the thought of being separated from him was mind-numbing. She turned away from her brother, covering her face again with the cloth so he couldn't see her expression.

Jebediah walked with her in silence to the hotel and left her as she went up the stairs to the hallway. "It's just me," she called out before using her key.

Jack crossed the room and pulled her into his arms, holding her close, nearly crushing her with his strength. "You scare the hell out of me, Briony."

She wrapped her arms around his neck, careful to try to keep her weight off of his chest, although he was pulling her hard against him. "That's funny coming from a man who runs around alone in a jungle with a crazed army after him." She kissed his lower lip, teased at the corner of his mouth. "Jeb sent a satellite phone. I have no idea where he got it, but you're supposed to call Ken. They're coming for you tonight. I'll go take my shower while you make the call."

Briony pushed the phone into his hands and moved away, not wanting him to see or feel how much it was going to hurt when he left. Their relationship had blossomed to intense too fast — yet for the first time in her life she felt as if she belonged. She let the hot water pour over her face, washing away tears. Of course he had to go. He had no other choice — it was far too dangerous for him to stay. She took her time drying her hair, needing the extra minutes to compose herself.

Jack was already in bed when Briony came out of the bathroom wrapped in a towel. He held up one corner of the sheet and patted the mattress invitingly. "Don't bother with clothes. I'll just have to take them off of you."

Briony laughed. "You sound like such a tough guy." She lit a single candle before turning off the light and sliding into bed beside him.

"I am a tough guy. You're the only one who doesn't notice." He framed her face and bent to kiss her, long, lingering kisses that helped to soothe the pounding of his heart from watching her perform under such duress.

Briony's lips were soft and welcoming, her mouth innocent and passionate, hot and spicy, the mixture intoxicating. He breathed deep, laid his brow against hers. He wanted to kiss her forever, hold her close. *Keep her.* Because he was Frankenstein with more stitches than skin, she hadn't been able to touch him, and he wanted to feel her hands on his body. He needed to feel her hands on him. *How was he ever going to give her up?*

Jack propped himself up on one elbow, resting on his side, one of the few positions he could lie in without extreme discomfort. He brushed silky strands of hair from her face, his fingers lingering against her skin. "Tell me about your life."

"My life?" She raised an eyebrow. "My parents were wonderful people. Circus people. They loved the life. So do my brothers. My mom was born in Italy and my father was from the United States. I have four brothers, all of whom think they need to boss me around."

His hands tunneled in her hair, rubbing the strands back and forth between his fingers. "They probably do."

She laughed. "I should have known you'd side with them. It's some sort of male bonding thing to think women aren't capable of running their own lives."

He nuzzled the top of her head with his chin. "It's ego and sheer desperation. We have to keep you thinking we're the superior species."

"News flash, Jack — no woman on the face of the earth believes that anymore."

He trailed kisses down her cheek. "But *men* don't know women know that. We still

161

live in our little fantasy world, so don't muck it up for us."

"I'll try to be good about it."

"You were telling me about your life."

She shrugged. "There really isn't all that much to tell. I'm adopted. My birth father insisted on designing my education as well as being responsible for any medical problems, mostly, I think, because I'm so different. He was aware of my differences and had a special doctor flown out whenever I had so much as a stubbed toe. He also insisted on developing my physical training. Running, gymnastics, martial arts, under water, that sort of thing. I liked it most of the time. I could use the skills for our performances, and it just felt good to use the speed and endurance I actually have, instead of hiding it all the time. Mom didn't want our friends to know I was different."

"Why did you all stay with the circus?"

She gave a little shrug. "They love the circus life, the camaraderie, the traveling — especially the traveling and, of course, performing in front of thousands. I think that's as big a thrill as the actual aerial act. Jeb loved it so much he didn't stay in the SEALs and you know he loved that. The money Whitney gave my parents when they adopted me and agreed to his terms enabled them to buy in as full partners of the circus. Performing and the circus are in their blood. We've been offered so much money to perform in Vegas, but it isn't the lifestyle any of them want. The circus has their hearts."

"But not yours."

Briony turned over to stare up at the ceiling, a small smile curving her mouth. "*They* have my heart, so of course I perform with them. We're family and it's what we do."

"And you know their act wouldn't be quite the success without you. It's your stunts that set them apart from other top aerialists."

"I contribute, but the boys are awesome flyers. They invent tricks most of the other performers copy. I've always been stronger and faster, and obviously it gives me an edge. I do a quadruple somersault, but truthfully, I could rotate five or six times before Jebediah catches me. I just wouldn't do that."

"Why not?"

"It would be too dangerous for others to try — and it would set me apart. I don't want the spotlight shining too heavily on me." She reached up and touched his face. She loved touching him, but there were few places on his body she could do so without hurting him. "What about you?"

He caught her hand and carried it to his mouth, nibbling on her fingers. "What about me?"

"What do you do when you aren't being sent into jungles to rescue people?"

"My brother and I own a piece of property up in the mountains. It's wild and suits me just fine. If he'd ever stop with his plans, we might be able to sit on the porch and enjoy it."

Briony heard the affection in his gruff response. "His plans?"

"Ken always has plans. He designed the house, and every time I think we're finished and I can just sit and enjoy the mountains, he comes up with a new idea for me to work."

Briony laughed softly. "He makes you work, does he? Somehow I'm having trouble believing that."

Embarrassment flickered in his eyes and was gone. He shrugged. "The man whines. I don't know. He wants it done and he just keeps at me, so it's easier just to give him what he wants so he'll shut up."

Briony's smile widened. "You pushover you. Who would have guessed?"

He found himself fascinated by the shape of her mouth and the laughter in her eyes when she smiled. "Yeah, well, don't tell anyone. Ken loves to design, but he doesn't necessarily like to do the carpentry work."

"And you do?"

"I like working with my hands." He shrugged. "Of course, it might be out of necessity. Ken brings me all kinds of ideas and someone has to keep him quiet."

"Ideas?" She tilted her head, one eyebrow raised. "What kinds of ideas?"

"Furniture. New rooms. Buildings. All kinds of things." He sighed as if greatly put upon, but there was too much admiration and affection in his voice to believe he was annoyed with his brother.

"You make furniture?"

"I made all of our furniture. And the cabinets." He shrugged. "Just about every-thing in the house. I told you, I like working with my hands. There's something satisfying in taking wood and making something long-lasting out of it."

She took his hand, running her fingertips over the calloused skin. "I love your hands." Briony smiled up at him. "If you do all the building, what does he do?"

"The ideas are his. And he talks to people, does all the ordering. Handles details. I'm not good at any of that. Ken thinks if someone screws up an order I might shoot them." He bent to brush a kiss along her temple. "There might be a little truth to that. I can't take incompetence."

She burst out laughing again, the sound playing through his body like a musical instrument. He could feel the vibration of every note running through his veins, heating his blood.

"I've always wanted to do stained glass," she confided. "I sketch. I'm not that good, but they're all original designs."

Jack caught the wistful note in her voice. "Have you tried making stained glass?"

"I took a few classes and made small pieces. I have a lot of books. It isn't practical when we travel so much, but someday, I'm going to have my own studio. I see differently. More bird than human, I think, and sometimes, especially in the evening, I sense people through heat and have no idea why. I actually see images in colors. When I look at things in nature, I see it all differently and want to use the colors in glass." She traced his tattoos, her fingers stroking caresses down his arm.

He was silent for a moment, savoring her touch. "I see the same way. Heat imaging. And I have a highly developed sense of smell." He bent to bury his face in her neck, inhaling her fragrance. "You always smell so good."

"Probably not when I finish performing. I'm hot and sweaty."

"You're beautiful, Briony." He kissed her throat, lingered for a long foray over her neck, sending shivers through her body. "I like you hot and sweaty." He pushed the sheet down to her hips, exposing her bare breasts and flat belly.

"You would." Briony relaxed under his wandering mouth. She could feel the urgency in his mind, but it never dictated to his hands. He might kiss her with fierce hunger and ravenous possession, but he stroked tender caresses over her body, slow and easy, as if memorizing every detail. His mind might be in chaos, howling for her, demanding he take her as if she were nothing to him but a female body he craved, but his hands were gentle — reverent — his hands spoke of deep emotion.

Briony traced his weathered features, her fingers lingering over the stubborn set to his jaw. He trembled beneath her touch, turning his head to draw her finger into his mouth. He looked at her with eyes filled with raw desire. Her breath caught in her throat. She could see that look forever and never get enough.

"Lie back, baby. We're a little hampered by my stitched together body, but we can try a few things that might make you feel good."

"*Might?* Looking at you makes me feel good."

He pushed her gently back onto the bed so she was lying down. Jack ripped back the top sheet and shoved it aside, kneeling between her legs. His hands massaged her calves, moved up to her thighs. He bent to kiss her inner thighs, using small circles with his thumbs to heighten her awareness of him. He leaned forward to press kisses over her ribs, to trace each indentation with his tongue and nibble at the underside of her breasts. He closed his eyes to better savor the feel and texture of her, to memorize every square inch of her. He didn't want the memory of her to ever fade, and this night was all he had to give her — to take for himself.

She relaxed into him the way she had earlier; once making up her mind to give herself to him, she did it wholeheartedly. She reached back with her hands to grip the bars of the headboard, to keep from accidentally forgetting, in the heat of the moment, not to grab and hold on to him.

Her bare body lay out before him like a

feast, and Jack took his time, tasting every inch of her, suckling her breasts, teasing and biting, deliberately heightening her pleasure. He waited for every gasp, every arc of her body, the movement of restless hips to tell him exactly what she liked — what drove her mad — what pushed her over the edge.

She gripped the bars tighter as he made his way down her body. He could feel the building tension in her spiraling out of control. His fingers caressed the slick heat between her legs, dipped deep to push her higher and higher until she cried out. He wanted more. He wanted to hear his name on her lips, hear her cry out with pleasure. He bent his head and feathered kisses along her inner thigh, feeling her body jerk in response. His tongue teased and caressed, drawing gasps of pleasure, plunged deep to dance, to stroke, to draw the honey out of her. Her womb contracted, stomach clenching, and her hips rose off the bed as she gave a little sob — somewhere between utter ecstasy and fear of losing her mind.

Jack took a firmer grip on her hips, drawing her even tighter into him, needing to hear her cries, to know that he was the man giving her such pleasure. His hands began a slow exploration of her body, deliberately seductive while his teeth and tongue sent her nearly spiraling out of control. Hot licks and teasing bites, he drove her higher and higher. Her hips thrashed and bucked under his assault, the searing heat setting off a series of small explosions. Instead of relieving the terrible ache, it only built it into a stronger tidal wave of pulsing heat.

Briony pulsed with fierce need, arousal so strong she thought she might not survive. Her mind was a haze of need, so that she began to plead with him, afraid of the nearly savage intensity of pleasure. Jack knelt between her legs and drew her to him, his eyes glittering with raw possession — with stark craving. He thrust hard, burying himself deep, driving through her tight folds, taking her over the edge. She exploded — imploded — strong currents of electricity dazzling her while her body simply fragmented and wave after wave of pleasure pulsed through her.

And then Jack began to move. Every movement of his hips sent a shiver of pain through his body, but it mixed with the building heat, the building pleasure. She surrounded him with hot friction, her slick folds tight, her muscles strong, gripping him as he surged deeper and deeper, and all the while she stared up at him with dark chocolate eyes, dazed with heat and passion.

He shifted her slightly to get the angle that would press him hot and hard over her most sensitive bud, and he picked a faster, rougher rhythm that had her crying out his name. *Jack.* Not aloud. Whispered in his mind. Aching. Stunned pleasure consuming her mind. He wanted to pound into her with a frenzied need, but the innocence in her eyes, the emotion on her face, forced him to keep some semblance of control. He wanted her to remember this moment forever, because it would be forever etched in his mind. He watched her face, saw the intensity increase, felt her body grip his. She gave a soft cry, the sound mingling with his harsh yell, and he emptied himself into her, pouring everything he was into her, body and soul.

"Again," he growled.

Jack sat on the edge of the bed staring down at her face. She looked so young — not a line on her face. Her eyes, when she looked at him, held so much innocence. She saw him as the man he could have been — not the man he was. He killed without remorse. Demons sat on his shoulder every minute of the day and drove him hard. He wanted her — but if he kept her, there was every possibility of becoming the man his father had been. His father had looked at his sons with cold, empty eyes, eyes filled with hatred for being near their mother. It was time stolen from him and he wouldn't put up with it — not from them — not from anyone. No one could touch her, speak to her — she was his possession.

Jack and Ken had made a pact together, a sacred oath, that neither would ever risk destroying a woman the way their father had their mother. His father had loathed them, twin boys who took up their mother's time, received her smiles — and her love. There were beatings that became more and more vicious as his obsession grew.

God help him, Jack felt that way about Briony — that terrible need to keep her to himself, to hold on too tight. He couldn't fool himself into thinking he wasn't already a little obsessed. He was capable of killing — had done so before he was in his teens — and now, faced with looking at the monster he'd become — he had to give her up. She deserved a normal man — one capable of loving without possession and jealousy and fear. It was the only gift he could give her. He knew, when he walked away, that no other woman would ever do, but he couldn't take her and watch her innocence and light slowly fade, to be replaced by fear the way it had been in his mother.

Briony stirred, murmured his name in her sleep, and reached for him. His heart clenched hard. He leaned close to her. "Once I'm gone, Briony, don't come near me again," he whispered. "Not ever, because I'll never be able to give you up twice."

Her eyes opened and she smiled at him. "I was dreaming about you."

His stomach churned and he bent to kiss her. He shouldn't. He knew better, but it was damned hard to let go. "I've got to get out of here. My ride's waiting."

She sat up, pushing at the silky hair, a small frown on her face. "Is it safe? Are you certain it's safe, Jack?"

"It's safe enough." He stood up and slung the rifle around his neck. "Thanks for everything."

Briony swallowed hard, resisting the need to cling to him. Of course he had to go, but he hadn't said one word about seeing her again. Not one. She caught his hand. "Jack." She said his name softly. "How are we going to find one another?"

He pulled his hand away, rubbed his palm down his thigh as if the gesture simply wiped her away. "We aren't. You didn't think this was going to go anywhere, did you? I'm not the kind of man who settles down with a woman and kids in a house with a white picket fence. You knew that going into it. You'd be a liability to me."

Briony never took her eyes from his face. His features were set and hard — carved of stone — eyes as cold as ice. Jack betrayed absolutely no emotion. She could have been looking at a total stranger. Her heart crumbled into tiny pieces. She heard her own wail, a long, drawn-out cry of anguish, but it was only in her own mind — and she had enough pride to keep her shields up stronger than ever so he couldn't hear the weeping in her head. He couldn't know just how much she'd invested in him — how much of a fool she'd really been.

"I see." It was all she could get out. She should have looked ahead, should have known he would be capable of walking away without a backward glance. She kept her eyes on his face, hoping for one small sign that she'd meant the same things to him that he had to her. "Good luck then, Jack."

He turned away from her, an abrupt motion, and walked out the door. Not once did he look back. Briony knew because she watched him through the window, all the way, until he was out of sight. She sat on the bed until dawn, unmoving, without a single tear, feeling numb — frozen — feeling as if he'd torn out her heart and taken it with him. She felt a fool for even thinking they had something special. Jack took her gift of love and trust and flung it back in her face. She stayed very still — very small — wishing she could just disappear. She stayed there on the edge of the bed until Jebediah pounded on her door to tell her it was time to face the day and another performance.

# CHAPTER 6

*Twelve hours earlier . . .*

The Special Forces GhostWalker team gathered together in the California home of Lily Whitney-Miller, daughter of Dr. Peter Whitney. They grouped together in the war room, where they met regularly, knowing the room was impossible to bug.

"Do we know if he's still alive?" Kadan Montegue asked as he spread the aerial maps of the Republic of the Congo across the table.

"If there's one person who has a chance of escaping the rebel camp and making it out of the jungle alive, it's Jack Norton," Nicolas Trevane replied.

"General Ekabela is the most bloodthirsty of all the rebels in the region," Captain Ryland Miller added with a small sigh. "The general's troops are mostly veterans in combat. Most of his men were in the military before everything went to hell there."

"It seems to me, as long as I can remember, it's always been hell in the Congo," Nicolas said. "Ekabela had done more damage to that region, destroying entire villages and towns, committing genocide, but he's as elusive as hell and well funded."

"He controls the marijuana traffic and has major backing by someone here in the U.S. None of his prisoners have ever lasted more than a couple of days. He's particularly ruthless when it comes to torture. Ken Norton was in bad shape and they'd only had him about ten hours. Ken's still in the hospital," Ryland pointed out. "They nearly skinned him alive, not to mention sliced his body into tiny pieces. If Ekabela has Jack, he has only a few hours to escape before they do worse to him."

Kadan tapped his finger on the map. "Ekabela is on the move. He isn't going to take any chances with Jack. What the hell was that senator thinking, flying over the Congo in the no-fly zone? And what was some hotshot military scientist doing in a region as hot as the Congo?"

"That's just the thing," Dr. Lily Whitney-Miller said. She stepped out of the corner where she'd been observing the Ghost-Walker team as they met together for the briefing. "The small jet that was shot down in the Congo is the same plane that landed at the airport outside of New Orleans when Dahlia's home was attacked."

"What's even more interesting," Ryland said, "is that Ekabela didn't kill the pilot or the scientific team. And when Ken Norton's squad went into the Congo to rescue the senator, Ekabela was waiting for him."

Kadan held up his hand. "You think Ekabela was tipped off that the GhostWalker team was conducting a rescue? How would that be possible?"

Ryland nodded. "I'm sure of it. Ken was able to get the senator, the research team, *and* the pilot out. Why would Ekabela keep the pilot alive? He wasn't worth anything at all."

"Of more significance," Lily added, "the plane went down with supposed engine trouble, yet no one was injured, and Ekabela didn't have the pilot and research team tortured and killed as he normally does with anyone not of monetary or political use to him. The rebels were waiting to ambush the rescue team. Even with that, the Ghost-Walkers were able to pull out the senator, and everyone else, although in the process, Ken Norton was captured. Ekabela didn't waste any time torturing Ken."

"Even of more significance is the fact that the rebels went for Ken — singled him out. That's how he was cut off," Logan Maxwell added. He was the only member of the SEAL GhostWalker squad present. Ken and Jack Norton were both members of his team. "They were waiting for him. I was there. They could have fought to keep their prisoners, but they were more interested in acquiring Ken."

"Specifically Ken? Not just any Ghost-Walker?" Lily asked.

"Specifically Ken," Logan reiterated. There was sudden silence in the briefing room. Members of the GhostWalker team sank into chairs around the table. "Who could have tipped Ekabela off?"

"I don't know how much you know about Dr. Whitney's original experiment, when he first began to use human subjects for physical and psychic enhancement," Lily said to Logan.

"Jesse informed us, ma'am," Logan Maxwell admitted. "We know he took orphans from overseas, all girls, and enhanced them first. After perfecting his technique, he enhanced the first team." He gestured around the room to encompass the men and women. "And then ours."

"Everyone, including me, believed my

father, Dr. Whitney, was murdered. We no longer are certain that's true. We suspect not only that he is alive, but that he has enhanced his own personal army and is conducting experiments with the sanction of someone in the military and someone very high up in the government. We believe there is a conspiracy to engineer the perfect human weapons and that conspiracy involves my father, perhaps the senator you rescued, and definitely members of the military and/or other covert government agencies."

Logan looked around him. "This place is a fortress. How could Whitney, or anyone else, get ahold of your plans? Or *our* plans, for that matter. It was my team that came up with the plan to rescue first the senator and, then again, Ken Norton. They were waiting for us when we went in after Ken. Jack provided covering fire, took a hit, and went down. He signaled us to get out of there, and frankly, if we hadn't, we'd all be dead. Ekabela wasn't playing games; he wanted us dead. And they wanted Jack. We've tried twice to rescue him or recover his body, but they're moving camps so fast our information is always hours late. General Ekabela definitely tried to kill all of us, and he's had traps in every camp we've hit.

Fortunately we've managed to avoid them."

"Which just reinforces the idea that Ekabela should have killed everyone but the senator. So why didn't he?" Ryland asked.

"We've known all along that all of the computers we use here at the house and at the Donovans Corporation belonged to my father. Most of the software programs were either written or modified by him. The datastores use a proprietary, encrypted format. There's no way to even access data except by using the program he wrote — although the raw data could be manually transferred from his programs to another by pulling it up on the terminal and transcribing it into another terminal . . . but that wouldn't get you whatever evaluation formulas were written into his software codes. Obviously if he were alive, and had planned to disappear but wanted to see what we were doing, he would have left himself a back door to monitor the computers. There are fifteen computers here in this house, counting mine, the ones in the lab, and the ones in his office, as well as his personal one in his room. There are over a hundred at the Donovans Corporation, where both of us worked. Dad was the majority shareholder and now Whitney Trust is."

"And you need his data so you can't very

well wipe everything clean, can you?" Logan asked.

"Exactly." Lily tapped the end of her pencil on the tabletop. "If someone could access our computers, they would know every move we make. And they could certainly make educated guesses based on data collected on any given move we make." She glanced at the woman sitting quietly in the back of the room. "Flame brought it to our attention and we all owe her a lot. We've been working on the natural assumption that my father planted back doors in the software programs. We assumed he used the main Internet connection."

Ian McGillicuddy, a tall Irishman, raised his hand. "I'm not very good on a computer, Lily."

She smiled at him. "Actually, Ian, don't feel alone. I use them on a daily basis, and it was Arly, our security expert, and eventually Flame who tracked this down. Flame? You want to explain to everyone what's going on? You're the one who finally figured it all out."

Flame made a face and touched the cap on her head to make certain it was in place. Raoul Fontenot leaned over to bite her ear and whisper something that made her blush. She smacked him hard. "You're such a perv, Raoul."

"Don't call me Raoul, Mrs. Fontenot," he whispered overly loud. "I told you, *Gator.* They have to call me Gator."

"Don't you call me Mrs. Fontenot," she hissed between her teeth, the color creeping up her neck.

"You married him," Ian pointed out with a wide grin.

"I was tricked." Flame shoved at Gator to move him away from her, but he didn't appear to notice, not budging an inch.

"The computers," Ryland reminded them.

"Sorry," Flame muttered. "There's a single Internet line coming into the house, a high-speed cable modem. The cable line hooks up to the cable modem. The modem, in turn, hooks to a router, which then distributes the cable signal to all computers. In this case, Dr. Whitney used a high-end snazzy, heavy-duty router because he has so many computers. We presumed Whitney," she glanced at Lily, "or someone who knew about his work, tried to get access to his computers via the Internet connection, through the router. The router has a built-in firewall, as do each of the individual computers. We used the firewall software to monitor any attempted intrusions. There were random attempts here and there that you can expect to find on any computer these days. The attempts were easily rejected by the firewall and didn't have the kind of systematic pattern I would have expected to see if someone was trying to get in."

"Arly and Flame monitored the computers for several days with no luck at all of spotting evidence of my father attempting to break in," Lily explained.

Flame nodded. "We kept daily logs on each computer." She took the notebook Lily slid to her and opened it to a random page. "Here's the event log for the last week. There were several random attacks from different IPs on UDP port 25601, like this one on Thursday at 10:39:17 a.m. from IP address 152.105.92.65. Or this one on Friday at 5:23:58 a.m. from IP address 59.68.234.64. They were all caught and stopped by the firewall and were all probably SeriousSam gamers looking for playmates — you can tell the game by the port they were trying to enter through."

Ian scratched his head. "Sheesh, Flame, and I thought Lily couldn't speak English."

She smirked at him. "And you thought I was just a pretty face."

"I thought you were a pain in the ass," he said. "Now I know you are. You're going to be holding this over my head, aren't you?"

"Darn straight." Flame tossed the log on the table. "At a certain point we realized someone was reading the key files on Lily's computers. We found that out by noticing that the last accessed date on several files was very recent."

"Wait." Ian held up his hand. "I'm really trying to follow this. How can you know when someone accessed a file?"

"Every Windows file has three associated time stamps. Creation date, last modified date, and last accessed date. You can access or read a file without modifying it, hence the distinction between last accessed and last modified."

"Okay, that makes sense," Ian said. "Did you catch him?"

"I wish. We ramped up our monitoring of the firewalls, but we couldn't link any of the random attempts to the reading of the files. We looked in all the usual places someone could insert a back door into the Windows operating system, but couldn't find any evidence of any such back door. We were completely stumped."

Lily laughed softly. "Arly and I were stumped. Flame suddenly jumped up and yelled, '*Hardware* back door.' I had no idea what that meant, Ian, if that's any consolation."

Flame shrugged. "It was so obvious. We forgot the most obvious advantage Dr. Whitney had over other hackers. These are *his* computers. He could do anything he wanted with them. Unlike the usual hacker, he doesn't have to sneak a virus, worm, or Trojan through the firewalls. Unlike software manufacturers, he doesn't have to sell someone software with a back door in it. No, he has complete control over his own computers. He could literally drill a hole in the side of his computer and run a cable into it creating a private tap. All that time we wasted looking for a software back door when it *had* to be a hardware back door."

"Then she went a little crazy," Lily explained.

"A *lot* crazy. I just knew I was right, and for once we were going to have the opportunity to the turn the tables on Whitney," Flame admitted.

"She was crawling around all the computers in the laboratory, picking up wires and following the network of cables from one computer to another. Then she held up the router and started yelling, 'Look at this, look at this.' I had no idea what I was supposed to be looking at."

Flame grinned at her. "It had one too many wires coming out of the box. I knew we had him by the —" She broke off. "I knew we had him. The file protection system on these computers is set up on the local area network, or LAN, to be able to access the files on any other computer — and why not? They're all the doctor's computers — it would only be the doctor working on one computer and accessing another. We'd been looking for an intrusion from outside via the Internet. All the firewalls are protecting us from outside intrusions. Dr. Whitney is getting in by masquerading as an insider, as another computer on his own LAN. One of the lines was bogus, and I knew it would take us to the doctor. I traced the line straight to a wall."

"This is where we get a little technical," Lily said.

"Not too," Flame assured Ian. "We discovered the network cable is hooked via a CSU/DSU box into what we realized is a leased T3 line. And before you ask, a CSU/DSU box is a channel service unit/data service unit or digital service unit box, and that's what identifies the fact that it is a leased line. This is a superfast dedicated connection across the phone lines. The DSU connects to the LAN inside the house and the CSU connects to the lease line."

Ian frowned and glanced around the

room. "I don't get this. The line goes through the wall and goes to a leased line? He rents a line?"

"A leased line is actually composed of three parts," Flame explained. "Two local loops and a long haul. The first local loop runs from this house to the nearest POP, which basically is point of presence of the long distance carrier or carriers. There has to be a similar local loop running from wherever the doctor is currently to the POP nearest him. The long distance carriers, one or more, use the normal phone lines to connect the two local loops. The fact that two local loops are completely private, plus special equipment on the hardware/software long haul, guarantees the entire connection is private."

"So he has to be in the country," Ian said.

"Not necessarily," Flame replied.

"There have to be records of who leased the line," Kadan pointed out.

"Of course. Dahlia broke in and looked for us. It wasn't very shocking to discover that an import company in Oregon, one owning a private jet by the way, a jet able to land in restricted military space all over the world, leased that line," Lily said. "Shockingly enough, the man who signed for the purchase of the private jet also signed for the purchase of the one that went down in the Congo. That man doesn't have a Social Security number or birth certificate that we could find."

There was a small silence. "It is Dr. Whitney, isn't it?" Ian asked. "He's alive then."

"We don't know. Certainly if it isn't him, it's someone he worked closely with who was privy to all of his experiments," Ryland said.

Lily cleared her throat. "No matter who my father was working with — or for — he would never have shared all of his information. He has to be alive. In my opinion, he's alive and he's continuing with his experiments." She pressed her hands protectively to her stomach. "He's out there, and he's watching us."

Ryland put his arms around her, leaning to nuzzle the top of her head. "But aren't we watching him now?"

Flame nodded. "He isn't going to be able to get to you, Lily. Not you and certainly not the baby."

There was a murmur of agreement through the room and Lily relaxed visibly.

"How are you watching him?" Ian asked.

"I hoped I could access his computer as easily as he was accessing ours. I actually identified all of our computers and isolated his, so I knew I had the right one, but he had disallowed access." Flame smiled. "So I changed tactics. I knew he was accessing certain files on a regular basis. He follows all of Lily's findings and wants to see her updated reports on each of us." She smirked. "He was particularly interested in my file."

"What a shocker, *cher*," Gator murmured. "I'm interested in it too." His hand swept down her arm, his fingers tangling with hers.

Flame relaxed, leaning back against Gator. "I created a little surprise of my own for Dr. Whitney. I created a Trojan and embedded it in one of the regularly viewed files. First I had Lily update my file in order to entice him to take a long look at it."

"What does that do? How'd you do it?" Ian asked.

Flame shrugged. "I assumed he was using Windows XP because all the computers here are XP. So I programmed the Trojan to do one thing. It goes into the controls for Remote Desktop on his computer and adjusts the settings that allow users to connect remotely to this computer across a LAN. Of course, we had to wait for the doctor to read the file embedded with the Trojan so he could unwittingly activate the program for us, but with Lily updating, he took the bait."

"That's amazing, Flame. You can actually read his computer files?" Ian asked.

Flame nodded. "It's so perfect. If he weren't masquerading as another computer on our LAN, we couldn't turn around and return the favor by using Remote Desktop control, which is only possible for other computers on a LAN. But now we've activated the Remote Desktop setting on the doctor's computer, we have access to his computer as if it were our own."

"So what is he up to?"

Flame nodded toward Lily. "She can explain it better than I can."

Kadan held up his hand. "First of all, by reading the files, is there any way to positively identify who is spying on us?"

Lily shook her head. "We can't *see* who is creating files, but certainly I recognize my father's type of notes. He likes to put everything into numbers, a kind of code, and definitely there are many files filled with numbers. In order to read the data, I have to break the code. It's rarely the same in each file."

Kadan glanced at Ryland. "Someone very high up in the government has to be helping him. How sanctioned can Whitney be?"

There was a small silence, no one wanting

to mention the inevitable suspicion. They were under the direct command of one man, General Ranier.

Lily shook her head. "I know what you're all thinking. General Ranier has been a close friend of my family for years, but he can't be involved."

"Why not?" Logan asked.

Lily ducked her head. "Because if one more person I love is living a lie and betraying us, I don't think I could live through it."

Ryland swept his arms around her and pulled her up against his body. "We've got Dahlia back and now Flame. We'll find the rest of the girls and we'll have our own family, Lily. No matter what happens, you have us."

"I'm scared, Rye," she admitted. "I'm really scared this time."

"We're not going to jump to any conclusions about General Ranier, Lily," Kadan assured her. "And, Logan, you've got your own worries with the admiral who runs your unit. If we have a line into Peter Whitney's computer, we might get lucky and come across an indication if either the general or the admiral is in any way associated with the doctor. In the meantime, we'd all better be very careful when our orders come down."

"To call me here, you must have found something on Jack or one of my other team members," Logan said.

Lily took a deep breath and nodded. "For purposes of simplicity, we're going to refer to whoever is behind this as Dr. Whitney. Most of us believe he's alive and pulling all the strings. Dr. Whitney appears to be trying to bring the women he first experimented on together with the men he later worked on. We believe he's doing so as part of a much larger plan. Each of the women so far has been both psychically compatible and sexually attracted to one of the men. The couples work well together as a single weapon. As a team, they're fully functional in a combat situation as well as being able to live and function in the world, which they cannot always do alone. Dahlia, if you recall, could not be out of the sanitarium for any length of time, but with Nico, she's able to live a seminormal life."

"So far, that part doesn't sound half-bad," Logan said with a faint smile.

"There are a few perks to the job," Gator said, waggling his eyebrows at Flame.

She rolled her eyes. "I don't have a clue how I got into this." She flashed a small smile at Logan. "Raoul is right, there are definite perks."

"So the doctor wants the men to hook up with the women," Logan said. "What's the big deal?"

Lily frowned. "He made us all into weapons. Together, as a couple, we seem to be far more powerful, complementing or even amplifying the enhancements. Where before, a team could be sent in and the odds of success went up tenfold, imagine how much better if only two people could be sent in to clean up a mess, especially if the couple were as powerful as, or more so than, an entire team."

Logan switched his gaze to Gator and Flame Fontenot and Nicolas and Dahlia Trevane. "Do you think it's true? The two of you could handle a mission without the entire team and do just as well?"

The couples looked at one another, then nodded. "There's no doubt, Logan, depending on what needed to be done," Gator answered. "Flame and I manipulate sound, and without using Kadan — or someone else — as a shield to stop the corridor, it would get tricky, but we could definitely get the job done. Our abilities are amplified when we're together. Both Flame and I are physically enhanced as well as psychically."

"We are too," Dahlia said, taking Nico's hand. "And like Gator and Flame, we work very well together."

Logan sighed. "This physical enhancement you've all mentioned . . ."

"And you know perfectly well your entire team is enhanced," Lily broke in.

Logan ran his finger around the collar of his shirt. "It's just gene doping. Inserting our own DNA into our cells to pump them up, right?"

"That would be what most doctors are doing these days, but Dr. Whitney took it a step further," Ryland said. "He developed a chromosome in order to insert DNA and enhance the entire body both physically as well as psychically."

"Now I'm not understanding," Logan admitted, frowning.

Lily tapped her pencil on the table again, the only sign that her earlier nervousness remained. "Actually, chromosomes come in pairs. Technically, he developed an extra pair of chromosomes. And that gave him eighty thousand extra genes to play with, which can encode a lot of capability. Whatever psychic attributes you already have, the experiments increased, but more were added when he inserted the extra chromosome for physical enhancement. For instance: there is a huge evolutionary distance between man and mosquito, but in spite of

195

that, at a molecular level, both are equipped with the same chemosensory system."

Logan whistled softly. "Whoa there. That's a darned big jump from computers to chromosomes and mosquitoes. I'm guessing there's a reason for that."

"I found a file on Dr. Whitney's computer relating to Jack Norton and one of the women he first experimented on. Apparently Jack and Ken Norton had, prior to undergoing physical and psychic enhancement, tremendous talent already in both areas. Both have extensive military training and are highly skilled."

"They're legendary as snipers," Nicolas volunteered.

"Apparently Dr. Whitney believes so as well. He has been attempting for some time to manipulate Jack Norton into meeting a woman named Briony Jenkins. I want you to note Briony is a type of plant just as Lily, Dahlia, and Iris are." She sent a faint apologetic smile to Flame for using the name Dr. Whitney had given her. "You know how he liked to dehumanize us. No real names and no birth dates."

"Briony is one of our lost sisters," Flame said softly, her fingers tightening around Gator's. "I don't remember her. Even when I try." She rubbed her temples, frowning, trying to ease the headache that always accompanied working at remembering the girls Dr. Whitney had experimented on.

"In this case, Flame," Lily explained, "I don't think we've forgotten her just because he tried to erase our memories, it's because she was very young when he sent her off. He actually did adopt her out."

Flame leaned forward. "What? It's not one of his elaborate stories to cover what he really did with her? He pretended Dahlia was adopted and he locked her up in a sanitarium. He certainly wrote a wonderful tale about my adoption when all the time I was locked in a laboratory being given cancer. Are you absolutely certain Briony was really adopted by someone?" There was a hitch in Flame's voice.

Beneath the cover of the table, Gator wrapped his arm around her waist to give her comfort.

Lily inspected her hands before speaking. "My father was a man who believed in having as many controls as possible. I wasn't enhanced physically, so I'm the control for that experiment. Briony was enhanced both physically and psychically, and he chose the parents he wanted for her, a circus family living in Europe. The father was a United States citizen and the mother was Italian.

They already had four boys and wanted a daughter desperately. They were also in need of a lot of cash to buy in as partners for the circus."

Lily looked around the room. "Flame and Dahlia were raised in a closed environment. Briony was raised with a family, although her training was directly overseen by my father. Detailed reports were sent weekly of Briony's physical and psychic training. It was rigorous, although certainly she didn't suffer from the training, but there were huge problems. Her family believed her to be autistic because she couldn't function around people. She isn't an anchor, and the toll on her not being able to filter out sound and emotion from those around her must have made her life hell. It's obvious from his notes, Whitney wanted to see if, after being raised in a loving environment, Briony would have the same abilities as Flame and Dahlia. He feels a child raised by loving parents may lack determination. He deliberately sent a child, who wasn't capable of living in close proximity to others without suffering severe pain, into a very crowded and public environment to see if she was tough enough. Whitney has many notations saying she surprised him with her abilities in the face of continual pain. From what I've read, in spite of numerous physical problems, she performs with her family, is extremely intelligent, and every bit as well trained as any GhostWalker. And he provided his own doctor for her care and designed her education, which her parents agreed to follow to the letter."

Lily's eyes glistened with tears for a moment. "I think he had her parents murdered when they objected to his sending her to Colombia. Jack Norton was in Colombia at the time. The parents were beginning to object to Whitney's continual interference in their lives now that she was grown, and he wrote that they were in the way. Later he wrote: problem solved."

Flame pressed her fingers against her mouth, her hand visibly shaking. "We have to find her, Lily. What does Whitney want from her?"

"He wants a baby. He wants the child to be a product of Jack Norton and Briony Jenkins. He's spent millions maneuvering behind the scenes in order to bring them together. Right at this very moment, she's in Kinshasa. She and her brothers were paid an exorbitant fee in order to get them to perform in a music festival there."

There was another small silence. Logan broke it. "You're saying Whitney was behind the senator's plane going down in the Congo? That he tipped off General Ekabela that Ken Norton was leading a rescue mission?"

"*Jack* was supposed to lead the rescue, remember?" Lily corrected. "Ken stepped in when Jack couldn't get back from Colombia in time. This was all about watching Jack perform. Was he worthy of donating the sperm? Jack is one of the more powerful GhostWalkers. We all know that. He has extreme talents, and I'm willing to bet Briony matches him in every way. Jack was the one meant to be captured. He was the one meant to escape and make his way to Kinshasa. Ken was used to draw him to the Congo, that's why Ekabela didn't have Ken killed immediately."

"Kinshasa is no small place," Kadan pointed out.

"Briony's brother is a former Navy SEAL and served with Jack. They have a history. Jack saved his life. I'd say the setup is more than perfect. Jack is going to go straight to him if he's escaped."

Kadan shook his head. "I can't see Ekabela letting him get away no matter how much money Whitney pays him. Ekabela has wanted Jack for a long time. He knows Jack is capable of taking him out and would if the order came down. The general is going to kill him."

"Certainly Whitney expects him to try. Whitney created the ultimate weapons. What's the use if he can't see them perform?" Ryland asked.

Logan swore softly under his breath. "Can we get to Jack?"

"We've tried. We hit two different camps where he was reputed to have been held. They were long gone. In the last one, it looked as if a fight had taken place. There were bodies and a lot of blood, but no Ekabela and no Jack."

"What about Briony Jenkins? Can you get to her?"

"We need a way to extract Jack. If we warn her . . ."

"So you're using her as bait." Flame's head snapped up, her eyes stormy. "Is that what we are to you, Kadan? Is that what *she* is? Something to use so you can get your GhostWalker back?"

Gator put a restraining hand on her arm, but she shrugged it off, glaring at the other man across the table.

Kadan shrugged with his usual calm. "We're all GhostWalkers, Flame. Neither Norton nor Briony is expendable as far as I'm concerned. If Whitney has targeted

Briony, he'll eventually try to reacquire her. Jack Norton is her best bet for protection. I'm not willing to give up either one of them. Even if we did manage to send word to Kinshasa, and the chance of getting there before this is over is not good, why would she even believe us?"

"But she isn't an anchor?" Ian asked.

Lily shook her head. "No, and it's surprising that she's managed to exist in the environment she has. My father has written copious notes about her ability to withstand pain and carry out her mission. In this case, performing with her family in front of so many people. She's a strong telepath as are both Jack and Ken Norton. She has the same abilities that both of them have."

"Which are?" Kadan prompted.

"Which brings us back to mosquitoes," Lily said. "Mosquitoes can sense carbon dioxide and lactic acid up to one hundred feet away. When we breathe, humans, along with other mammals and even birds, give off these gases. The chemicals in sweat also attract mosquitoes."

"Are you saying Jack and this woman, Briony, can do that as well? Scent people by breathing and sweat?" Ian asked.

"Yes. Absolutely they can. They were born with the same olfactory system in their noses, as we all were. Mosquitoes have receptors that allow them to use that system efficiently. Briony and Jack both have receptors." A small smile escaped. "Although their receptors are not in antennae. Mosquitoes also have heat sensors, as do Briony and Jack. And last, but not least, mosquitoes have visual sensors."

"I'm seeing a pattern here." Ian flashed a grin around the room. "No wonder the man is good in the jungle. He can just home in on his targets."

"Actually you're right, he can. He also has the ability to change his skin color to match his surroundings."

"Like a chameleon?" Ian asked.

"Contrary to popular belief, chameleons can't display limitless colors and do not change colors in a camouflage response to their surroundings. Their skin changes in response to temperature, light, and mood," Lily explained. "The hormones that control the melanin-containing cells can vary in concentration over the chameleon's body, producing elaborate colored patterns. Some patterns are good camouflage, while other patterns are more showy stripes or spots in contrasting colors that signal the chameleon's mood."

"But chameleons don't have the same skin

we do," Kadan pointed out. "So far, Whitney hasn't introduced any alien DNA into us, has he?"

"A chameleon has four layers of skin. The outside layer has both red and yellow color cells. Inside that layer are two more layers, both reflecting light, one blue and one white. The inner layer is complicated and contains pigment granules called melonophore cells. The melonophore has dark brown pigment called melanin."

"The same stuff that colors human skin brown or black?" Ian asked.

"Exactly the same stuff," Lily acknowledged. "Humans, by the way, also have red and yellow color cells. So if you could independently and precisely control the hormone levels for each of the melanin-containing cells, you could create a wide variety of color patterns within the ranges allowed by multiple-color cell layers."

"In a human? How could you do that?" Kadan asked.

"Through a distributed network of nano-computers associated with the melanin-containing cells: one such nano-computer."

Ian shoved a hand through his red hair. "I hate it when you start talking like this. It makes me feel stupid."

"Each nano-computer is a few hundred

molecules in size, and its primary purpose is to regulate the hormone level of the melanin-containing cell with which it's associated. It has one more function — something like a sperm cell, if injected into the bloodstream, it will find its way to a melanin-containing cell that currently doesn't have a 'nano-computer' and latch on to it."

Flame frowned. "So you're saying the idea is to inject a zillion of these into the bloodstream, and they will sort themselves out into a distributed computing network, one nano-computer per melanin-containing cell? What controls them?"

"The nano-computers change the hormone level they are allowing — and hence the colors those color cells are displaying — when they are exposed to a magnetic field of a certain strength."

Logan burst out with "Damn it, Lily, are you sure?"

She nodded. "Jack and Ken Norton have extensive files. They're very strong telepaths as well as having many other talents on a lesser level. Both can use telekinesis. Psychokinesis, more commonly referred to as telekinesis, is the ability to move things or otherwise affect the property of things with the power of the mind. Of all psychic abilities, true telekinesis is the rarest — and the most difficult to control. I know because I have some small talent — nothing like theirs. And I believe Briony must have this talent as well. Not only did both men test strong in that area, they were enhanced even further. They've apparently had the ability to communicate telepathically from the time they were toddlers."

"Let's go back to the ability to change skin color into camouflage," Logan said. "If they need a magnet to control the nano-computers, do they carry it? And if hormone levels trigger the capability, how can they keep from revealing their mood swings like the chameleon does?"

"Good question. They're trained with bio-feedback, and both men have amazing control. Dr. Whitney implanted an MRI-like device inside both of the Nortons. It radiates the magnetic pattern outwards to the surface of the body. The device responds to a mental signal the brothers first learned in biofeedback training, but because of their extensive talent, it has become second nature to them."

"If Briony was adopted, how could they do the same thing to her? Surely he didn't have this technology before he adopted her out," Kadan said.

"The parents took Whitney's money believing he was a grieving husband who had lost his wife. They agreed to educate Briony in the way he wanted and he paid for all medical not only for her but the entire family. Every time she was sick, his doctors treated her. Whitney had access to her the entire time. And I believe he still does. They use his doctor when she's ill. She has a lot of trouble due to the fact that there's no respite for her from the continual assault on her senses. Quite frankly I'm surprised she's survived this long without a breakdown."

There was a small silence as the enormity of the implications sank in. Ryland pulled Lily into his arms and buried his face against her shoulder. "What impact will all this have on any children?"

"I don't know. I don't know what he's done to any of the rest of you. And I sure don't have a clue what would happen if Jack Norton and Briony Jenkins have a child together. The one thing I can say for certain is that it *will* affect the baby." Lily placed both hands protectively over the small rounded evidence of her pregnancy.

"If Ken Norton carries the same genetic code," Kadan said, "why is it so important to Whitney that Jack, not Ken, meet up with Briony?"

"I'm guessing the pheromone reaction is specific to one man and one woman. I haven't run across a mention of that in the files yet, but there is no other explanation. Dr. Whitney" — deliberately Lily distanced herself from the man she'd known all her life as her father — "is looking for a second-generation soldier and wants Jack Norton and Briony Jenkins to provide him with one. With their enhanced olfactory systems, the chemistry between them would be zinging off the charts."

"Well," Logan said, "he looked to the wrong man. No one controls Jack Norton. He's a dangerous man and Whitney made the mistake of making him more so."

"Maybe so, Logan, but if what I suspect is true, he wouldn't be in control, he'd be at the mercy of his body's demands — and so would Briony," Lily explained.

"How is it going to help the Nortons to change skin color when they're wearing clothes?" Flame asked pragmatically.

Lily sent a small, wan smile in her direction. "I forgot to tell you about the 'smart' shirts Georgia Tech developed to monitor soldiers and patients for medical problems. The Natick Soldier System Center in co-operation with Crye Precision developed the MultiCam Multi Environment Camouflage system. Companies have a line of personal clothes as well as combat clothes. The hottest thing is microscopic mirrors sewn into the fabric to reflect the environment around them. You'll never guess who is testing these clothes."

"Jack and Ken Norton," Flame said. "Of course. And Whitney had to pull some strings to make that happen."

"Whitney seems very adept at pulling strings," Kadan agreed. "You're right. He isn't alone in this."

# Chapter 7

"You're pregnant."

Briony stared at the doctor in shock. "That's impossible. I'm on birth control pills. You prescribed them yourself." She *detested* the man; the way he looked so reptilian, she often thought scales would erupt all over him at any moment. He had the coldest smile, almost a smirk when he looked at her. She didn't trust him — had never trusted him. Even as a child, she had wanted to run screaming from the room whenever he entered. When she left the office, she was going to go out to the car and wring Jebediah's neck for calling him. She'd only agreed to come because she wanted a few answers. This was definitely the last visit she would ever make to Dr. Sparks.

"You're pregnant, Briony, about eight weeks. Perhaps you forgot to take a pill when you should have." His shark-toothed smile flashed at her, but never once reached his eyes. "The father will be overjoyed."

A shadow slid into her mind. Her body went into alert mode — she felt the alarm shooting through her, but she maintained her shocked look and swung her leg back and forth in agitation. "Tony? I'm sure he will. He's wanted to marry me forever and this will be his big chance. My brothers will all get out shotguns and side with him."

For the first time his smirk slipped. The eyes grew even colder. "Tony?"

She shrugged, trying to look casual. "One of the tiger trainers. We've had a steady relationship for a while now." She looked him straight in the eye, determined to carry off the lie just to see his reaction, because something wasn't right and she had a very bad feeling that she was in more trouble than just being pregnant.

*Pregnant?* Was it really possible? Was he lying to her? She was sick all the time, unable to keep any food down. He didn't feel as if he was lying, but she never could tell with the doctor, almost as if his mind was shielded from hers.

Sparks cleared his throat. "I thought you told me you couldn't stand to be touched and doubted you'd ever have a relationship. Has that gotten better?"

She rubbed her temples. Funny, with the

doctor she didn't get pain, but a strange buzzing noise in her mind always persisted when she was close to him. "The exercises helped a lot and I've been working with bio-feedback and meditation." That part was true, but no amount of meditation would free her from pain enough to allow a close relationship with anyone other than maybe Jack — and she wasn't going to *ever* think about trusting him with her heart again. She tried a small smile, pursuing the lie. "For some reason, when I'm with Tony, it's not nearly as bad, although I don't know about marrying him."

"Will you want to keep the baby then?" Dr. Sparks asked, watching her closely.

She fought back her first reply. Of course she was going to keep her baby — she *wanted* the baby, even if its father was a complete bastard. She was quite capable of taking care of a child on her own. She shrugged again. "I'll think about it. I hadn't thought in terms of having a baby right now — or ever for that matter. My brothers are going to go psycho on me and Tony will lose his mind too, all wanting me to do the right thing and marry, so I'm not going to say anything to anyone until I decide."

Dr. Sparks turned away from her and opened a cabinet. "Let me know, Briony, and I can certainly help you with whatever you decide. In the meantime, you'll need prenatal care, just in case you decide you want to keep the child." With his back to her, he glanced over his shoulder, busying himself with a syringe. "Did any of your brothers come with you? Perhaps if I spoke to them they'd understand that it would be difficult for you to remain in a relationship for any length of time."

"No, I came alone." She had no idea why she lied. Jebediah drove her, afraid she'd be too sick to stay on the road, or — more likely — afraid she wouldn't actually see the doctor. Her eyes were on Sparks's face as he turned, and her heart jumped with fear. His reptilian features seemed nearly alien, twisting with a kind of fanatical glee as he approached her with the needle. Briony drew back. "What's that for?"

"Vitamins, for you and the baby. You look a bit pale to me. You don't want birth defects if you decide that you're going to have the child after all."

She inhaled and knew immediately there were no vitamins in the syringe. "Back off, Dr. Sparks, I'm not getting a shot of anything." She was in danger, every sense on full alert. Adrenaline flooded her body, rushing through her veins with certain knowledge.

"Don't be silly, my dear; this is necessary and it's just a small stick. You've had stitches and far worse than this."

"Maybe, but I'm leaving now *without* a shot. If I need vitamins, I'll get them the old-fashioned way — over the counter in pill form."

Dr. Sparks raised his voice. "Luther, will you come in here, please?"

The door burst open and Luther blocked the only exit. He was big, and Briony knew immediately he was enhanced. Maybe it was his scent, but more likely she simply sensed the enhancement in him the way she had in Jack. Briony inhaled sharply and found herself frowning. There was something about Luther that repelled her.

"Sit still, Briony; we don't want to make this harder than necessary," Dr. Sparks said smoothly, still smiling at her.

Luther grinned at her.

*The ape and reptile,* she thought a bit hysterically.

Briony held up her hand as if to ward off the doctor, her gaze on Luther, mind racing to figure a way out of the room. "What exactly is that? And don't tell me vitamins. What's going on?"

"I can't have you running out and getting

an abortion. I think we'll just calm you down until you're more reasonable." Sparks stepped closer.

"I'm more than reasonable," Briony said. "I don't understand." She lowered her hand as if in surrender, but kept her gaze on the huge man in the doorway.

"That's a good girl."

"Incubator you mean," Luther said with a little smirk. "I even volunteered to be the donor."

Dr. Sparks glared at Luther. Briony kicked out hard as Sparks turned his attention from her. She wrenched the syringe from the doctor's hand as he went down, screaming, clutching at his groin.

The smirk fading from his face, Luther rushed her, leaping over the doctor, his arms outstretched to wrap her close. She was grateful for her smaller size — one that allowed her to perform all kinds of aerial tricks, and to slip through small spaces. She used the gurney to kick off of, going up and over the arm reaching for her, and stabbing at Luther with the syringe. She couldn't push the plunger to release the liquid — liquid she was certain was a knockout drug — but she managed to complete a full somersault in the air and kick out, going feet-first through the window. She protected the baby with one hand and her face with the other, although her feet pushed most of the glass out onto the street.

She landed in a crouch, and was up and running toward the parking lot. Luther was too big to get through the window, but strong enough to smash the frame out. She heard him swear as he hit the pavement.

"Start the car, Jebediah," she yelled, putting as much urgency and command into her voice as she could.

Fortunately Jebediah, sitting in the driver's seat, threw his newspaper, started the car, and pushed open the passenger door.

"Go! Go!" she ordered, gesturing with her hands, running at top speed toward the car. She dove into the seat as he pulled away from the curb. Slamming the door, she glanced back to see Luther racing toward a vehicle with two men in it. He had a gun in his fist and fury on his face. "Hurry, Jeb! He's coming after us. He's got a gun."

Jebediah didn't ask questions, but reacted the way she knew he would, grim-faced, driving like a pro, turning off the main street the minute he could and taking a back route through narrow streets toward the circus grounds.

"What the hell's going on, Bri?" Jebediah demanded when they were racing down the highway.

"Sparks tried to drug me," she said. "I don't know what he wants, but it has something to do with the baby." She pressed both hands over her stomach.

He glanced at her sharply, shock written on his face. "The *baby?* What baby?"

"I'm pregnant."

"You can't be pregnant. You're never with anyone. Where the hell have I been? And why would Sparks drug you for your baby? Look in the small compartment under my seat and get out the gun and ammo. Hurry, Bri."

"I don't know, Jeb, but he asked me if you were with me and I had the feeling you would have been in danger too." Briony found the gun and hastily slammed the clip in. She handed it to her brother. There was a certain comfort in being swamped with his emotions. There was no doubt Jeb loved and wanted to protect her. "Something isn't right about my adoption and the story they gave Mom and Dad. I think whoever these people are, they murdered Mom and Dad as well." She kept her gaze glued to the back window. "Because of me."

Jebediah's jaw tightened. "Whoever murdered Mom and Dad is responsible, Bri, certainly not you, and I never want to hear you even imply that again. They loved you every bit as much as they did all of us. There were no regrets adopting you. None whatsoever, not for them and not for us. Damn it, Briony." He hit the steering wheel with the flat of his palm. "I should have picked up on this. You knew something was wrong. You always knew. I didn't want to know." He swore again. "How many with guns back there?"

"I only saw the man Sparks called Luther with a gun, but Sparks probably has one as well. I've always detested that snake. He gave me the birth control pills. All my medications came through him, not a pharmacy. How can I get pregnant on birth control pills? Doesn't that bother anyone but me? Why would a doctor fly in to see me every time I managed to catch a cold?"

"You didn't get colds, Briony. You've never had one in your life; that's why I was so worried about you being sick now. You don't get the flu and you didn't get childhood illnesses. Mom and Dad agreed to allow Whitney's doctor to have your full health care. That was part of the adoption agreement, and I've always insisted because you're so different and another doctor might not be able to treat you adequately. Sparks knows your history — knows how to treat your special circumstances." All the while he talked to keep her calm, Jebediah drove through the streets with the precision of a race car driver, the gun at his hip.

"And that's another thing. Why am I so different? He knows my history all right, a lot more than he ever told us."

"Both Whitney and Sparks said you have a form of autism, that's why you can't connect with people."

"I connect, Jebediah. I love you and Mom and Dad and the other boys. You know I do. I feel pain when I'm too close. I can tell what you're thinking, not exactly, but your emotions. Right now you're afraid and feel guilty and you're really pissed off because Sparks tried to kidnap me. You think you should have seen the danger a long time ago."

"Well, I should have." He spun the wheel and took them onto a dirt road out away from the city. "I've got a few connections, Briony. I'll see what I can dig up on Sparks and Whitney both. Mom and Dad kept all the original papers pertaining to your adoption in the safe in the trailer. We can take a look and see if anything in the papers will help us sort this out. And who the hell got you pregnant? I didn't know you went out on a date."

She shrugged, careful to avoid meeting his eyes. "I was curious, thought I couldn't get pregnant, and slept with a hot guy just to see what it was like."

"That doesn't sound like you. Who are you protecting? Tony? Randall? Which one? They have to assume some responsibility."

Briony burst out laughing. "Do you know how ridiculous that sounds when we have someone trying to drug and maybe kidnap me? The big man called me an incubator." She closed her eyes briefly. "He said he volunteered to be the donor."

Jebediah hit the steering wheel with the flat of his hand. "This doesn't make sense, Briony. What do they want with you?"

"My differences maybe. Jack Norton told me that Whitney is supposed to be dead, that he was murdered last year, but we were still sending updates to him, and Dr. Sparks still came as well. Remember, last year when he told me it was so important to work harder on my water skills? And right after Mom and Dad were murdered, they ordered me to go to Colombia for something stupid. I refused. It was the first time I ever refused them anything, but I couldn't function after finding the bodies."

Jebediah glanced at her. "I was afraid for you. You were nearly comatose. Of course I told them no. And later, when we did the water training, you nearly drowned staying under water so long. I was a wreck. Why the hell didn't I question any of this? What was wrong with me?"

"Mom and Dad allowed the training; you wouldn't ever question their judgment. A better question would be why was my training so important to them? They want me for something, Jebediah." Her hand massaged her stomach. "Or my baby."

Her brother shot her a sharp glare. "And what would Jack Norton know about Whitney? You aren't corresponding with him or seeing him, are you?"

"I don't have a clue where he is and haven't seen him since he left Kinshasa. We talked a lot, that's all."

"He's not a man you want to be around, Briony," Jebediah cautioned.

"I thought he was your friend."

"Men like Jack Norton don't have friends. We know one another. I respect him, but he's dangerous and I don't want him anywhere near you."

"I've never understood why you use that word whenever his name comes up. Does it mean he suddenly erupts in rabid rages and shoots people? I'm already pregnant; it's not like he's going to want to have mind-blowing sex with me."

Jebediah winced. "The last thing any brother ever wants to hear is that his sister is having mind-blowing sex. Geez, Bri." He pulled through the gates of the circus "town" and drove straight to their trailer. He signaled her to stay put and got out, leaving the car running as he surveyed the area around them. "Slide into the driver's seat and if I don't come out of the house in one minute, take off. Get away from here, and call this number." He scribbled a telephone number to the United States on a torn napkin. "Don't trust anyone else."

Briony nodded and sat behind the wheel, anxiety rushing over her. For once Jebediah believed her, instead of insisting she was paranoid — and that was just plain frightening. She was relieved when he stuck his head out the door of the trailer and gestured for her to come inside. The moment she was in the house, Jebediah slammed the door closed and ordered Tyrel to keep watch outside.

"They'll be coming for her," Jebediah told the brothers. "Pack up now. We're going to have to get out fast. Grab everything important and leave the rest. Seth, break out the weapons stash; we're going to need them. Don't say more than that. Briony, get moving, hon; we don't have much time."

"The rain's beginning to really come down," Ruben said. "That will help us if we get on the road."

"What should we tell the others?" Seth asked.

"Absolutely nothing. We don't want to put anyone else in danger," Jebediah answered. "The big bastard pulled a gun. Our people here can't tell them anything if they don't know anything."

"His name is Luther." Briony's hand fluttered to her throat. "Do you think he was going to shoot me?"

"No, hon, he was going to shoot me."

Briony's eyes widened with shock. "Jeb, I can't stay with you — any of you. One of you could be hurt, or worse, dead like Mom and Dad."

"Don't get dumb on us, Bri," Ruben said. "Whoever these people are, we'll sort it out." He threw files into a duffel bag and held it out. "Throw some clothes in here and let's go."

"She can't be carrying anything heavy," Jebediah objected. "She's pregnant."

"How?" Seth demanded.

"Who?" Ruben roared.

"Oh for heaven's sake." Briony rolled her eyes. "I'll get my clothes."

"Hurry," Jebediah urged.

She hurried to her bedroom, ignoring Ruben shouting questions after her. As she stuffed clothes into a small bag, she heard her brothers arguing over where to go. Rain fell in a steady rhythm, adding to the dark gray of her world. No matter what, her brothers would protect her, and she had a terrible feeling that if Whitney really wanted her back, he wouldn't stop until he had her — that he'd go right through every member of her family.

Screams pierced the night, and the tigers roared a challenge. Briony stiffened, adrenaline flooding her body. The rain beat down with hard strength, and the tigers continued, a constant unrest, their voices menacing, carrying through the circus town. Shrill screams grew louder, galvanizing her into action. She ran for the door.

Jebediah stopped her. "You stay here. Let us find out what's going on. Tyrel's making a sweep around the houses."

Her brothers raced toward the animal cages to help with whatever emergency there was. As soon as they were out of sight, the back door crashed open. Briony didn't wait to see what happened or who was there. She ran out the front after her brothers. She refused to call out, not wanting to draw Tyrel into possible danger. She was very fast and she had a good chance of catching Jebediah.

Rain poured down on her, drenching her hair and clothes as she sprinted toward the sounds of disaster. As she flashed past the wind-lashed shrubs, a huge man emerged from the bushes, streaking toward her. *Luther.* And he wasn't alone.

Briony nearly ran into a second man, switched directions to avoid him, and found herself trapped between the men and the next trailer. She stopped moving and turned to face them, resolve on her face. She kept her feet beneath her shoulders, standing sideways to present the smallest target, one hand held loosely across her waist and the other up gesturing as she spoke. "What do you want, Luther?" She looked at her hands. They were beginning to shake and her head felt crushed, as if in a vise. The pain was too severe to be just the emotions of the two men, but she could feel the backlash from the crowd over near the tiger cages.

"You. Just come with us now and no one else has to get hurt."

There was something vaguely familiar about him, something just out of her reach. "What did you do?" Her stomach cramped, and she pressed her hand protectively to the baby.

"Your boyfriend wasn't feeling too good so we gave him a place to sleep it off," Luther said. He rubbed his shoulder where she'd slammed the needle into him. "He isn't going to be helping you with the baby, so you'd better make up your mind to come with us or you won't have any of your so-called brothers alive either."

She took a deep breath and glanced toward the animal cages where the crowd had converged. "You hurt Tony?" They had to have, or she wouldn't be so violently ill. Blood began to trickle from her right ear.

"Worthless piece of trash. You could have had the pick of a dozen men to father your baby. Men worth something. Why the hell you picked that gigolo is beyond me. He screamed like a girl."

Briony's mouth went dry. "Why would you hurt him?"

"He had no right to touch you."

"He —" She broke off abruptly. She didn't dare tell them Jack Norton was the father of her child. They might decide to kill him. "This is crazy. I don't understand any of this." She wiped at the small trail of blood at her ear.

"Come on. You don't want your brothers

hurt," the other man said, a trace of sympathy in his voice. "Just come with us and no one else is going to die. We'll explain everything to you. You can't take much more of this. What if you have a seizure? That would hurt the baby."

"Don't play nice with her, Ron, she's a hellcat," Luther warned.

"He's *dead?* You killed him?" Tony was a handsome man with a ready smile who pitched in without complaint wherever needed. "Why would you do that?" She rubbed her pounding head. Of course they'd done it, because she'd named him the baby's father. She'd aimed a gun at Tony's head with her thoughtless statement. "Why does Whitney want my baby?" She was going to be sick in another minute if the pressure in her head didn't let up. Her vision was beginning to blur.

Ron held out his hand. "Come on. You know they aren't going to let you run around loose when you're so valuable to them."

Briony pushed back her rain-slicked hair and rubbed her eyes to try to clear her vision. "That's right. I'm valuable. The baby is valuable. I guess that means you can't use your gun on me."

"I could shoot you in the leg," Luther

warned, "and after that stunt you pulled with the syringe, I'd enjoy it. Get your ass over here right now."

Briony shook her head. "I don't think so. Come and get me."

"No one wants to hurt you," Ron said. "Let's just get this over. Get in the car and we'll sort it all out."

Luther pulled a gun and aimed it past Briony. "Your brother is coming this way, and I sure as hell don't mind shooting him. Get in the car now."

Briony turned her head to see Tyrel hurrying through the downpour toward her. There was no time for anything but action, and she took it, somersaulting across the ground and going in low to sweep Ron's legs out from under him. As he went down, she came back up and stomped hard on his wrist, reversing to kick him in the knee, hoping to incapacitate him.

The gun went flying and she dove for it using a second somersault. She was able to scoop it up and continue forward her motion toward her brother. "Catch!" She tossed the gun. With the tremendous reflexes gifted to the Flying Five, Tyrel picked the gun out of the air, shoving his sister behind him as they backed toward their own trailer.

"We can't get trapped, Tyrel," she cautioned.

Luther dragged Ron into the cover of the bushes and sent a warning shot that sprayed leaves all over them. "Just hand her over and no one will get hurt," he called.

"Did they really kill Tony?" Tremors wracked Briony's body from the violence rushing into the spaces around her. The emotions choked the breath out of her and pounded at her head. She bent over and vomited, unable to stop the cramping in her stomach.

Tyrel kept pushing her back behind him with one arm as they retreated.

"Someone hit him over the head and threw him in with one of the tigers," her brother answered grimly.

"Damn them. I told them Tony was the father of my baby. I shouldn't have done that, Tyrel. I shouldn't have said anything at all." Deep inside she was crumbling, going to pieces, screaming even. She was directly responsible for Tony's death, and a big part of her was certain she was connected to the murder of her parents. "Maybe I should go with them. If I stay with you, they'll try to kill you, Seth, Ruben, and Jebediah."

"Pull yourself together," Tyrel snapped. "Do you think for one minute we'd let them take you away from us? Get as far away from this as you can. You're already sick. In another minute you're going to go down, Bri, and I can't watch over you and keep them off of you."

Briony backpedaled until she reached the edge of the trailer. She *wouldn't* allow her disability to compromise Tyrel's safety. She took a deep breath, let it out, and ignored the shards of glass piercing her skull. She loved Tyrel, and Luther could just go to hell if he was counting on her crumbling under the pressure. She glanced up at the roof while Tyrel exchanged another shot with Luther. Someone would hear the shots and come running right into the middle of a war zone.

"I'm going over the roof, Tyrel, and get behind him."

He glanced back at her, his expression furious — protective. He could see the sweat on her body, the toll of violence already ripping at her. Pain shot through Briony, but at the same time she was humiliated to think that in spite of all her special gifts, her capabilities, her brothers had to protect her because she was unable to use her speed and agility or marksmanship.

"No, you're not. These people are playing for keeps. Seth and Ruben and Jebediah will be here any minute and we'll get you out of here. Just stay put."

Luther was moving, trying for a better angle on Tyrel. Briony couldn't stop to think about it, the emotions of all the men swamping her. Anger. Resolve. Luther had an eagerness to destroy — to kill. He was really angry with her — not because of the syringe, but thinking Tony was the father of her baby was somehow a blow to his ego. It made no sense to her, but he was broadcasting loud and clear.

Briony crouched and leapt straight up to the roof, bending low to stay out of sight, running lightly and leaping to the next roof and then the next. From her vantage point she could see the crowd gathered around the tiger's cage and Randall, the other trainer, inside. Jebediah stood outside with a tranq gun and the tiger lay, sides heaving, head lolling from the knockout shot. Randall bent down to pull Tony's body away from the big cat.

Below her and just to her right was Luther. He lay flat on the ground, gun in both hands, arms extended, determined to line up a shot on Tyrel.

Beside him, Ron cursed and moaned, holding his kneecap. "I think my leg's broken. She broke my leg, Luther."

"Idiot. Why do you think they picked her to mother the kid? I warned you, but you had to fall for her big brown eyes," Luther spat contemptuously. "Go to the car and get it running. We'll need to get out of here fast. She can't hold out much longer, and when I shoot her brother, she'll go down hard. I've been studying her for a while."

Luther had been studying her? He thought her knew her capabilities and her weaknesses? Briony wiped a smear of blood from her mouth with the back of her hand. He didn't know the first thing about her determination. The man wasn't killing her brothers, and he sure wasn't getting her baby. She lay flat on the roof, anchoring herself as the wind and rain slashed at her, making the roof slick.

Briony focused on the gun in Luther's hands. Ron began to inch his way back through the brush, toward the car running a few feet away. He dragged his leg, cursing every few feet. She refused to allow her mind to wander, holding to one thought, one action, her entire being focusing on the metal object Luther clutched so tightly.

The metal appeared dark in the rain and shadows, but as she continued to stare at it, it took on a slight glow. Luther suddenly swore and dropped it in the grass. The gun shone with hints of yellow and orange through the gray of the rain. Luther looked around, a small smile suddenly appearing. *You're good. Better than we thought — or hoped. Come home where you belong.*

The voice was pitched low, and the vibration running through her body made her stomach knot. Alarm spread through her. What was he doing? It was an attack — but not on her — on the unborn child. *Stop it.* Feeling desperate, Briony pressed one hand to cover the baby and clutched at the roof with the other to keep from slipping.

*The baby should be mine. Come with me or I won't stop and the useless kid you're carrying is going to die.*

Briony didn't bother to argue. She could feel Luther's resolve. He wouldn't stop until he had Briony. She blocked out her fear for the baby and for herself and concentrated once again on the gun.

*You'd better listen to me. I know you can hear me. You were promised to me — meant for me. Get in the car or I'm killing your brother. You know I can do it too.*

The gun wiggled in the grass, began to rise, and dropped back to earth. Briony took a deep breath and forced calm into her mind. It didn't matter what he was thinking or feeling or saying. Only the gun mattered.

It was the only thing in her world. It rose slowly, and swung around until the muzzle was aimed straight at Luther.

The most difficult part was to keep the gun in levitation while she focused on the trigger. She'd never actually fired a shot this way, but anything was possible.

Luther turned his head, the movement catching his eye. He rolled out of the line of fire, his hand snaking out so fast it was a blur, knocking the gun back to earth. *You should have listened to me.*

Briony saw the determination on his face as he slipped back into the bushes. He was going after Tyrel. Without hesitation, she rolled backward, straight off the edge of the roof, turning in midair the way she did during a performance, to land on her feet. Sprinting around the corner of the trailer, she raced back toward her brother.

Luther burst out of the shadows, slapping the gun out of Tyrel's hand, knife gleaming as he sliced viciously at his jugular. The blade missed by a scant half an inch as Tyrel stumbled back. He did a series of back springs to put several feet between them, but Luther was just as fast, covering the distance in a single leap, the knife slashing fast, over and over, cutting Tyrel's arms as he tried to defend against the unbelievably

234

fast attack.

Blood splattered in all directions — drops hit Briony as she burst from the garden to strike Luther with the heel of her hand flat on his chest, putting her weight behind it and using every ounce of adrenaline and enhanced strength she had. He slashed with the knife as he fell backward. Briony felt the bite of the blade along her forearm, but she kept going straight at him, kicking at his hand to try to get rid of the blade. She missed his arm, but nailed him in the ribs.

As she attacked again, she caught movement out of the corner of her eye. Ron emerged, limping, gun in hand. Briony leapt at Tyrel, knocking him back as Ron fired off several rounds in rapid succession. Briony and Tyrel hit the ground, rolling away to shelter.

Luther rose and glanced toward the animal cages, where the people were beginning to turn heads. "This isn't over," Luther snarled. "And when I get my hands on you, you're going to wish you were dead."

Briony kept her head down, trying not to be sick, the pain squeezing her head almost as bad as the day she'd found her parents. Was it possible Luther could amplify what she was feeling?

Tyrel stroked her hair. "How bad, honey?

Did he cut you?"

She waited until she heard the car leave before she pushed herself into a sitting position, rocking back and forth. "I'm going to pass out, Tyrel. I can't have a seizure, I don't know what it would do to the baby." She raised her hand to press her palm against her head. Blood dripped steadily.

Tyrel swore. "That's deep. You need stitches."

"Maybe we should call Dr. Sparks," Briony suggested a little hysterically and leaned over and threw up again.

Pounding footsteps announced the arrival of her other brothers. Seth reached down and plucked her out of the wet grass, while Ruben wrapped her arm in his shirt.

"How bad, Tyrel?" Jebediah asked. "You're all cut up to hell."

"They're shallow," Tyrel confirmed, "but Briony's needs stitches."

Jebediah swore. "Get her in the house. I'll take care of both of you, and then we have to get out of here."

"Where are we going?" Ruben asked. "Why are they suddenly after Briony?"

"She thinks they killed Mom and Dad," Jebediah said. "And I'm beginning to think she's right. Get everything out of the safe and let's go now."

"Jebediah." Seth's voice stopped them all. He was standing in the doorway of Jebediah's room.

They turned slowly to stare at him. He stepped back to allow them to see the chaos in the trailer. The place had been torn apart and the safe door was open — the contents gone.

"There were three of them," Briony whispered. "I didn't even smell them." She looked at her brothers with horror on her face. "Who are these people?"

# CHAPTER 8

Briony stared out the window into the pouring rain. The small villa where Jebediah had taken them belonged to an old friend of her parents, a fellow circus performer now retired. They traveled most of the night to get there and arrived tired, hungry, and irritable. Being in the close confines of the car had been hell for Briony. Her brothers were angry and scared and worried. Tyrel was in pain and trying to hide it. No one said a single word about Tony's death — but it was on all of their minds. She threw up so many times Seth even began to curse, frustrated by all the stops they had to make.

"Briony?" Tyrel stood in the doorway. "Are you up to talking or do you need to be alone for a while?"

She turned away from the rain to look at her brother, love for him overwhelming her for a moment. He always inquired, and that meant a lot to her. "What are you doing

238

up? I thought you'd be sound asleep by now." Deliberately she curled up on the sofa to indicate she didn't mind company.

"I was asleep, but my arms were hurting so I got up to try to find some aspirin. I brought you some just in case." He held up the tablets and a glass of water.

"Thanks, Tyrel, I appreciate how thoughtful you always are. I'm not really sure if I should take aspirin. I didn't ask Sparks how to take care of the baby." She flashed a rueful smile. "It never occurred to me I'd ever be having a baby, so I never bothered to research what to do if I got pregnant. I wouldn't want to take anything that might be harmful."

Tyrel dropped into the chair opposite her. "I still can't believe you're having a baby. I had no idea you were seeing anyone."

"I wasn't — not exactly. I can't be around anyone long enough to get intimate with them as a rule."

"Are you saying Tony isn't the father?"

She ducked her head, looking down at her hands. "I told Sparks he was. I wanted to see his reaction. He was acting so strange and I didn't want to name the real father, so I used Tony's name." She looked up at her brother, horror in her gaze. "I swear, I had no idea they would kill him."

"Briony." Tyrel laid his hand over hers in an effort to comfort her. "Of course you didn't."

With anyone else, Briony would have drawn away, but Tyrel was always genuine. She could easily read his thoughts filled with love and concern. She let his hand stay over hers even those it was uncomfortable.

"Whatever these men do, it isn't your fault. No one could have known they were going to harm Tony. We just have to figure out what they want."

Briony frowned. "At first I thought they wanted the baby, but then the big man — Luther — seemed upset that Tony was the father. He even said I was promised to him — that he had volunteered to be a sperm donor." She rubbed her temples. "I have a strange feeling that I'm supposed to give birth to a superchild."

Instead of laughing at her, Tyrel nodded his head. "That makes sense if you think about it, Bri. You can run faster than anyone I know and you're far stronger than even Jebediah."

Briony took a deep breath and moistened her lips. "I think I was an experiment — genetically engineered. I don't think I was Whitney's daughter at all, Tyrel."

Tyrel sat back in the chair, regarding her

240

with his serious gaze. Before Sparks had tried to kidnap her, any one of her other brothers would have laughed and accused her of watching too much sci-fi, but Tyrel always took everything she said seriously. "It never made sense to Mom that Whitney insisted on providing his doctor for you. It bothered her, especially as you got older. We traveled so much, and it was inconvenient to wait for Sparks to fly in to see you when we had a doctor traveling with us."

"I detested going to Sparks." Briony shivered and looked at her gauze-wrapped arm. "I think this was an accident. I honestly think Luther would have killed you, but I don't believe they want me dead at all. I think I'm the baby carrier."

"Are you going to tell me who the father is?"

Briony sighed. "Jebediah will kill me." Even as she said it, she knew her oldest brother was close. She caught his scent and looked up. He lounged in the doorway, beefy arms folded across his chest.

He shrugged lightly. "More likely I'll pound the guy into the ground. Who?"

"Jack Norton." Even saying his name still hurt. She bowed her head, waiting for the firestorm to erupt around her.

There was a stunned silence. Jebediah

looked as if someone had punched him. "He touched you? That son of a bitch put his hands on you? After we risked our lives for him?"

"Jebediah," Tyrel cautioned. "It's been a long day. She's gone through enough."

*"Jack Norton?"* Jebediah repeated, obviously dazed. He sank into another chair and put his head in his hands. "Briony, you have no idea what you've done."

"I got pregnant, Jebediah," Briony said, allowing exasperation to creep into her voice. "I'm not a teenager. I grew up a long time ago, and being pregnant isn't the end of the world. If you don't want me around, just say so."

Jebediah's head jerked up, shock showing on his face. "I'm not upset that you're having a baby. Shocked maybe. Traumatized that my baby sister actually had sex, but nieces or nephews are fine with me. But Jack Norton . . ." He broke off abruptly.

Briony sighed. "Does it really matter who the father is, Jeb? He isn't ever going to be in the picture. He's in the States, far away, we're in Italy. What does it matter?"

"Oh, honey," Jebediah assured her, "it matters. Jack Norton always matters. He's totally unpredictable and he lives by an entirely different set of rules than the rest of us. Do you remember when I first saw him in your room and I was yelling at you for going out into the jungle by yourself?"

"Of course."

"Do you remember the threat he made?"

"He said he was going to rip out your heart if you kept talking to me like that," Briony said.

"That's right. It wasn't a threat, Bri. Jack would have done it." He leaned forward. "I'm serious, honey. Jack Norton is a straight-up killer. He has a code and all that, but when push comes to shove, Jack's going to be the one standing. There's something different about him."

Pain twisted her heart. "He's like me."

"He's *nothing* like you," Jebediah objected. "Where did you ever get an idea like that?"

"I thought you liked him."

"You don't *like* Jack Norton. You respect him. You might fear him — but you don't like him. Jack's someone you want on your side in a tight spot, but you're never going to invite him home for dinner."

"That's strange, Jeb, because for the first time in my life, I *was* comfortable. I didn't hurt at all when I was with him, not a single headache. I relaxed. I laughed. I enjoyed being with him."

Jebediah exchanged a long look with Tyrel. Her tone had wavered, alerting both brothers that she was close to tears. "I've never known Jack to talk much and I sure have never seen him laugh. You must have brought out the best in him, Briony. Did I ever tell you that he saved my life once?"

"He did?" It didn't make sense to her the way Jebediah felt about Jack, yet now, when she needed it the most, her brother had given her a gift and she was grateful. "You never mentioned it — and neither did he."

"Jack would never say a word. We were running a rescue, going after two Rangers caught in enemy territory. The Rangers were supposed to hump it out to the extraction point but ended up right in the middle of a hornet's nest."

"Where were you?" Tyrel asked.

Jebediah shot him a quelling look. "Somewhere we weren't supposed to be and would never admit to being, so it was imperative to get them out of there without anyone getting caught. We came in on the north side, wanting to be able to cover them. Jack lay up in some trees and waited, and I moved into position on the ground. We just needed to provide them with enough time to get into the ravine, where the team members had set up an ambush. The Rangers would go in, drawing the enemy after them, and the canyon was going to be blown all to hell. That would give us time to get back to our ride."

"Something went wrong?" Tyrel prodded when Jebediah fell silent.

Jebediah smiled, but the amusement didn't quite reach his eyes. "You could say that. A guy came out of the ground, practically in my face. I swear his knife was the size of Texas. I didn't even hear the shot, my heart was pounding so loud, but I saw the hole right in the middle of his forehead. Jack took him out before he could finish his first slash with the knife. Later, I thanked him for saving my butt and he just shrugged. Never said a word to anyone about it. He probably saved a lot of us that day."

"He said I was a liability."

Tyrel's head jerked up. "He doesn't deserve you, Briony."

"It still hurts."

"Of course it does, honey," Jebediah said. "But it's for the best. Life with Jack would be difficult at best. He's not a man easy to be around. I don't know why he was so good with you, but that isn't the norm. He'd go days without speaking a single word. His brother, Ken, joked around some, but not Jack. He never seemed to sleep. Some of the guys liked to play pranks, but the smart ones knew better than to try to creep into Jack's area. More than one found themselves on the floor with a knife to the throat, and he wasn't gentle about it. You ever look into his eyes and you could see death there." Jebediah spread his hands out. "You wouldn't want to raise your child with him, honey. You want a place where there's laughter and joy. We'll help you. You know we love you and want you with us."

"I feel very lucky to have you all. Thanks, Jeb. It was very sweet of you to tell me about Jack. It's something for the baby, you know. I don't know much about him."

"I know a little," Jebediah admitted. "I'll tell the baby Jack stories."

"The rain is so loud," Tyrel complained. He rubbed his head, his bandages very white in the dimly lit room. "I'm tired tonight."

The rain was loud — too loud. A small alarm bell went off in Briony's head. Somewhere, a window or door in the house was open, allowing the force of the storm to penetrate into the villa. Her gaze jumped to her two brothers. Both had gone very still, awareness hitting them at the same time.

*Wake up! Seth! Ruben! Danger!* She sent the warning with as hard a push as possible, hoping she penetrated their sleep.

Jebediah touched Tyrel, gesturing him toward the back of the villa, where Seth and Ruben were sleeping in the guest rooms. He signaled Briony, and she rose in silence and followed him into the hall. As she passed the small room where she was supposed to sleep, she caught up her backpack and shrugged into it, wincing as the strap scraped over her bandages.

Jebediah pushed her in front of him, pointing with three fingers toward the left hall leading to the courtyard. Briony crept to the wide, lace-covered doors and willed them not to creak as she pushed them open. At once the rain poured in, driven by the ferocious wind. At his tap on her shoulder, she turned to look at her brother.

Jebediah leaned close, put his mouth to her ear. "Get to the car."

She knew he was going back for her brothers. Tyrel was going to wake them, but they should have been right behind them. Tyrel would have got them moving immediately, yet there was no sign of any of them. She hesitated, but Jebediah pushed her toward the night — the shadows. At his urging, Briony slipped into the courtyard among the overgrown shrubs and the wind-bent trees.

She took on the colors of the night, the

stripes of shadow, black and green and a multitude of shades of gray. She moved with the wind, matching the flow of energy as leaves and twigs swirled around her in the midst of the storm. The mosaic tiles were slippery, so she abandoned the path and took to the grass and shrubbery, trying to avoid the branches as they swayed, reaching out with thorny brambles to catch her clothing. She was only steps away from the small hidden spot where Jebediah had secreted the car when the wind shifted subtly.

She caught a familiar scent and halted, looking around, trying to find her enemy. He was close. She could smell him, knew him by the mixture of sweat and cologne he'd worn in Sparks's office. He wasn't masking it, and she glanced up just as Luther leapt from the roof. He was blindingly fast, giving her little time to react. The best she could do was take one step to the side and strike him as hard as she could, hoping to knock his legs out from under him so he'd fall.

Luther caught her hair in his fist as he went down, dragging her backward with him so that she landed heavily on top of him. "I'm running out of patience with you," he snarled. "Behave before I do something we'll both regret."

She slammed her elbows into his ribs, followed with the back of her head to his face. He jerked his head out of the way just in time, but she was already rolling back from him, scrambling to come to her feet. "Stay away from me."

He feinted to his left and jumped to his feet, landing in a crouching position, his fist streaking out too fast to block. She tried to slip the punch, whipping her head to the side, but he hit her hard enough to send stars dancing momentarily in front of her eyes. Briony staggered back, slipped on the tiles, feet going out from under her, and went down.

Luther was on her in seconds, pinning her down, hand over her mouth. "Damn it, you gave me no choice. Stop fighting me. I was careful not to hurt you, but you keep this up and it's going to happen."

Briony went still. He was incredibly strong, and the more she struggled, the tighter he held her. She tried to curl into a ball; an attempt to protect the baby.

"I don't want to hurt you," Luther said. "And I certainly don't want to upset you by killing your brothers, but you're giving me no choice. You *have* to come back to the lab with me." He brushed the hair out of her face and probed her swelling jaw with the pads of his fingers. "You shouldn't have pushed me so far."

Briony winced and jerked away from him. Her mind raced with ideas to get away. She had only seconds. He would be somewhat vulnerable when he shifted to his feet. It might be her only chance. She turned her head away from him, and colors danced for just a moment, yellow and red heat sensors, just a brief blur alerting her to the presence of her brothers. Briony quickly looked up at Luther, hooking her fingers in his shirt. "I'll stop fighting you if you tell me the truth. Are they going to harm the baby?"

"No. No! Sparks should have told you. They want the baby alive. Both you and the baby are valuable to them. They don't want to harm either of you. They can't take chances with either of your lives. There are others who want you dead because they're afraid of the power we wield."

Briony scented her brother just as Luther turned, a whisper of sound warning him. Jebediah hit him hard over the head, knocking him from Briony's body. Seth and Ruben quickly wrapped yards of duct tape around his legs, wrists, and mouth as Jebediah reached down to help his sister to her feet.

"You okay, honey?" He caught her chin in

his palm to inspect the swelling. "He really nailed you, didn't he?" He turned and kicked Luther in the ribs, using all his pent-up rage at the situation.

"He's not conscious," Briony pointed out.

"I don't give a damn."

"Did you hear what he said?"

Jebediah nodded. "I heard. They killed Tony because they thought he was the father of the baby. The rest of it is bullshit. Can you walk?"

She nodded. "Are there others? He couldn't have been alone."

Tyrel winked at her. "Seth and Ruben woke up. Both said they heard a voice warning them. They got the drop on the intruders and tied them to the bed."

Luther opened his eyes and glared at her. The more he looked at her brothers, the more afraid she became. Even tied, Luther had powers and skills her brothers couldn't conceive of.

"Let's get out of here," she suggested.

Jebediah wrapped his arm around her as he glanced at Luther. "I agree. We need to go now."

*Thought he was the father of the baby?* She heard the voice, loud and clear in her head. Whirling around, she stared at Luther. Jebediah had been careless, and Luther was no fool. She could see the dawning comprehension on his face.

Briony dragged Jebediah to the car. "Hurry. They can't follow us this time."

Jebediah slid behind the wheel of the car. "Did you check for a tracking device, Ruben, like I told you?"

"I didn't find anything," Ruben said. "Maybe I missed it."

"We'll ditch the car," Jebediah decided. "We're not taking any chances."

"He knows," Briony whispered. "Luther knows about Jack. He knows Jack is the father."

Jebediah glanced at her, put his hand over hers. "I'll find a way to get word to him, to warn him, Bri."

"Thanks, Jeb. I have no idea where we can go, do you?"

"Tonight we're going to put as many miles as possible between Luther and us, and then we're going to hole up for a while and sort this out. If we're not moving, we're not leaving tracks for them to follow. Let's pick up another car and ditch this one as soon as possible."

It was easier said than done. At night, with the storm still raging, it wasn't easy to find another car. Jebediah wanted something fast with good maneuverability in case he had to try to outrun someone. Ruben stole a Mercedes and switched plates with a second one they found several miles up the road.

Briony covered her face with her hands, appalled that they had been reduced to stealing cars. She slept on and off, and her brothers took turns driving through the night and morning. They got rid of the stolen car, after first washing it inside and out, leaving it parked on a narrow, deserted street while they walked over to a little store.

Ruben hurried down the street to purchase another car at a used-car lot they'd passed. While they waited for him, her other brothers went inside the store to stock up on food and necessities. Briony opted to stay outside, needing a little respite from the constant company in the small confines of the car.

There were few people on the street, and she breathed deep to calm her churning stomach. "Come on, baby, don't be making me sick this morning," she crooned. "My brothers are getting a little freaked out by it." As she talked to the baby, she noticed a man sitting in his car parked just down the street from the store. Her heart leapt, began to pound. At once she got up and started toward the store. *They'd been followed.*

The man got out of his car, removed his

dark glasses, and walked toward her with long, confident strides angled to intercept her before she could make it to safety. "Ma'am, my name is Kadan Montague. I need to speak with you and your brothers about a matter concerning you and Jack Norton."

Briony turned away from him, wary of the stillness in his eyes, the calm expression, but most of all, the instinctive knowledge that he was enhanced. He lifted his arm and his shirtsleeve pulled up, revealing the same tattoos Jack wore. She stared at them, knowing the strange dye only showed up using enhanced vision. "You must have the wrong person. I don't know anyone named Jack Norton."

Tyrel emerged from the store, knowledge flaring in his eyes, and he snapped a command at his brothers over his shoulder before hurrying to her. He took Briony's arm and pulled her protectively toward him.

"It's important, ma'am. Just hear me out. We can sit out in the open, maybe at that table over there." Kadan indicated a colorful umbrella over a round table on the sidewalk where she'd been. "I've been traveling nonstop to find you and I could use a cup of coffee about now."

Her brothers poured out of the store,

rushing to surround the man. He calmly handed Jebediah his identification. It was his stillness — his complete control — that worried Briony. This man reminded her too much of Jack. She didn't trust anyone, and without a doubt, Kadan Montague was enhanced both physically and psychically. More than that, she realized right away, he was an anchor. Out in public, her body trembled continually and she had to fight off the pain squeezing her head like a vise. The moment he'd approached, the symptoms had receded.

She pressed both hands over her stomach. She was never going to feel safe again. Worse, her brothers were running with her. They had no plan. No clear direction. They didn't even really know why they had to run. She knew Jebediah could read the desperation in her eyes, because he put his arm around her and pulled her close to him.

"Please, I'm only asking for a few minutes of your time."

"Are you armed?" Jebediah asked.

"Yes. And you should be as well. I arrived too late to help at the circus, tracked you to the villa, and followed you here. I'm not the only one on your trail."

Seth cursed under his breath. "I watched the entire time; I never saw a tail."

Jebediah gestured to indicate that Kadan precede him to the table. "Seems like half the world is on our trail. What is it you want?"

Kadan waited until the Jenkins family was seated around him, the brothers forming a protective ring around their sister. "Did you meet up with Jack Norton in Kinshasa?" he asked bluntly.

"I'm not going to answer that," Jebediah said.

"Maybe this will help you understand what's going on," Kadan said, opening his briefcase. Before he could retrieve anything, Jebediah pinned his wrist. Kadan merely looked at him, one eyebrow raised. Jebediah slowly removed his hand.

Kadan took out a file. "Once upon a time, many years ago, a brilliant researcher, with more money than good sense and morals, came to Europe and went through the orphanages looking for specific children. He wanted children, all female, who showed promises of superior intelligence, but also — more importantly — a psychic gift."

Tyrel leaned forward. "How would this researcher be able to tell if a child was bright with psychic gifts? How old were these girls?"

"Many of them were infants. He bought

the girls and took them back to his lab, where he proceeded to conduct experiments on them. Later, when he feared he might get caught, he devised a plan to make it look to the world as if he had adopted the girls out. In the meantime, he conducted his experiments on volunteers, military men trained in Special Forces."

Jebediah let out his breath in a slow hiss of comprehension. "He was developing a superior soldier, a weapon, using physical and psychic enhancement."

"Exactly. Briony, you're one of his girls."

"Dr. Whitney," Jebediah said. "My parents were approached by a man named Peter Whitney. He was a billionaire. Checked out completely, had all kinds of ties to several governments, here in Europe as well as in the States. He knew the president and just about anyone who was anyone. He said his wife died and he just couldn't raise his daughter alone. He wanted her in a loving environment, but somewhere she could develop her unusual skills."

Kadan nodded. "We don't know every-thing. Supposedly Whitney was murdered, but none of us believe he's dead. We've retrieved three of the girls, now grown women, of course. Lily, Dahlia, and Iris, and now you, Briony. We've been looking everywhere. I know you're not an anchor. How have you managed to survive all these years without one, in such close proximity to others?" There was open admiration in his voice.

Briony gripped Jebediah's hand hard. "Do you know a man named Luther? Enhanced physically and psychically just as you are?" Deliberately she hit him with her certain knowledge.

Kadan shook his head. "I'm sorry, no. There are two teams of men I'm aware of. If there are others, Whitney enhanced them in secret."

"What did he do to them?" Tyrel asked.

They all had questions. *She* had a hundred questions, but they didn't know this man. If Luther and Sparks were after her, it was possible Kadan Montague represented the other persons Luther said wanted her and the baby dead.

"It's an involved process," Kadan said. "If you come back with me, to the States, Lily can explain it. She's one of the girls bought from the orphanage. She's been working not only to find the other girls, but to find a way to help those who aren't anchors to better be able to live in the world without constant pain."

"You mean that's real?" Seth asked.

"Oh, yeah, it's real," Kadan said. He leaned across the table. "You've been able to do that, Briony, when even most of the men have problems, and they were adults and strong. Your input would be invaluable to the rest of us."

Jebediah's face darkened with anger as he read through his sister's file. Much of it was in scientific terms he couldn't understand, but the gist was there and it was horrendous. "Does Jack know about this?"

"Not yet. We believed Briony was in the most immediate danger. Is she pregnant?"

There was a long silence. Kadan looked around at the set faces. He tapped the file. "We just received the information that you're pregnant or we would have moved sooner to alert you. We hacked into Whitney's computer and this indicates she's pregnant. If the child is Jack's and both of you are enhanced, do you have any idea what that could mean? Whitney would do anything to get his hands on the baby. And from what I've been told, Briony, he'll do whatever it takes, including killing everyone you love, to get you back. He'd like to use you in his breeding program."

"This is scaring the hell out of me, Jeb." She looked to her oldest brother. "I couldn't bear it if any of you were hurt because of me."

Kadan tapped his briefcase. "They won't stop, Briony, and sooner or later they'll kill your brothers and take you back to the lab. You need protection. Come back with me, and we'll make certain Whitney never gets his hands on you or the baby."

Jebediah continued to frown down at the file. "Why would you be so willing to put yourself in harm's way for my sister?"

"Because she's one of us," Kadan said.

"Luther volunteered to protect me too. He murdered Tony," Briony said, watching Kadan's face carefully. It didn't do her much good; the man never changed expression.

"Who is Tony?" he asked.

"The father of my baby," she lied.

Kadan blinked, his only reaction. "Not Jack?"

Briony shook her head. "Not Jack. Unfortunately when I went to the doctor, thinking pregnancy impossible because I was on birth control . . ."

"They were giving her placebos," Jebediah snapped. "Damn them. Where did you get this file?"

"We hacked into the doctor's computer and stole it. He's been trying to maneuver

Jack Norton and your sister together for this past year. He didn't count on her being able to be with another man. Not being an anchor was his safeguard against Briony finding a relationship." Kadan's voice was devoid of expression as he imparted the information. His eyes stared straight into Briony's. "Like Whitney, I can't imagine how you could possibly have a sexual relationship with a man who isn't an anchor."

Briony shrugged. "He didn't think I could stand living with my family either, but I have for all these years. I also perform in front of thousands of people. Did anyone think I could do that?"

"Briony." Jebediah simply said her name softly, emotion moving through the depths of his eyes. "We should have known about this. We would have been . . ." He broke off, looking helplessly at his brothers.

"Better with you, more understanding," Tyrel finished.

"I'm fine. Mom always said I was strong enough, and I am." She touched Jebediah's arm because he looked so distressed. Fortunately, with Kadan so close she couldn't feel his distress.

"Wait a minute," Ruben interrupted. "None of this makes any sense to me. Why would this Dr. Whitney want to get this guy

261

Jack together with Bri?"

"Dr. Whitney was — or is — a genius, a man with connections all over the world, well respected, the highest of security clearances and a drive to succeed at everything he does. We know for certain that he conducted experiments on orphans, the young girls he basically bought in Europe and brought back, hiding them away while he perfected his method of enhancing them psychically and eventually physically. Everyone thought those girls were adopted out, but we've since found that Briony has been the only one we know of. Whitney then conducted tests for psychic abilities among the Special Forces and performed his experimental operations on several of us. No one at that time knew about the girls. We only found out after Whitney was supposedly murdered. We believe he is still alive and now is continuing and escalating his experiments, sanctioned by some covert organization within the government."

"Son of a bitch," Ruben growled. "Is this for real?"

"Unfortunately, yes. I'm giving you information that could get us all killed. At the very least, if he finds out we have it, that we know he's alive, Whitney will go underground and cut off the leak and we'll never find him. I risked my life coming here to warn you, to offer protection. The least you can do is give me the truth."

"What makes you think I'm not telling the truth?" Briony asked.

"I'm psychic too. The things he did to you, he did to me. I can help you. My team can help. You know as well as I do, Briony, that as your pregnancy advances, you won't be as fast. You won't be able to escape and it will fall to your brothers. They might get one or two of the men he sends after you, but not the enhanced soldiers. Those soldiers will wipe out your entire family and never look back."

"That's enough," Jebediah snapped. "We have to think about this, not go off half-cocked. I have friends who will check you out for me. I'm not turning my sister over to anyone until I know who they are and what they want."

"You may not have the luxury of waiting for an answer," Kadan said and signaled the waiter over. "I don't think these people are going to wait while you call your friends. If I can find you, they can find you." He looked at the bandages on both Tyrel and Briony, his gaze jumping to her swollen, black and blue face. "Again."

Briony smiled at the waiter and took

between her palms the cup of coffee he placed in front of her, her mind racing with the things Kadan had said. There was no way she could trust her baby to a stranger, but she did have a choice. She stared into the black liquid, her stomach fluttering with fear. Could she do it? Was she strong enough?

"Where are you staying, Mr. Montague? We'll talk it over and let you know what we've decided to do. I have to think about this."

Kadan sighed. "Read the file. Whitney is a monster, and if he gets his hands on you — or the baby — your life is not going to be worth much. At this time we have no idea where he is, so there wouldn't be a rescue team showing up to bail you out. Come back to the States with me. If you're worried, your brothers are welcome. At least stay until the baby is born. You're enhanced; you've had a great education. We can teach you survival skills, maybe enough to protect you and the baby."

*Survival skills. Don't open the door. Stand to the side of it. Walk on my left side. Go up to the roof, not into the alley.* The words played over and over in her head. Who better to learn from than the master?

"Why haven't you gone to Mr. Norton

264

and told him all of this?" Briony asked. "There must be more than one of you. Did you send someone to warn him?"

Kadan watched her with his unsettling direct stare. "Norton disappears, and when he doesn't want to be found — no one finds him."

Briony poured cream into her coffee and stirred it. "He's missing? Then you did try to find him."

"One of his team members was with us when we discovered this information. We left it to him to decide whether or not to try to contact Jack and tell him."

Seth took the cream from Briony, dumping it into his coffee as he glanced at Kadan, a challenge in his eyes. "If they killed Tony thinking he's the father, wouldn't they go after this Norton character on the off chance he is?"

Briony glanced up when Jebediah groaned. He covered his eyes with one hand and whispered in her ear. "The thought of you having *two* partners is more than I can take."

"They might go after Jack. They have a lot of intel. Whitney had a high-security clearance. He has access to files on Jack that few people have. In my opinion, he won't go near Jack unless he has no other choice. He would be stirring up a hornet's nest."

"What does that mean, exactly?" Seth demanded. "Why would he kill Tony and not Jack?"

Kadan sat back in his chair. "Tony was an easy target. Jack's not. Whitney has only so many men. We had a run-in with him recently and he lost a few. If he sent a team in after Jack, few of them, if any, would make it back alive. Jack isn't alone up there. He's got Ken with him, and his twin is every bit as lethal as he is. They're an unstoppable team. They've worked together for years and each knows exactly what the other is going to do at any given moment. Whitney would have to be insane — or desperate — to go after Jack Norton — especially on his home turf."

Briony looked at her brother, despair in her gaze. Resolve. She blinked away tears, and Jebediah swallowed hard, reaching for her hand.

"Briony's right, Mr. Montague. We appreciate the warning and the information, but we need to talk this over as a family. Give us a few minutes."

Kadan nodded. "I could use food. I'll order while you all talk. Anything I can get for you?" He scooped up the file and put it in his briefcase.

Jebediah wanted breakfast, and the others followed suit. They waited for Kadan to go into the café.

"He wasn't fooled," Briony said. "He knows we're going to leave. That's why he took the file."

"We are?" Seth asked.

"Ruben's back with the car," Jebediah said grimly. "Let's go."

# CHAPTER 9

Briony stared out the window at the wild scenery as they climbed higher and higher up the mountain in the Montana wilderness. At times the road seemed more of a faint, pitted track, overgrown with shrubs and grasses. The more she learned about Jack Norton, the more she could see him in this wild environment. He was a throwback to earlier times, a man who made his own rules and was as dangerous as the predatory animals surrounding him. He could disappear anytime he wanted and survive quite well off the land. She doubted anyone could find him, and that's why she needed him. He could teach her those same skills and protect her while she was learning them.

It didn't matter that he didn't want her. *Liability.* The word echoed through her mind. She pressed her hands over her stomach, her mouth tightening with determination. Too bad for Jack. She was not only arriving on his doorstep, she was bringing a *kid.* Granted, it wasn't born yet, but he was going to have to live with it. She couldn't see him turning them away once she told him their child was in danger.

Her fingers curled around the window as she leaned out to look down to the valley floor. They were on the right track. She *felt* him, the same way she'd felt his presence long before she'd ever laid eyes on him. He was closer than she'd anticipated, and she tasted fear in her mouth. Her heartbeat accelerated, and slowly, involuntarily, her fingers curled around the window jamb until her knuckles turned white. She felt the heightened danger with each mile they traveled.

"Are you certain, Bri?" Jebediah asked, his voice tight with strain as night fell. "It's becoming harder to see, even with the moonlight, and I don't want to use the headlights unless we absolutely have to. We've managed this far without a tail, and if we tip off Norton we're coming, he could slide away from us and we'd never find him." He glanced at her. "Once we do this, there's no turning back."

"You feel the threat too, don't you?" Few things worried Jebediah, but he definitely had a sixth sense when it came to danger.

"We *are* in danger, Bri. Jack could just as easily decide to shoot us for trespassing as listen to us. How many signs have we seen warning us away?"

"About ten." Briony offered him a faint smile. "If he bothered to put up signs, he doesn't want to kill anyone."

"You can bet every cent you have his brother Ken put up those signs."

"I hope I can trust the SEAL you contacted for Jack's address."

"Jess Calhoun was the closest thing to a friend Jack and Ken had."

She shrugged. "Who knows if what I'm doing is right? I don't trust anyone I don't know. None of us can right now, but Jack Norton is the baby's father. I'm not asking him to take responsibility. I'm not looking for a lifetime commitment, but if he's the badass you keep saying he is, then, for certain, he's my best chance of protecting our child. Even Kadan Montague said if he wanted to disappear, no one could find him. That means he can teach me."

Jebediah shook his head. "He scares the hell out of me, Bri, and the thought of you with him . . ." He stopped the SUV right in the middle of the narrow track and turned toward her. "Some men live by their own rules, and Jack is one of them. He'll never be an easy man, won't ever fit into society, and he's dangerous as hell if you cross his sense of justice. The government uses men like him, trains them, hones their natural instincts, and calls them when they need them, but they don't acknowledge them, because they're killers. Jack is extremely intelligent, and he's got more recorded kills than any sniper I know of — unless it's his brother." He tapped his fingers in agitation on the steering wheel. "I don't know if he was born that way, or if Dr. Whitney's enhancements made him that way; he doesn't talk much, but didn't you feel the danger when you were around him? Didn't you look into his eyes?"

Briony looked away from him. She'd glimpsed too much emotion in those eyes he spoke of. That intensity still haunted her sleep at night. Jack hadn't looked at her with the eyes of a killer. He'd been all man and he'd been dominant, loving, and frightening all wrapped into one. As inexperienced as she was, she still recognized that Jack could have taken things further than he had. He could have tied her to him sexually, left her craving only him, wanting only him — but he hadn't — not deliberately. He wasn't nearly as cold or unfeeling as those around him credited him as being, and that was what she was counting on.

"There's a chance he'll want to protect the child. He protects his brother. He's part of a military unit, and you said yourself he doesn't leave his people behind. He must have a sense of responsibility."

"That's a hell of a big leap of faith."

"What choice do I have, Jeb?" Briony asked. "If what Montague says is true, and he had enough proof that a madman is after me, where can I go? Especially if Whitney is part of some secret government project. We don't know one way or the other, but you told me you found enough proof in Mom and Dad's papers to know I was adopted and *Whitney,* the same name Kadan Montague used, insisted I be brought up with a very strange training program. Sparks tried to drug me and Luther tried to kidnap me. I don't think there's much doubt I'm in trouble here."

"Don't sound bitter, Bri. Mom and Dad absolutely loved and adored you." He flicked her a quick glance. "The money makes sense. They wanted to buy into the circus as partners. They wanted a child, a girl, and they wanted to give you the best education possible. You speak several languages, you're a genius, and you can kick serious butt when you need to; it wasn't as if they didn't genuinely love and want the best for you. They *loved* you — don't ever forget that in all of this."

"I won't, Jeb." She put her hand over her already rounded tummy. "But that doesn't change the fact that we won't be able to protect the baby indefinitely. I'm not willing to let Whitney, or anyone else, take my child for experiments. I'm a strong person. I'll do whatever I have to do to keep my child safe. Where else can I go? You tell me and I'll do it."

"They offered protection, Briony," Jebediah reminded her.

"And what do we know about them? That man — Kadan — was enhanced both psychically as well as physically. I not only felt the difference in him, he admitted it. And I had the feeling he was more powerful than Luther. What's to say he wasn't sent to bring me back? We don't know. At least you know Jack Norton. He saved your life. You told me he's got integrity and that he'll never stop if he takes on a job. I'm going to ask him to take on this job, to keep me safe until the baby is born. He can teach me how to hide, and once I have the baby, I can disappear. We should be able to figure out a way to make that happen. People disappear all the time."

"What if he says no?"

"He owes us that much, but if he's that big of a bastard," she shrugged, "then I guess we'll investigate these people and try to figure out who the good guys are."

"Look me in the eye, Briony," Jebediah challenged. "Look at me and tell me you aren't harboring any girlish fantasies about Jack Norton falling in love with you. This is no fairy tale and he's no Prince Charming. The last thing you want is to try to live with a man like that. I'm terrified of leaving you alone with him."

She touched her brother's arm. "I have no silly notions, Jebediah. You know me. I have above-average intelligence; I'm enhanced, and I certainly have more than my share of pride. I read the file on me thoroughly, especially the part where I would react to a certain scent. Jack said I'd be a liability and that he wasn't the kind of man to have a woman around. Those are almost his exact words. Obviously, whatever it is between us was simply manufactured by this doctor so we'd have a child. It has nothing to do with emotion and everything to do with scent. I was inexperienced and got caught thinking Jack could love me. He made it very clear he can't. I won't make that mistake twice."

"It scares me more that he actually *might*

fall in love with you, Briony. He would take over every aspect of your life. You saw a glimpse of him, a tiny one. He isn't an easy man. He's got demons on his back, and they aren't going to magically disappear. I hate saying these kinds of things to you, but Jack *is* different. When we're out there with guns in enemy territory, we're praying we don't come up on anyone, and if we do, that he doesn't spot us, because we don't want to have to pull the trigger, but Jack . . ." Jebediah shook his head. "He doesn't give a damn either way."

"Believe me, I respect your opinion, Jeb. If you say he's dangerous, I'm not stupid, I believe you. But I also see how much you respect him and his abilities." Her body shook with sudden adrenaline pouring in. "*No one* is going to take my child away from me. I can be absolutely ruthless if I have to be. And Jack Norton will underestimate me, just like everyone else does. I'll have the advantage."

Jebediah hit the back of his head several times against the seat in frustration and slammed the flat of his hand against the steering wheel. "This sucks. I should be able to protect you myself. How could something like this happen, and why the hell didn't Mom and Dad suspect something was wrong when Whitney demanded all that specialized training for a child? No one makes a child stay under water for long periods of time and do all the crap you had to do."

"I enjoyed it," Briony pointed out. "If I hadn't enjoyed it, they probably would have objected — just like they did when Whitney demanded I go for field training in Colombia." She flashed him a wan smile. "At least I'm equipped to handle anything thrown at me."

She looked out the window again, at the surrounding wilderness. She loved the outdoors. She loved the night. But — Briony sighed. Right now, darkness made her feel vulnerable instead of cloaking her in safety as it normally did. The trees and shrubs took on a sinister quality, rising high and dark and ominous, as if lurking in the shadows were monsters ready to leap out and devour her.

"I've spent my entire life feeling a coward — always afraid — but this situation is truly terrifying." She blinked back the sudden tears burning behind her eyes. "I've never been without you and the circus. I knew I was different; Mom used to tell me I had to hide it all the time, and maybe that was the appeal of Jack Norton. I finally found someone like me. The moment I laid eyes on him, I knew he was like me. I wanted to belong. Just once."

"Damn it, Briony, you've always belonged with us. *Always*. We wanted to have a sister as much as Mom and Dad wanted to have a daughter."

"I know that. It has nothing to do with adoption. You're my family and always will be. I didn't feel unloved — just different." She struggled to make him understand. "I didn't have to hide who I really am from Jack. He *saw* me and I saw him. I didn't have to hide the fact that I'm stronger and faster and can see people in ways others can't. More than that, I didn't hurt." She closed her eyes. "Can you imagine what that was like for me? For the first time I could be around someone and not know what they were thinking or feeling. Emotions didn't swamp me or make me sick. It was such a relief."

"I wish to hell we could give that to you, Bri," he said.

"I know, Jeb. And I know you all love me."

"That same appeal is going to be there when you see him again," he warned.

She turned her head to look at him. "I know. But I'm not so inexperienced this time. He was honest with me, and you and

I both know how tough I am. I look fragile to the world, but I've got the baby and you and the boys, and I'm not going to *ever* sell myself short. I won't get caught in the same trap twice." She looked around her at the trees swaying with the rising wind. "It's very dark, Jeb, and I'm determined to go through with this, so let's just get there, feel him out, and get it over with."

"Has it occurred to you he might decide he wants the baby?"

"Of course I considered that. What would he do with a baby?" She turned her gaze on her brother, and this time the fire in her eyes made him wince. "I'll do whatever I have to do to protect my child, Jebediah. Jack Norton, or anyone else, isn't going to take this baby away from me."

Jebediah swore under his breath as he started the SUV. "I knew you were stubborn, Bri, but I had no idea you were impossible."

Briony rested her head against the seat and kept her eyes on the scenery passing by. She prayed she was doing the right thing. Jack Norton terrified her on so many levels. She'd waited until after three kidnapping attempts, *three,* before making the decision to contact him. And it wasn't because he might want to kill her — or take the baby. It was because Jack Norton was the only person in the world she feared might take her over. He was stronger, dominant, definitely light-years ahead of her sexually. She had voiced aloud to her brother the hurtful things Jack had said, just to remind herself, to keep them in front of her so she wouldn't be taken in again. It was all too obvious to her that she would be swallowed up by Jack's dominant personality if she wasn't careful.

*Don't come near me again. Not ever, because I'll never be able to give you up twice.* Had she heard him whisper that as she was coming out of her sleep, or had it been an inexperienced girl's last hope? Maybe it had been her own warning system, screaming — shrieking — at her to stay away. Self-preservation demanded she obey, yet she was sticking her head right back into the lion's mouth.

The Lolo National Forest was on all four sides of them, completely surrounding the property they were trying to find. The mountain was lush with trees, and she often caught glimpses of wild animals.

"I think this is it, Briony," Jebediah said, slowing the SUV and staring at the narrow trail leading off to his right. "You have to be absolutely certain this is what you want to do. I think we follow this creek for another four miles and we're there. Once we arrive, it will be too late to change your mind."

For a moment she couldn't breathe. She held up her hand and her brother stopped the vehicle. Briony jumped out and was sick, over and over, leaning against the door, while her stomach protested the need to ask Norton for help. Pride alone dictated she stay away from him, but to have to ask him for protection — Briony shook her head as she took the cloth Jebediah handed her. The idea of leaving the safety of her family when she needed them the most, to go to a man who didn't want her, left her cold inside.

"You all right?" Jebediah rubbed her back in sympathy.

"Don't tell him about the baby. Let's tell him about Whitney. We can see how he reacts."

"If we even get that close," Jebediah said. "Be careful, Briony. We could get killed."

"I know." She nodded her head, her stomach cramping again. "I'm sorry I'm putting you in danger. Maybe I should walk from here."

"Not a chance. If you go in, I do too."

A sound awoke him, something out of tune with the familiar night noises. Jack lay for a moment fully alert, all senses flaring, seeking the disturbing break in the rhythm of the night. He rarely slept for any length of time, and always very lightly. A low, one-two hoot — like an owl, without the proper resonance — sounded from somewhere nearby; not the yard, more likely the forest just before the entrance to his home.

Jack dropped his feet to the floor in complete silence. He caught up his jeans and shirt, pulled them on, and strapped on a long leather sheath containing a razor-edged knife. A Smith and Wesson in his hand, he padded silently to the door. He moved down the hall unerringly in the dark and eased through the door to his brother's room.

He touched his twin's shoulder lightly. Ken was already alert, dragging on his jeans, aware of the need for silence. They used hand signals, as they had since they were children, preferring to use telepathy when distance separated them. Ken caught up his rifle, a night scope, and a box of shells.

Jack chose to leave by a side door, moving into the night silently, stealthily. He signaled Ken to high ground and then made his own way through the yard, a shadow among the shadows, first a boulder, then a tree, a part of the night.

Once in the cover of the forest, Jack picked his battleground carefully — good cover, good escape routes, a clear shot for Ken. Jack whistled softly, calling in the intruder. Ken would use a scope to get the exact number of intruders.

"Jack." The voice was a soft hiss of a sound. "It's Jebediah, Jack," the voice continued. "Jebediah Jenkins."

"Come on in," Jack said softly into the night, a challenge more than a welcome. He closed his eyes briefly, fighting back the memory of Briony, of soft skin and sheer ecstasy, a haven of pleasure that took him outside himself and the hell he constantly lived in. He was never going to be free of her.

*He's not alone.* Ken's voice filled his mind.

Jack sighed softly. Surely Jebediah wouldn't be a big enough fool to come after him because he found out about Jack sleeping with Briony. The idea was too childish for words, and not Jebediah's style. *Let them come, Ken.*

The wind shifted just a bit, just enough for him to catch their scent. Need slammed into his body, pheromones spinning out of control, enfolding him in her feminine allure. Briony was with Jebediah, and her scent called to him, heady and intoxicating, threatening his tight control. Jack let his breath out slowly. How could he ever give her up a second time? He wasn't a man who lived by rules. He wanted Briony, and the temptation to take her, to keep her, to tie her to him irrevocably was overwhelming. He had no doubt he could do it. He'd warned her. Why the hell hadn't she listened? And what was wrong with her brother that Jebediah didn't keep her safe — away from Jack, a continent away?

Jack waited there in the darkness, seeing the heat of their bodies before they stepped through the foliage to approach him. He needed to be watching Jebediah, but he couldn't take his eyes from Briony. *Stay on him, Ken. I've got the girl.*

She was everything he remembered and more. He'd filled his nights and his days with the memory of the feel of her skin, her body surrounding his, the fierce, almost primitive need to possess her. Stark, raw emotion surged and poured through his veins until his blood pounded with heat. Mostly he remembered the way she looked at him — as a man, so that he could see himself in her eyes — the man he should have been, if he'd met her years earlier. She looked like the most beautiful woman in the world to him, and here he was, up in the mountains where no one would ever be able to take her away from him.

Her hair was short and thick, platinum and wheat, sassy and inviting so that he itched to bury his face in the soft strands. Her eyes were as large, as beautiful as he'd remembered, so dark they were nearly black. As she and her brother approached him, she reached out to Jebediah, taking his hand, as if she was afraid. Jack could see the strain around her mouth, the shadows in her eyes. As she neared, he caught the minute difference in her scent. Even more feminine, as if chemical changes in her body had occurred since he last saw her. He remembered his own scent mixed with hers, powerful and appealing. The raw sexuality of their union, lust and overwhelming emotion mixing until they were both so wrapped in one another they were locked in another world.

Damn. He wanted her with every cell in his body. Every part of his brain. She walked out of the night looking too young. Too innocent. Too soft and sweet for a man like him. She was the epitome of everything he wasn't, would never be. Home. Family. Children. She was good and he'd lost that so long ago. All he had left was his honor, and if she didn't get the hell off his mountain, she'd rob him of that. She'd fight his possessive nature and eventually he'd break her spirit. In that moment, as she came closer, he truly hated the monster he had become.

"What the hell do you want?" he spat out, remaining in the shadows, knowing Jebediah wouldn't be able to spot him. He was less certain of Briony. He knew she was every bit as enhanced as he.

Jebediah and Briony exchanged a long look. Jack could smell their fear. It oozed through their pores and permeated the air around them. The tension shot up a notch. Jebediah stepped protectively in front of Briony, and that annoyed the hell out of Jack. He wanted their fear, but at the same time, if anyone was protecting her, it should have been him. She belonged with *him.*

"If you came to challenge me to a duel because I fucked your sister, Jebediah, you're a hell of a lot stupider than I gave you credit for." The words were out before he could stop them. The rage, usually hidden deep, boiled over with Briony being in such close proximity, his craving for her driving him to stupidity. He detested standing there watching Jebediah put his hands on her. For a man with the need of tight control, she was dangerous, shattering Jack's every protective shield. He needed to drive her away. Even as the thought came, his heart sank. It was too late for him — for her.

Fierce anger clouded her face, and she leapt across the distance at him, her hand moving so fast it was actually blurred. The slap was loud, reverberating through the clear night. Fear galvanized him into instant action. "Down, Jeb, get down!" He yelled the command even as he slammed his body hard into Briony, driving her backward to the ground, covering her smaller frame with his larger one. *Stand down! Stand down!*

The bullet tore through the tree right where Briony's head had been, splintering wood and sending bark raining over them. Jack kept Briony pinned down, holding her still beneath his body. He knew she could feel the merciless hard-on pressed so tightly against her stomach, and it gave him the utmost satisfaction to see the edge of fear mingled with her fury. His fingers dug into her shoulders and he gave her a little shake. "Damn you for your stupidity. Did you think I wouldn't have someone out in the shadows with a scope on you? You could have been killed."

His body blanketed hers. Imprinted onto hers. Wanted hers. The scare of nearly losing her sent a deep tremor through his body, shaking him. He was never shaken, yet just her closeness had him off balance. *Damn it to hell, Ken, don't you shoot at her again. I'll fucking kill you myself.*

His brother's amused laughter echoed through his head. *It was a warning shot.*

*My ass, that was a warning shot.*

"Get the hell off of me." Briony's eyes, so dark with anger, nearly threw off sparks. "I forgot what an utter bastard you are. Get off now." There was a definite threat in her tone.

Somewhere deep in his gut, the admiration rose, just as it had when she'd shot a man to protect him. Briony might be sweet and innocent and far too good for the likes of him, but she was a fighter through and through. "Or what?"

Behind him, Jebediah sat up cautiously, looking around him for the shooter. "Or I'm going to beat you to a bloody pulp. Get off of her."

The shadows shifted with the trees, the moon spilling across her face. Jack saw the swelling, the bruise spread across her jaw, chin, and cheek. He'd noticed the gauze wrap on her arm, but someone had hit her? Raw fury poured through his body — raged ice cold and deadly. "Who hit you? Damn it, don't lie to me either. If your brother dared lay a hand on you . . ."

"My brother wouldn't hit me, you moron. Let me up now."

"Get the hell off my sister or I'm going to knock you off of her," Jebediah threatened, uncaring of the shooter.

"Who hit her? Tell me now, Jebediah, or Ken's going to blow your brains all over the place."

"A man named Luther hit me. Get off before *I* hurt you," Briony snapped.

"What were you thinking bringing her here?" Jack demanded, ignoring the threat.

"He was thinking about saving your life, you jackass." Briony shoved at the wall of his chest, this time hard enough that it rocked him. Touching his chest brought back the memory of fresh knife carvings, of kissing her way down the jagged wounds, lower and lower until . . . She slammed her mind closed on her wayward thoughts.

Jack had forgotten how strong she was. "That was thoughtful of him. Who is Luther and who wants to kill me?"

"Who doesn't," Briony snapped. "You're hurting me. Get off."

Jack shifted his weight immediately, dragging her up with him, retaining possession of her arm when she tried to get to her brother. "Who is trying to kill me? Jebediah, stay right where you are. You wouldn't want my trigger-happy brother to take another shot at you."

Jebediah froze in the act of getting up. Sweat trickled down his armpits. "We had a recent visitor, Jack," he explained. "A man calling himself Kadan Montague. He told us about experiments a Dr. Whitney had performed first on orphan girls and then on men in the military."

"Keep talking."

"Apparently Whitney is still alive and looking to reacquire some of the ones who've slipped away from him."

Jack studied Jebediah's face. There was righteous fury there. And truth. But not the whole truth. He switched his gaze to Briony. She was still, no longer struggling against his hold, but she didn't meet his gaze. Up so close to her, he could smell the heady scent of her, reminding him of satin sheets and candlelight. Of finer things. Things he couldn't have.

His fingers tightened on her arm and drew her closer, until they were nearly skin to skin. His gaze narrowed on Jebediah. "You wouldn't have brought your sister to tell me that. You would have come alone." He leaned closer to Briony, inhaled the scent of her hair, of her body. Something was different. Subtly so, but different.

"I insisted on coming with him."

Her voice was low. The faint tremor running through her body shook him enough that he had an urge to pull her into his arms and comfort her. He studied her face for a long time. Jebediah was afraid of him. Briony might fear his possession, but she hadn't been afraid of him. Where was all the fear coming from? He let out his breath slowly. "You're one of the orphans he experimented on. That's why Kadan told you. It's all classified information." He'd suspected all along that Whitney had experimented on her and adopted her out, but he hadn't pursued it. Being so close to her had had him thinking of other things. Like the taste of her in his mouth. The sound of her laughter.

Briony hesitated so briefly he nearly missed the quick glance she shot at her brother. "Yes. Kadan came to warn me. He's legitimate then? The things he said were true?"

*Kadan.* He didn't want Kadan Montague anywhere near her. Kadan was an anchor and a hell of a lot better man than he was. Jack's thumb slid over Briony's bare skin in a small caress. The feel of her soft skin set his heart pounding. What was different? Her scent. The chemistry of her body. *The feel of her body.* The air rushed out of his lungs. Where before her stomach had been rock hard and flat, she was now soft and round. Knowledge flooded his brain. Adrenaline flooded his body. His hands slid up her arms to her shoulders.

She'd let another man touch her the way he had. Be inside her body. Kiss her. Lie with her and laugh with her. How could she? His heart accelerated until he thought it would burst out of his chest. *How could she lie with another man after being with me — belonging to me?* He knew there would be no other woman for him. "Son of a bitch. You're pregnant."

Briony stood perfectly still under his hands. Jack's fingers were around her neck as if he might strangle her. He stared down at her, his eyes black and ice cold, the hard angles and planes of his face without expression. His skin had changed color, to a darker, much more violent hue, mirroring the turbulent emotion he refused to allow to rise to the surface. She felt the first real surge of fear of him, but then the pads of his fingers began stroking small caresses over her frantically beating pulse. She deliberately took a breath and let it out slowly to calm herself and stay in control.

She was unprepared for her physical reaction to him. Even now, knowing it was planted, pheromones designed especially to attract her to this man, she couldn't help the rush of heat flowing between them. "I can see you're thrilled with the news."

There was a bite of anger in her voice, but something else, something deeper, sorrow maybe. Regret? Was it possible the child was his? Hope was stirring when he didn't dare allow it. He tried fishing. "Why the hell didn't you tell me right away?"

"Obviously I didn't know where the hell you were. Do you think you could stop swearing at me? I realize we aren't welcome here, but it seemed the only thing to do under the circumstances."

"And what are the circumstances?" He held his breath.

"Dr. Whitney wants our baby. He's already made three attempts to kidnap me." She put her hand to her cheek. "I can't stay with the circus because I'm endangering my friends and family. As I get further along, it's going to be more difficult to defend myself. I thought if I came to you, you might be able to protect us until the baby's born and teach me survival skills at the same time for afterward. I'm not asking for financial help or anything else, and I realize it's dangerous. Whitney is sending enhanced soldiers against me. The man they sent, Luther, did this. And for some reason he's very angry that I'm not carrying his child, so I'm afraid for our baby." She looked up at him, her dark eyes meeting his gaze squarely. "They aren't taking this baby from me."

Jack was stuck back on *our baby.* Her voice echoed through his mind, repeating the words in that soft, almost loving tone. He let his breath out slowly, arms coming up to enclose her small frame, drawing her back against him so his hand covered the small, soft, rounded stomach. His child lay beneath his hand, nestled deep inside her body, protected by her. *Wanted* by her. Deep inside where he was hard and cold and carved of stone, he felt a curious shifting, melting, a softening he couldn't explain, and it scared the hell out of him. For a moment she stiffened, tried to pull away from him, but he tightened his hold in warning.

Briony went very still in his arms. It seemed too intimate to have his hands over her stomach, covering their child, protecting it, yet he said nothing, gave her no indication of what he was thinking or feeling. But it was obvious he wasn't going to let her go. "Kadan Montague offered us protection, but I don't know anything about him."

Jack's body jerked and his arms tightened around her. *"No one* is taking this baby from *us,"* he corrected.

Briony held herself stiffly away from him. "Aren't you going to ask for a paternity test?"

"You said the baby is mine, then it's mine."

Briony sagged against him in relief. She could feel tears burning behind her eyes. She hadn't realized how she'd been holding herself together under such rigid control. She drew in a deep, ragged breath and tried to stop the sudden trembling. "I thought, if you were willing, we could work something out."

Jack ignored her statement, pinning his gaze on Jebediah. "Did you fly into the Superior airport? Is that how you arrived?"

"No, we were afraid to. Whitney's managed to find Briony everywhere we stashed her. All of my brothers flew to the States, rented cars, and went in different directions in the hopes of throwing them off. We took great care to keep anyone from tailing us, but they're good, Jack. Tyrel, my youngest brother, fought them off of Briony about a week ago. Tyrel nearly was knifed and he's good. Briony saved our butts that time, but she's worried about taking a hit in the stomach and losing the baby. They found us again at a villa and nearly managed to get Briony; that's where she got the bruise on her face. He punched her."

Jack's hands went to her shoulders. "You fought someone with a knife while you were carrying our child?" He bit out the reprimand, the words all the while echoing in his head: *He punched her.* He hoped Luther found Briony again because Jack was going to be right there, and if the man wanted to hit a woman, he was going to get a lesson in manners he'd never forget.

Briony jerked away from Jack, forcing him to drop his hands. "What did you expect me to do? Meekly go with them? Let them kill my brother?"

"Your brothers are big boys. The only thing you need to be worrying about is keeping the baby safe."

She backed up two more steps. "I've been keeping the baby safe, tough guy. You ran off, after *fucking* me, remember? Being the baby's biological father doesn't give you the right to dictate to me. In fact you have *no* rights when it comes to me. I asked for help protecting the baby, not someone to order me around."

Jack inwardly winced as she threw his words back in his face. He'd made a big mistake using that word, implying that making love with her meant nothing at all to him. She tried to act confident, but she'd hesitated, just that little bit, telling him she wasn't used to that kind of language — not even being around her brothers. She was a lot more sheltered than he'd first thought, and that only made the gap between them that much wider.

He ignored her outburst as he turned back to Jebediah. "Are they specifically tracking Briony, or all of you?"

"I think Briony," Jebediah said.

"I can't figure out how they're tracking me," Briony interrupted. "I've gone through my clothes and even my jewelry. I've been so careful."

"They sure as hell didn't follow us up here," Jebediah said. "It was easy enough to watch the back trail on the switchbacks." He glanced around uneasily. "I just have a bad feeling about these people, Jack. I don't want them to get their hands on my sister."

"You won't be able to communicate with her for a while," Jack said.

"We can set up something safe," Briony said in contradiction.

Jack shook his head. "We're going to play it my way. No communication between you and your brothers. Jebediah gets the hell out of here and goes back to Europe immediately. When I know you're safe, Briony, we'll contact them."

"That's not going to fly," Briony said calmly. "I don't care how bad it gets, I want to know my family is safe at all times and they'll need to know I am."

*Hello! I'm getting a little tired of sitting here with my finger on the trigger. You want them dead or you going to invite them up to the house?*

*You're out of shape, Ken. Go on in. It's safe enough. I'm not letting the woman go. She'll be staying with us.*

*Like hell. Until you're under cover, I stay out here.*

"Did you hear me?" Briony challenged. "I asked for help, not a dictatorship."

"I heard you." Jack shrugged. "I don't believe in arguing, so there's really not going to be a problem. Where are your things?" He could breathe again. He didn't have to find the strength to let her go a second time. He didn't have to compromise his honor by forcing her compliance. She'd made the decision on her own. The knots in his gut began to relax.

*And what do you mean, she's staying with us?* There was shock in Ken's voice as Jack's message sank in.

*She's carrying your niece or nephew.* There was immense satisfaction in revealing the news to his brother. By telling his twin, it made the news real.

*Holy shit, Jack. You could have told me. What the hell have you done?*

"I only brought a small bag and it's still in the SUV. If anyone was watching, I didn't want them to think I intended to stay for any length of time. Besides, I'm going to get a lot bigger and I'll need new clothes, so there wasn't much point in bringing a lot of my things." Briony rubbed her temples. "Who are you talking to?"

Jack's head jerked up. *No one* had ever been able to tell when he carried on a conversation with his brother. They'd been doing it as long as he could remember. Instead of answering, he caught her wrist, his touch gentle this time. "Do you have a headache?" His fingertips brushed over her temples in exactly the same spots she'd been rubbing.

"It's been a long trip and I'm just tired," Briony said.

"She was pretty sick on the way up here," Jebediah volunteered.

Jack removed his shirt and held it out to Briony. "I want you to strip. Take off everything including underwear, jewelry, and your watch. Put on my shirt and give your brother the rest of your things. My shirt will be long enough on you to be a dress."

"Oh for heaven's sake, I'm not taking my clothes off and parading around in your shirt. We checked for bugs and didn't find any." His tattoos glowed at her in the dark. She couldn't help looking at his chest, at the terrible scars carved so deep into his heavy muscles. Her gaze traveled lower, following the series of slashes to the waistband of his jeans before she could stop herself.

His eyes darkened, slashed at her face. "I'll be more than happy to help if you can't manage on your own."

There was a very seductive note in the command, and Briony's body responded. Her gaze jumped to his. She felt the rush of heat. Her breasts ached. There was a welcoming dampness between her legs. Just like that. A note in his voice. Taking off his shirt. Even when he was being a bastard, her body wanted his.

She retreated, taking several steps away from Jack, back toward her brother. "This isn't going to work. I thought you'd be reasonable." She glanced at Jebediah. "It was a mistake to come here."

"Maybe," Jack conceded. "But you did come here. Go into the trees and take off your clothes, Briony." He gentled his voice. "If you make me force you, Jebediah is going to get all protective and then we're going to have a problem. He can't take me, and there's a high-powered rifle trained on him. Ken has an itchy trigger finger."

Briony went very still, her stomach churning, her heart beating too fast. Jack sounded so matter-of-fact. He never raised his voice. Even when he gave commands, his voice was always soft, but he expected to be obeyed. The knowledge was there inside of her, a dawning realization that he truly didn't live by the rules of society. She was surrounded by forest, deep in the mountains with a man who made his own rules, and she'd chosen that path herself. Worse, she'd put her brother's life in danger.

Jebediah waited for her answer. He was willing to try to get her out of the situation. She saw it on his face.

Jack stepped toward her, breaking the tension, his shirt in his hand. "We've got a few kinks to work out, but I can promise both you and your brother, no harm will ever come to you or the baby as long as you're in my care. Put the shirt on, Briony, and let

Jebediah get out of here. The sooner he goes, the easier on you it will be."

# CHAPTER 10

Briony stepped with great reluctance behind several large trees. It had seemed such a good idea coming to ask Jack Norton for assistance, but the reality was far different from thinking about it. He could take her breath away with one smoldering look, but when he spoke, she just wanted to strangle him. And for some reason he seemed to have no problems touching her a little too intimately. She'd have to remind him what a *liability* she was.

She'd never been without her brothers watching her back. She was deliberately separating herself from them because she was terrified they were going to be killed protecting her. She tilted her chin. She couldn't lose her resolve now. The danger to her family and friends was all too real. She just had to be strong. Briony put both hands over her stomach, wishing she were far enough along that she could feel the baby move. Once that happened, she wouldn't feel so alone and vulnerable.

"Briony?" Jebediah called to her. "Are you okay?"

She tossed her clothes aside and enveloped her body in Jack's shirt. His scent enfolded her close, teased her senses so that she couldn't help inhaling sharply. "I'm fine, Jeb," she lied, careful to keep her voice from shaking as she picked up her clothes. *How could just his scent alone make her want him?* Whatever Whitney had done to her was frightening in its intensity.

She didn't look at Jack as she walked back to the two men and handed her things to her brother. "Don't worry about me. I'll find a way to stay in touch with you."

Jebediah stared down at her. For one horrible moment she thought there were tears in his eyes. "Are you certain this is what you want, honey? I swear we can find a better way to protect you."

Briony shook her head. If her brother broke down, she would cry a river. She held herself rigidly. "Not without all of you being in danger."

"Give him your earrings." The order came from behind her. Too close behind her. Jack crowded her so that she felt his body heat. She felt his warm breath on the nape of her bare neck.

Briony stiffened but didn't turn around, her palms covering her earrings, holding them to her. "These belonged to my mother. They mean a lot to me."

"Give them to him. You can have them back later."

She was going to cry. She blinked furiously as she removed the small diamond studs. Jebediah closed his fist tightly around them as he bent to kiss her.

"I'll take care of them, Bri."

She nodded, afraid to speak, biting her lip hard to hold back the tears. She wanted to cling to Jebediah, to the love and comfort of her familiar world. Now, when she needed her family and friends the most, she was thrust into a world of uncertainty — of fear. She didn't want to be afraid of Jack or her reaction to him, but she was.

Jebediah gathered his sister into his arms, pulling her close to whisper into her ear. "You don't have to do this, honey. We're a family. We'll take care of you ourselves."

Jack heard the soft entreaty, heard the small sob she tried to suppress, and his gut twisted hard. He wasn't used to emotion. He'd trained himself not to feel anything, and now here she was again, and just like before, he had the same instant bond with her, the same flood of raw emotion that had nearly ruined him months ago. He put a restraining hand on her arm — or maybe it was to comfort her — he honestly didn't know which, but if she cried, he was afraid it was going to tear him up inside.

"It isn't helping prolonging the good-byes, Jebediah. Get out of here and make it easier on her." His voice was gruff — too gruff. He felt her stiffen beneath his hands, and she shot him a quick, quelling glance over her shoulder. There were definite tears swimming in her eyes. His heart turned over. Violence was his world. His first re-action was to smash something, his next was to pull her in to the shelter of his body.

Briony held herself away from him at first, but as her brother dropped his arms in resignation, she dug her fingers into Jack's restraining arm where it circled her waist, almost as if by holding on to him she could prevent herself from following Jebediah.

"I love you, Bri," Jebediah said.

"I love you too." She choked and pressed her hand against her mouth to keep from telling him she'd made a terrible mistake.

Jebediah looked at Jack for a long time, as if memorizing every detail of his face. "You know I would never have brought her here unless I thought she was in real trouble."

Jack nodded. "I know."

"If anything happens to her — if you harm her in any way, Jack, and that includes breaking her heart, I don't give a damn if you are the baddest ass around, I'll hunt you down."

"I know."

Jebediah remained staring at Jack a moment longer and then touched Briony's arm before turning away.

Briony bit her lip hard as she watched her brother disappear into the thick trees surrounding them.

Jack felt her trembling. Felt her pain. It got to him as few things could. He had the mad desire to snatch her up into his arms and carry her back to the house. "Let's go up to the house where it's a little warmer."

"Not yet." She couldn't move. As long as she stayed where she was, separating herself from her family wasn't a reality. She couldn't breathe, panic setting in, her throat closing down, stopping her air until she was choking, fighting just to stay alive. *She was alone.*

"Breathe." Jack's hand came up, fingers curling around the nape of her neck, massaging gently.

"I can't." She took a step after her brother.

"Sure you can; you're just having a little

panic attack. Let out your air and draw it back into your lungs." Deliberately he turned her around to face him, to keep her from staring at the spot where her brother had disappeared. Placing her hand on his chest, he took a deep breath, willing her to follow his lead, capturing her gaze with his own. "That's it. You're fine. They won't take our baby from us, Briony. I may not be the best man in the world, or the easiest to live with, but I take care of my own."

Briony stared up at him, looking more vulnerable and forlorn than she could possibly know. Jack wrapped his arms around her and held her, offering the only comfort he knew how to give. He wasn't a man of words; he never had been. Everything he said to her seemed to come out wrong.

She leaned her forehead against his chest. "I'm afraid. I don't think I've ever been this afraid before — not even in the Congo."

"Of me or of Whitney?" His fingers tunneled into her hair because he couldn't help himself. Her scent was impossibly feminine, a mixture of flowers and rain and the outdoors. She was made for candlelit dinners and satin sheets, not for the end of the world out in the middle of the Montana wilderness.

"I don't know," Briony said honestly.

"I'll get you through this," he said. "I give you my word." She wouldn't know that he'd never quit once he gave his word, or that he'd die to protect his unborn child and its mother. He didn't want to examine his re-action to Briony too closely. It didn't feel right thinking she was part of an experi-ment and they were both no more than pup-pets on a stage, but he couldn't stop his tremendous physical attraction to her, or even the way he responded emotionally.

The trembling in her body slowed and she lifted her head, determination on her face. "I hesitated to come here, not only because of what happened between us, but because I knew I'd be putting you in danger. I can only apologize for that, but I knew that as the baby grew, I wouldn't be able to defend myself. If you don't want to do this, now's the time to say so. I can still catch my brother and you'll be out of it, free and clear."

A faint smile touched his mouth, but didn't reach his eyes. "I warned you I wasn't going to give you up twice. You're here. We'll work things out."

"I'm here so you can protect us. So I can learn survival skills, no other reason. You made it very clear to me that you weren't a man who wanted a woman or a kid around

— that I was a liability. Now that we both know the attraction was forced on us for breeding purposes . . ."

*"What?"*

"Didn't I tell you that part? Whitney apparently wants a supersoldier, our baby. He's been trying to manipulate us to be in the same place at the same time. I was supposed to go to Colombia when you were there, but didn't, so he paid the music festival a great deal of money to arrange for us to be there. Once we met, whatever he did to make us attracted physically was supposed to do the rest."

"Son of a bitch."

"Luther said they wanted the baby and they wanted me for their continuing breeding program. He was willing to be the donor, so you may very well be expendable."

"I thought you were on birth control pills."

"So did I. Whitney supplied all of my medical care, and it was Dr. Sparks who gave me the birth control pills. They were mailed to me like clockwork. The file said they were placebos. I'm sorry, but I didn't know, and now we're in this situation, we both just are going to have to deal with it. Now that I know it's just sex, we both can guard against any entanglements."

For one brief moment, amusement flared in his eyes. "We can?"

"Yes." Briony drew away from him, suddenly aware of being naked beneath his shirt — and he was aware of it too. She could see the knowledge in his eyes. She shivered. "I don't have any clothes."

"I have some things you can wear, and tomorrow I'll go into town and get you a few things to tide you over until you can make me a list."

"Make you a list?" she echoed. "I'm capable of shopping for myself. I have money."

"I don't want you seen in town unless we have to go for the baby. And are you talking credit cards, or cash?"

"I brought plenty of cash. It's in my purse." She spun around, taking two steps toward the forest, before he caught her arm to stop her. "Call Jeb back. I gave it to him."

"We don't need your money."

"There isn't a bug in my purse," she protested. "I checked it. I'm not stupid, just pregnant." On the other hand, she felt stupid for getting pregnant. Jack had been virtually a stranger, and birth control or not, she should have been more careful. She didn't dare allow her body to overrule her brain again. She was part of an experiment.

Nothing between Jack Norton and Briony Jenkins was real — or would ever be. "I need that money."

"No, you don't." There was finality in his voice.

"Look, I'm not going to be stranded here with no clothes, no money, and no vehicle. I'm not a prisoner. I have to have a way to get out if it doesn't work."

Jack sighed, his expression bleak. "I'm not a man who argues. That's the second time I've told you and I'm not going to keep reminding you."

One minute she stood looking at him, the next she turned to run, opening her mouth to call out to her brother. Jack caught her in his arms, one hand covering her mouth hard, his arm biting deep into her body just beneath her breasts. That fast, the heat flared, enveloping them both, the need so strong, so primitive it was all she could do to stay on her feet; her body, of its own accord, melted into his. She tried to bite his hand, self-preservation stronger than her fear of retaliation.

"Stop it," he hissed, his mouth so close to her ear she felt his lips moving against her earlobe. "You're going to get someone killed."

She stopped struggling, and he removed

his hand from her mouth, but didn't let her go, pressing his body closer into hers. He was rock hard, his body without any give to it, no soft spots, and his erection seemed merciless, a thick, long bulge pressed tightly into her flesh.

"It's not real. It's just chemistry," Briony said desperately. Her own body ached, dampened, breasts too full and nipples too hard. Lust curled through her relentlessly, thick and needful, making her body throb and her womb clench. "It isn't real."

"It's so fucking real, baby, I want to pick you up, wrap your legs around my waist, and bury myself deep inside you right here. Right now." His voice roughened. "I can taste you in my mouth. I'm breathing you in with every breath I take. Don't tell me it isn't like that for you. It's real and we both know it."

She struggled again, this time more against her own body, than him. There was no controlling the fierce physical attraction arcing between them. It was electric, all consuming, crackling in the air around them, the intensity so strong, he actually shifted her in his arms, turning her around, his mouth coming down hard on hers. She was lost, the waves of need so powerful she thought she might die if she didn't have him.

His tongue swept into her mouth, and there was nothing teasing or gentle about his kiss. It was purely dominant, commanding, taking her over until Briony was swept into a world of sensuality as his hands roamed possessively over her body and then cupped her breasts beneath the shirt, finding soft bare skin.

Jack abruptly jerked his head away from her, swearing eloquently. "Stop it. Stop crying. Damn it, Briony, I haven't hurt you. Why the hell are you crying?" His hands framed her face, and he stared down into her wet eyes and spiky eyelashes before bending to taste her tears.

Even that small gesture was impossibly intimate, sexual, his mouth tracing the path of her tears. She felt the light touch of his lips on her face all the way through her body.

"Stop," he pleaded again, more gently. "Come on, baby, you're just tired. Maybe I was a little rough, but I couldn't have hurt you."

Briony hadn't been aware that she was sobbing. She was only aware of her body, so unfulfilled, so needy. The craving for Jack was like a terrible claw scraping her raw, tearing at her insides, yet all the while her brain screamed a warning, screamed she didn't really matter to him — or he to her. A madman had performed an experiment and they were the results. Two people in heat like animals. She was disgusted with herself.

She couldn't blame Jack Norton, even if she wanted him to assume the responsibility — which she didn't. He couldn't help his reaction to her any more than she could hers to him. "Don't you see what he's done to us? He's taken away everything. We won't ever have a chance at a family. At love and marriage and all the things that matter in life. Once we're away from one another, do you think this is going to stop? This terrible craving? It's an addiction. He's managed to make us into addicts for one another. You can't tell me you haven't thought about it night and day ever since you left. He's taken our lives away from us and made us into mindless animals."

Jack pulled her into his arms and held her tightly against him, wrapping his arms around her head as she sobbed against his chest. The sound wrenched at his heart and wreaked havoc with his normally nonexistent emotions. Hell. The woman was going to make him into a wuss. He put his head down on hers, holding her tighter. "Stop it, baby. You're going to make yourself sick.

None of that matters right now. We're here and we can make our life whatever we want it to be. He isn't going to get our child." He put his mouth against her ear to whisper. "You hear me? He isn't *ever* going to take our child from us and experiment on it."

She lifted her head to look at him. "I'm sorry. It must be all the hormones. I'm not usually such a crybaby."

His fingers tangled in her thick hair. She looked so forlorn, her eyes too big for her face, still swimming with tears. For years he'd thought all gentleness had been driven out of him for all time, but it was there, hidden deep inside, rising as fast as his every protective instinct. Whatever Whitney had done to them might have been all about sex and coming together in heat, but for Jack, the relationship with Briony was developing into something altogether different. His feelings for her were every bit as strong and real as the need for sex. Briony had managed to slip past his guard and find that small spark of humanity, of tenderness he never knew existed.

Jack didn't think too closely about how his emotions had become entangled with the violent chemistry sizzling between them, but he knew it was dangerous for a man like him to get attached to anyone. He wasn't normal and he'd never be normal, no matter how much he wished it different. He'd given up wanting it to be different, until he'd walked away from Briony.

"You're just tired," he murmured.

"I'd like to tell you I'm sorry about the pregnancy. I should have been careful. It never occurred to me I could be intimate with anyone, let alone lose my ability to think about something so important as protection. I had no idea the birth control pills weren't the real thing."

Jack felt relief sweeping through his body. Her being intimate, even thinking about being intimate, with another man might have gotten that man killed. He took a breath and let it out slowly to keep his thoughts from going in that direction. He ran his finger down her face just because he had to touch her. "The idea of you being intimate with another man is something I'm not willing to entertain."

Briony hesitated, frowning. "I can't be around many people without it really affecting me physically. I can't seem to develop the barriers other people have to filter out sounds and emotions, and I've really tried." She tilted her head back further, staring up at him, blinking back the last of her tears, determined to regain control. "When I'm with you, it's much easier. My mind can rest. I'm trying to understand what Whitney did to me, and I'm hoping you can explain it better than the file did. I didn't understand half of it."

"It definitely helps that I'm an anchor and can filter everything for you." So was his brother. The thought that Ken could filter for her just as well came unbidden, and he was ashamed of the rush of adrenaline surging through his body that fast. Whatever Whitney had done to push them together was potent — and dangerous. "I draw the emotions and sounds away from you to me."

"But how? I've tried all kinds of exercises because I had to perform with my family in public, but it was so painful. I end up with terrible headaches. If I can figure out how you do it, maybe I can teach myself to get above the pain before the baby comes." Her brief description didn't begin to describe the agony she was in after every performance, and it was frightening to think that if she had a baby, she wouldn't be immune to the child's distress.

Jack brushed back stray strands of hair from her face. "You're looking tired now. And you have a headache, don't you?"

She shrugged. "Crying like a baby didn't help. I was confined in a small space with

Jeb for hours. He was really afraid for me and it was coming off of him in waves."

She'd spent hours on an airplane as well, Jack realized. And she was incredibly honest with him. He hadn't expected her to be so forthcoming. She didn't trust him — or herself. The shadows in her eyes told him that. Every time he touched her, she stiffened just the slightest bit, although she was trying to hide how uncomfortable she was.

"Let's get you back to the house," he urged.

Briony pressed both hands against her stomach protectively. The baby was the only person she had left, her only ally, only family. Already she could find comfort in the presence of the child.

Jack's hand tightened around her wrist. "I like that you're telepathic." He loved the intimacy of communicating with her. It was familiar to him. Jack and Ken had been using telepathy as long as he could remember and it meant *family* to him.

She twisted her hand, a subtle attempt at getting him to release her. He didn't appear to notice. "I'm a lot of things," she said. "Right now, tired is the number one thing I am. I need to rest." She needed desperately to be alone.

He turned back toward the house, tugging

at her wrist to get her to follow him. "Stay on this path."

"You have your property booby-trapped?"

He shrugged. "I don't like visitors."

"That's ridiculous. Some camper could accidentally stumble onto your land not realizing it isn't part of the national forest."

"Because they wouldn't notice the two hundred signs Ken put up everywhere?"

There was a hint of humor in his voice, but his features remained expressionless.

She flashed a small smile up at him. "A lost child?"

"If a parent loses their child all the way up here, the kid's better off without them."

"Better off *dead?*" She stood absolutely still, studying his face, her heart beating too fast. If he really believed that . . .

Amusement might have crept into his eyes briefly, but it was gone so quickly she wasn't certain she'd seen it. "Nothing lethal. Just some fun ones to sound the alarm and slow down any neighbor wanting to borrow tools."

Relief swept over her. "I'm sure that happens often. Don't tease me like that."

Other than Ken, he hadn't ever teased anyone that he could remember, but it felt good. Just having her there felt good.

"Jebediah told me Ken is your identical

twin. Is he much like you?"

"No." Jack's voice turned gruff. It was almost as if she could read his mind even with his barriers up. "He's much nicer. You'll like him." His gut twisted again. He spoke the truth. Ken was tough, but he'd always been the social twin, the one who was thoughtful and kind. People naturally gravitated toward Ken, and he was much more sensitive than Jack. Jack respected and admired few people; Ken was at the top of his list. He just hadn't considered that Briony might put Ken at the top of her list.

He actually hesitated, stopping abruptly on the trail leading up to the house. He couldn't feel jealous of his own brother. He couldn't conceive of such a thing. Briony was messing up his thinking if he was that far gone.

*What is it?* Ken reached out to him the way he'd done since they were in diapers. When one was in trouble, the other knew it immediately.

*I don't know. I've got some things to work out.*

*You upset over the baby? Are you absolutely certain it's yours?*

Jack looked at Briony's face. She looked far too young. Too innocent. She hadn't been with another man any more than he'd

320

been with another woman — and now it wasn't ever going to happen for her, because he couldn't allow it, even if it was the right thing to let her and the child go. *It's my baby.* There was utter satisfaction in his voice. It resonated in his mind so strong his twin couldn't fail to feel it. "Can you feel what I'm feeling?" he asked Briony aloud.

"If I try."

"Don't try." He detested the clipped way he had of talking, so abrupt as to be rude. Funny, he'd never considered that before. Most of the time, he left the niceties to Ken. People avoided Jack just as he avoided them. "And, Briony, if this chemistry thing is the same between you and Ken, stay the hell away from him."

"It won't be."

"How do you know that?"

"It was in the file. They used him as bait to get you in the Congo. The order was to capture him at all costs."

"That was in the file?" His voice was tight. "Did it say something about skinning him alive? Cutting him into tiny pieces?"

She glanced up at him. There was no expression on his hard features, but she shivered all the same. "Is that what they did to him?"

She sounded sympathetic. Compassionate. "Like I said, don't get interested in him. He's not in the market for a woman."

"Like you? There's no need to warn me. You don't have to worry that I'm going to get silly and romantic," Briony assured him as she pulled away from all contact, straightening her shoulders. "You made it perfectly clear we had nothing but sex. No emotional attachments. I'm a big girl. I can handle things myself. It's my choice to keep the baby, and I really do feel bad that I've had to ask you for protection for us. I'm not stupid enough to fall for your brother and compound the mistake."

His eyes were dark and fathomless. She couldn't read his expression, but there was something almost predatory about him, something cold and dark and very dangerous. She could feel it emanating off of him in waves. He stared at her without blinking, and she knew he missed nothing at all. Her heart was pounding almost out of control. Every breath she took. The beads of sweat forming on her forehead, the ones trickling down between her breasts. The way her lips were dry and her palms sweaty. There was no hiding from his heightened senses, and she didn't try. She wouldn't apologize for her fear.

"Stay right behind me."

The moment his back was turned, she tugged on the tails of the shirt, making certain it adequately covered her. With anyone else, she might have thought he was forcing her to dress in his shirt to make her feel more vulnerable, but Jack was already too aware of her sexually. He didn't need her naked beneath the shirt to be aware of her as a woman. He was matter-of-fact about it, almost too much so.

Briony cleared her throat. "I'd prefer not to meet your brother until I have clothes on. I'm very uncomfortable."

"I'd prefer it that way as well," he said, without glancing over his shoulder. "I'll get you clothes right away." *Stay out of sight, Ken, until I get her clothes. She has Whitney's new army after her and I didn't want to take a chance on bugs.*

*Whitney? I thought he was dead.*

*So did I. Ken.* Jack hesitated.

*I'm here.*

*Don't be too charming. I don't want her falling for you.*

There was dead silence. Jack cursed under his breath. Ken was the type of man all the ladies fell for. Few women gave Jack a second glance, and if they did, they moved away quickly. Never once, in all their years

323

together, had he warned Ken off of a woman.

*You okay with her here?*

*I don't want her anywhere else.*

*That wasn't what I asked. You know how you are. Is it safe for her to be here?* Ken persisted.

*Damn it, Ken, how the hell would I know. She's here. She isn't going to leave, so we all have to find a way to live with it.*

*She doesn't want to leave or you aren't letting her leave?*

That was Ken, going right to the heart of the matter. Ken knew him, knew every black mark on his soul. Jack didn't answer, taking Briony through the trees to the front yard. She stopped abruptly when she saw the house.

"It's beautiful. It never occurred to me that there would be a real house way out here. It's perfect."

Secretly pleased at the appreciative awe in her voice, he gave a casual shrug. "Ken and I built it together. We own a little over twenty-four hundred acres, and the property is completely self-sufficient. We have acres of tamarack and fir trees, and if we ever need to make a little money, we can harvest some of them. We also have a gold mine. The water supply to the property is gravity-fed. We don't need power to get it into the house. The hydroelectrical system powers the batteries, and we only use a small amount of the power available to us."

"It looks like a log cabin, but it's huge."

"Over three thousand square feet. Ken has one wing of the house and I have the other. We share the kitchen, dining, and great rooms. The garage nearly doubles the space, so we have the room to expand into offices if we ever want to."

"Why offices?"

"Ken thinks we're going to run a high-priced camp for bored businessmen to practice survival skills."

"That's not a bad idea."

"It requires actually talking to them."

Briony laughed. It was the first time he'd heard her laugh since he'd left her months earlier, and the sound played down his spine like caressing fingers. "I see. What did you make the house out of? I love the fact that it looks like a log cabin."

"The logs are Western white pine. We fitted them together with Swedish cope and used oil for the finish. The original mine is still on the property, as well as the first cabin built."

"You really have a gold mine?"

He tucked a strand of hair behind her ear,

his fingertips lingering against her skin. "There's gold up here, although Ken and I have never bothered to pursue it. We have all the wildlife and trout in the streams we need and are completely independent when we're here. No telephones, so no one can bother us."

"Jebediah said you're still in the service. How do they get in touch with you if they need you?"

"Radio. We have a helicopter if we need it and a small plane at the airport."

"Well, your house is absolutely beautiful and unexpected. I think you're a secret artisan."

He waved her toward the porch, inexplicably pleased that she liked his home. It was a sanctuary, plain and simple, a place few would ever find and fewer would dare to enter. "The road goes out in the winter, but we have snowmobiles."

"What do you use for heat?"

"Wood. There's plenty of it."

"I especially love the verandah. I've always loved covered wraparound decks, and yours is perfect." Briony touched the railing and stepped up onto the porch. She did love the house, but now that she was about to enter, her heart was beating too wildly. It took all of her courage to flash a tentative smile and act as if she entered strange men's homes in nothing but a shirt every day of the week. "Funny, with all the warnings about you, Jack, you have more of a home than most people do. And it surprises me. This is beautiful."

"It's very isolated. Most women wouldn't like it up here."

Briony shrugged. "Most women can be around people without any problems. Me, I like solitude. And I've never had the chance to be in the mountains like this. It's especially beautiful at night."

"Tomorrow, I'm going to show you any alarms or booby traps on the property so if you're out walking, you won't get in trouble."

She rolled her eyes. "Can we just say paranoia?"

"I prefer to use the term *prepared.*"

He led her through the kitchen. She glimpsed a stove and refrigerator, but little else as he hurried her through the house, down a wide hall to push a door open and step back for her to enter.

His scent was everywhere. She glanced back at him, hesitating. Her womb clenched, and she could feel the slow heat moving through her body. "Your bedroom?"

Jack drew in his breath. This was going to

be a hell of a lot harder on both of them than he'd first thought. "Where else? I'll get you something to sleep in and something to wear tomorrow morning." He crossed to the dresser and pulled out a pair of drawstring pants. He'd never worn them. Ken had been trying to dress him for years, but so far Jack had resisted, preferring his jeans and camouflage clothes. "Are you hungry? I can whip something up for you."

"I'm just really tired, Jack. I'd like to take a shower if you don't mind, and just go to bed." Because she couldn't face him anymore. Looking at him hurt. And her body was out of control. She was ashamed of her lack of control. More than anything, she wanted to be alone where she could pull the covers over her head and cry her eyes out where no one could see — or hear.

Jack opened the door to his private bathroom. Her scent was already mingling with his. Once she was in his bathroom, he would have no respite from her — and he didn't care. She had her plan to keep him at a distance. He wasn't going to let that happen. Briony Jenkins was going to have to learn to live with him. It wouldn't be easy for her, but there was no alternative, and he wasn't going to allow her to back away from what was so obviously between them.

# CHAPTER 11

Briony curled up into a tight little ball in Jack's big bed. She could smell his masculine scent everywhere. The hot shower had taken some of the stiffness from her body, but the dread inside of her grew until her heart seemed to be in her throat choking her. She couldn't get away from him. She drew him into her body with every breath she took. It might have been okay if it had just been her body betraying her, but her emotions felt raw and she couldn't stop thinking about how gentle his hands were when he touched her.

*She would not get caught in that trap again.* It wasn't real — it would never be real. Jack had made his feelings clear and she had to respect that. He was a man who, in spite of his roughness, treated women gently, and she was simply more susceptible because her hormones were running wild. Emotional and sexual at the same time. It was a difficult combination to cope with.

*If you came to challenge me to a duel because I fucked your sister, Jebediah, you're a hell of a lot stupider than I gave you credit for.* Briony felt her cheeks grow hot remembering Jack's accusation. Damn it all. She'd already fallen into his seductive trap. He just looked at her, touched her, and she practically threw herself into his arms. What was wrong with her? Didn't she have any pride? How was she ever going to be able to stay in his home — his bedroom — with the scent of him driving her into some kind of mindless heat?

She sighed, flung off the covers, and padded barefoot to the window to shove it open and lean out to inhale the night, trying to clear her head. The air was far cooler than she was used to, but it felt good on her hot skin. She sat on the windowsill and watched the trees dancing in the wind, ignored the tears that streamed down her face. She was so emotional lately someone should just put her out of her misery. She blinked until she brought the landscape back into focus. The branches swayed and bowed, leaves glittering silver in the moonlight. Sitting quietly, she saw several deer wander into the yard, and something larger, almost horse-size, much farther off.

Curious, Briony climbed out the window and padded barefoot across the porch to the railing, leaning out to get a better view. She didn't dare go wandering around the property until she knew where any alarms or traps were hidden, but she was intrigued with the large animal foraging in the forest so close to the house. She'd never seen an elk wandering free before, and she was fairly certain she was looking at a herd of them. For the first time in what seemed like weeks, she could breathe again, not have her mind in a whirling chaos of emotions. Out in the night air, there was no scent of Jack and no reminders that she was so susceptible to him.

Hand to her throat, she walked softly along the wraparound porch, keeping pace with the herd, following them around the large house, determined to think of something other than Jack — other than her situation. The covered porch was wide and the railing high enough that, holding on to one of the support columns, she was certain she could push off, swing up to the roof, and get an even better view, without disturbing anyone. She climbed up on the railing, keeping one eye on the huge animals, afraid they'd retreat farther into the forest before she could get a good look at them.

She wrapped her arm around the pole and judged the distance to the roof. It wasn't very far for someone as enhanced as she was, but she'd have to swing out and flip her body up to get above the overhang. She leapt and caught the edge of the roof.

Two hands bit into her waist and yanked her back down, pulling her tight against one very hard body. Jack's eyes glittered like twin diamonds, slashing at her angrily. "Just what the hell do you think you're doing?"

The man was built of iron, no give in his body, and where she was cold, he was hot, heat radiating off his skin. Her heart immediately went into overdrive. Worse, her body reacted, breasts full and aching and her womb clenching. She tasted him in her mouth, felt him in her body. The memory was instantly vivid and alive. Just like that — so simple for him to reduce her to nothing but need. Desperate to escape her own reaction to his scent, Briony struggled to break his grip, but even with her enhanced strength, he didn't budge.

"I wanted to see the herd of elk — at least I think they were elk. Thanks to you, I didn't get a good look at them. Let go, Jack." He was the last person she wanted to see. She needed to be alone — and she wasn't sleeping in his room — or in his bed, where his scent was everywhere. She wanted to weep with frustration. She wanted to strike out at someone. This was a totally impossible situation. She wasn't strong enough to be around him and not want him. *And why was he always touching her?*

"Anyone creeping around my house is liable to be killed."

"I'm not a prisoner, am I? If I want to look at some animals in the forest, I don't think that's a killing offense. Go back to bed. I'm fine out here alone." Because she couldn't lie in that bed and not want him with every cell of her body. *If you came to challenge me to a duel because I fucked your sister . . .* Deliberately she repeated the words in her mind, needing something to keep her from being an even bigger fool than she already was.

"It's cold, Briony, go in the house."

She pressed two fingers just above her eyes, feeling humiliation that she couldn't control her own physical needs. He *had* to get away from her, had to stop touching her body. "Go to hell. I have every right to be out here if I prefer it."

He tipped his head to one side to study her furious expression. "Why are you trying to pick a fight with me?"

"I don't like being told what to do." *Be-*

*cause he was all she thought about, and he had already made it clear he didn't want her.* Because he'd said . . . *fucked your sister.* She shouldn't want a man who'd been *programmed* to sleep with her. It was utterly humiliating. A man who wanted nothing but a cheap, mindless *fuck.*

*Damn it all to hell. That's not true. That was never true.* Jack stepped close, and Briony backed away from him, throwing up one hand to ward him off.

"Don't!" She said it sharply, terrified she'd burst into tears. Already her eyes were burning and she felt a lump rising in her throat. "Just don't say anything more about it."

Jack reached for her anyway, not giving her personal space, but crowding her body so that the heat of his skin seeped into the ice of hers. "You're shaking like a leaf." He ran his hands up and down her arms in an effort to warm her. He forced gentleness into his voice. Why the hell had he ever said such a stupid thing to her brother? "Your body is freezing and you aren't even aware of it. What were you going to do? Get up on the roof?"

"As a matter of fact, yes."

"And did it occur to you that you might slip and fall and hurt the baby?"

"I'm a flyer. I do stunts for a living. I think I can manage to climb up on a roof."

"Well, don't. I thought you were tired." Jack wanted to comfort her, but she was too far away from him emotionally, trying to distance herself, and he wasn't good at this sort of thing.

She reached up to her earlobe, needing the comfort of touching her mother's earring, found bare skin and dropped her hand. "I am. I just need space. I can't do this."

"Yes, you can."

"Well, maybe I don't want to do this." She backed away from him until she was up against the railing. He couldn't touch her again. Every brush of his fingers brought acute awareness of his body and the desperate needs of her own. She'd come outside to escape him, yet there seemed to be no escape.

"You should have thought of that before you came to me."

Briony clenched her fists. "At the time, I didn't feel I had a choice." Her chin went up. "Look. Obviously this isn't going to work. I can leave. There are other ways to disappear, and there's always Kadan Montague. He offered his protection."

Jack's jaw tightened, the gray eyes suddenly turning a peculiar silver — ice cold —

frightening. "Kadan Montague is not going to be protecting my child or its mother. That's my job, not his. Don't try bringing another man into this mess, Briony. We have enough to worry about without that."

"Oh really?" Furious, not even knowing why, she turned and in one smooth move leapt over the railing onto the ground below. "This *mess?* My being pregnant is such a mess, isn't it? I don't need your help and, quite frankly, I don't want it."

Jack swore and leapt after her. So much for tact — he didn't have it, never would. He shackled her wrist in a viselike grip and she whirled, throwing a punch at his face. He caught her fist in midair. "Keep it up and I'm going to turn you over my knee. What the hell is wrong with you? You should know better than to pick a fight you can't win." She looked wild, angry, and embarrassed. She looked vulnerable, young, and all too fragile. She *felt* alone and frightened. The fear moved in his mind — not of him, but of the situation. Of him callously saying he'd fucked her. Of expecting a baby and having no one to turn to. She was terrified Whitney would find her and take her baby from her. Jack glimpsed the roller coaster of emotions jumbled in her mind.

He gentled his voice in spite of his exasperation. "I didn't say the mess was your being pregnant. Stop putting words in my mouth. And, baby, you know damned well I wasn't fucking you. Not like that. Not how I made it sound to your brother."

She shook her head. "I can't breathe here. I can't. I'm just going to go."

Jack's expression hardened. His jaw flexed and the gray eyes glittered silver. "You're going to calm down and go into the house and get some sleep." He made another effort to gentle his voice. "You've been under a tremendous strain. Once you get a good night's rest, you'll see things differently."

"Stop talking to me in that superior tone. Do you think it was easy to come here and ask for help after the things you said to me?" She shoved at his chest, barely rocking him when she put all her strength behind it. "I left everyone I love. My child's in danger. I'm sick. I have no clothes or money, and I'm at the mercy of a man who doesn't want me around." She pushed at him again. "Get away from me. I was going to sit on the roof, not wander around like an idiot when you have the property booby-trapped."

"What are you thinking of doing now? It's the middle of the night. You know I have traps set up."

"I have a very good sense of smell. I can

track my way back out of here the same way I came in."

She probably could too, but she was making him crazy, and his calm was going to disintegrate very soon. "Stop crying. I mean it, Briony, you have to stop."

"Or what?" She was angry that she was crying. Once she'd started, she couldn't seem to stop. Maybe she was hysterical, but if she wanted to sit out in the middle of the night and cry her eyes out, it was her business. "You're going to beat me? Someone else already did that. I'm not intimidated by you."

Jack dragged her close, holding her tightly against his body in spite of her struggles, one hand cupping the back of her head to press her face against his chest. He bent his head to find her bruised cheek, his mouth feathering kisses over the swollen side of her face. "Shh," he said to soothe her, closing his eyes against the pain in her mind. She radiated sorrow — grief — and he couldn't bear it. "I'm not the enemy."

"I know. I know. I'm sorry." But she couldn't stop. Her world was gone and her hormones were running wild and there was nowhere to go to escape him.

"It's going to be all right. Everything will be fine. You're overtired and you need to sleep." His fingers began a slow massage of her neck, then slowly crept into her hair to massage her scalp, tunneling deep, moving with sure, circular strokes.

"I don't want to go in the house, Jack. I can't go into that room." How could she make him understand? At least outside, the wind and forest helped to dissipate his scent — give her a breathing space from her need of him.

Jack had never had a weeping woman in his arms before. He stood quietly, just holding her while her body shook with the force of her sobs. His chin nuzzled the top of her head. Soft strands of her hair caught in the shadow along his chin. He didn't try to stop the flood of tears — she had enough to cry about — he simply reached down, positioning his arm beneath her knees, and lifted her, cradling her against him.

"All right. We'll stay out here. Shh, Briony. You're going to make yourself ill." She was light, easy enough to lift, and Jack simply jumped with her, landing back on his porch, Briony cradled in his arms. He settled on the front porch rocker, the one he'd built with his own two hands. They fit comfortably, and he rocked gently, rubbing her hair with his chin, hands gently massaging her neck.

He should have felt like a damn fool, but he didn't. She felt right in his arms. He sat in the night, rocking on his porch, watching the trees swaying and listening to the night sounds of the forest. She wept silently, her tears soaking his shirt as she slowly struggled to regain control.

"It's strange with you," he said aloud. "When I'm with you, I feel like an ordinary man. Everything else falls away, and I can see how beautiful things around me really are. I've sat on this porch hundreds of times, and the night has never looked like this. I've stared into the forest, and I saw a million places to hide, to set up an ambush, to find food. I didn't see the way the leaves look silver in the moonlight, or the way the trees seem to dance and lift up their branches to the stars. Why do you suppose that is?"

Briony swallowed hard and turned her tear-wet face up to him, her dark, liquid gaze searching his face.

Jack wiped the tears away with his fingertips, hands gentle, almost reverent. "It's the truth, Briony. I see the world differently when you're around me."

"Don't, Jack. I'm very susceptible to you, and right now I'm pregnant so it's probably worse. Don't say things like that to me."

Briony tried to look away from him, but he held her chin.

"I want you here," he admitted gruffly.

"But you said . . ."

"I know what I said. That doesn't matter now. We'll have plenty of time to sort it all out. I can feel your headache, and you aren't making it any better by crying. Just listen to the night and relax, go to sleep. One of the reasons we chose to build up here is the quiet, the peace."

Briony closed her eyes and fit her body more comfortably into his. As a rule she didn't cry in front of anyone, and she was embarrassed that she was still sniffing. He held her like she mattered to him, and she didn't know if that made it better or worse.

"Just over there, through those trees and down a little slope, is my shop. I thought I'd add onto it and give you a place to make your stained glass."

"I didn't bring my sketchbook."

"I'll get you a new one. You'll have plenty of time to draw."

Briony's lashes lifted. He was looking down at her, and there was something in his eyes, something close to admiration, when she didn't feel she was at all acting in an admirable way. Her heart responded in spite of her determination to remain at an emotional distance from him. She lifted her hand to his face, traced the hard lines with her fingertips. "I missed your face, Jack."

He turned his head enough to brush kisses over her hand. "I'm sorry for the things I said to you that night. I know I hurt you."

"You did hurt me. I knew you had to go, but you didn't have to do it that way. Why did you?" The pads of her fingers smoothed over his lips.

"I have some things to sort out, Briony, but it isn't about you — or the baby. It's about me and my character and who and what I am. Never you." He caught her hand and held it against his throat.

"I swear I was on birth control pills, Jack. I didn't get pregnant on purpose. I wouldn't do that to a man. And I'm capable of raising a child on my own. You won't have to worry about me asking for money or anything. I need survival skills . . ."

"Briony, stop," Jack ordered. His hand curved around her neck, fingers working to massage the tension out of her. "It's my child too. I want you here. I want the baby here. I'll teach you the things you need, and after the baby is born, we'll both protect him together."

Her heart jumped, but she wasn't ready

to hope again. "Why do you think it's a boy?"

"Because my heart couldn't take a girl. Can you imagine some boy trying to date my daughter? I'd be sharpening my knives when he came calling."

Briony's soft laughter was muffled against his chest, but the sound played through his body with the strength of a tidal wave. He'd expected the rising, urgent need, but not the contentment, the joy. He didn't know joy, didn't understand it, was even wary of the emotion. It crept over him, stealing into his heart whether he wanted it or not — brought by a woman, by the sound of her laughter.

"You're so silly, Jack."

"I've never been called that before. I know it was difficult for you to come here." He knew that was a mild way of putting it, but Briony always did what she thought was right — no matter the cost to her — and going to Jack had come with a high price tag.

The smile faded from her face. "I want this baby. I know we weren't looking for it to happen, but the minute the doctor told me I was pregnant, I was happy. I'm really serious about being able to do it on my own."

"I know you are. I'm really serious about being a part of your lives."

Her smile lit her eyes. "Boy or girl, a child is such a miracle, don't you think?"

*She* was the miracle. "Yes, it is," he replied quietly. "Go to sleep, baby. I can feel how tired you are." He stroked caresses through her hair. She was bone weary — more, she hadn't felt safe in a long time. He wanted her to feel safe in his home — in his arms.

He rocked her gently, letting the night work its magic. So many times Ken and he had come home weary and wounded and sat on the porch listening to the night. Insects hummed, owls fluttered wings, bats dipped and whirled, and deer moved with grace through the surrounding forest, comforting them. His heat seeped into the cold of her body, warming her as her lashes drifted down and her body relaxed fully into his. Her breathing became soft and even, as she snuggled like a broken child in his arms, sheltered close to his heart.

*Boy or girl, a child is such a miracle, don't you think?* Jack thought about her innocent statement for a long time. He sat in the dark with the moonlight spilling into the trees, listening to the sound of water running over the rocks and the night insects calling to one another while he rocked her to sleep. *A*

*child is such a miracle, don't you think?*
Briony boiled everything down to such simplicity. Was a child a miracle to him or not? Did he want the child? Or only Briony? Was there room in his life for a baby? How did he feel?

There was no sound, but he was aware that he wasn't alone long before a shadow fell across him. He looked up to see his brother standing, hands on hips, bare feet, dressed only in drawstring flannels. Scars covered his face, ran across his shoulders and down his arms, over his chest, and disappeared into the low waistband. Even now, the skin was raw and red, shiny and raised, an ugly mottled remembrance of falling into the hands of a madman. For one moment Jack felt the stirring of anguish. He hadn't been there, hadn't been protecting his brother's back. Ken had been sent in *his* place. Jack should have been there, and he would carry that sin to his grave.

He looked up, voice casual. "Can't sleep?"

"Nope." Ken sat on the edge of the railing, swinging one foot. He looked easygoing and relaxed, but Jack knew him too well. "She all right?" Ken indicated Briony with his chin. His eyes glittered like silver in the moonlight, a warning of impending battle.

"She cried herself to sleep. She's had a

rough time," Jack said.

"We've got to talk about this, Jack."

Jack closed his eyes, rested his head against Briony, and inhaled her scent. It wrapped him up like a heady dream. "I know. I know we do. I should have told you when I came back from Kinshasa, but there didn't seem much point. I walked away from her. I did the right thing; I just walked out and left her to have a life with a decent man. Damn it, Ken." His eyes snapped open to glare at his twin. "I walked. It was the hardest thing I ever did in my life."

Ken nodded. "I've felt it, ever since you came back. Our connection is too strong for me *not* to feel how difficult it was. But this is dangerous." He passed a hand over his face. "I came out here to tell you you've got to give her up, that you can't risk it — but seeing you with her — *feeling* what you're feeling . . ." He shook his head. "I don't know how you could."

"For the first time in a long time, I'm afraid, Ken. I always figured if I went psycho, eventually they'd send someone better than me and I'd get whacked. I knew I'd never turn on you — but now . . ." He stroked his hand down Briony's hair. "I couldn't stand it if she looked at me the way Mom looked at him." He shook his head slowly. "I've already got the beginnings of his ways. I'm too obsessive over her. I can't think about anything or anyone else. I don't want anyone close to her."

"Does that include me?"

"I was afraid it might, but you're close to her now and I don't want to shoot you, so maybe not."

A faint smile crept into Ken's eyes. "That's a relief."

"I can't let her go. I just can't, Ken. It's like looking through different eyes when I'm with her. I *feel* hope again." He shook his head again, feeling a fool. "When I came back this time, I wanted it all to end. After having her — and walking away — I just wanted it all to be over."

Ken scowled. "I knew you felt that way. What are we going to do?"

"You're going to give me your word of honor . . ."

Ken stood up, shaking his head, hand raised to stop his brother. "Don't. Don't ask me to do that. It's not an option."

"It's the only option we have. I'm telling you I can't let go of her. I swear, Ken, I don't know what I'd do if she tried to leave me."

"You'd harm her?" Ken's voice went quiet, his gray eyes once again catching the silvery light of the moon.

"No! Never! Never that. I'd destroy myself before I'd ever do anything to hurt her." Jack caught Briony closer, held her protectively. "I'm totally fucked, Ken. You have to give me your word on this."

"The baby?" Ken persisted. "How do you feel about the baby?"

Jack sighed. "How would I know what I feel? I don't recognize feelings anymore. You're beginning to sound like those shrinks they always want to send us to." He'd been sitting in the dark contemplating that very question and still had no real answer. Did he want the baby because it was a tie to Briony or because it was his child?

"When you told me, I felt that same flash of joy in you."

"I'm happy she's pregnant. She's here. I don't know what the hell I'll do with a baby, but I'll figure it out. I was sitting here thinking I might start a crib or one of those little things they sleep in with rockers on it."

A small smile escaped Ken. "A cradle, you cretin. And just to give you an added glow, you might also consider that our dear old dad gave us one more legacy aside from his monster genes."

"And that would be?"

"Twins. He was a twin. His father was a

twin. His father before him was a twin. See any pattern here?"

Jack groaned. "Briony will be especially pleased with me for that one." He stared into the woods, at the trees with their dark trunks and dazzling leaves, one hand sliding down to cover her rounded tummy. "He drank, you know. Do you remember that? He was always drinking. I tried to remember what he was like without alcohol." He looked at his brother. "Promise me, Ken."

"It's a hell of a thing for you to ask me."

"I have to ask."

Ken swore and turned away from him. "Damn that man to hell for what he did to us. I have to think about it. I don't know if I could do it. I'm not giving my word unless I know I'll keep it."

"I've lived my entire life trying to do the right thing, Ken. I'm not ending it by hurting the people I care about." A faint, humorless smile touched his mouth briefly. "There's so many of you — you and Briony."

"And the men. You've never left a man down, Jack. You don't give yourself enough credit because you're always watching yourself so closely, so certain you're going to be like him. He was vicious when he drank. It was like poison to him."

Jack raised his head, forcing his twin to look into his eyes. "You know we're different. We've always been different. I refuse to pretend otherwise. If I know what I am — what I'm capable of doing — I have a chance to stop myself. If I can't, then you have no choice."

"I'm not doing this with you. We both agreed there would be no woman, not one we cared about, not one who mattered."

"She saved my life. She's a GhostWalker, same as we are. Whitney's after her for the baby."

Ken swung around. "What the hell are you talking about? Peter Whitney is dead. He was murdered. How could he have anything to do with this?"

"Apparently he has a lot to do with it. Aside from enhancing us, he programmed us to respond sexually to one of the enhanced females — at least that's what I'm told. And if it's true, it's potent. I'm a walking hard-on around her."

"Great. Like we didn't have enough problems." Ken sighed. "Are you certain about all of this, Jack?"

"Just as certain as I was that someone set us up in the Congo. That someone had to be Whitney. He has the money, the resources, and the clearance — and someone very high up is helping him. They'll be coming after Briony and the baby."

"They won't get her, Jack, but we'd better be prepared. How is she in a fight?"

"She needs an anchor, but she's tough as nails if she needs to be. She'll stand."

"So there's a woman out there who is going to turn me into a raging testosterone bull."

"Yeah, that's about it," Jack said.

Ken whistled softly. "Well, there are always compensations in life."

"Yeah? Well, don't be too sure about that. The way I understand it, Whitney's not having much luck getting us lab rats together so he's trying to round up the women and establish some kind of baby factory with a few of his enhanced soldiers volunteering for donor duty."

"Okay, that's just sick." Ken frowned. "So this woman — the one I'd react to — might be locked up in Whitney's basement as a broodmare?"

"Makes you want to meet the son of a bitch on a dark night with no one around, doesn't it?"

Ken crossed to his brother's side and bent close to Briony's neck, inhaling deeply. He was acutely aware of the rising tension and Jack's sudden stillness. He straightened slowly, winked at his brother, and backed up. "Doesn't do a thing for me."

"Well, next time you're going to get personal, you might warn me."

"Get used to it. If you're keeping her, then she's my sister and that child is my niece or nephew. I'm a hands-on kind of man."

"You just like to piss me off," Jack said.

"Well, there's that. On the other hand, we'll find out really fast just how much of a bastard you're going to be to live with — with your woman around. You get out of line, and I'll have to take you out behind the barn."

"We don't have a barn."

"I told you we needed a barn, damn it," Ken said. "You had to have a shop. It doesn't sound the same saying I'm taking you out behind the shop." Ken dropped his hand on his brother's shoulder, a silent gesture of camaraderie — of solidarity. "It's getting a little cold out here for me. I'm for bed."

Jack watched his brother walk into the house. Ken's shoulders were straight, his gait even and fluid, but his heart was heavy, aching with the weight of dread — of the nightmare both had always feared. The savage wounds on Ken's body had healed, but the scars were everywhere, inside and out.

Jack didn't like contributing to his brother's burden, but there was no help for it.

Briony stirred in his arms, shivered, and snuggled closer, her body squirming against his groin. The feeling was different than any he'd experienced. The painful, aching tightness was there, a swift response he was becoming used to, but there was more, a rush of emotion threatening to choke him. He should have felt reluctance — he did feel it, but the wakening sensations, affection, stirrings of love mixed with passion and his heightened senses were all unexpected.

He stood up, cradling her slight weight against his chest. She lifted her head, blinked, and looked around her. "I was dreaming."

"What were you dreaming?"

"That there were two of you."

He took her into the house, striding down the hall toward his room. "That must have been frightening. Two men to order you around."

"Not really." She laid her head back down on his shoulder. "I'm used to four brothers, all with loud opinions."

She sounded amused and drowsy all at once. It wasn't just her scent, he decided, as he laid her on the bed and stretched out beside her. She trusted him on some instinctive level. No one trusted him — not even his twin brother, not even Ken. He turned on his side to wrap his arm around her, pressing his body close to hers.

"Don't try anything," she warned. "I'd have to smack you around."

"I was just going to tell you the same thing," Jack said.

"Really?" She turned her head to look at him, amusement creeping into her dark eyes. "What are you doing in here?"

"Keeping you from sleepwalking. It's the only way I'm going to get any sleep."

"I don't sleepwalk."

"It's safer, trust me, baby."

It wasn't, but she wasn't going to get into the reasons why. She turned completely over to study his face. "What if they find us? They could hurt your brother, Jack. I didn't think about that. I was so busy protecting my brothers, I didn't think about yours, and I should have. I'm sorry."

"You had no way of knowing Ken and I shared a house."

"Yes, I did." Her gaze slid from his, flicked up to the ceiling. "You were worried about him when you were in Kinshasa. The rebels had tortured him, worse than what they did to you, and you were upset that you didn't

354

get to him fast enough. I caught glimpses of your home and knew he lived close — or with you. I just should have thought about how you'd feel if something happened to him."

"You were thinking about the baby. You didn't want to come here," Jack pointed out. If she was going to be honest about the things she'd glimpsed, so could he. They had to come to an understanding at some point. She wasn't ready yet, and he didn't blame her, but he wasn't going to pretend with her. She'd come to him. She had to know what kind of man she was dealing with. "I intend for you to make this your home."

"I'm going to take one day at a time. I'm too comfortable with your touch, and I don't trust myself around you anymore."

"Don't worry, baby, if you try to jump me, I'll fend you off."

She smiled, just as he knew she would. "Don't think it couldn't happen."

The smile faded slowly and she looked frightened, so much so that Jack wrapped his arm around her waist. "What is it?"

"Doesn't that bother you? What he did to us? You don't have to even like me as a person, Jack. All that matters is having sex together."

He reached for her hand, held it close to his chest, rubbing her skin with his thumb. "I've got news for you, Briony. Most men are just fine with that."

She yanked her hand away. "So I found out." Hunching one shoulder, she turned on her side. "Isn't there another bedroom where I can sleep?"

"No. You can sleep in here. I have to be able to watch over you."

That low note of command was back in his voice, the one that grated on her nerves and implied that he was in complete control, while she was a victim of her runaway hormones.

"Do you ever ask?"

Jack didn't know why her sarcasm made him want to smile. "No. What would be the point? You're so tired, Briony, you don't know what you're doing or saying anymore. I'm not about to let anything happen to you. If you'd rather I sat in a chair all night, I will, but it won't change how we're both feeling."

"You don't know anything about my feelings."

Exasperated, he caught her hand and forced it between his legs, over the thick bulge pulsing with heat and urgent need. "It's not going to matter a damn whether

I'm sitting six feet from you, in the next room, or lying beside you. This isn't going to go away until I'm buried deep inside of you where I belong." He let go of her hand, nearly shoving it away from him. "Now go to sleep before I forget all my good intentions and get a little relief."

Again Briony surprised him. He expected tears — or anger at his rough response, but she laughed softly. "There's some comfort in knowing I'm not the only one suffering."

"You don't have to. You give me the word and we'll both be sleeping like babies." If she said no, he might have no recourse but to head for the shower as soon as possible and relieve the terrible ache. It would be fast and cheap and unsatisfying, but hell, he was going to explode. And he had the sinking feeling the solution wouldn't last more than the next lungful of air he drew.

"I think a little suffering is good for your soul," Briony said.

Her voice was muffled in the pillow, but he was absolutely certain she was laughing at him. Jack contented himself with smacking her on her pretty little rounded ass, and was more than satisfied when she yelped and glared at him. He closed his eyes and tried not to think of her body naked, stretched under his while he drifted off to sleep. He hadn't embarrassed himself since he was twelve, but tonight might start a new phase in his life. Even with his physical discomfort, there was something right about lying beside her, having her close enough to hear her breathing and touch her soft skin — just to know she was there.

He heard her even breathing, slow and rhythmic, and knew she'd finally drifted off. Turning on his side, wrapping his body protectively around hers, he pushed his throbbing groin against the curve of her buttocks, one arm around her, his hand splayed over her stomach to hold their child as he allowed himself to drift into a light sleep.

# CHAPTER 12

Briony wandered through the large house, surprised by how spacious it was. The ceilings were high and the rooms open, one running into the next. The house itself was shaped in a U, the kitchen, dining room, and great room separating the two wings. She peeked into the rooms in Jack's wing and found only his bedroom and the bathroom finished. The second bedroom was still under construction, with the walls bare Sheetrock.

In the great room, the furniture was sparse but well made, and she examined it closely, running her hand along the large, wide sofa, remembering Jack admitting that he made all of the furniture. It was beautiful, as were the other pieces, all made of the same hardwood. She didn't know if it was milled from their own trees, but she suspected it was. The cushions were thick and made of leather, obviously custom-made to fit each piece of furniture. Jack continually surprised her.

She followed the rich aroma of fresh coffee into the spacious kitchen and stopped abruptly when she saw the stranger sitting at the table. Even from the back, he looked like Jack, but there was a subtle difference in his scent. She stood in the doorway, reluctant to intrude.

He turned his head and smiled at her. "You must be Briony. Come in and have some breakfast."

He looked like Jack — not as hard, but far more ravaged. The scars marring his skin looked painful and deep, but somehow he managed to look not only confident — but good-looking in a rough pirate sort of way.

He stood up and crossed to the sink. "Coffee or orange juice with breakfast? I'd choose coffee if I were you. Jack's already handing out orders about what you can and can't have. It may be the last time you get close enough to even smell a cup of coffee in a while."

She laughed. "Both then." It was difficult not to stare at him, and she didn't know if it was his resemblance to Jack or the scars. Although Ken was much more mutilated, she recognized the patterns and symmetry of his scarring, so much like those on Jack's body. "Where is he?"

"Left for town before sunup. I think he's buying clothes, groceries, and making you a doctor's appointment." He grinned at her as he held out a chair. "I'd love to be a little fly on the wall when they try to tell him he has to wait a week or two to get you in."

"Want to make a bet whether or not I'll be going today?"

"Hell no. Jack has no social skills. If they give him a hard time, he's liable to pull out a knife this big" — he measured a foot with his hands — "and start cleaning his fingernails. If he wants you seen by a doctor today, you will be."

Briony sank into the chair. "He didn't say anything about a doctor to me."

"You'll get used to him. He doesn't talk much. He's more of a man of action. He muttered something about prenatal care while he was drinking his coffee. I didn't know he knew what prenatal was." Ken placed a plate of food in front of her. "I'm not the best cook, but it's food."

Briony laughed again. "He definitely takes charge. And the food looks good."

Ken lifted his coffee cup, the smile fading from his eyes. "Jack's always had to be in charge, and that won't change. He's a strong man, and he knows what he can and can't have in his life to stay balanced."

"Just say whatever it is you need to say," Briony encouraged.

"Don't push him too hard. And don't hurt him."

Her eyebrow shot up. "That's it? That's the best you can do? I was expecting wisdom, something to make sense of all this, but that's no help." She ran her fingers through her unruly hair. "Give me something else."

Ken glanced right and left and leaned over the table. "He's bossy," he added in a conspiratorial whisper.

"He's a dictator," Briony corrected. "Don't try to soft-soap it for me. You should hear the man throwing out orders left and right."

Ken smirked. "At least now he can order you around instead of me. I owe you for that."

"Don't count on it. I'm betting he has plenty for both of us."

"You have no idea."

There was a short silence, a little awkward in spite of the fact that both of them were trying. Briony took a deep breath and forced a smile. "What are you working on today? Can I help?"

"I'm tiling one of the bathrooms. As you

may have noticed, only a few rooms are actually finished. We've been taking our time and trying to get each room exactly how we want it. Jack wants to start on the second bedroom in his wing so by the time you have the baby, the room will be ready for it."

Briony shook her head. "Don't go to a lot of trouble and expense. I'll be able to protect the baby after it's born. It's just now, when they come at me, I worry they'll hurt the baby, and as I get bigger, I'll probably get slower. I'm not asking Jack to take on the responsibility forever."

"Is Jack the baby's father or not?" Ken asked, his gray eyes darkening, reminding Briony of thunderclouds.

"Jack's definitely the father, but I can understand why you'd ask. I'm not trying to trap him, Ken." Briony felt dark color creeping up her skin.

"I asked because you don't seem to understand my brother. He'll *never* walk away from you or the baby. You're in his life now. It won't always be pleasant or easy, but he'll protect both of you with his life. He'll make certain you have everything you could ever need — or want — because that's the kind of man he is."

"I know he's honorable," she conceded.

She couldn't very well blurt out she wanted more than sex from Jack. She wanted to be loved. She wanted him to love her child, not just feel responsible. Of course Jack would take care of them. His code of honor dictated that he give them his best — but his code wasn't his heart.

Ken tapped the table with his finger, a small rhythm that told her volumes. She studied his face, the gentleness there, the concern, the flicker of unease.

"Jack is . . . different — extraordinary, but different. It would take a very special woman to live with those differences," Ken said.

"You admire him."

"I know him." He leaned back in his chair, legs sprawled out in front of him. "Most people don't. You'll be living here a long time, Briony. My advice is to get to know him."

It was heartbreaking to stare into the man's ravaged face when he looked so like Jack. Not broken, not unbending — just accepting, as if he took whatever fate threw at him in stride and lived the best he could. That was Jack — and it was apparently his brother too. Briony ducked her head to keep those piercing eyes from reading her expression. She felt at home here. It made no sense, but these men, this house — all of it felt right to her.

Restless, she stood up and crossed to the window. "Is the yard really booby-trapped? I'd like to be able to walk around outside. It's so beautiful."

She heard the chair scrape. No footsteps. For such stocky men, the Norton twins walked softly, but she caught his scent as he neared her — almost the same as Jack's, but with that strange, subtle difference. His hand came over her shoulder with a piece of paper in it.

"My orders," he said.

She took the paper and read the words scrawled in a masculine hand across the sheet. She spun around to face him. "He made you get rid of them all?" For some reason the vise gripping her heart so hard began to ease.

"Every last one, which, I might point out, he insisted we put there in the first place, the jackass. He dragged my butt out of bed at four-thirty this morning to do it too." He grinned at her. "I'm usually much better looking, but he robbed me of my beauty sleep."

Briony burst out laughing. "I slept in. It's almost noon."

"Little slacker. You just didn't want me to

put you to work." He winked at her. "Now that I'm thinking about it, can you cook? Because my brother leaves a bit to be desired in that department."

Briony instinctively turned her head. Ken had known all along, but she didn't feel him until his scent reached her. *Jack.* She breathed his name in her mind. Soft. Intimate. Before she could think, before she could stop.

*Jack.* That soft sigh of his name was enough. Walking in, hearing the laughter, the easy banter between Ken and Briony had nearly stopped his heart. *Jack.* The sound of his name brushing along the walls of her mind, almost as if she cherished him, gave him peace, made him a part of that laughter, brought him into a secret world of true intimacy between a man and a woman — one he'd never experienced.

She looked up to meet his gaze, and her face lit up, a welcoming smile curving her mouth, lighting her eyes. "Hey you." It slipped out before she could stop it, and gave away instantly her growing feelings for him.

He walked across the room, arms filled with packages, straight to her, leaning close to brush a kiss along the corner of her mouth. "Has Ken been taking care of you?"

"Yes. He's been wonderful. What in the world is all this stuff? I thought you were getting a few clothes." She tried to cover the rush of excitement, of pleasure, at seeing him; the embarrassment she felt for her behavior the night before.

Jack frowned. "I should have sent Ken. The salesladies kept adding things to the list. I don't know what half of it is. You have an appointment with the doctor this afternoon, and I have vitamins you're supposed to be taking." He dumped the packages on the kitchen table, frowning as she rescued her coffee cup. "Ken. Didn't I tell you that she shouldn't have caffeine?" He held his hand out for the cup.

Briony bared her teeth at him. "Back away from my coffee if you want to live."

"I heard it wasn't good for you."

"You heard wrong." She put both hands around the cup and gave him her most fierce look. "Don't make me hurt you, Jack. If you touch this coffee cup, you're going to lose some fingers."

"Ouch." Ken grinned at his brother. "The woman isn't going to put up with your shit for a minute."

"Ken," Jack cautioned. "We're going to have a baby in the house — clean up your language." He couldn't stop looking her.

She was dressed in his shirt and drawstring pants, barefoot, hair rumpled, and she looked so damned sexy he wanted to eat her up.

Ken groaned. "I'm so out of here." *Have a little mercy, Christ, Jack.*

*Sorry, I didn't realize I was thinking without putting up our barrier.*

*I'm going to be getting hot and bothered with that kind of crap. I'm going to work. You can find me tiling the bathroom if you ever pry yourself away.* Ken stalked off, glaring at his brother over his shoulder.

"Well, at least I know how to get some work out of you now," Jack called after him.

"Thinking what?" Briony asked. She took a sip of her coffee.

"That you looked so damned sexy I could eat you up."

Briony nearly spit the coffee all over the floor. "Good grief, Jack. I look terrible. You need help. Look at me, I don't even have a brush."

"You look beautiful." He opened the bags and began to pull things out. "Brush, toothbrush, toothpaste, and all the stuff you need to wash your face."

Her eyes widened with surprise. He'd obviously asked for help, and the salesladies had been more than happy to steer him to the most expensive products in the stores. He brought out beautiful soft sweaters and designer jeans as well as expensive, very sexy underwear. He'd even remembered shoes and socks, and a dress so elegant that she'd never have a single place to wear it.

Briony sank into a chair, staring in awe at the wardrobe he'd laid out. Each item had been picked with great care. He hadn't just grabbed things off a rack, he'd taken his time and made certain everything was soft and comfortable and the latest fashion. Tears welled up. She was so emotional lately. "Jack. I don't know what to say. This is amazing. Everything I need."

"Not really, but it's a start." He pulled a small box out of his pocket. "These aren't your mother's, but you have a habit of touching your earrings for reassurance. I thought they'd do until we get your mother's back." He slid the box over the table to her and turned to pace restlessly across the kitchen.

He'd rather face a firing squad than watch her face while she opened the box. He hadn't been certain if getting her the earrings would upset her, and already tears were glistening in her eyes. He was beginning to sweat. How did other men find it so easy to be around a woman they cared for?

She opened the box slowly and stared down at the earrings. "They're beautiful, Jack. Really beautiful." He hadn't gotten her diamonds like her mother's, but exquisite rubies, burning with fire. They resembled fireworks bursting in the sky. She swallowed the choking lump in her throat. "Jack. This is so incredible, but how can I possible accept them?" She wanted to — the earrings were so beautiful, but more than that, they were from him.

A slow smile lit up his face, and it occurred to her that it was the very first time she'd seen his eyes really light up. "Call it a celebration of the baby. Take them. No one else around here is going to wear them — well, maybe Ken might — but they'd look better on you."

Briony removed them from the box and fastened them in her ears, holding back her hair for him to approve. "What do you think?"

"I think they were made for you." He leaned down again and brushed a kiss on the top of her head. "Were you sick this morning?"

"I'm sick every morning. And often during the day. It comes and goes. I think it's part of the experience." She touched one of the sweaters, rubbing her fingers over the soft material. "I know it's stupid — it's not like Whitney can be everywhere — but I'm afraid to go to the doctor. He wanted us to get together, isn't there a chance he planted a doctor here?"

"I considered that," Jack said. "I asked around to find the doctor who'd been around the longest."

She nodded. "Okay. Thanks, that sounds good."

Jack's eyebrow shot up. She wasn't guarding her thoughts that closely, and it might have sounded good to her, but it didn't feel good in her mind. She was still worried that Whitney might expect her to go to Jack and that he'd bribe the doctor.

Jack caught Briony's chin and tilted her face up to his. "First, let me explain this. I'll be going with you to these doctor visits, and Ken will be right outside the window with a rifle and scope. He doesn't miss. Second, Whitney would never think I'd take you in. He doesn't know me; he only thinks he does. And thirdly, if you don't get that little worried frown off your face, I'll be obliged to kiss it off and then we'll both be in trouble."

For a moment her heart seemed to stop beating. She could only stare up at him, lost in the intensity of his gaze. There was nothing at all easy about Jack, even when he was doing the sweetest things. There was too much dark possession, too much raw, driving need, and — God help her, something in her responded like an addict.

He swore under his breath and reached for her, hauling her into his arms. His mouth came down on hers, his kiss rougher than he'd intended when her scent drifted around him and her taste drove him right to the edge of control. He shifted her into his arms, pulling her close, fitting her smaller body into his larger frame, his mouth moving with urgent demands.

She gave the briefest of hesitation, a slight resistance, and then her arms crept around his neck, and she leaned her body into his, and her tongue, soft as velvet, slid over his in a hot tango. He captured her soft little sigh, and tasted spice and honey, her mouth a dark mystery of heat and passion. He could feel the soft weight of her breasts pressing into his chest. The familiar rush of heat raced through his veins, to settle into a terrible ache in the center of his groin, so that he was full and tight, but along with the physical need, he felt as if he had come home — as if he belonged.

Taking his time, Jack gentled his kiss, savoring the moment and every separate sensation. The full, painful ache of his body, the beating of his heart, her soft skin and heady scent, the potent combination of sex and something far, far deeper.

Briony slid her hands to his chest and over the thin barrier of his shirt and traced the letters carved into his body. "I dreamt about you last night." But it hadn't been a dream. She'd been aware of him as she lay drifting, his body wrapped closely around hers, so protective. He'd held her close, one hand over their child as if he could keep all monsters at bay while they dozed. Briony rarely slept, and never with anyone close, yet she had gone straight out, Jack's scent surrounding her, his body next to hers, and it had felt so right — as if, for the first time in her life, she belonged.

"I dreamt about you too, but I don't think our dreams were quite the same," he said, his voice rueful.

She caught a glimpse of desperate relief in the shower, a mind filled with lust and need and awakening emotions all jumbled together. Briony pulled away from his memories, feeling like a voyeur.

"I don't care if you know, Briony," Jack said softly. "I'm not going to hide the fact that it's difficult to be around you and not want you. We're in this together. I don't want you to be influenced by what I feel. I can take it as long as you can." He didn't know if that were true, but he was going to do his best to respect her wishes and do a little old-fashioned courting — whatever that entailed. His thumb slid over her full lower lip in a small caress. "I can wait a long time if I have to."

Her heart jumped again. Maybe she didn't want him to wait. Maybe she needed him to make the decision for them. Ashamed of her cowardly thoughts, Briony busied herself with looking at the clothes spread out on the table. "How are we going to get past it, Jack?" She glanced at him and was caught and held by the strange look on his face as he watched her folding a pair of soft black cotton pants. "What is it?"

"You. Watching you do the smallest, most ordinary things makes me happy." He crossed to the sink and poured himself a cup of coffee. "You have no idea how strange that is."

"What? Feeling happy?"

"Feeling anything at all. You make me feel, Briony, and that is a fucking miracle."

Her heart nearly stopped beating, then jumped in her chest, accelerating until her pulse was pounding. "Jack." She said his name softly, wanting it to be the truth —

afraid of believing they had a chance. This man could hurt her where no other had ever come close. He'd rip out her heart and she'd never recover.

"It's the simple truth, Briony."

Tears filled her eyes. She didn't know what to say — how to react — afraid to take the next step and trust him all the way. To cover her reaction, she held up a pair of designer jeans. "All of these clothes are so beautiful, but nothing I can work in."

Jack didn't pressure her, choosing to give her some room. "Work? What are talking about?"

"I'm going to help Ken tile the bathroom."

"No, you're not." He leaned one hip lazily against the sink. "You don't need to be crawling around on your knees and breathing in chemicals."

"It isn't that bad, and it will be fun. I've always wanted to learn to tile." She didn't look at him, keeping her voice light and cheerful as she carefully put the purchases back in the bags. She wasn't going to argue with him, even though he was using his drill sergeant voice. She'd overlook it and stay in a great mood.

"Nevertheless, you aren't tiling the bathroom. If you want to learn, I'll teach you after the baby's born."

Briony's hands stilled and she turned to face him, holding on to her smile. "Jack. This isn't a dictatorship. I'm quite capable of deciding what I can or can't do. While I appreciate your concern, it isn't necessary to make my decisions for me."

He nodded his head, his features as always expressionless. He shrugged his broad shoulders. "Well, baby, do me a favor and decide *not* to tile the bathroom right now. That way there won't be a problem, will there? Would you like me to help you carry those things to our room?"

Briony drew her breath in sharply, smelled blood, and whirled around to stare at Ken as he stood in the doorway cradling his bloody arm.

"Give it up, Bri," Ken advised, casually walking to the sink without looking at his brother. Blood dripped down his arm. "Jack's a mule, stubborn as hell, and you're not going to be tiling the bathroom."

Jack moved fast to Ken's side, taking his arm and turning it over to inspect the cut. The wound was over a particularly rigid scar. "You didn't feel it until it was too late, did you?" he asked his brother.

Ken shrugged and flashed Briony a small, humorless grin. "You probably should wait until you go to the doctor. You can ask him what you can and can't do and what you can drink or eat, so if jughead starts with the orders you have some ammunition." His eyes begged her not to notice the blood dripping down his arm, to continue their conversation as if Jack wasn't washing the wound and treating it with antiseptic.

Briony tipped her head back to meet Jack's unfathomable gaze. His expression was unreadable. She winked at Ken as Jack dried the cut and bandaged it. "And if I decide I'm going to do it anyway, what kind of temper tantrum does he throw?"

A sudden wisp of a smile softened Jack's hard jaw and relaxed his mouth for a fleeting moment. The approval in his eyes warmed her and sent little flutters of excitement to her stomach.

"I throw a caveman tantrum," Jack answered and swooped her up, lifting her into his arms, caging her against him. "Brute strength, baby. It works when all else fails."

Ken gathered the packages and piled them high in Briony's lap. "I've never seen an actual temper tantrum," he admitted. "Just do what he says; it's so much easier."

"We're going to head into town," Jack reminded his brother. "I'll need you to go with us. Another hour and we'll take off. You'll need to be ready for combat, Ken."

Ken shrugged. "I'm always ready."

Jack carried Briony through the house toward the bedroom. "Thanks," he said gruffly. "It happens sometimes. The scarring makes it difficult for him to feel anything until it's too late. The scars are all over him — everywhere."

Briony felt his pain like a knife stabbing through her heart. It took a moment to realize she was in his mind. "He doesn't want pity."

"Hell no, he doesn't. He'd shoot me first. He insists on doing the tiling, though."

"He needs to do it, Jack," Briony said, recalling the desperation in Ken's eyes.

"I know. I don't say anything, but it's damned difficult some days." Jack tossed her on the bed, ending the subject because if they continued to talk about it he might cry like a baby. "Before I left this morning I cleared out a couple of the top drawers and there's plenty of room in the closet. Make sure you take a good look at the spare bedroom so you can tell me how you want to fix it up for the baby."

"I will."

"And stay the hell out of the bathroom. I don't want you near the tile saw."

"Jack." Briony traced the pattern on the cover, looking around her at all the bright packages. Her fingers crept up to her ear-lobe, stroked the fiery rubies, and slid to her throat. "You can't order me around, no matter how charming you are."

Pain swirled in the depths of his eyes for just a moment. She caught the surge of sorrow in his mind. He turned away from her to open the closet door. "I told you I wouldn't be an easy man to live with."

"What does that mean?" Briony asked, frowning, trying to grasp what he *wasn't* saying to her. She sank down onto the edge of the bed. "I'm a grown woman, Jack."

He glanced at her over his shoulder, rubbed his brow with the pad of his thumb, and sighed. "I'm a control freak, Bri. It's one of the biggest reasons we live here, so far away from everyone. It's why I mostly work alone. I go out on my own and I control the situation. If I work with a team, I run the team. It's who I am."

"That isn't big news, Jack," Briony pointed out. She pulled clothes from the packages and began removing tags. "It isn't an excuse to take away my rights as an adult to make my own decisions. Control is an illusion anyway. No one can control another person."

"I control what I can, and it helps to keep everyone safe."

"You don't trust yourself."

"No. I realized a long time ago I don't think or react like other people. Under the right circumstances, things could go wrong."

Briony busied herself with putting clothes in the drawers, all the while trying to grasp what he was saying. Jebediah, Ken, and now even Jack were all warning her about something in Jack that even he feared. She turned to look at his face. Whatever it was, he was more afraid of it than he was of a sniper's bullet.

"I don't think you'd ever hurt me, Jack. Not ever. You don't have it in you. Is that what you're afraid of?"

He looked at her, something moving in his eyes. Pain? Sorrow? Haunting fear? She couldn't read his emotion. "I don't know," he answered honestly, ashamed.

She went to him, framed his face with her hands. "I do. Remember Luther? He hit me with no problem. I made him angry and he punched me. He didn't slap me. He didn't try to restrain me, he punched me with his fist. Maybe if I were your enemy . . ."

He caught her wrists and yanked them down, holding them hard against his chest. "That's just it, baby. That's just it." He dropped her hands and went out of the room. She heard the door slam as he left the house.

Briony let out her breath and sank down onto the bed more confused than ever.

The cursory knock didn't startle her; she already knew that Ken's stocky frame filled the doorway. "You okay?"

She nodded. "Where'd he go?"

"He's probably headed to the shop. He hangs a bag there and works out when the devil rides him too hard." He shrugged. "Either that or he'll soothe himself with woodworking."

"Why would he think I could ever become his enemy, Ken? I told him I knew he'd never hurt me, maybe if I was his enemy, but *never* otherwise. He's afraid of hurting me, isn't he?"

A muscle jumped in Ken's jaw. He rubbed his thumb along a scar down the left side of his face. "He's afraid of hurting everyone. He has to tell you himself, Briony. It has to come from him — and then you have to decide if you're strong enough to live with him."

"This is temporary."

He shook his head. "You're deceiving yourself and you know it."

"He walked out. He said I was a liability. He told me he wasn't the kind of man who would ever have a woman or kid."

"I'm sure he did say those things. He believes he shouldn't have a family. It doesn't mean that he doesn't want a family. He isn't going to walk away from you ever again."

"I don't want him like that. Trapped because we were forced together by an outside source and now he's stuck because I needed help."

Ken leaned his hip against the doorjamb, a gesture very reminiscent of Jack. "What do you think he would have done had you been kidnapped and word got back to him? Even if he didn't think the child was his, what do you think he would have done?"

Briony plucked at the comforter. "I have no idea. I barely know Jack, and when I think I do know him, everyone warns me off — everyone including Jack."

"He would have come after you and he would never — *never* — have stopped until he found you and got you out — or they killed him. Jack would never abandon someone who did what you did for him."

"My brother helped him get out of Kinshasa. I just slept with him."

Ken's eyes darkened to a turbulent gray. "Don't do that, Briony. Don't cheapen what you did and don't belittle yourself. You saved his life. He told me what happened."

"He doesn't owe me anything. If that's why he's doing this . . ."

"You're here because you're carrying his child and he never wanted to walk away from you in the first place. He did it for you. He walked out of your life so you could have a normal life. And this time, if you want out — you'll have to be the one to walk away, because he isn't going to do it."

Briony burst out laughing, but it sounded too close to hysteria, so she hastily crossed to the drawers and began looking through them for something to wear to the doctor's office. "I don't have a normal life, Ken. I can't have a normal life because some megalomaniac dragged me out of an orphanage and experimented on me." Her voice was getting louder, swinging out of control, but she couldn't pull back. "And when he adopted me out, he made certain he could still experiment on me. And as an adult — well . . ." She threw a sweater into the drawer and spun around, spreading her arms wide to encompass the room. "Here I am. Not like any other mother-to-be. No, I've got a man who doesn't mind having sex with me because of the experiments, but would much rather I didn't come near him, so no, Ken — my chances at a normal life frankly suck."

"You in here upsetting my woman, Ken?" The voice was pitched so low — so soft — that for a moment Briony wasn't certain she'd actually heard right, because those soft-spoken words sounded like a threat, but her body went still and her heart accelerated into high gear.

Jack moved into the room. His shirt was off, and a fine sheen of sweat covered his body as though he'd been working hard. Muscles rippled beneath scarred skin, and he crossed to her side, taking a T-shirt from the top of the bureau and wiping his face with it. He looked at his brother over the shirt, his eyes a peculiar silver.

"I thought you'd already done that," Ken said easily.

Briony frowned. Ken sounded easygoing enough, but his body shifted slightly into a much more defensible position. She looked from one brother to the other. "*Hello!* Are you both morons? I'm *pregnant.* That means emotional. I'm not supposed to be the one with the cool head here. I'm supposed to fall apart at the drop of a hat; it's my prerogative. You two are supposed to smile and nod and agree with everything I say."

Ken's eyebrow shot up, and a ghost of a smile played for a moment with his mouth, and then disappeared. "Was I upsetting you,

Briony?"

"I'm in a perpetual state of upset," she reiterated. "I've never been pregnant before. I never even thought about having children." She sank down onto the bed again, looking up at Jack. "*Never.* I have such a difficult time being around people, it never occurred to me the opportunity would be there."

Jack stood in front of her, forcing her chin up with his thumb so she had to meet his gaze. "You want this baby."

She nodded, swallowing hard. "It's just scary. Everything is so frightening right now. I wish I wasn't such a coward."

The pad of Jack's thumb rubbed over her lower lip. "It's all right to be afraid, Briony; fear doesn't make you a coward. Why shouldn't you be afraid?" He crouched down in front of her, framing her face. "I want you here more than I've ever wanted anything in my life. And I have every intention of seeing you through this. You came here because you trusted your own instincts. I'm sure your brothers objected."

A faint smile teased her mouth. "*Strenuously* objected."

"But you knew to come to me anyway. I may be a lot of things, Briony, and I'm hell to live with, but you came to me for protection and *that* is guaranteed. Just keep trusting me."

Ken came up on the other side of her, looking so heartbreakingly like Jack. He put one hand on his twin's shoulder and the other on her shoulder. "We're in this together — all the way, Briony. Here, where we live, we have a policy that it's okay to be who we really are. Jack gets a little dicey sometimes and I have my own demons. If you're afraid or sick or want to stand outside and scream, it's all good."

Briony nodded, struggling not to cry. She didn't know what acceptance was. She'd never had it. She had always fit into the circus world because her family needed her to — not because it was her choice. She'd fought every day of her life to appear normal. Here, with Jack and Ken, she felt no pain at all being near them. They both shielded her, not only from their thoughts, but Jack had been able to keep her from feeling the effects of violence up close.

Was it really that simple? She touched their minds and found sincerity. They both had concerns and both were a little leery of the new situation, a woman — nearly a stranger — in their comfortable, safe world, but both were more than willing to accept her and learn how to live with her.

*How to live with her.* They were willing to

adjust for her. Was she willing to adjust for them? She looked up at Jack, at his peculiarly colored eyes that seemed to go from charcoal gray to glittering silver, depending on his mood. Could she put herself totally in his hands? She already liked and respected Ken. She might be willing to try for Jack — but could she hand Jack her heart when she knew the attraction was because of genetic manipulation? She needed to go slow — take one day at a time and see where it led her. She took a deep breath and let it out. "Thank you both."

Jack felt relief sweep through him. Briony was afraid, but she was accepting their offer. He didn't know what he would have done if she'd tried to run. "You'd better get ready to go, babe," he said. "It's a long drive down the mountain and we don't want to miss the doctor appointment."

"We can eat dinner in town," Ken added, flicking his brother a warning glance.

"I'll cook tonight," Jack offered as he stood up, tousling Briony's hair.

"We can eat dinner in town. I got up at four this morning and removed the traps and set alarms. I've still got the tile job to do. Don't give me grief on this."

"See how he whines." Jack appealed to Briony.

"I'm being reasonable, Bri," Ken protested. "You've never tasted his cooking," he added, following Jack's example and ruffling her hair.

She sat very still, just absorbing the affection in that simple motion. It should have made her feel like a child, but even Jack's persistent orders had nothing to do with thinking she was a child. "I'd like dinner out," she ventured.

Jack groaned. "Don't help him, Briony. It won't just be dinner. He'll want to go listen to music. Every time, every *single* time I'm dumb enough to agree to dinner, we end up at the Last Saloon listening to his country music. He flirts all night and I sit there watching his back."

"I'm trying to get him to work on his social skills," Ken explained. "And the music is awesome. You do like country music, don't you, Briony?"

"Yes."

"And you do agree Jack needs a little work on his social skills," Ken prompted.

"He flirts just fine," Briony said.

"Jack? Flirts?" Ken looked shocked. "If he does, he's only flirted with you. The ladies sashay up to him, and he gives them that deadpan look, and they scurry away. It's embarrassing."

"Really?" She glanced at Jack.

"You're not taking Briony to the bar," Jack decreed. "Some drunken idiot cowboy is going to take one look at her and decide he's going to dance with her, and I'll have to bury his body out in the forest."

"Or you could just dance with me yourself and not have to kill anyone," Briony suggested. "It might be easier."

"Dance?"

"You do know how to dance, don't you?"

"You'd distract me," Jack said.

"From what?"

"I watch Ken's back. Now I've got two of you to look after."

"How about this," Briony suggested. "Ken can dance and we'll both watch out for him. And don't worry, Ken — if one of the ladies starts groping you on the dance floor, I'll be all over it in a heartbeat. But then, Ken can watch out for us while we dance. Ken, you could do that, couldn't you?"

"It's a deal, as long as you let the ladies grope me."

Jack threw his hands into the air. "So this is how it's going to be. You're going to double team me, aren't you?"

Ken and Briony exchanged a grin and nodded, unrepentant.

# CHAPTER 13

"Briony, look at the monitor," Dr. Casey instructed. "Jack, do you see what I'm looking at."

"Two hearts," Jack said.

Briony went still, the color draining from her face. She reached for Jack's hand for strength. It wasn't possible. She'd never considered having one child — let alone two. She was beginning to think she was in the middle of a nightmare and just needed to pinch herself very hard to wake up.

Jack bent close to her, close enough that his lips brushed her ear, but his words were in her head, not spoken aloud. *Don't panic on me, baby. We'll get through this.* His fingers tightened around hers.

Briony swung her head around slowly and stared at the small screen. There was a black cone and a lot of swishing and not much of anything that she could see. "No way. Don't even joke like that, you two. I almost had a heart attack."

The doctor pointed and made a small circle first over one spot and then over another. "You're definitely carrying twins."

*What's wrong, Jack? I can feel Briony from here. She's very upset.*

*Don't go shooting the doctor. He just told her we were having twins, and she's not prepared for the news.*

*She's very distressed.*

*I'm aware, Ken. I'll deal with it.*

Jack brushed the hair back from Briony's face. Small beads of sweat dotted her brow, and her skin was clammy, so pale it was nearly translucent. One hand fluttered to her throat.

"Jack. No." She shook her head, her gaze desperately clinging to his. "I've never held a baby in my life, let alone changed diapers. I don't know the first thing about babies." *What if they cry and I freak out and throw up everywhere? I can't be with anyone when they're upset. A baby can't control that. I thought with one, I could, you know, take a breather every now and then, but not with two. Jack, I can't do two.*

The doctor held on to his smile, looking cheerful. "I know it's a bit of a shock, but many women have twins and do just fine. Everything looks good. You should be able to carry without any problems. We'll want to keep a close eye on you."

Briony nearly crushed Jack's fingers. "Are you absolutely certain? Two babies?"

"Yes. I heard two heartbeats, and you can clearly see them on the sonogram. If you'd like more clarity, the hospital has a newer model and you could have it confirmed on their machine. I can set up the appointment."

Jack pressed his free hand into Briony's shoulder in warning. "That won't be necessary." *We don't need more of a paper trail than necessary. Let's just stick with Dr. Casey as long as possible.* "It's a shock, that's all, but a welcome one, isn't it, baby?"

She swallowed the fear crushing her and hung on to his tender tone. If only he really loved her that much — wanted her that much. A woman could put up with a lot to have a man love her so much. How could he fake that look? That caressing tone? He actually sounded happy about the babies. She wished she had Jack's strength.

The doctor casually wiped the smears of gel from her stomach. Jack pulled down her shirt. "Thanks, Doc. We'll go celebrate. Do you have a nutrition expert who can give us advice on what she should or shouldn't eat?"

"Ask the receptionist for our comprehensive tip sheet and don't forget to take your prenatals," Dr. Casey advised. "Any more questions?"

Briony shook her head. The man had already said a mouthful.

"Is there any reason why we can't make love?" Jack asked.

Briony bit back a squeak of shock. Her gaze jumped to his face, but he was looking at the doctor.

"I'd like to know what we can and can't do," Jack added.

Briony closed her eyes. Just the thought of Jack touching her was enough to get her wet, make her body go into hormone overload. What was he thinking, bringing that up when they already had so many problems avoiding it. She should have influenced the doctor to say they *couldn't* have sex, but no, he was going into great detail and Jack was just soaking it up. She lifted her hand limply as the doctor left.

"What were you thinking?" she hissed.

"I'm taking precautions. If you're with me, Briony, it's going to happen. We both know it, and we need the answers. I don't want to take a chance on hurting you or the babies."

She let Jack help her into a sitting position. She wasn't going to go there. Not now, not when there were other, much larger problems. *Babies.* "What are we going to do? One baby I might be able to take care of, but two of them? Do you have any idea what this means?" She couldn't disappear with two babies. It would be nearly impossible to protect two children from Dr. Whitney. "Can you see me running with a front and back pack, fighting enhanced soldiers off? This is getting worse and worse."

Jack's jaw tightened. "What do you want to do? The doctor said you're eleven weeks along. What's the cutoff time?"

Her breath caught in her throat, and both hands covered her stomach protectively. "For what? I'm not having an abortion, Jack. I might not be able to take care of my children myself, but I'll be damned if I'll have an abortion. They feel a part of me already. No." She shook her head. "No way."

"We'll take care of them together the old-fashioned way, by ourselves."

"Jack, you've never seen me around people without you there to buffer me from all the emotion."

"I watched you perform. I didn't protect you then because I wanted to see and feel what your life was like."

She shook her head. "You did protect me. Not all the way, but it wasn't nearly as bad as usual. You weren't even aware of it. I'm just so afraid that if the babies get sick, or are upset . . ." She looked up at him. "What if I can't take care of them?"

"You performed night after night because you loved your family that much, Briony, why would you think you'd do any less for your children?"

She couldn't pull her gaze from his. He was so certain, not in the least ruffled by the news. She was impacting his life in ways she hadn't expected, and *he* was the one handling it, not her. "Okay. You're right. We'll just do whatever has to be done — one day at a time."

Jack's fingers circled the nape of her neck. "We can do this." He flashed a small grin. It faded quickly, but fascinated Briony all the same. There was no softening of his hard, weathered features; rather, his eyes went from dark to light. Her stomach somersaulted in response, proving she was still way too susceptible to him. "And we always have Ken to do diaper duty."

"Aren't you worried about Whitney's men finding us?"

"They'll either come for you or they won't, baby. We can't stop living our lives because Whitney may find out where you are."

Jack didn't leave the room as she got back

into her jeans; in fact he didn't even avert his eyes. "You're incredibly beautiful, you know that?"

"No, I'm not, but it's nice of you to say so." She tried not to blush as she zipped up her jeans. It seemed natural to have Jack in the room with her, and it added another layer of intimacy between them.

"You are, and I have good taste in women and underwear." He bent to brush a kiss against the corner of her mouth. "Ken's on the roof of the building next door. Maybe we should sneak out back and make our getaway."

She laughed and took his outstretched hand. "I still can't believe we're going to have twins. Do you have any idea how large I'm going to get? You won't be able to push me through the door."

It took a few minutes to get out of the doctor's office. Jack made certain they had another appointment and that he picked up the tip sheet on nutrition. Briony was fairly sure she was going to be sorry she allowed him to get his hands on it.

Ken joined them at the Jeep. "Congratulations, you two. When you decide to do something, you really go all the way, don't you?" He stowed his innocent-looking case containing the sniper rifle in a well under the seat floor before locking the vehicle.

"Keep it up and I'm going to kick you in the shins," Briony warned.

"Stay between us, Briony," Jack cautioned as they started down the street to the restaurant Ken insisted had the best food.

The twins walked with easy, fluid strides, eyes restless, gaze constantly moving — up over the buildings, examining the shrubbery, watching the people. Briony should have been nervous, but she was too excited. She didn't walk down streets in the middle of a town, have dinner in a restaurant, or go listen to music in a bar in the evening. This was a luxury — a gift from Jack. She felt no pain at all, just a wonderful sense of freedom. She smiled at a couple walking toward them, and joy blossomed when they smiled back. She didn't read anything terrible, such as that the man was having an affair, or the wife wanted out of the marriage, or that they'd just lost a child. She could take them at face value — a happy couple walking on the same sidewalk.

Jack glanced down at her face. Briony was beaming, and he could feel the change in her with every step they took. The air was cool and crisp, a light breeze with night beginning to fall. She was nearly dancing, the elation coming off her in waves.

"Don't you love this?" She looked up at him, flashing a smile. "I love this."

"What?" He tried not to be distracted by her excitement, but something about her jubilation was catching. He was happy just walking down the damn street with her. She fit right beneath his shoulder, her head brushing against his arm as he walked with her and he felt — whole.

He glanced at Ken. *Why the hell does a woman complete a family?*

Ken shrugged and exchanged a small smile with him. *I don't know, but let's keep her. She's mellowed you out, and I didn't think that was possible.*

*I've always been mellow.*

Ken snorted aloud, drawing Briony's attention. He reached past her head and opened the door of the restaurant. "My brother is living a life of total illusion. He thinks he's mellow."

"He does?" Briony's eyebrow shot up as she tilted her head to look up at Jack. "You do?"

"We want that table," Ken indicated a table near the exit door, up against the wall facing the front.

"We have a nicer table over here," the hostess said, "in the section that's open." She stared at the scars on Ken's face and neck and glanced briefly at Jack, then quickly averted her eyes.

Briony took a step to place herself between Ken and the hostess, bristling with indignation that the woman would stare with such naked horror at Ken's wounds. Jack's fingers settled around her arm — gently, but firmly — preventing her from moving out from between them.

"That table," Ken said with another engaging smile, stepping in front of Jack, who didn't move, didn't speak, but suddenly appeared menacing.

The hostess took the bill Ken slipped her and led them to the table without further complaint. Ken waited until they were seated and had water and fresh baked bread before he pinned his brother with a steely gaze. "There's no need to intimidate anyone, Jack. You be nice."

"You have to bribe them to get your way," Jack pointed out. "I'm never out any money."

Ken shook his head. "Cretin."

Briony rolled her eyes. "Are you two like this all the time?"

"Yes," Ken confirmed. "I'm trying to integrate him into society, but he's resistant. Without me, Jack would be some old mountain man with a bad attitude, chasing people around with his bowie knife."

"I don't much care for society — and I'd use a gun."

"Were you always in the military — I mean, before Whitney?" Briony asked.

"Went in as soon as we were old enough," Ken replied. "It got us off the streets and we had a knack for it. Pain didn't mean much to either of us, and we're both right at home behind a weapon."

"How did Whitney find you?"

Ken sprawled his legs out under the table, forcing Jack to turn sideways. Both watched the doors and windows and people, rather than looking directly at Briony. "We've always been telepathic; used it to communicate when we were kids. In fact, we were pretty damned strong and had never met anyone else like us. We trained in the SEALs program and served a few years, then we were asked to take a test for psychic abilities." He flashed her a brief grin. "We scored very high, and Whitney was drooling over us."

"*Both* of you scored high?" She flashed a small, teasing grin at Jack.

"I'm sure my score was higher," Ken said, breaking off a piece of bread and slathering butter on it.

"Do both of you have the same abilities?"

"Yep, right down to being anchors. And we seem to be enhanced the same as well," Ken added.

"So if he's so interested in getting a baby out of Jack, why isn't he pushing a woman on you, Ken?"

"That's a good question," Jack said. "Why didn't we ask that question, Ken? Why is it that Whitney went to all the trouble and expense of maneuvering Briony and I into the same place to see what would happen, but not you and whoever he's matched you up with."

"Maybe there is no match," Ken said. *And I'm not certain how I feel about that. I should be elated that he hasn't messed with me to that extent, but hell, I wouldn't mind a woman of my own, not after seeing you with Briony.*

The wistfulness in his brother's voice had Jack's gaze jumping to his face. Ken couldn't stop the brief flow of information, the fear that his appearance would stop any woman from wanting to be near him. Ken looked away quickly and stuffed another piece of bread in his mouth.

"Or maybe he already has her," Briony ventured. "I'm betting that Luther was my secondary match and that's why he was really upset that I was pregnant. The thought that someone other than an enhanced soldier had taken his place was too much for him. He was really angry. I think Whitney had nearly given up on getting us together."

"And he was counting on the fact that I'd walk if he did manage it," Jack added.

"I don't like that idea, that some woman could still be held prisoner by Whitney," Ken said. "Jack, let's get ahold of Lily and her team and find out how much they know. If they have an idea where he is, we can do a little recon."

"The problem that we're facing, Ken, is that we don't know who we can trust. Whitney always had contacts. Hell, he knew the president. If he's alive and pulling all the strings in this experiment, he isn't alone. We don't know who's behind any of this. Whitney may have the know-how and the money, but he's in solid with someone directing all this."

Briony cleared her throat. "If Whitney really has contacts in the military, and there is some huge conspiracy going on, if they thought I was with you, wouldn't they send you out on a mission so I had nowhere to go?"

The twins exchanged a long look.

"Oh God." Her hand went to her throat. "I'm not going to like this, am I?"

Jack pulled her hand to his heart. "We were contacted late last week, but we're on leave. We were both injured and neither of us has a doc's okay to return to service, not that that ever stopped us before, but we said no." *I said no because Ken needs far more recoup time.* Jack made sure his barriers were up against his twin to keep him from that private contact. "Both of us intend to extend our time with personal leave as well."

"They can't make you go back?"

"I think they counted on us never turning them down. We never have. And they figured the target would be too personal for us to resist. They want General Ekabela taken out," Jack said. "My guess is, the man knows too much and they need him dead."

"In other words," Ken added, "he isn't useful to Whitney anymore."

"Why didn't you tell me?"

Jack raised her knuckles to his lips. "You were a bit upset, Briony, and you needed sleep last night, and in any case, we didn't think about why they would send us into the field, we go all the time." He shrugged. "I thought they offered it to us because of what Ekabela had done to us."

"But that means they know I'm with you. How would they know?" She nearly jumped out of her skin as the waiter approached.

Jack laid his hand on her arm. Gently. Just touching her. Warmth flowed into her mind, and almost at once she felt calmer, more able to breathe away fear. "Not necessarily. They may have wanted to make certain we were out of the country in case you did try to contact me."

"It makes sense," Ken added.

As the waiter hovered, Jack glanced up, eyes suddenly going from warm gray to ice steel. Briony buried her face in her menu to hide her expression.

The waiter cleared his throat. "Are you ready to order, ma'am?"

Jack drew out the paper on nutrition and began to study the menu, comparing items with the paper. "The chicken pasta looks good, Briony," he ventured. "And the vegetable salad."

Ken nudged her foot under the table and flashed a quick grin from behind his menu, winking at her.

"Yes, it does, Jack. I think I'll have that." Briony gave the waiter her menu and smiled at Jack.

"And she'll have a glass of milk as well," he added.

Ken nearly spit water over the menu. "Milk? You having it too, Jack?"

"Sure. Why not? And I'll have the chicken

pasta as well," Jack said, handing the waiter his menu.

"I'm driving, so I'll have a very hot cup of coffee," Ken said. "And a steak, rare, with a baked potato and everything on it."

"Ken?" Briony widened her eyes in help-less innocence. "That might make me sick just to look at it. I've been feeling so nauseous lately."

Ken jerked his head up, a suspicious frown on his face. "You wouldn't joke about something like that, would you?"

Briony covered her mouth with a delicate hand. "Just saying steak and rare made my stomach upset."

"Fine. Give me the chicken pasta as well. But hold the damn milk." Ken glared at her. "Just how long do you plan on being sick?"

She grinned at him. "A long, long time, now that we've had the good news about the baby and all."

"Babies," Jack corrected.

"Comes in useful, does it? I had no idea you had a mean streak in you, but I should have guessed, with Jack adoring you and all."

Briony took a sip of water, looking away so he wouldn't see her expression. She didn't seem very good at hiding her thoughts from either of them. Jack didn't adore her. The chemistry was there, exploding all over the place, but he didn't adore her — that was never going to happen.

*Don't count on it.* The warmth of Jack's voice caressed her mind, touched her intimately, and spread through her body.

For a moment she could barely breathe with wanting him.

*You can't look at me like that, baby. Not here. Not where I have to keep my mind on protecting you.*

She had to remember to shield her mind from him. She wasn't used to having anyone around who could catch her thoughts, and worse, her face seemed to be an open book.

"Don't look at him, Bri," Ken suggested. "Pay attention to me. As soon as we hit the bar, he's going to go all bossy and possessive and act like an idiot and annoy the hell out of you anyway, so don't even think nice thoughts about him."

"Are you, Jack?" she asked. "Are you going to go manly and possessive and act like an idiot?"

He shrugged his broad shoulders. "Probably."

"Why? I'm pregnant and on the run, Jack. Do you think I'm likely to fling myself at another man and beg him for wild sex?"

Jack groaned. "You can't say wild sex. You

can't think it. I have the hard-on from hell now, thank you very much."

Briony flushed, damp heat soaking her panties and her breasts suddenly aching and full. She lifted her chin. If he could admit it, then so could she — just not aloud. *You can't say hard-on from hell because then I want to touch — and taste, and have you buried very deep inside me.* She took great care to keep her barriers up against Ken and hoped Jack was doing the same.

*Son of a bitch, Briony, you're going to fucking kill me talking like that.* Jack caught her hand and drew it under the table, pressing her palm tightly against him.

His reaction was definitely gratifying. She could hear the need pulsing in his voice, hoarse and clipped and edgy, feel it in the thick bulge throbbing under the thin material of his jeans. *Nice to know I'm not alone.*

"Would you like me to go check you into a hotel room?" Ken asked, glaring at them. "Because it's getting embarrassing sitting with the two of you." *Hell, bro, we've been mind-to-mind so much we don't even think about it and certainly have never cared how hot either of us was for a woman — but it feels different with Briony. I feel like a damned Peeping Tom.*

*I'm sorry. I'll try to be more careful about*

*protecting you.*

*I'd appreciate it.*

"You'll be doing a lot of babysitting, Ken," Jack said, releasing Briony's hand as the waiter arrived with their dinner.

Briony busied herself with her pasta, not wanting to think too much on her confession and what the repercussions might be. She was getting used to the tremendous pull between them. It wasn't waning in strength — if anything, it was growing by just being in close proximity and getting to know each other better, but she was learning to handle it. Even so, she sat eating her dinner, listening to the sound of the two brothers' voices, and all the while she was acutely aware of every move, every gesture — no matter how small — that Jack made.

He watched the doors and the people passing by. The table was situated where they could look out, but no one would see them. She realized that they were acting as they always did — her being there didn't mean added security. They were always watching — always aware. What did that say about their lives? She studied them closely. The same shadows were in Ken's eyes. That same wariness. He looked more relaxed, maybe even more easygoing, but she realized it was a façade. And they knew each other so well, had worked with each other, could communicate silently — they were definitely a team, and a lethal one at that. It occurred to her that it was somewhat of a miracle that both of them had allowed her into their lives.

It was Ken who paid the bill, and all the while he was busy talking to the waiter, Jack was at his back, gaze flat and cold and watchful. How long had they had to be afraid someone wanted them dead? Too long. It had to have been too long.

Briony stayed between them as they made their way out into the dark of night. Music blared down the sidewalk, pouring out of a building just up the street. Neither man said anything, but they turned in the direction of the sound.

"I've never actually gone in a bar," Briony confided, sliding closer to Jack as they went into the darkened interior. "I couldn't go into such a confined, crowded space. There were too many overwhelming emotions — desperation and loneliness seemed the most prominent when I'd pass by an open door. I wasn't taking any chances."

"I'm forced to come here," Jack said, scowling at his twin.

Ken grinned unrepentantly. "Should I order you milk, Briony?" He turned to go to the bar.

"You do and I'm going to prove to you that I'm enhanced." Briony heard his laughter as Jack ushered her toward a booth near the back where he had a clear view of the room. The crowd parted like the Red Sea as he walked through.

"You really don't like it here, do you?" she asked. She had to sit close to him in order to be heard above the music and the noise of the crowd.

"Too many variables. All it takes is one really drunk cowboy and things are going to go to hell fast."

She patted his thigh. "Don't worry, I'll take care of you."

He looked so startled she couldn't help but smirk. At once he relaxed, taking her hand. "I do enjoy watching Ken have fun. He loves country music. He plays the guitar and sings like you wouldn't believe. Don't tell him, but he has a good voice — really good. Before Ekabela had him tortured, all the women flocked around him like bees to honey."

"And now?" She watched Ken. He didn't look at the women. He sat on a bar stool and talked to the bartender, and after bringing them both drinks — hers Coke — he talked to several men who were obviously friends. He didn't look like he had a care in the world, but she knew differently when Jack took her hand and nearly broke her bones squeezing it.

*Can you feel him? He tries to shut me out, but this is hell. Still he makes himself come here. He doesn't have retreat in him. See why I admire him?*

There were a lot of reasons to admire Ken. Watching him make the rounds, she sat quietly enjoying the music, holding Jack's hand, all the while feeling the warmth of his body so close to hers. Ken took about an hour and then slipped into the booth and waved them onto the dance floor.

"You sure, baby," Jack asked. "You don't have to, if you're tired."

"I'd love to dance with you." She wasn't certain why he looked so leery until she slipped into his arms.

His scent enveloped her, his arms surrounded her, and his chest felt real and solid beneath her cheek. His body responded to her nearness with a tight fullness pressed close to her belly. It was a slow, dreamy song, and she let herself drift in a haze of need and lust, of urgent desire, matching the sway of his body, finding a perfect rhythm with his body. It was a moment in time no one could ever take away from her.

His hands held hers while he guided her through the swaying crowd. He bent his head to brush his mouth along her temple. She'd never danced with a partner — she couldn't touch anyone so intimately — but Jack was sure and strong and led her as if they'd been dancing forever.

She closed her eyes on the way home, not letting the conversation between the brothers take away from the experience. She was tired, but happy — in spite of the fact she was having twins. She must have fallen asleep, because she woke to Jack carrying her into the house.

Briony took a long bath, and when she came out, Jack was already lying on the bed, his hair still damp from a shower. She raised an eyebrow, but her body reacted immediately, breasts aching. Beneath the thin tank top, she felt her nipples peaking. "Are you sleeping here again tonight?"

He pulled back the covers. "It's the only way I'm going to get any sleep. If you don't want me in the bed, I'll take the chair."

"No, we managed last night." She slipped between the covers, her heart beating a little too fast. "I'm going to have nightmares about babies everywhere."

Jack rolled over and shoved the blankets off of her to expose her before pushing her tank top from her stomach. His hands passed over her rounded tummy, then surrounded it, and he bent forward to press his lips against her skin. "Hello in there. Come to attention. This is your father talking. Your mom's a little afraid of this twin thing. We're going to have to ease her into it, so don't go kicking too hard at first. Give her a little time to adjust."

"The baby book says the baby can hear and eventually recognize our voices, but not this early."

"But they aren't talking about our babies, Briony. They hear me. They know. And they aren't going to be little soldiers for Whitney and his fucked-up plans."

Briony smiled. "If you're really so sure they can hear you, stop swearing. They'll come out saying the F word and I'll tell the doctor you taught it to them."

"Sorry. That was a slip, boys. Don't be saying that word."

"Boys?" She caught his head in her hands, forcing him to look up at her. "*Not* boys. Boys are difficult. They do all sorts of boy things."

"Not girls, Briony. Can you see me trying to keep up with two little girls? And what happens when they get older and some boy wants to take them on a date?" He groaned and once again stretched out, turning on his side to prop himself up with one elbow. "I'd either lock the girls in closets or spend my life picking off hopeful horny teenagers."

"Hopeful horny teenagers?" she echoed.

"We'd have to homeschool the girls and put up a twelve-foot barbwire *electric* fence complete with a security system."

"Let me get this straight. If we have boys, they can run wild and be free, but our daughters will be locked up in closets and behind fences for all time."

"That's about right," Jack agreed. "Ken and I can handle boys, Briony, but no girls, so keep that in mind when you have these babies."

She patted his hand. "I hate to be the one to give you the bad news, but you determine the sex of the baby, so if we have a girl, it's all your fault."

The touch of her hand, light and teasing over his, squeezed the air out of his lungs. He stared up at the ceiling and wondered how he'd gotten so lucky, to have her in his home, in his bed, lying in the dark teasing him. It didn't seem possible. His life was what he'd chosen and he had no complaints. He was used to silence. To being alone. There were days when he didn't talk to another human being, and weeks when he went without conversing with anyone other than Ken. He had always thought of himself as solitary — it was safer for everyone that way — but now, with Briony lying beside him, her body warm and soft and her scent teasing his senses, he felt an odd sense of peace.

"Strange thing." He made the confession aloud, not knowing why, but wanting her to know. "I've never actually relaxed with anyone around, not enough to sleep. Even out in the field, I have to move away from everyone or I don't close my eyes — but you relax me. Before, when we were together, first I thought it was exhaustion, and then the sex, but it's you." He pressed his hand over his heart. "It's just you."

She was going to rip him apart when she tried to leave him, and it would come — maybe not now, or a month from now, but sooner or later, his domineering ways would make her need to rebel. She couldn't understand the demons that drove him. Hell, he couldn't — why should he expect that she would?

"I thought I could relax with you because you shield me from emotion, but that's not the reason either." She turned toward him, her fingers brushing his face as if she could read his expression. "You don't think Whitney could do that too, do you?"

"No." His voice turned grim. "Whitney doesn't want to make it easy on anyone, Briony. He could have kept you with an anchor, but he deliberately put you with a family where you'd be out in the public on a daily basis. You *had* to interact. That was on purpose, for his little experiments. What were you made of? Could you find a way to overcome the pain? Overcome your differences living in a normal family? Bastard. He knew you were going to suffer every damn day of your life — and that there was every possibility your family would reject you eventually."

"They thought I was autistic at first. Mom would hold me, and I felt everything she was feeling, knew what she was thinking, and it hurt so bad. I used to curl up in a ball under my bed and hide. She cried and cried, and I knew I was failing her."

His hand found her hair. "That's bullshit, baby. You've never failed anyone in your life. You did whatever it took to live in that family and fit in. Whitney needs someone to cap his ass."

Briony snuggled closer to him, so close he could feel her breath against his chest. "Well, don't do it tonight. I'm thinking I'm going to have nightmares about little boys running wild in the forest and me chasing them all. If I wake up screaming, it's your fault."

He loved the soft, drowsy note in her voice; it was as sexy as could be. What would it be like to be normal? He didn't know. Ken didn't know. And he doubted if Briony would ever know. But she was with him now, and he could wrap his arms around her, and somehow the memories of blood and death seemed far away.

# CHAPTER 14

"Oh you angel!" Ken leaned across the table and pressed a kiss to Briony's temple. "Who knew the woman liked to cook? Marry me right now. We'll run away together."

"Get the hell off of her," Jack said, his tone mild. He forked another bite of fluffy omelet into his mouth. "I had the good sense to get her pregnant, so you can just back off."

"Good food and a beautiful woman haven't improved your disposition much," Ken grumbled. "And having a baby hasn't improved your language either."

"Not one baby," Jack corrected, *"two."*

Briony laughed softly, shaking her head at him. There was a note of pride in his voice he hadn't bothered to conceal — one totally at odds with his tough, scarred features. "You're so conceited."

The sound of her laughter slid over his skin like fingers trailing over his nerve endings, stirring his body into yet another erection. He could sit across from her every morning, drinking in her tousled hair and her bright eyes and sunny smile. Even if Ken was deliberately provoking him by making goo-goo eyes at her.

"Well if you're going to insist on twins every time I get pregnant, this is it, buster," she said and reached over to pour coffee into Ken's cup.

"Even your coffee is great," Ken said.

Briony's eyebrows drew together in a frown. "How would I know? Every time I try to sneak a cup, your brother dumps it down the sink."

Jack lifted the book he had open at the table. "It says right here, caffeine isn't good for you or the baby. And we need fresh fruit, not juice. Do you have any idea of the amount of calcium you need?"

She yanked the book out of his hand and flung it across the room hard enough that it hit the wall. "You've got to stop reading from the Book of Satan. You're clearly becoming obsessed."

"Rebellion!" Ken grinned at her. "I knew it was coming. You can't mess with a woman's coffee, Jack. See, hon, if you marry me and cook three meals a day with a snack or two thrown in daily, I'll let you have all the coffee you want."

"How good of you to *let* me." Briony kicked his shin under the table. "You just pretend to be the sweet, easygoing brother. I'm not marrying you so you have a cook."

"That's not right," Ken complained, rubbing his shin and trying to look pathetic. "I'm still growing, and all I get around here is lists for work." He held up a small notebook and scowled at his brother. "No fuel to keep me going."

"She's not cooking your meals, Ken, so stop whining." Jack glanced over at Briony. "I told you he whined."

"Wheedle," Ken corrected. "I wheedle. It sounds so much better than whining."

Laughing, Briony shook her head. "You two are so crazy. So is it okay for me to walk through the yard now?"

"We just have alarms set," Ken said, "small strobes that will go off to alert us if anyone has breached the parameters. It's safe enough."

Jack looked up alertly. "Are you planning on going for a walk today?"

She nodded. "If I have the time. I want to do a little cleaning and put together something for dinner."

He shook his head. "You don't have to do that."

"Idiot," Ken hissed, wadding up a napkin

and throwing it at his brother. "Are you insane? Don't listen to him, Briony. You want to cook, get on with it, I say."

"I like to cook, Jack. It's always been something I've been interested in doing. I didn't have a chance to do a lot of it, but now I've got several months to play."

"I bought you some sketchpads the other day," Jack said. "I left them in the great room on the coffee table along with a few other drawing supplies."

"You did?" Briony's eyes lit up. "Thank you for remembering."

"He's been looking all morning at a furniture book," Ken confided. "Thinks he can make a better cradle than you can find anywhere else, and he probably can too. Believe it or not, my brother's gifted that way." There was a singular note of pride in Ken's voice.

Jack flicked a repressing glance at him and then caught the expression on Briony's transparent face. She looked at him almost as if the sun rose and set with him. Her expression turned his insides out and made him uncomfortable. She was getting the wrong idea about him. Part of him loved it and part of him — the sane part — hated it. And damn him to hell, there were the beginnings of love in her eyes. Between Ken and Briony he felt like a fraud. They were killing him with their belief in him.

He rose abruptly, nearly knocking the chair over, shoved it out of his way, and caught her chin in his hand. He hadn't intended to touch her, or even acknowledge her, but he couldn't stop himself. "Stay close to the house," he warned gruffly and bent to brush her mouth with his.

Heat flared instantly, the moment his lips feathered against the soft curve of hers. His hand slipped to the nape of her neck, tilting her head for a better angle, so his tongue could delve deep, teasing, stroking, exploring her incredible mouth. He pulled away abruptly — self-preservation required it — and pressed his brow to hers, breathing deep. "You remember one thing. You decide you want to get married, it's going to be to me."

Briony watched him stalk outside, slamming the kitchen door behind him. Both eyebrows raised, she turned to Ken.

"Close your mouth, honey. That's Jack trying to be romantic and failing miserably. *Don't* let him get away with that shit either. If he's going to ask you, make him do it all the way. You know — down on one knee, looking stupid."

Briony nearly choked. "That's just mean, Ken."

He leaned close to her. "If you do it, Briony, tell me first so I can videotape it. I could blackmail him for the rest of his life."

"He would never get on his knees for anyone," she pointed out, gathering dishes and taking them to the sink. "It would never happen."

"You could just be wrong, Miss Jenkins." Ken pushed back his chair and caught up his hat. "I think, for you, he'd do just about anything."

Briony watched him saunter out the back door and walk along the path toward the shop, taking the same direction Jack had. She took a deep breath and turned around, surveying the large kitchen with its wood floor and large beams. It was beautiful to her — the wide open spaces. It looked — and felt — like a home to her.

She glanced back to the window, her gaze searching for Jack. "Why do I feel so strongly about you? Why do I feel like I know you better than you know yourself?"

She set the dishes in the sink and wandered through the house, exploring the various rooms. It was obvious to her that the two men had planned each section of the house carefully. Ken's style was distinctly different from Jack's — yet there were touches here and there that reminded her of his twin. He liked Western motifs and music, yet he had a gun cabinet beside his bed and another in his office — just as Jack did. Jack had shelves of books everywhere.

Briony retrieved the pregnancy book and carried it into his office. She stood in the doorway frowning. The office was finished, walls in place, a beautiful one-of-a-kind desk that she suspected Jack had built, piles of papers, and a box containing a brand-new computer. Beside the box was another carton containing paper, but it was open and there was a column as long as or longer than her arm of paper spread across the desk and onto the floor. She went closer to examine the handwritten notes.

Two separate masculine scrawls, one stating in very crude terms that Ken could shove the computer somewhere impossible to shove and Jack wasn't opening the thing. Ken answered with a long dissertation about computers being a necessity in their new business venture and Jack could just come out of his cave and quit bellyaching. The rest of the notes were a daily ongoing argument about who would get the computer up and running. Ken was adamant that it was Jack's job since he was going to have to deal with all the actual people, and Jack stated that he absolutely wasn't touching the machine under any circumstances.

Briony took the computer out of the box and found that it was a fairly decent model, one that certainly could be used for the type of business Ken wanted to try. She spent the next hour putting it together and hooking up the various cables and connectors, along with backup batteries and surge protectors and finally the printer. She doubted if Jack would actually use it, but she loaded the software programs Ken had purchased for it anyway.

Sinking into the chair, she opened the pregnancy book, and skimmed each chapter carefully before retrieving a black permanent marker from the desk drawer. With great care and precision she blacked out every reference to caffeine she could find in the book. "Don't ever try to come between a woman and her coffee, Jack," she murmured aloud.

Briony sat back with a satisfied smirk before going through the book again, this time reading with much more diligence, blacking out everything she didn't approve of and making her own notations in the margins, before closing the book and taking it into Jack's bedroom. She left it on his dresser, right where he would be certain to find it. Laughing, she went back into the kitchen to make the men lunch.

She found the brothers in Ken's wing of the house, in his bathroom, finishing up the last of the tile, wrangling with each other, much like all the notes on the computer. Both men wolfed down the sandwiches and lemonade while she surveyed the large room.

"This is beautiful, Ken. Both of you really like space."

Ken nodded. "We thought a lot about what we'd need before we designed the house." He grinned at her. "Of course we hadn't really considered children."

"Well, the second bedroom would easily make a room for the baby," she pointed out. "The room isn't finished in Jack's wing, but it doesn't seem like it would take that much to get it ready before the baby comes."

"Babies," Jack corrected. "We're having two."

"I'm not thinking about that." She gave him a quelling scowl. "One is all I can assimilate right now, so stop saying that to me. The doctor could be wrong."

Jack raised an eyebrow. "We saw the two hearts and heard two heartbeats. I don't think there's much doubt, baby."

Briony glared at him again and flounced off. "Go back to work."

The feeling of being home stayed with her throughout the day as she did laundry and thoroughly went through the pantry to get an idea of what she had to work with for meals. As she did, she made lists of anything she thought they could use, so the next time one of the twins went into town he could pick up more supplies. It didn't matter how much she told herself not to get too comfortable, this place — and this man — seemed to fit.

The sunset was spectacular and Briony went out onto the porch to watch it. Both men were in the shop now, working away on something she couldn't see yet. She was fairly certain Jack was starting the cradle and they were making plans for the spare room in his wing to be finished.

Briony stepped off the porch and inhaled the slight wind, taking the crisp mountain air into her lungs. The house was spotless and dinner was simmering. She'd even managed to whip up a pie for dessert. She felt safe and secure. Jack and Ken left her alone to do whatever she wanted while they went about their business. Occasionally, Jack would touch base with her, brushing her mind with some anecdote about Ken, and it made her feel even more a part of him — of the bond the twins shared — as if she really did belong.

She had found herself smiling throughout the day, and the strange part was that although she really missed her family, there was no pain, there were no migraines, no forcing herself to do things that hurt like hell. She could be happy here in this place — she *was* happy.

Briony examined the front yard first, noting where she'd put in flowers if the property was hers. There were two really good locations, and on the side of the house there was a garden already planted in long, neat rows. Fencing caged the area in, to keep out the deer and other animals, and she could see it was on a water system, fed by the spring.

She'd never considered that Jack and Ken would have a garden, but she should have. They could probably live on their mountain for months — maybe years — without needing anything from the outside.

She began to jog, enjoying the feel of her muscles as they stretched. Twice she jumped into the lower branches of trees, just because she could. It was no wonder the men loved it up here.

■ ■ ■ ■

"It's about time to quit," Ken said. "You can't work all night anymore, Jack. You've got yourself a woman and she's not in your pocket yet."

"What does that mean?"

"It means you have to do a little courting, bro. You know, actually make nice."

"You're really enjoying yourself, aren't you?" Jack demanded, giving one last pat to the wood lying on the table. His head jerked up and he suddenly took off running, snatching up the rifle beside the door.

"What the hell?" Ken snapped, breaking into a run to match his brother's.

"Someone triggered the alarm just inside the grove of trees to the left of the house," Jack said, tossing his brother his rifle as he sprinted past. "The strobe started flashing. Make sure Briony's safe. Get her into the tunnel and wait for me."

Ken picked the weapon out of the air on the run, breaking off to sprint for the house. He burst through the door, shouting Briony's name, heard the echo ring through the empty rooms, and his heart sank as he turned to follow his twin.

*Not here, Jack. She's gone.*

For a moment Jack thought a vise squeezed his heart. Pain flashed through his chest — real, physical. His gut twisted into hard, cramping knots. *Damn it! Briony! Answer me now!* He kept running, staying in the shadows of the trees, using scent, breathing away fear for her, anger that he hadn't been watching her close enough.

*What is it, Jack?*

The sound of her voice brushing through his mind like a caress was almost more than he could comprehend. For a moment he didn't believe it and he kept running, using enhanced speed so that he was a mere blur flashing through the grove. The guns were solid in his hands, so familiar they seemed a part of him, and all the while his mind was working, planning out his strategy to ferret out the intruder and eliminate the threat. Then he comprehended — knew she was alive, knew they hadn't taken her. His legs actually went weak in reaction — something that had never happened to him before in his life.

*Take cover; go up into the trees and blend in with your surroundings. Stay very still. Ken will come to you.* His voice turned hard, as his heart settled. She had a lot to answer for and it wasn't going to be pleasant. Damn her for making him feel what amounted to terror, for causing him to lose — even for a moment — his equilibrium.

Briony didn't ask questions. The icy cold in his voice warned her — Jack was beyond angry with her. She glanced right and left to ensure she was alone, and leapt into the lower branches of a tree, climbing fast to the thicker canopy, changing colors as she did so to blend with the foliage. She wore beige trousers and a soft gray and beige shirt. She hoped the neutral colors helped to camouflage her in the dense leaves.

It wasn't that she'd forgotten she was in danger — it was just that she'd felt safe. Stupid, stupid mistake. She'd come to Jack Norton for lessons in survival, and she had the feeling she was about to get one she'd never forget. There was nothing politically correct about Jack; he was quite capable of extreme violence, but never once, not for one moment, did she believe he would hurt her. And where had that trust come from?

Briony crouched in the tree, trying to figure out how and why she was with Jack. Why were they such a good fit? Because she knew they were — even if he didn't — and she was going to hold on to that when he came for her, fiercely angry for her stupidity.

The wind was stronger in the canopy, and

she inhaled, hoping to catch the scent of any intruder and to figure out just where Jack and Ken were. Jack, she picked up right away, moving fast toward her. There was someone else, someone who didn't bathe often and smelled of animals, pungent sweat, and dirt.

*There's a man just south of you, Jack.*

Her warning wasn't needed. Jack knew the precise location of the man wandering through his property — and he knew by the smell who it was. He whistled and signaled Ken to circle around and get behind the intruder. *Stay where you are, Briony. I don't want him to see you.*

Ken moved into position, settling into the high branches of a tree, rifle in hand, eye to the scope. *It's old man Brady.*

Jack swore softly. *Could be a trap. It would be like the bastard to use a helpless old man. Watch your back, Ken, and keep an eye on Briony.*

*I'm watching your back. You be careful. I'll take him out if I have to.*

Jack snapped his teeth together to keep from swearing at his twin. He took a deep breath and let it go, letting the ice replace the adrenaline rushing through his veins. *We do this one by the book, Ken. We have no choice. She's primary, you're second. I take out the enemy and you protect Briony.*

*You're going to be a father, Jack. Your life . . .*

*Don't you fucking argue with me over this. Get to the primary and provide protection.*

For the first time in their working relationship, Ken hesitated. Jack bit back another command, still running, until he was within a couple of yards of the intruder. He was wearing the color of the forest on his skin, and his clothes reflected his surroundings so it was nearly impossible to see him. He froze in place, making no sound, waiting for the old mountain man to come to him. Ken had no choice but to protect Briony and leave the target to Jack.

Brady O'Conner had lived in the forest for more than thirty years. He lived mostly in a cave several miles to the east of the Norton property line, and lived by trapping animals and eating roots. He sometimes came to Jack and Ken when he was hungry, mostly in the winter, or if he was injured and needed medical aid. He didn't talk much, and as far as Jack knew, he had little contact with anyone off the mountain.

*If he's not alone, they're good. I can't spot anyone. The forest is quiet; animals and birds going about their business. I say he's alone,* Ken reported.

Jack couldn't detect the scent of another human through the ripe odor Brady gave off. He waited until the man was nearly on top of him before stepping out of the shadows. "Brady. What brings you my way?"

The older man startled, pulling back with a gasp. "I didn't see you there, Jack." The faded eyes darted left and right. "Ken around? He said you had extra from the garden this year."

*Ran into him about three weeks ago,* Ken confirmed when Jack relayed the information.

"We'll fix you a bag of food, Brady," Jack said. "You see anyone around in the last few weeks? It's been quiet here."

The old man shook his head. "Hikers and campers don't come up this way much. Good thing too. Too many damn people if you ask me."

Jack's built-in radar zinged off the chart. *Too many damned people, Ken.* He shared the answer with his brother. *I don't like the way he said that.*

*Neither do I. You stay on him, Jack. I'll get him the supplies.*

The blade lay up against Jack's wrist where it couldn't be seen. *I'm in position. Get it fast and let's get him out of here.* He indicated the ground. "You want to sit and

434

wait for Ken?"

"I'm outa coffee."

"He'll bring it." Again, Jack sent the information to Ken.

"Now you mention it, I did see someone nosing around the falls a couple a days ago. I think they took my supplies. I'd hid 'em in the root cellar." The old man cackled at his own joke. His root cellar was actually a network of roots in a small cavern just beside the falls.

"Who did you see nosing around, Brady? What did he look like?"

"Big fella, talked real low like you do."

"Did he want anything?"

Brady shrugged. "He just wanted to know about the elk. Said he was a hunter, but he wasn't hunting elk."

"How'd you know?"

"Tracks everywhere, but he didn't even look at them. I think he took my supplies. Saw a partial track by the cave, and it was his all right. Damn thief."

*Supplies are in the usual drop.*

"I'll look into it, Brady. Meanwhile, you take what Ken gives you and go to your winter place. Ken left the bag for you in the usual place. If the big guy was looking to tell the Rangers where you are, they won't be able to find you."

Brady nodded and muttered to himself. They exchanged a few more pleasantries and Brady shuffled off. Jack followed him, careful to stay out of sight, while Ken retrieved Briony.

She jumped down from the branches of the tree, landing in a crouch, her gaze touching on the hard angles and planes of Ken's face as she straightened. "You're angry with me."

He caught her wrist and began walking back to the house, taking her with him. "Damn right I am, but I'm angrier with jughead, so you can breathe easier, I won't take your head off like you deserve."

"You're angry with Jack? But I did this, put us all in this position, not him."

"No, he just has to make sure I'm tucked away where no one's going to shoot me while he's taking all the risks. It's time he knocked that shit off."

Her breath hitched in her throat. "I should have been more careful. I'm sorry, Ken. Neither of you should be in danger because I wanted to take a walk."

Before Ken could respond, Jack came striding into the yard. He moved fast, fluidly, a muscular fighting machine, his face dark with anger.

To Briony's horror, the men came together, faces hard, jaws set, gray eyes as turbulent as a lightning storm. In that moment they looked exactly alike — raw power — warriors of old, equally matched.

Ken swung his fist at Jack, a hard jab to the face. Jack barely slipped it and slammed both hands hard into his brother's chest. The blow rocked Ken, but he stepped closer, not away, staring straight into Jack's eyes.

"Back the hell off," Jack snapped. "You don't change procedure in the middle of a mission. We do what we've always done; it's how we stay alive. You know that. Get your head out of your butt."

"I'm not hiding behind you anymore, Jack. If anything had gone wrong . . ."

"What kind of crap are you talking? You've been guarding my back my entire life, not hiding behind me. Is the entire world going to hell? And you!" Jack whirled around to face Briony, fury in every line of his body.

He advanced on her, his fingers settling around her upper arms like a vise. "You *never* forget you're in a combat situation. Not for one minute. Do you understand me? You could have been killed, or you could have gotten someone else killed." He punctuated each word with a hard shake. "This isn't a game, Briony. Someone wants you in a lab where they can experiment, not only on you, but on our children."

Waves of fear — not anger — rolled off of him. He didn't even realize he was using his anger, whipping himself into a rage to keep from feeling the terror her disappearance had caused. She felt a shudder go through his body and saw that he was pale beneath his weathered tan; most of all she could see the terror for her behind the icy cold in his smoldering eyes.

"I know, I'm sorry," she said, meeting his gaze steadily, wanting him to know she meant it. "And I'm sorry for scaring you. I'll be more careful, Jack."

He dropped his arms as if she'd burned him, stepped away from her, and shook his head. "Damn you, don't you do that. Don't you look at me like that." He took two more steps away from her. She was looking at him with something far too close to love in her eyes — disarming him, making him feel naked and vulnerable and without an outlet for the terrible fear she'd put in him.

*Fear* — it tasted like bile in his mouth, churned in his gut until his only recourse was action to remove it. He turned on his heel and left her, heading to the shop and his workout bag, something he could hit until his hands were bloody and he was too damned tired to think anymore.

"Why'd you hit him, Ken?" Briony asked.

"Because he values my life more than his."

"And you don't feel the same about him?"

"I don't have you and the babies. He's got to consider that now before he stands in the line of fire."

"I don't think that's going to change. And I don't understand. It was just an old man," Briony said to Ken. "He shouldn't be so upset."

"Think, Briony, you always have to think. The old man comes here often for food or if he needs medical attention. We know him and we let him on the property. He's not quite right anymore, been living alone too long, but he's a decent man. If Whitney wants to find out where you are, what better way than to use Brady? He wouldn't even know they were using him. Plant a vid camera on him and give him the idea he needs to see us, and they've got their spy in the enemy camp."

Her hand went to her throat. "You don't think they'd actually do that, do you?"

"Whitney's seen our files, Briony. He isn't stupid. Why risk sending his men in without insuring you're here and getting the layout as well? You notice we didn't bring him up to the house? We *never* bring him up to the house. We feed him meals and give him supplies, but not up at the house — but they wouldn't know that."

"How terrible to live that way. You don't think it's just a tiny bit paranoid?"

"We've taken out targets in nearly every country in the world, Briony, and no matter how top secret our status, our names have leaked out a couple of times in the past. Someone comes for us every now and then. It's our way of life, and if you're going to stay — it has to become your way of life as well."

"And the baby?"

"Babies," he corrected. "They'll learn. We'll teach them."

"That's what he meant when he said I'd be a liability." She looked up at Ken. "He knew someone could use us to go after him, didn't he? If they captured and tortured us, he'd do anything to get us back, wouldn't he?"

"We'll protect you and the children. You couldn't be safer with anyone else. Jack and I both would stand between you and anyone who wanted to harm you."

"But who's watching out for the two of you? I've just brought more danger on both of you in even more ways than I imagined."

"Jack and I are a family. We'll always be

family. We'll always look out for each other. If you and the little ones live here, you're part of that family, it's that simple, Briony."

"Are you all right with me being here, disrupting your life, Ken?"

"Hell yes. You make him happy, Briony. I can't remember him happy." A slow smile curved his mouth, but never quite lit up his eyes. "And you can cook. You did make dinner, didn't you?" There was a hopeful note in his voice.

A ghost of a smile to match his slipped through the strain on her face. She couldn't bear for Jack to be angry with her. She hadn't thought about wandering through the woods alone — but she should have. And she certainly hadn't considered that Whitney might use an old, half-mad mountain man for recon — but she'd remember, and it would never slip her mind again. She could learn their ways. She was smart, fast, and strong, and she wanted to belong to Jack.

"I'll put biscuits in the oven, and by the time we clean up, it should be ready." She hesitated. "Are you going to call Jack?"

"No. You are. When you have dinner ready, just call him in. Don't let him brood about this. It happened. It's over."

"I really am sorry, Ken."

"I know, honey. It isn't an easy way to live, and Jack should cut you a little slack, but he's doesn't do scared well — and you scared him."

"I know I did."

Ken dropped his arm around her and walked with her to the house.

"Aren't you afraid he'll get more upset?"

"Because I have my arm around you? He can learn to live with it. If I feel affection toward you, I'm going to show it. Jack's a part of me. He loves you and you make him happy. Believe me, I feel affection for you for that alone, but it isn't sexual and he might as well find out what he can live with and what he can't." He dropped a kiss on her forehead. "It's good for him to see he isn't as bad as he thinks he is."

Briony washed her hands and put the biscuits in the oven. "You were worried about me coming to live with you at first. I could feel it."

Ken shrugged. "Jack is — Jack. There's no telling how he's going to react to anything. This is a completely new situation for us, and honestly — I didn't know how he was going to react. He feels things much deeper than most people, or he doesn't feel at all. It's a difficult trait for him to have to live with."

Briony took a quick shower and dressed in the soft cotton pants and tank top she liked to sleep in, before hurrying back to the kitchen to pull out the biscuits before they burned. It took that long to work up her courage. *Dinner's ready, Jack. Come in and eat.* She tried not to let her voice shake, tried to sound matter-of-fact, but she knew Jack would know she was upset. She couldn't speak telepathically and not have him know.

Ken sniffed the air appreciatively. "I'm falling madly in love here, Briony."

She forced a smile as she placed the pot of stew in the middle of the table. "I sure hope the woman you end up with knows how to cook."

For a moment his smile slipped, but he recovered fast. "Since we'd all be living here together, you could teach her."

"Lucky me." She heard the door open behind her and knew immediately that Jack had stepped into the room. He'd been working on the heavy bag. She smelled sweat and blood and the tangy masculine scent that sent her hormones into overdrive. She swung around, her gaze jumping to his, her heart pounding in her throat.

"Smells good," Jack commented, his gray eyes watching her closely. He crossed directly to her side, never once looking away.

Jack held her gaze captive. Briony felt mesmerized by him — was mesmerized. Her heart beat so hard she was afraid she might have a heart attack, but she didn't dare lift her hand to press against her chest; she was trembling too hard to hide. He bent his head to hers and brushed her upturned lips. Once — twice. "I'm sorry, baby. I was angrier with myself than with you. I should have given you specific instructions on where you should or shouldn't go. I'm sorry I frightened you." He kissed her again, so gently her heart did a funny little somersault and soft wings brushed the inside of her stomach.

"What did you do to your hands?" She caught his wrists and turned his hands over to inspect his knuckles.

"I'm fine. Let me get cleaned up for dinner."

"I'll do it," Briony said decisively, leading him back to his wing of the house. "Next time you decide to wig out on me, wrap your hands."

"Wig out?" His eyebrow shot up. He wasn't going to admit that there was a certain satisfaction in pounding flesh until it bled. She already had enough to condemn him.

He let her wash and apply antibiotic cream to his wounds, enjoying the way she touched him, her hands gentle and her eyes shy. In the close confines of the bathroom, with her clean scent enfolding him, his body zinged out of control, tightening and pulsing, blood engorging his groin. "I'm going to take a quick shower before dinner, and tonight, Ken does the dishes. You need to rest." He'd opt for a cold shower, but he doubted it would do much good.

Briony noticed the baby book was on the bed and bookmarked as she went through the bedroom on her way to the kitchen. Sometime during the day he must have retrieved it from the dresser and had been avidly reading again. She smiled to herself, secretly pleased. She hoped he found all her additional comments enlightening.

The entire time she'd been attending Jack's knuckles, all she could think about was running her hands over his chest, his belly, dipping lower to feel the hard strength of his very evident erection. She loved that she could do that to him, and most of the time she could block out the thought that Dr. Whitney had orchestrated the intensity of the chemistry between them.

She avoided Ken's eyes as she sat down. "Quit smirking."

"I've never heard him apologize. I wanted to record it, just to play back later so I'd know I hadn't lost my mind. He just might really get on his knees and propose," Ken said. "And the biscuits are great by the way. If Jack doesn't get out here soon, I'm eating them all. Every last one." To prove his point he dipped one in gravy.

Briony shook her head. "How did you survive before I was here?"

"I don't know. You're not just an angel, you're a goddess. A woman ought to know how to cook just to qualify to be a woman."

Briony choked on her milk. "And you think your brother is a chauvinist! Really, Ken, I ought to dump all the food in the garbage for that statement. Why haven't you learned to cook?"

"I can cook. I get by; I just don't cook like this," Ken said. "And of course I'm a chauvinist, but it isn't my fault."

"It isn't?"

"No, Jack was born first and I share his genes. I can't help it if he infected me inside the womb."

Briony burst out laughing. "I should have known that would be your excuse."

Jack stood in the doorway, leaning one hip against the jamb, toweling his hair dry while he listened to Briony and Ken bantering back and forth. She sounded happy, easy in her relationship with Ken already. Ken could do that. He genuinely liked people and they liked him. Briony looked past his scars and seemed to see the man Jack saw, the one to be respected and loved. Jack could see that Ken was relaxed and even happy in Briony's company.

Jack examined his feelings closely. Maybe there was a twinge of jealousy, but not because of the shared laughter and the way the two seemed to be growing closer, but because Ken was the better man and she deserved better.

Briony was reaching for the coffeepot when he stepped all the way into the room. "It clearly states no caffeine," Jack said.

Her gaze jumped to his face. "No it doesn't. I read the entire book and it's not in there anywhere. You'll have to read it again."

"You will." He pulled a red marker from his pocket and held it up. "The book is the latest edition, with new and important text."

She flashed a small, shy smile at him at their shared intimacy.

Ken reached for another biscuit, and a knife sliced through the air to bury itself in the table half an inch from his hand.

"Back off, biscuit thief."

Briony rolled her eyes. "Great, Jack. You'd better not be doing that in front of the baby."

"Babies," both men corrected simultaneously.

"Wonderful, surround sound," Briony complained.

Jack pulled the blade from the table and slipped it back into the scabbard at his belt. "She said I wigged out, bro. You ever see me wig out?"

Ken coughed into his napkin, nearly choked, and had to have Jack slap his back. Jack's hand went to his brother's shoulder and squeezed briefly before he sat down.

# CHAPTER 15

Briony watched Jack as he padded barefoot around the dark room. He had stayed up late reading, mostly, she was certain, in the hopes that she'd be asleep when he got to bed. Her close proximity had to be just as hard on him as being continually surrounded by his scent was on her. It was hard to lie in his bed and not fantasize about him.

"You should be asleep," he said abruptly, standing over her.

His shoulders looked wide, arms sculpted with defined muscle, and in the darkness she couldn't see the hideous name carved into his chest. He was breathtaking. Her pulse kicked up a notch. "So should you."

He stood for a moment, just looking down at her, almost hesitant. "You took your vitamins today, didn't you?"

He slipped into bed beside her — not under the covers, but on top, giving her a measure of privacy, but no real reprieve from the sexual need clawing at her so sharply. The moonlight caught him for just a moment, and his eyes gleamed silver, ice cold, and devoid of emotion, as if he'd stepped back away from her.

"You've been reading that book again, haven't you?" she accused.

"It's a good book, very informative, especially with all the new additions to it. I think we should find one specifically about carrying twins."

"You're just evil. You know I don't want to think about twins. Every time you mention it, and you've got your brother doing the same thing, I get a stomachache."

His eyes laughed at her. *Laughed.* Briony's breath caught in her throat. How could eyes so flat and cold and devoid of emotion one moment be warm and bright and move over her with such raw passion the next?

"Jack." She said his name and heard the ache.

He heard it too. She watched his face change, go hard, go blank, the light fading away. He lay back down close to her, but she felt his body tremble.

"Briony." Jack's voice was tight, maybe a little too husky, but he couldn't sound indifferent or casual when he was going to make one last attempt to do the right thing. "I want you to hear me out and really listen to me for once."

Her hand found his in the darkness. Comfort? An offer? Fear? He didn't know, because he wasn't opening his mind to her, not when he knew that what he was going to say would run her off. He wouldn't be able to bear her terror of him, her disgust of him — disgust of the monster he knew himself to be. Her fingers tangled with his, closed around his as if holding him close. He shut his eyes and reached for inner strength. Why was it easier to talk after night closed in?

Briony didn't say anything, but her hand, so tightly holding his, gave him the added strength to try to make her understand. He let out his breath and took the biggest risk of his life. "I'm not a good man, Briony. You keep thinking I am. I don't want you to come to me without knowing what you're getting into. When I go out on a mission and acquire a target, it's simply that to me. Nothing more."

"You've been trained that way, Jack," she said gently.

"No, baby. It's my nature. It's who I am. I escaped the rebel camp, and instead of high-tailing it out of there like anyone else would do, I went back and took out as many of them as I could. That's not training, Briony, that's my nature. You aren't someone who likes conflict, and you don't fight with me just for the sake of arguing, but sooner or later you're going to be opposed to my point of view enough to fight with me — and you won't win. You won't. I'll try to see it your way and I'll want to give in, but in the end, if I think your safety or health or something else important to us is compromised, we'll do it my way and you might want to walk out on me."

"Couples fight, Jack. No one gets along all the time, but it doesn't mean they walk out on one another. Look at you and Ken. He's a very strong man and definitely thinks for himself. You must have arguments."

"He knows my triggers and he backs off when we hit one. He accepts me the way I am. Believe me, Briony, if I could, I'd be different."

"What happened today was a stupid mistake on my part, Jack. I put our baby in danger. I didn't mean to, but I should have been thinking. I *asked* you to teach me. I want to learn. You had a right to be furious with me."

"Babies," he corrected automatically. "You're damned lucky I didn't turn you over my knee. I didn't because you're a


452

grown woman and you'd probably take a gun and shoot me after, but I swear, Briony, you ever scare me like that again and I'll risk it." He pressed the heel of his hand to his pounding head. "Damn it, I know I would."

Her fingers brushed his face. "You were so afraid for me — for us. Did you think I would blame you for being so angry?"

He could feel her struggling to understand what he was trying to tell her. He sighed. "My father was a very abusive man. He didn't want to just love my mother — he wanted to own her. She *belonged* to him. She was his possession, and he became more and more jealous of anything or anyone — including her children."

Memories flooded and he tried to hold them off, tried to keep from smelling the blood, Ken's blood, his blood, tried to keep from feeling the beatings, so many of them they all blended together until he couldn't remember not being beat. Broken bones, bruises, swollen faces, and hiding the evidence so no one would know. Moving constantly so no one would ever suspect, so none of them could make friends — so no one ever shared his mother, cared for his mother.

His fingers tightened around hers, his

thumb sliding over the back of her hand. "I feel possessive toward you. I don't like anyone else touching you or getting too close."

Briony drew in her breath, frowned, thinking of Ken teasing her, laughing with her, and Jack sitting there looking so relaxed. "Tell me what happened, Jack," Briony encouraged, because he had to get it out, needed to get it out.

"He got worse and worse, to the point where she hid us when he was drunk. He wanted us dead because we took her love away from him, because we took her time. She thought about us, tried to do for us, and God help her, she loved us. He was jealous even of his own children. Eventually she tried to leave him — for us — and he killed her."

"Oh God, Jack. How terrible."

"I walked outside the little shack she'd found for us and saw him standing over her with her blood covering him and the baseball bat in his hands. Ken had come up on him first and was covered in blood. He was still swinging the bat at Ken. Blood was everywhere, all over the ground, smeared on the steps, splashed on the walls, and Ken's arms were broken — both of them." Jack held up his hands. "I don't even know how it got on me — probably when I jumped him to get him off of Ken, but I remember her blood on me, Ken's blood." He shook his head as if to clear his vision. "It was everywhere."

She wanted to comfort him — soothe him, hold him in her arms — but there was no way to give a child comfort when he found his beloved mother murdered, and right at them moment, Jack was a young boy reliving his mother's murder.

"I swear, I felt something in me snap, Briony. I told Ken to run, but he didn't — he didn't — he wouldn't leave me." He pressed his fingertips to his temples. "You can never wipe the memory away, no matter what you do. You can never forget the smell of blood, or the hatred in someone's eyes. He wanted to kill us, and if he hadn't been so greedy to make us pay — because of course it was our fault he'd had to kill her — he would have succeeded."

Briony bit down hard on her lip to keep from allowing the small sound of horror to escape her throat. Jack was seeing every vivid detail, so much so that it was spilling over into her mind as well.

"He came at me so fast — he was always so fast — and big." Jack looked at her. "Like me. Damn him to hell, just like me. Big beefy shoulders and arms — natural muscle, not from working out in a gym. He was strong. When he hit me, I knew he meant to kill me. She wasn't there to stop him, and he was going to beat me to death with his bare hands. I tried to fight back, and instead of running, Ken jumped on his back to keep him off of me. Even with two broken arms, Ken tried to defend me. When I went down, my father kept hitting and kicking me, until I couldn't breathe. I think he thought, with so much blood, and the sound of the breath rattling in my lungs and throat, that I was dying. He left me there, lying in my mother's blood, and he turned on Ken. Ken could have gotten away, but he wouldn't leave me."

"Any more than you would have left him," Briony reminded him.

"I don't know how I got up, or where I found the strength to move, but my body had somehow separated from my mind. I didn't feel pain. I don't know if I was really breathing. Later, they said my ribs were caved in and it was impossible for me to stand, but I did. I could see Ken's face, the tears running down through all the blood. And I saw *him* — the monster who ruled our lives. My world narrowed to him. I picked up the baseball bat and I took him out just the way I take out every other target — coldly, precisely, and quite thoroughly."

"God, Jack."

"I didn't feel anything at all. I should have, he was my father, but I didn't, Briony. I didn't — and don't — feel remorse or horror or even joy or satisfaction that he's dead. I felt nothing then and I don't feel anything now. When I line up a target, it's always that same way. My mind separates and it's nothing more than a job."

She turned on her side, easing her body against his, sliding her arm around him. "You feel remorse when you've done something that hurts Ken — or me. I've seen it in you. You're careful with both of us. Is that what you're afraid of, Jack? That you won't love the baby and that if I walked out you'd follow us and murder us? Is that really what you think you'd do? You'd try to stop us?"

*"Babies,"* he corrected automatically. "And I wouldn't try, Briony, I *would* stop you." He sighed, the sound more sorrowful than hopeful. "I wanted you to have a decent man."

"You wouldn't murder us, Jack. It's unbelievable that you could conceive of such a thing. You wouldn't. It isn't in you. Of course you'd try to stop us if you loved us.

Any man would. You are a decent man, you dope. You're just a difficult man. There's a difference. And has it ever occurred to you that you're so afraid you're like your father that you examine your motives way too much? People get jealous and possessive and some try to hold on too hard. You know your weaknesses and strengths. Maybe you'd go a little overboard to keep a woman you love with you, but you'd never harm her. *Never,* Jack. I don't *think* it — I know it with absolute certainty."

"I frighten you sometimes."

"Everything frightens me sometimes. I'm ashamed to admit to you that I'm pretty much the biggest chicken on the face of the earth. You're an intimidating man — a little on the ruthless side — and I never know what you're going to do."

"Or what I'm capable of."

"I may not know what you're capable of, Jack, but I do know what you're *not* capable of. I'm a good judge of character and I've been in your head. You're not capable of murdering a woman — especially one you love. As for the babies, Jack, you would never harm your own children. You'd die to protect them. You're so far from being your father you don't even know it."

"I love you just the way you are, but I'd

want to dominate you, insist on you doing everything my way."

"Like I'm not aware of that? I was raised with four brothers, Jack. While I don't consider myself submissive, I also don't argue for the sake of it. If it's really important to me, I'll let you know, and if you don't back off, I'll probably do it anyway and you can yell all you want."

His eyes met hers, and there was something dark and dangerous flickering there, but looking beyond that, there was something else. Something deep and enduring, an emotion she wanted to wrap herself in.

"I'm giving you a last out, Briony. I'll get the other team to take care of you. You can stay with Lily. It's a fortress there. She's an anchor. You won't feel any pain around the others."

"I'm not with you because you're an anchor."

"Damn it, Briony, are you listening to anything I've said? If you stay with me, I'll never let you go. I'll make you crazy . . ."

"It's a nice kind of crazy, but if you don't want me here . . ."

He actually snarled, like a wolf. She heard the growl of anger and his hand caught hers and forced it between his legs to rub over his aching, full erection. "Does it feel like I don't want you? I can't think straight with wanting you, and damn it, it isn't all about sex either. Whitney may think he overdosed us with the right pheromones, but it's a hell of a lot more complicated than that. My need of you, *this* monster of a hard-on, comes from my heart, not just from lust."

There was a moment, a heartbeat, when she didn't think she'd have the courage to seduce him, to take what she wanted, but then her will took over, conquering fear as it always did. She wouldn't let Jack Norton slip away from her because she was afraid of the unknown. She wanted him with every breath she took, not because of the craving clawing through her body and making her breasts feel swollen and achy, but because she saw inside him and loved and needed what and who he was.

"Jack," she said softly. "You always come to bed with too many clothes on. Do you think you could do something about that for me?"

He wasn't wearing a shirt, but he had put on the soft flannel drawstring pants in concession to her modesty. His breath hitched and his body stilled, gray eyes moving over her face with something close to hope, something close to despair, and such a dark intensity of raw desire it robbed her of breath.

"You have to be sure this is what you want, baby," he said, even as he pushed the offending material from his body. He wasn't strong enough to keep her safe. He wanted her so bad he could feel her in his bones, right through his skin. He'd wanted her since the moment he'd seen her again, and the longer they were together, the more he knew she was right for him.

Part of him, the sane part, nearly pushed her away, knowing the outcome, but self-preservation kicked in, and he lay back, letting her hands caress his body, with soft, sweeping strokes that sent shudders of pleasure down his spine. *Save me, then, Briony, but God help you, I hope you know what you're doing.*

Her breath slid over him, teased his senses, heightened his sexual needs. She kissed his chin, nibbled for a moment, and then trailed kisses down his chest, over his scars, down his belly, until he couldn't find a way to breathe adequately. Her tongue darted out, moistening her lips to a silken slide. He couldn't think clearly anymore, could only gasp when her tongue curled around the thick length of his erection and began long, slow licks, as if she were savoring an ice cream. *I've never really done this, so if I do it wrong, tell me.*

*There is no doing it wrong. If you don't enjoy it . . .* She was killing him with that hot, wet mouth now, so tight, tongue moving and flicking with tiny teasing strokes that nearly took the top of his head off. She kissed her way down his shaft and across his tight balls, tongue going on a little foray that had his teeth coming together and a moan escaping. *For someone who doesn't know what she's doing, you're doing a damn good job of it.*

*I'm just following the little fantasy in your head.*

Hell. He didn't know he could fantasize that well. His imagination could never have taken him over the way her mouth was doing. She did little figure eights back up his rigid shaft and suddenly engulfed him, suckling, drawing the ragged breath from his body. Her mouth tightened again, sucked and tormented, this time sliding slowly down him almost to her throat. Electricity sizzled along his thickening cock. He was so hard he thought he might explode, but he didn't — couldn't — stop her.

It was more than the sensations her mouth created, it was her enjoyment, the obvious pleasure she took in loving him. He felt it in her — there was no faking it, and Briony was definitely enjoying herself. More than enjoying herself, she was getting hot and wet, her hips moving in an automatic rhythm to the glide of her mouth.

Her tongue lashed him with heat, circled, and probed, and then she was suckling again, and he couldn't stop the streaks of lightning racing through his body, or the need to take control. His hands fisted in her hair, pulling her head back to just the perfect angle so he could watch as he thrust deeper into her mouth, so he could take over the direction and pace.

She hesitated, and he tasted the fear in her mind at the loss of control over the situation. *That's so good, baby, so good. Relax for me, you can do this.* He pulled back, groaning as the erotic sensations rocketed through his body. He thrust deeper, holding her in place, the sight of his cock disappearing into the velvet heat of her mouth nearly driving him over the edge. *Harder. That's it, baby. Harder.* She was killing him and he couldn't stop, couldn't be gentle with her with his balls tightening and thunder roaring in his ears. He was going to explode down her throat.

He wanted to savor this moment, keep it in his memory for all time, but it was far too late, she was stroking his sac, gripping the base of his shaft as he thrust deep, and he felt the fire race up his spine and spread, spread hot and searing through him, until he was exploding, yelling hoarsely, as his shaft erupted in hot, spurting jets. Even then he couldn't let her go, holding her to him, so that he honestly didn't know if she was suckling him dry or he was forcing her to accept him.

Briony choked and then swallowed, her gaze holding nothing but longing, shy sensuality, a lingering doubt that she hadn't pleased him. Acceptance of who he was. His peculiar need to dominate and control every situation. There was no distaste, or repugnance, not even a shadow lurking in her mind — only her wanting to give him pleasure.

Anger at himself, despair, shot through him. *I'm such a fucking bastard. You're an innocent, and you hand me something incredible and special, and I take it instead of allowing you to give it.* Even now, he was holding fistfuls of hair in his hands as the streaks of lightning raced through his body with her hot moist mouth surrounding him. He let go of her, fingers sliding with reluctance from her hair. Jack threw one arm over his eyes, ashamed of his nature and his own lack of the ability to control it. He had too many demons forever haunting him, and he couldn't let go like that, couldn't give in to his baser nature. She didn't deserve that.

Briony moved, sliding out of the bed, away from him. He heard her in the bathroom, the running water, the pad of her bare feet as she returned and stood by the window, drinking slowly. "You're so silly, Jack. You're not supposed to have control when you have sex; isn't that the point? I wanted to drive you wild, feel you crazy for me, for the sensations I can bring you. That was the idea. I'm not fragile. I have the same tremendous drive that you do, the same pheromones, the same terrible hunger for you. For me, it was wonderful and exciting and very, very sexy. The feel of your hands on me, holding me to you, knowing I'd taken you over the edge, it was perfect."

His arm dropped down and he looked at her, eyes glittering silver in the moonlight. "Do you have any idea the things I want to do to you?" His voice was rough, already thickening with lust. "Whitney's potent brew, my feelings for you, and my need for constant control are a bad combination."

"Maybe they're a great combination — did you ever think of that?" She sat on the window ledge and sipped at the glass of water. "Maybe you're just afraid because the pull is so powerful. Maybe you need to control everyone and everything in your environment because you're afraid to lose them, afraid of being hurt. Guess what, tough guy, everyone loses people, everyone gets hurt — its part of life."

"Afraid?" He sat up, eyes narrowed and dangerous. His erection was back, and it was as heavy and as painful as before — as if the combined scent of them was a drug that filled him with a raw, aching hunger that couldn't be assuaged. "Look at me. Do you think this is normal for me? I'm shaking I want you so damned much."

"And that's a bad thing? Jack." Her voice caressed him, whispered over his skin until he swore he felt her mouth on him again, her breath. "You think I'm not feeling the same way? Empty and unfulfilled? So wet I can feel cream dripping along my thigh."

Jack raked both hands through his hair, a groan escaping at her words. "Damn it, don't say things like that. I want to be buried balls deep in you, and if you tempt me . . ."

"Am I supposed to never have anything or anyone for myself because of a little fear? I've lived with fear my entire life. You just deal with it, Jack, you don't let it conquer you."

"I'm *protecting* you."

"The way you do Ken? Has it ever occurred to you that you don't want someone to love you because then you'd have to accept a little protection back? Ken would die for you — nearly did die for you — and that's not acceptable, is it? Only you want that choice, but life — and relationships — don't work that way. Ken is part of who you are, but even then, you don't like to relinquish control to him, do you?"

"You're going to get yourself in trouble, Briony."

"Why? Because you can't take the truth? You want me on your terms. You want me to stay and accept you as you are, but you'll be damned if you'll accept me for who I am. I'm a woman with my own needs. I'm not going to let a little fear stand in my way — especially if the experience is pleasurable."

"You have no idea what my needs are, Briony, what you're asking for."

"I'm asking you to love me, Jack. If you can love me and accept me for myself, I can do the same for you. I can give you anything you need. I don't want to be here, forcing you to give up your life for me because we happen to have made a baby together. And I'm no martyr to give up my life for you with nothing in return but protection."

Jack spread out his hands, palms up. "This is it, Briony. This is me loving you. I've never felt for anyone else — or wanted anyone else — in my life the way I do you. I don't know how to romance a woman, or how to be gentle or tender . . ."

She shook her head. "You're so sad, Jack. You're very romantic and gentle and tender. You don't see yourself at all."

"*You* don't see me. You've built me up in your mind because I shield you from pain." He couldn't pull his gaze from hers, no matter how much he told himself to walk away, walk into the night. The demons raged tonight, demanding things better left alone, yet she stood there, with her soft skin and beautiful face and her too innocent eyes asking him to love her.

How the hell did he know what love was? Obsession — yes. Domination — yes. But love? Looking at her hurt. Did that count? Wanting to keep her safe — watch her smile, watch her eyes light up when she saw him. What the hell was love?

"I scared you when I took control. You couldn't stop me and you knew it. I saw the fear in your eyes, felt it move in my mind and I couldn't stop, couldn't let go and give you control back."

"Of course there was fear. I was doing something I'd never done before, but it was part of the excitement. I trust you, Jack, more than you trust yourself. You were in my mind, I felt you there, guiding my actions, and you knew I was loving every single minute of what I was doing. The fear doesn't matter — it never has. When you took control, I felt more powerful than I've ever felt in my life. More beautiful and sexy and hot. I wanted you so much and I wanted to make you feel exactly the way you were feeling."

He watched her throat work, watched her swallow. Even that small ordinary action was sexy to him. His skin was too tight for his body and his blood pounded in his groin. Hell yes, he was afraid. If he let her all the way in, and somehow, someway, the ugly shadow of the man who sired him — who hid deep inside where he never wanted to look — was let out, he would destroy the one woman who mattered to him. He was too weak to drive her away. He'd had her now, and the thought of endless days and nights without her was too much to bear.

"Take off your top, Briony." His voice had gone husky, but carried the ever-present command in it. He couldn't change that even if he wanted to.

"My top?" She set the glass on the window ledge and grasped the hem of her shirt, arms crossed, pulling up in nearly slow motion so that inch by inch the smooth expanse of her peaches-and-cream skin was revealed. Her ribs, the underside of her breasts, the firm, rounded globes and darker pink nipples. Briony drew the shirt over her head, trying not to moan as the material brushed over her sensitive nipples. She tossed the shirt aside to stand facing him, moonlight spilling over her, casting a silver aura around her.

The shadows caressed her body lovingly. Each breath she drew in lifted her breasts, so that her nipples moved from dark shadow to silver light. If it were possible, his body hardened and thickened more. He didn't deserve her, but he was going to take her — and keep her. Maybe it wasn't everyone's brand of loving, but he'd give her everything he had — everything he was.

Jack moistened his lips and waited until he could breathe. His cock was as hard as a rock, springing out from his body greedily, and his hand circled it, stroked, with the same casual way he wore his nakedness. "Get rid of the pants, baby, we don't need them tonight — or any other night."

For one moment, Briony hesitated, reluctance crossing her face. "I haven't gained a lot of weight, but my stomach is quite a bit bigger."

Impatience hardened his features. "I know exactly what you look like, Briony, and you're so damn beautiful to me and so is your belly. Just get rid of them."

His voice scraped like sandpaper, raw and urgent, eyes darkening with heat. Briony hooked her fingers into the soft pants and shed them, sliding them over her rounded hips and down her legs, where they pooled around her bare feet. She stepped out of them and stood bare — vulnerable — in the soft light of the moon. She couldn't look away, mesmerized by the way his hand slowly stroked his shaft.

"Look how beautiful you are with my children growing inside of you." His voice deepened, became nearly a growl. "Come here." He indicated a spot in front of him. All he wanted to do at that moment was love her — his way — pour everything he was or ever would be into her.

Briony crossed the room, her breasts swaying with every step, her heart quickening and the hot cream thickening in anticipation as her womb spasmed. Her mouth went dry just seeing the dark intensity in his gaze as it moved so possessively over her. He might be afraid of that trait in himself, but she reveled in it.

Yes, of course she felt fear of the unknown — he was far more experienced sexually than she was — but she was willing to go where he led, wanting the hot passion flaring between them. It spread through her belly and up her spine, little flicks of electricity sparking through her nerve endings.

His hand glided over her breast, the lightest of touches, but she was ultrasensitive and shivered beneath the pads of his fingers. He bent his head to kiss her, thinking to be ruthless, to show her what he was like, but his mouth gentled the moment he felt the curve of her silken lips. His tongue ran along the seam, savoring her softness, teeth tugging on her full bottom lip, a demand that she open for him.

He sank into the inviting heat of her mouth as he ran his hands over her body. Up her back, down her spine, massaging her rounded bottom — until the sensations of her mouth and her silky skin sent thunder crashing in his mind. Her arms crept up around his neck as she leaned her body into his, hard nipples pressing tightly into his chest as his touch and kiss aroused her more. He took his time exploring her body, letting her explore his. Her touch, light and hesitant, but eager, nearly drove him out of his mind.

"I didn't get to touch you," she confided. "You were so wounded, cuts everywhere. I still don't know how you were able to have sex. I watched your eyes and the pain was there, but not in your mind."

There was an ache in her voice that struck him at the very core of his being. He knew he was a hard man, but she got to him, and he didn't know if it was Whitney's pheromones, her courage, or just the fact that her need of him was as great as his own for her. "I wanted you to touch me. I spent more nights than I can count imagining your hands on my body."

Teeth nipped along her neck and shoulders, small pinpoints of pain, followed by the tender ministrations of his lips. His tongue tasted her skin, swirled like velvet over the tiny bites, sending whips of pleasure bursting through her.

Her hands traced each slice of the knife, injuries she'd attended to — wounds she'd stitched. They were everywhere, all over his body, front and back, small cuts and hideous burns. On his chest, she could make out the letters with her fingertips, the name of the man who had done such a thing, forever carved across Jack's chest.

He flicked her nipple with his tongue and she shivered with pleasure. Her back arched when his mouth covered her breast, hot and tight, tongue stroking and teasing, sending licks of excitement through her body. He lifted his head to kiss her again, and it was addicting, the hard press of his mouth, the dark arousal washing through her body in waves. He pressed his thigh up into the damp vee between her legs, sending a shaft of lightning whipping through her.

Briony cried out, her head falling back as she pushed against him, riding his thigh, so that the flashes of heat flamed through her. She stroked his neck, down his chest, and leaned forward again to flick her tongue over the deepest of the scars, as if she could heal it with her moist caress.

His touch became more demanding, losing the gentle glide as he explored her body. His hunger was so sharp, so terrible, his need of her so great he felt like an animal, a predator, dark and dangerous in a feeding frenzy. He dropped to his knees, his hands dragging her thighs apart.

Briony gasped as his finger pushed deep into her heat. Her muscles clamped hard, raging for release as another gush of fluids betrayed her own need.

He swore harshly, hands biting into her

hips, dragging her forward as he replaced his finger with his mouth.

Briony nearly fell, her legs turning to jelly, shudders wracking her body as she flung her arms out to try to anchor herself. "Jack." His name came out a sob, but he showed no mercy, his tongue sweeping through her slick folds, stabbing hard, so that she bit off a scream of ecstasy. He growled again, the vibration sending a spasm through her womb and a firestorm of flames through her blood.

"I can't stand it," she moaned. "It's too much."

He licked her hungrily, desperate for the taste of her, desperate to bind her to him in the one way he could be sure of.

Briony caught his hair in her fist, tried to yank him back as her legs went to rubber and the pleasure burst through her, her muscle spasms painful as his teeth and tongue fed at her silken channel. He added his fingers and she did scream, her mind fragmenting as he pushed her higher and higher. She couldn't control herself anymore, a mindless body thrusting against his mouth, riding his fingers as her body wound tighter and tighter, dragging her into a whirlpool of such pleasure she simply exploded, bursting into fragments, muscles contracting violently, heat searing her body and spreading through her — spreading more need, more hunger, until there was only Jack. Until she was more his than her own. She heard her own cry of release, the wailing sound shocking as she thrust helplessly against him.

*You're safe, baby. Safe with me. I've got you.* He lowered her shaking body to the bed, hips keeping her thighs wide as he stood between her legs and lifted her, dragging her until her bottom was off the bed and only he supported her.

Her eyes widened and another clenching release shot through her as he pressed the broad head of his erection into her. Flames threatened to consume her, racing over her body, inside and out, between her legs, up her belly, even to her breasts and nipples. He was shattering her with pleasure, turning her inside out, and she'd never be the same.

His face rose above her, dark with passion, eyes like steel, his hands gripping her hips as his hard shaft began to push inch by inch through tight, spasming muscles, as he slowly invaded her channel. A strangled groan escaped his throat as he looked down at her body stretched so tightly around his.

"Stay with me, baby. Don't fight me."

She didn't realize she was thrashing under him, every move of her body, every tightening of her muscles sending pleasure crashing through her — pleasure so intense it bordered on pain. "It's too much, Jack. I'm losing myself." Her voice was hoarse and panicked as she choked out the words.

He withdrew and her heart nearly stopped; then, without preamble, he drove through the slick, tight folds to bury himself deep. Briony screamed his name, hands digging into the sheets for an anchor as her body pulsed around his, dragging at him, clenching and burning like a fire that could never be put out. He was ruthless, holding her hips to accept his harsh, pounding thrusts. The fire raged hotter, the tension winding and winding until she was certain she would shatter into a million pieces. Her head thrashed from side to side and she twisted her fingers into the sheets, trying to hold on, but he was relentless, pushing her further, until she was nearly sobbing for release.

"Jack. Jack." She was chanting his name. "Please."

"You can take it, baby, everything. All of it — all of me." He pressed hard into her, stimulating her most sensitive area deliberately, feeling her body's instant reaction, the sudden jerking of her muscles all around him, contracting harder and harder, until the fury of her orgasm rocked both of them. It powered through her body, her stomach and breasts, sent shock waves through her thighs and a series of major quakes through her groin, until her muscles squeezed like a vise, forcing his hot release to fill her in hot jetting spurts.

Jack fought to catch his breath, her hips in his hands, body still buried balls deep, exactly as he needed, real peace settling into his heart and mind for the first time that he could remember. His pulse was racing, and he thought for a moment that she might have killed him, might have given him a heart attack, with the pleasure shooting through his body, from his toes to his head. "Son of a bitch, Briony."

She took a breath. "Yeah. Me too." She closed her eyes and drifted in the sensual storm of small quakes. She felt him move, sliding out of her, dragging across too-sensitive nerves, so that she shuddered again with another wave of pleasure, and then he was running a wet cloth between her legs.

Jack picked her up as if she were no weight at all, shifting her back to the top of the bed and pulling the sheet and comforter over her. This time he slid under the covers with her, shaping his body around hers. "I think we're going to have to look up vigorous sex. The book said it was okay, but our sex may not be what they're talking about."

She snuggled closer to his warmth, her heart still racing out of control, body still so sensitive that even the feeling of the sheets against her heated flesh caused her muscles to clench with pleasure. "We won't survive another round like that, Jack; at least I won't."

He took her mouth, soft gentle kisses of reassurance. "That was me loving you, baby, and I haven't even gotten started."

# CHAPTER 16

The window beside Briony's head shattered, spraying glass all over her. Something hit the floor just as a second and third window shattered. Jack rolled Briony off the bed onto the floor, covering her body with his own as smoke poured into the room from the canister bouncing and rattling on the floor.

*Ken!*

*I'm on it.*

*Don't breathe, Briony, keep your eyes closed tight. Don't take a breath. If you get in trouble, let me know, I'll help you.*

*How do they keep finding me? I don't understand. They shouldn't have been able to find me.*

*Don't panic, baby. We knew they'd come eventually. It's no big deal.*

Jack was so calm. She squeezed her eyes closed and held her breath, wishing she'd managed to take a gulp of air as she hit the floor. She wanted to reach for him, cling, but she heard him moving with purpose around the room.

*What are you doing?*

*We'll need your clothes, the baby book, a few things.* He pushed jeans and a shirt into her hands and pressed her shoes close before shrugging into his own clothes.

*The baby book? We're under attack and you're calmly packing up the baby book? Jack, you're nuts! We need weapons.*

*I've got weapons stashed; we'll be fine.* Jack sounded every bit as calm as he acted. *Just stay put and keep your eyes closed. Ken? Where the hell are you?*

*They're breaking in through the living room. Send Briony into the tunnel.*

Jack stuffed the last of the clothes into the backpack and shoved the rug out of the way to lift a trapdoor with a smooth, practiced motion. There was nothing hurried about his deliberate movements. He tapped Briony's shoulder.

*Three steps to the trapdoor and then you're going to jump straight down. I know you can't see where you're landing, but trust me, it's safe. You can open your eyes once you're in the tunnel; no gas there yet. When you hit the floor, follow the tunnel. Ken will meet you.*

He held her right at the edge of the hole,

letting her feel empty space with her foot. She felt his mouth touch her neck, a brush of his lips, and it felt too much like good-bye. *Wait! Aren't you coming with me? Jack, come with me.*

He ignored the fear and desperation in her voice. *I'll be there soon. Go, baby. Do what I say.* He pulled her tighter against him and kissed her mouth, holding her close. *Get out of here before we run out of time.*

Briony wavered and Jack dropped her into the darkness. *Jack!* Her startled protest was more shocked than anything else as she landed in a crouch, waiting for her eyes to adjust to the darkness.

*Get the hell out of here, baby. I've got work to do.*

*Stay alive, Jack. For me. You stay alive.*

Jack's heart twisted in his chest at the worry in her voice, the love that washed through him. He couldn't afford to think about anything but the enemy, and she was turning him inside out. He yanked on night vision goggles and calmly slung a rifle around his neck, tucking two handguns into his belt and adding clips of ammo to the loops. He covered the trapdoor and replaced the rug before stepping to one side of the broken window. Shadows flitted through the trees, surrounding the house. The strobes in his room and probably in Ken's began flashing as the alarms were tripped. Someone had used the tree branches to get close enough to fire the canisters of gas through the windows, and that told Jack that at least some of the soldiers were enhanced.

He lobbed two smoke bombs into the yard, one right after the other, and followed them out, leaping onto the rail and grasping the edge of the roof to somersault up. The moment his feet touched, he knew he wasn't alone. He smelled sweat, heard air rushing eagerly through lungs — and he spun toward the sound, firing quickly, blindly, relying solely on his enhanced senses. As he pulled the trigger, he moved fast, a blur of speed across the rooftop, making his way toward the wide chimney, the only possible cover.

The enemy returned fire, ribbons of color streaking in the darkness. Jack dove for the chimney, rolling partway and flattening his body as best he could while he lay still, allowing the shadows to absorb him. He waited, listening, inhaling to track his enemy by sweat and smell, body heat, whatever worked.

Smoke drifted over the house and into the canopy of the trees. Along the ground the smoke rolled in strange shapes, so that the trunks of the trees seemed to emerge out of dark, turbulent clouds. He heard shuffling, the sound of boots running through his home, voices reporting into radios — but not the sounds he needed to hear. He smelled sweat and fear and excitement along with the chemicals of gas and smoke — but couldn't find the scents he needed to tell him where his opponents were. The rest didn't matter yet. He had to take out the enhanced soldiers first, and they were trained enough to keep still and try to wait him out.

Ken would be returning as soon as Briony was safe, and he would run into a buzz saw if Jack didn't get the job done. The hell with it; the soldiers knew exactly where he was. Let them come for him. He lay flat, fitting his rifle with care, scope to his eye and sighting a soldier working his way through the woods, moving bush to bush, tree to tree. Jack squeezed the trigger and sighted the next target.

A hail of bullets fell all around him and he kept his head down. The whisper of movement on the roof tipped him off, and he drew his handgun and fired off three rounds toward the sound.

*Talk to me, Jack,* Ken demanded.

A curse told him he'd scored a minor hit

— still, it was a hit. *Whitney must have wanted these yahoos dead,* he informed his twin as he calmly turned back to his original target. *And they're fuckin' idiots for coming after us. They know who we are and their egos are going to get them killed. I can smell the blood on one of them now. He's a dead man if he's stupid enough to move.* Again he squeezed the trigger, watching his target slump to the ground. *And why would Whitney send these infants after us? It's like picking off ducks in a pond.*

*Just don't let your ego get you killed,* Ken warned.

Two soldiers on the ground opened fire on Jack, but Ken had designed the roof to make it difficult to get a clear shot from the ground. Jack took out both shooters, then set the rifle down, picked up the handgun, rolled out to his left, toward the smell of blood, and fired three shots in rapid succession again, before rolling back to cover just as efficiently. He and Ken had practiced the moves on the roof hundreds of times. He knew every square inch of it, every depression, every place an enemy might think he was safe.

*One enhanced down, Ken,* Jack said. *There's no way I missed. I shot him between the eyes just in case he was wearing body armor. They can get the hell off our property or die here. It's their choice. Doesn't much matter to me.*

*You're a mean son of a bitch, bro,* Ken informed him. *You recognize the enhanced soldier? I'd kind of like to know who our enemy is.*

*Didn't see him, shot by smell. He's dead, though, heard him drop, and that was a dead man hitting our roof.*

*Not the roof. Damn it, Jack. I'm not hauling his dead ass down; you can clean up your own mess.*

*What the hell did you want me to do?* Jack fit the scope to his eye again.

*Wait until he stood up near the edge of the roof and shoot him so he falls over. Is that too much to ask?*

Jack lifted his eye away from the scope, a small, humorless smile escaping. They had always talked to each other, years ago, as children, long before the death of their mother, using banter to get through the scary moments when their father was home and searching the house for them. Later, it was the same in the numerous foster homes, and then on the street. The habit never left them, the reassuring touch of mind to mind, to know the other still lived, still breathed, that no monster had managed to swallow him.

*You're such a damned wimp, always wanting the easy way out. You can drag his ass off the roof. It's a good workout for you. And quit messing around and get back here. I'm a little outnumbered.*

"Give me a gun, Ken," Briony demanded as she raced toward him. "Jack didn't make it into the tunnel."

"Relax, hon; he had no intention of coming into the tunnel. He'll meet up with us near the mine. He'll hold them off, give us a chance to get out just in case they decide to torch the house."

Briony skidded to a halt, sucking in her breath. "You planned this? Without saying anything to me? Why would you let him risk his life that way, Ken?"

"Jack is Jack, Briony. There's no arguing with him in certain situations, and this is one of them. If he had to, he'd knock you out and have me haul your ass to safety. That's how serious he is when it comes to your life — and mine."

"They might kill him. If we help . . ."

"We'd distract him. He's not going to let you near those men, so forget about trying to help him and get moving."

487

"Ken, I know you're a marksman — so am I. I just can't leave him to fight off however many enhanced soldiers Whitney sent." She could barely breathe with the thought of Jack in danger. She began to edge away from Ken and back toward the ladder.

"Get over here now, Briony." His voice hardened unexpectedly, his easygoing façade fading away, to be replaced by the same commanding tone Jack used. "He entrusted me with your life and I take that seriously. You're carrying his children. Get your ass over here and stop thinking with your heart."

"This isn't right," Briony protested, reluctantly making her way to his side. He looked capable of throwing her over his shoulder like the proverbial caveman. It occurred to her that Ken was every bit as dominant as his twin — he just hid it better.

"Right or not, get moving." His voice softened even as he gave her a little push. "Right now, everyone Jack comes into contact with is the enemy. He doesn't have to worry about shooting either of us. He'll take out as many as possible and disappear."

"They're enhanced."

"So is he, and I'm betting he has far more combat experience than all of them combined. Keep moving straight ahead. Double-time it."

Briony pressed a hand over her lurching stomach. She'd come to Jack for protection, to protect her baby — babies — but she hadn't counted on falling in love. She was torn between wanting to keep the unborn children safe and rushing back to help watch Jack's back. "You should be with him, Ken. You're always with him. You fight together."

"I'll stash you in a safe place and then I'll join him. But I have to know you're going to stay put, Briony. No heroics."

"I'm not stupid, Ken. And I can take care of myself if I have to."

"Which is why you showed up with bruises and a cut down your arm. Some man does that to you now, and Jack will rip his heart out — or I will. No one touches you, Briony. You fight only as a last resort."

"I promise, Ken. I'm not looking to lose the babies, or get taken by these maniacs."

The tunnel began to curve upward, and Briony sprinted, wanting Ken to get back to Jack as soon as possible. "Give me a gun and several clips of ammo if you have it to spare," she called over her shoulder. "I'm a good shot, Ken."

"We have a weapons stash in the mine,

here in the tunnel, and out in the shop, as well as the house. If anything happens, get to a man named Logan Maxwell or Kadan Montague. You can trust either of them. Don't go near your family; they'll be watched."

She rounded a corner and skidded to a halt. There was a dead end. "How do we get out?"

Ken indicated straight overhead. "Trapdoor. We open it up there. Anyone coming in and not knowing how to get out is trapped. They aren't going to get us on our home turf, hon." He handed her the rifle and leapt up to catch a ring painted black to blend in with the darkness. He inverted, planting his feet on either side of the trapdoor and, using toe rings to brace his body, he heaved upward.

Briony realized only an enhanced person could move the door, another guard in place for the brothers. "If they do follow us into the tunnel, they might not be able to find the door," she said aloud.

"They'll die if they come in the tunnel. Each section has an activation switch with very precisely directed blasts. Don't go back in there for any reason until we deactivate the security."

"This place is a death trap."

"For anyone coming after us or ours," he agreed. "Can you make it out, or do you want a hand?"

"That's an insult." She leapt up, caught the lip of the doorjamb, and inverted easily, pushing through with her feet and shoving to launch herself out the opening. She did a flip and landed nearly at his feet.

"Show off. I'm carrying the pack."

Briony looked around her. They were in deep forest, some distance from the house, but she could hear shots being fired. "I'm afraid to distract him even to make certain he's safe."

"He's safe. Worry about the other guy. If this is some kind of test for his soldiers, Whitney must have more than we thought, because these must be expendable."

"Do you think he guessed that I was here?"

Ken frowned as he shook his head. "Whitney has access to our complete files. He has high security clearance. He'd never send men against us to get killed unless he was certain. Even if they planted a camera on Brady, he was treated the way he's always treated and sent on his way. He never got close to the house — or to you. They couldn't have known that way."

"But they knew, didn't they?"

Something quiet in her voice alerted him, and he stopped in the act of concealing the trapdoor to look at her sharply. "Whatever you're thinking — don't. You aren't putting us in any more danger than we're normally in."

"Yes, because you have enhanced soldiers coming after you all the time. These are *military* men. We can't tell the good guys from the bad. For all we know, Ken, some of them are soldiers thinking they're doing a job their commander sent them on. We have no idea what they've been told."

"Whitney isn't going to chance letting someone else acquire you. These are his men. He may have gotten military equipment using his clearances, and no doubt someone, an admiral, a general, maybe the senator I pulled out of the Congo, is helping him, but these are definitely his men. Don't do anything stupid, Briony, like try to leave. It wouldn't be heroic — it would be the dumbest thing you could do. Jack would come after you. You know him now. He's not going to let you go."

"I'm going to get you both killed."

"Have a little faith, woman. And think about my nephews. I'll be damned if they're raised in a laboratory."

Briony turned away from him, into the

deeper forest, hurrying along the faint animal trail in the direction Ken indicated, but her mind was working furiously. She had come to them with nothing. Jack had even insisted she get rid of her clothes. She touched her earlobes and felt the rubies — not her mother's diamonds. Everything had been left behind. So how were they tracking her so easily?

"Shift to your right. I want you to walk along the boulders. The original mining camp is still here along with the original cabin. We've never actually done any mining, but we went through it to make certain it was safe and it's a good place for you to wait for us. You can guard the entrance; no one can sneak up on you from behind, and anyone trying to come in is going to be a large target. I'll get rid of the tracks leading to the mine and make a few branching off from the trail so anyone tracking us will head in the wrong direction. The stream winds through the property along here for a good four miles."

Briony glanced at him sharply.

Ken sent her a reassuring smile. "I like to cover all of the bases. If by some miracle Whitney's soldiers get lucky, you need a route out of here."

"If you're not coming back to get me, I'll

be looking for you," Briony said. "I mean it, Ken. I could help."

"You can help by staying put so we don't have to worry about you."

*Where the hell are you? You'd think this was a tea party.*

*As a matter of fact, Briony and I were just pouring a cup. You can handle it, Jack. I'm still a little sleepy.*

"Just up ahead is the shack. See the bushes just to your right, Briony? Behind them is the entrance to the mine. I'll check it just to be certain." He handed her a gun and several clips. "Just don't shoot me." Ken slid the pack to the ground and motioned her to stand aside.

Briony watched him disappear into the thick shrubbery. All around her leaves were turning red and gold. Deep colors of vibrant green carpeted the ground and adorned the trees towering above her. A gentle breeze brought the first lights of day streaking across the sky. It was beautiful — breathtaking, hardly a day for anyone to die.

Both Ken and Jack exuded confidence and spilled it over to her. She was afraid, but it wasn't the heart-pounding, gut-wrenching fear she normally experienced. Both of the Nortons were men who knew themselves and their capabilities — and were ready to do whatever was necessary — but most of all they were utterly calm in a crisis. And more than all of that — she didn't experience a single consequence of witnessing violence. There was no pain stabbing through her head, making her so ill she could barely breathe. With Jack and Ken close by, she could handle even a full-scale assault.

Ken returned to lead her into a clearing, past a shack to the mine itself. It was old, but solid. Briony stood just inside the entrance. "If I have to go back into it to hide, how do I find my way out?"

"It's not a huge labyrinth like a lot of mines. It has two tunnels. Either has an exit. The left tunnel is your best bet; it comes out in heavy wood, so more cover. You're good, hon. One of us will come for you. If we don't warn you ahead of time, shoot anything coming your way." He handed her the pack with her clothes. "I've got to get rid of the tracks and go help my idiot of a brother. He might go psycho on us and I'd have a hell of a mess to clean up."

Briony nodded, managing a small smile. "Stay safe, Ken."

Ken leaned in to hug her, in a clumsy attempt to reassure her, and then shouldered his rifle and sprinted back toward the house.

Jack was surrounded, trying to pick off the soldiers one by one, but he was pinned down by the second enhanced soldier. Ken hurried as he wiped out the tracks leading from the mine back to the tunnel. *I'm on my way. Don't shoot me.*

*Go up, Ken. Get the son of a bitch off my back. Whitney can't afford to lose too many of his enhanced soldiers. He might be able to enhance some of them physically, but you have to start with some psychic ability before you can strengthen it.*

*I've got a few soldiers between us.*

Even as he sent the thought to Jack, a soldier rose up in front of him, covered in leaves and twigs, a handgun spouting flame. Ken whipped his body into a spin, lashing out with his foot, managing to avoid getting shot, but the knife in the soldier's other hand sent a streak of fire racing down his thigh. He caught the soldier on the hip and sent him staggering back. The gun went off a second time, the bullet zipping through the trees, shaving leaves from the branches.

Ken sprang into the air, cartwheeling over the soldier's head to avoid the next shot. He banked off a tree and kicked the soldier hard in the head, driving the toe of his boot into the back of the man's head. He dropped like a brick, and Ken was on him, quickly snapping the neck and letting the body fall to the ground. He removed weapons, ammunition, and a tiny radio, and once more began to follow the stream back toward the house, using much more caution. Obviously the ground soldiers had spread out and were circling the house.

*I'm approaching from the east.*

*About damn time.* Jack inched his way to get a better angle on one of the soldiers moving through the yard toward the east. He had to cover Ken's approach, but the enhanced soldier wasn't giving him anything to work with.

The air around him shimmered, turned opaque. He felt the impact in both his chest and head, as if something squeezed the air out of his body. The enhanced soldier was making his move, forming a shield around Jack.

Jack rolled, bringing up his rifle, but there was no target. He wasn't certain a bullet could penetrate the psychic shield. Only two men he knew could do such a thing. Kadan Montague and Jesse Calhoun. Jesse worked with the SEALs team and Kadan belonged to the other team — a mixture of several of the special forces under General Rainer. Had either the admiral or the general set them up? Someone was working with Whitney and they had to find out whom, or sooner or later both teams were going to be set up to be murdered. Now that Whitney was acquiring his own army, all of them had to be expendable.

"So you're Jack Norton. I hear about you all the time. Elite. The best. You and your brother are so unstoppable. No one can shoot you from the ground. Let's see how good you really are. If you want me, put the rifle down and let's have at it."

Jack was silent, trying to get an exact location from the sound of the voice. "You're looking for a reputation."

"I have a reputation. You're the older, flawed model."

"You mean I can think for myself." Jack tried to inch his way to the edge of the roof, but a bullet slammed into the shingles beside his boot, warning him to stay still.

"I'm going to kill you," the other man said, confidence in his voice.

"Who the hell are you?"

"Name's Will Gunthrie. You remember me. You put a gun to my head when we were out in the jungle in Colombia. You didn't like my attitude."

Jack had him now, the memory bringing bile into his throat. The kid was a straight-up killer, liked inflicting pain. It was more than a job; he wanted to hurt. He hadn't gone for a straight kill, but had left two guards with slashes in their bellies, trying to put their guts back inside. Men like Gunthrie sickened Jack.

"You've been practicing with your knife, haven't you, Willie?" Jack asked softly. "I took it away from you and stuck a gun in your mouth and you pissed your pants. You wake up at night in a cold sweat, don't you, thinking about me taking out your sorry ass."

The shield expanded and contracted as if Will's temper had flared, but when he spoke, his voice was as cool as ever. "I want my chance, Jackie boy. You're such a bad-ass, the boogie man of snipers, you and that ghost of a brother of yours. Funny how no one ever sees or hears him until it's too late. But you're the one they talk about. Big Bad Jack."

"Yeah, he's out there, somewhere in the shadows, Will, got a bead on you right now. Are you sweating again? You're starting to feel him, aren't you? Is your left eye twitching yet? I go for between the eyes, but Ken likes the left eye."

"You want to kill me, Jack, come at me with a knife. Your guns aren't going to do any good this time."

Jack sighed. "I don't have time for this crap, Willie, but if your ego needs stroking, let's do it and get it over with."

*You know it's a trap, Jack! I can't even see up to the roof. There's some kind of light reflecting back at me. I'm in position; I should be able to see both of you, but the haze is covering the roof. Can you get out of there?*

*I don't think so, Ken. I'm going to have to do this his way. He's been waiting a long time. I should have capped his ass in Colombia when I found him torturing the guards. I would have, but we had to fight our way out of there and we needed every man.*

*Did you know he was part of the psychic experiments, Jack? Did you see him taking the test?*

*No. I thought he was killed a couple of months after we took the test. I'd been keeping tabs on him and word came down he took a hit in Afghanistan.*

*It could be a trap, Jack. There are two helicopters, and one is buzzing back and forth over the roof. I've got a radio, and they're ordering your boy to stand down and remove the shield. As soon as you show yourself, he could do it and let the helicopter boys have themselves a regular turkey shoot.*

Jack pulled the strap of his rifle over his head and set the weapon aside. He patted the Glock in his shoulder harness and pushed his rifle out away from the chimney, where Will could see it. *Maybe, Ken, but I think he's got too big of a hard-on for me. He's been thinking about this for a long time. This is his one chance and he knows it. And it might be my only one as well. If he removes the shield, I've got to contend with both helicopters and with him.*

Ken swore. *Get it done then. I'll see what I can do about the helicopters.*

"You want to really do this, Will?" Jack asked. "Put your rifle where I can see it. I know you've got a handgun, but so do I. You bring that shield down and I'll kill you before they get to me. If you don't believe anything else, you believe that."

Will Gunthrie laid his rifle in plain sight on the roof and stepped out. Jack was tempted to shoot him right there and be done with it.

"You can shoot me," Will said, "but I'm looking down my sights right at you and you're a dead man as well. Keep your hand away from your gun. This is personal to me, Jack, and that's why you're going to die. Everything is business to you."

"Are you looking to talk me to death?" Jack asked softly.

Gunthrie whipped up his hand, wrist flicking, sending a knife streaking through the air. Jack dove under it, rolling, coming up directly in front of the younger man, knife slicing up the thigh and going for the soft parts of the body. Will leapt back, drawing a second knife, circling warily. "I'll give it to you that you're fast. Didn't expect that."

Jack watched him, his eyes taking in every detail, registering the slightest movement, the tensing of muscles, the tic in the jaw. Jack smiled, a mere baring of his teeth. "You're sweating, Gunthrie, and we haven't even started yet."

Will feinted to draw Jack in. Jack just watched him without reacting, his stare unblinking, the flat, cold eyes never leaving his target. Blood dripped down Gunthrie's leg from the slice along his thigh, but he had jumped away before the cut could go deep enough to do major damage. "Come on! What are you waiting for?" He beckoned with his fingers, but Jack just watched, never reacting.

Will moved with blurring speed, slashing with the blade, up toward Jack's stomach and across the midsection, narrowly missing skin, laying open Jack's shirt. Jack's shoulder moved, a flick of his wrist as he engaged and leapt back. There was a shallow slice along both of Gunthrie's forearms and one across his chest — right over his heart. Jack's expression never changed. His gaze remained flat and cold, his eyes gleaming silver as he watched for Will's next move.

It came fast, Gunthrie leaping into the air, aiming a spinning back kick at Jack's stomach and lashing out with his knife as he came around. The kick never connected — Jack caught his ankle, but as his opponent spun around, and the knife slashed a burning cut across Jack's bicep.

Jack drove his blade deep into Gunthrie's thigh, twisting as he withdrew it, shoving the man away from him and leaping back, only to rush forward again, knife slicing several times, making shallow cuts so that when he stepped away again, blood welled from half a dozen small cuts.

Will Gunthrie swore savagely and stepped in close, driving his knife upward in a classic attack, wanting to finish it. Jack slapped his wrist away and repeated the figure-eight attack, the shallow cuts to the arms and belly, adding one to Gunthrie's face. Will staggered back and stared down at the blood welling up from so many sites. "You fight like a girl."

Jack didn't respond, merely watched him, refusing to be drawn into a conversation with a man he already considered dead. On some level he was aware of the helicopter hovering overhead, trying to find a way around the shield Gunthrie had built, and he was very much aware that when that shield came down, he would have to move faster than he'd ever moved in his life. His mind plotted every step, even to collecting his rifle, and all the while he watched Gunthrie, waiting for that one mistake he knew would come.

The soldier lifted his hand to wipe the blood from his face, and Jack went in fast, slamming the knife deep, tearing through the wall of the chest and burying it in Gunthrie's heart. They stood toe to toe, staring into each other's eyes. "It's *very* personal this time to me, Gunthrie, and you should have taken that into account."

The light faded from the other man's eyes, leaving them opaque, flat, and as lifeless as the body slumping to the rooftop. As Gunthrie died, the shield shimmered into transparency, dissolving to leave Jack standing on the roof with half a dozen guns aimed at him and a helicopter circling.

The soldier manning the machine gun let loose with a hail of bullets. Jack dove for the edge of the roof, catching his rifle with one hand and slipping the strap over his head in a smooth practiced move as he flipped over the eaves and swung hard to bring his feet back through the window, into the relative cover of his bedroom.

*Down, down. Incoming.*

Everything around him exploded, taking out part of the wall and burning down his leg, charring his pants and searing flesh as he crawled to the reach the protection of the bathroom. He slapped his smoldering jeans, rolling over and over to put out any flames. He swore as blisters rose along his calf and thigh and his skin turned bright red.

*Take that fucking guy out.*

*I'm on it.* Even as Ken spoke, Jack squeezed the trigger, focusing first on the shooter with the machine gun and second on the soldier lobbing grenades. *I'm going for the helicopter.*

*Wait until the damn thing is clear of the house. I don't want it coming down on my head.*

Ken squeezed off three rounds in rapid succession, and the helicopter began to spin wildly. Jack lifted his head enough to take aim and add another two rounds. The helicopter slipped sideways and spun again, black smoke pouring off of it.

*Damn it, Ken. It's going to hit the garage. My Jeep is parked there. Your Rover just happens to be in the shed. How did that happen?*

*Bitch-bitch-bitch. Get out of there. Someone just jumped from the helicopter, and the way he landed, he's a supersoldier.*

The helicopter slid to the ground, crumbling, almost in slow motion, metal grinding loudly and more smoke choking the air. Clouds of smoke burst all around them.

*He's blanketing the area, Jack, could be coming at you. Are you hit?*

*Not exactly, but I'm really pissed you blew up my car.*

*I didn't blow up your car, you jackass. I saved your life. I told you to park the thing in the shed. I was cleaning the garage out and you wouldn't move it. Serves your happy ass right.*

Something stilled inside of Jack. *Where's the second helicopter?*

*I shot at him a couple of times and he drew back.*

Jack shook his head, trying to force his mind to rise above combat mode. *Something's not right,* he said. *They're engaging with us, Ken, but they aren't trying all that hard. You think they're afraid?*

Ken turned that over and over in his mind, frowning as he did so. *I think they're obeying orders.*

*So they're keeping us occupied. Whitney ran his computer probabilities like he did for*

506

*every mission, and his damn computer said we'd stash Briony somewhere safe.* Jack's gut knotted — not a good sign. Warning alarms were beginning to shriek at him.

Ken's alarm rang just as loud. *Briony was worried because they keep finding her. How, Jack? How are they finding her?*

## CHAPTER 17

Briony crouched in the tunnel leading down into the mine. Something wasn't right, but she couldn't put her finger on it. *How were they finding her?* If Ken was right, they would never have sent soldiers against him and Jack. How could Whitney get away with sending soldiers after members of the military? They had no one they could trust.

The tunnel was far darker than the woods, and she sat at the entrance, where she could hurriedly escape back into the mine should someone come, but there was solace in being close to the woods. She occasionally saw a flash of light in the sky and heard the sound of gunfire, but it seemed far away. *How were they finding her?*

There had to be logic in what Whitney had done. He'd brought her from the orphanage where he found her, and experimented on her, but unlike some of the other girls he'd kept, he'd adopted her out to a loving family. *But that was still an experiment.* He had wanted to see how she would develop and function in comparison with someone he'd kept. What exactly did one need for an experiment? Briony sat up straighter, her heart beginning to pound, knowing she was on the verge of an important discovery. Her temples throbbed and her stomach twisted. Too many times in her life she'd felt the same stabbing pains, the terrible churning in her stomach, and she'd stopped trying to remember her past. Who did Whitney control and who was he comparing her to? Whitney needed his experiments the way others needed to breathe. There would be someone — another child he'd kept behind, raised without a family, raised in a stark, difficult environment — one he kept.

"Oh God." Horrified at her own thoughts, she began to rock back and forth, pressing her hands over her stomach. One of the other girls? What would that show Whitney? Only that she reacted differently under duress? Under pain? No — Whitney would need more than that. Why was she chosen to be adopted out? What was special about her that he sent her out when he kept so many others?

She tried to remember, forcing her

thoughts back to her childhood before her adopted family. She'd been five — old enough to have memories. Her skull pounded. Blood trickled out of her nose in warning, but shadows moved, eluded her, small wisps. A childish voice. Crying. Begging. Was that her voice? Were there two voices crying? Hard hands tearing her away when she clung . . . when *they* clung together.

She rubbed her hands up and down her arms, suddenly chilled to the bone. There were *two* voices. Pain shot through her head, stabbing deep into her brain, but she wouldn't let go when she was so close. Blood dripped steadily from her nose and began to leak from her ear. She pressed her palms to her head. It felt like someone was squeezing a vise there, but she pushed through the barrier, the pain — and saw . . .

Briony choked back a scream, and covered her eyes as if that would block out the knowledge. Two little girls with the same tow heads, blond hair falling around their faces, their dark brown eyes enormous, walking and talking and holding each other until . . . Briony ran deeper into the mine, bent over, and threw up.

*She had a twin sister.* Whitney had ripped them apart, buried her memories behind a wall of pain, and sent her out alone while he kept her sister. How could she have let him erase the knowledge she had a sister? All the years that had passed, what had he done to Mari? *Marigold.* Had he taken her memory as well? Or did her sister know Briony was out there somewhere free, while she remained locked up with a madman and his experiments? Did her sister wait for rescue? Would he be so cruel as to torment her that way? Did her sister wonder every day of her life why Briony didn't come for her?

Tears streaked her face as Briony staggered back to the entrance of the mine. She remembered bits and pieces only, but she knew she was right, she *felt* it, the clawing emptiness, just the same as when Whitney had torn them apart all those years ago. There had to be a way to find her. Briony *would* find her, but first, she had to find out how Whitney's men continued to track her. Before she could turn the tables on the doctor, she had to get completely away from him.

Briony's head came up. Whitney had never really relinquished control over Briony. He had full control of her education and certainly her medical needs. She'd been available to continue with his experiments, even to being given the ability to change her skin color. So if that were the case, he had the ability to plant anything else he deemed necessary — such as a tracking device.

She swore softly under her breath. Of course there had to be a tracking device. He wouldn't want her getting away from him when she was the future mother of his supersoldiers. When had he planted it? Not when she was a child; it was too many years ago and the technology advanced too fast. He'd want the best, the latest. When was the last time Dr. Sparks had done anything of importance on her? Two years ago she'd been hospitalized on an outpatient basis for surgery. Sparks had his own team there, not the regular hospital staff.

Briony touched her hip. She'd woken up with stitches, and Dr. Sparks had told her they'd found and removed a suspicious lump, and with her super physical abilities they couldn't be too careful. He hadn't specifically mentioned cancer, but he'd implied it and her mother had obsessed over every bruise and bump.

Briony ran her finger over the small scar, pressing deep to try to feel if there was anything beneath the skin. Her breath caught in her throat. If she pressed very hard, there were small ridges distinctly against the pad of her finger. Whitney had to have had the device implanted. And that meant that it wouldn't matter if Jack and Ken held off an entire army as well as hid her in the deepest jungles — she would be found.

Her heart beating wildly, she opened the pack Jack had hastily put together. Weapons as well as a medic's kit lay on top of her clothes. She pulled the knife from the scabbard and turned it over to inspect the blade. Jack and Ken seemed to have the best of equipment. The knife had a nice balance to it as well as a comfortable grip. She stared at the blade for a few moments, indecision warring with resolve.

Briony touched Jack's mind, needing reassurance, hoping the danger was past and he could come for her, but his mind was totally occupied with a target. She withdrew from Jack and stared again at the knife. Very slowly she opened a packet of antiseptic and wiped the blade of the knife. She swirled some more over her bare flesh, right above her hip. It was cold and a shiver went down her spine.

She took a deep breath and pressed the tip of the knife against the corner of the small ridged disc in her hip. Her body shuddered and broke out in a sweat as the knife pierced her skin. She dug deeper, feeling her way to find the dimensions of the foreign object. She began to shake, the pain streaking through her, clawing at her stomach, but she was determined to cut the thing out. Once she knew the size, she ran the blade carefully along her skin, creating a flap. It was only about three quarters of an inch, but it seemed like half her hip was involved, with pain radiating down her leg and up her back. Even her stomach hardened. Once cut, she put down the knife and used the tweezers to extract the object, all the while whispering reassurance to the babies, afraid they might be aware.

She had to rest for a moment, breathing deep to keep from getting sick again. It was an awkward place to stitch, and blood was flowing freely, making everything slippery. The medical kit contained several needles, sutures — thankfully — already threaded. She'd practiced field stitching before, but somehow it seemed a lot more painful and difficult than she remembered.

Her hands trembled, which didn't help, but she bit down hard on her lower lip and forced the needle through her skin. She worked at making tiny stitches as she closed the flap. By the time she was finished, Briony felt sick to her stomach and she leaned back to close her eyes briefly. The scent of her own blood was overwhelming in the small confines of the tunnel. She closed her eyes and tried to concentrate on stopping the churning in her stomach.

A small sound alerted her, the snapping of a twig. Her eyes flew open, and she caught up the nearest weapon, a rock, flinging it hard, using every bit of strength she had to launch it. Her hand was still bloody and the rock slipped as she threw. Luther's face darkened with anger as he trapped the rock against his chest where it struck him. He stepped into the entrance of the cave, looming over her.

"If it isn't the little whore, back with her man. That's his defective brat in your belly, isn't it? Not the lion tamer, you lying bitch." Luther kicked at her.

She rolled over at the last minute, as the toe of his boot drove directly at her stomach. She kept rolling until she ran out of room, trying to scramble to her feet. Luther was too fast, following her, his large body trapping her against the wall of the tunnel. She drew her knees up in an effort to protect the babies, and waited for the next attack. Luther was breathing hard, the rage in his eyes terrible.

*Jack!* Forget calm. Forget being stoic.

*Jack, Luther found me!*

He answered at once and she could have wept. His voice was utterly calm — completely confident. *We're on our way. Stall him if you can. If not, cooperate, baby. Don't give him any reason to be pissed off at you.*

*Good thinking, but a little too late. I'm really afraid he's going to try to hurt the babies. I don't know what his deal is, but he seems to think I've betrayed him in some way. I've got the knife, but I don't know if I can take him.*

*Has he seen your weapon? Does he know you have it?*

*No.*

*Keep it as a last resort. And, baby, keep your mind open to mine. I might be able to shield you from emotions even from this distance. And I'll be able to find you if he takes you before I can get there.*

"I'm getting really fed up with you, Briony," Luther said, bending down to stare into her eyes. He wanted her to be afraid of him; she could see it on his face. "You lied about Jack being the father."

Briony shrank back farther into the shadows, felt the pack behind her, and found the bloody knife still lying on top of it. She leaned against the pack, the knife blade concealed by her body. "I know. I'm sorry. I'm so confused. Nothing makes sense anymore." She kept her tone low, submissive even.

It was the last thing he expected her to say, and he stopped in his tracks, suspicion on his face. Deliberately Briony lifted a shaking hand and wiped at the sweat from her face, smearing blood on her forehead, looking as fragile as possible.

"You found the tracking disc." His entire demeanor changed. He even sounded proud of her. "I knew you would — and you cut it out of your body. You're just like . . ." Luther broke off abruptly, crouching beside her, removing a canteen. "Here, take a drink. It's only water. Let me take a look at that."

"Like my sister?" Briony took the canteen from him and drank, her gaze never leaving his, watching his reaction.

"I *knew* you'd figure it out. I chose you because you're tough as nails and our kids are going to be incredible." His fingers brushed her hip as he examined her handiwork.

Briony bit down hard on her lip, forcing herself to stay still and not jerk away from his touch. "Where is she?"

"You'll see her soon enough. She's not in very good shape at the moment. Brett has to discipline her often. She's highly combative."

"Who is Brett? And why is she combative?"

"She doesn't want to cooperate with him." He shook his head. "I don't want to have that kind of trouble with you."

"My sister is with someone named Brett? And he disciplines her? See why I'm so confused? I thought Whitney wanted certain pairs to have children together and he made certain they were attracted physically." She took another drink of water, trying to slow down the inevitable — stall for time.

Luther pulled out his own medical kit and wiped the area around her hip with more antiseptic before applying a topical antibiotic. "We realized it isn't necessary for the woman to be attracted to the man — only that the man wants her."

Briony frowned. "That's ridiculous. Why would she ever agree to have someone's baby if she isn't attracted?"

"She doesn't have to agree. *You* don't have to agree. We can force compliance. It isn't easy if the woman is a fighter — but on the other hand, it's a good thing, and we all recognize that. If the woman is willing to fight, and she's tough enough to cut a disc out of her body, she's definitely someone we want as the mother of our children." He put gauze over the wound and taped it in place. "That should hold until we get you back to the lab."

Briony bit back her opinion that he was crazy. "Will I be able to see my sister?"

"If you two want to see each other, you'll have to do whatever is necessary."

"You mean have sex with someone we don't want to be with? Why doesn't Whitney use in vitro rather than force a woman to be intimate with someone she's doesn't want?"

"Because when we have the soldiers we want, no one can say they were genetically engineered. They'll be human and beyond any outcry or protest."

"It's rape," Briony pointed out.

"Only if you make it rape," Luther argued, his fingers settling around her wrist to pull her to her feet. "The woman has a choice. We always give her a choice. The easy way or the hard way. Don't be like your sister."

The fanaticism on his face sickened her. He believed every word he said. He didn't think there was anything wrong with what he was proposing — forcing her to have sexual relations in order to produce a child of superhuman strength and abilities. It made no sense that they wouldn't use in vitro to produce a child — there had to be other reasons.

She staggered against him as he pulled her from the tunnel into the night. That quick he was on her, whirling her around, slamming her up against the side of the entrance, pressing tight with one hand while he clamped down on her wrist with the other, exposing the knife. He pried it out of her fingers and sent the blade skittering along the ground.

"Do you really think I'm that stupid?" He slapped her face, hard enough to rock her, following it up by pushing her back against the wall again. "I'm already angry with you, so don't piss me off."

"Why?" The slap brought involuntary tears to her eyes. "What did I do besides try to get away? You would have tried too." She tried to think, to keep from panicking. Jack was on the way. Just stall. There would be a moment, one moment when Luther wasn't paying close attention, and she'd find a way to get away — or kill him.

He inhaled, pressing his face into her neck. "You stink of him. You slept with that killer. That's all he is — all he knows. He's no soldier. He doesn't understand loyalty to the unit. He's a killer and you're carrying his baby. You're going to a doctor before we get you to the lab, and you're getting rid of it. You'll tell them you lost the baby. Understand? If you don't, your life is going to be hell for a very long time. I'm tempted to cut the thing out of you myself, just like you did the tracking disc."

Briony couldn't stop the shudder that ran through her as his hands wandered over her body. He kissed the side of her neck, bit her shoulder hard, a punishment for her sins. "You were always meant to be mine — never his. Why they wanted his child, I'll never know, but they aren't going to get it. I'm not going to be able to wait long for you, but I at least want his stench washed off."

He was pressed up tight against her, so tight she felt him rock solid, his hands exploring her flesh. The sound of gunfire echoed through the night, off in the distance, and she knew Jack was still far away.

She shouldn't react. If she showed Luther how much she detested his hands on her, he might beat her and force a miscarriage, but his tongue lapped at her neck and his hands crept up her shirt to grab her breasts, and she couldn't stop herself.

"I know what you're thinking, and you don't want to try it, Briony. You're tough enough, but in a fight, I'd take you every time. You're not mean enough. I've studied you, every training tape they have of you, every move you have." His lips traveled up to the lobe of her ear and his hand cupped the weight of her breast.

For one small moment she tried to understand what it was like for him, driven by Whitney's diabolical mind to pursue her, *needing* to pursue her because his body made relentless demands. No other woman was going to satisfy him ever. Why couldn't Luther see he was every bit a victim as she was — as Jack was — her sister and probably Brett? Whitney moved them all around like pieces on a chessboard.

Luther shoved up her shirt and lowered his mouth to her breast, the urgent needs of his body overcoming all reasoning.

Briony stomped down on his foot as hard as she could, kicking back to drive her heel into his knee. She missed the knee, but hit his shin. He grunted in pain, but his hands tightened to try to hold on to her. Bending forward, she caught him around the neck and threw him, using her back to roll him off of her. Luther hung on to her wrist grimly as he sailed over her head, yanking her arm nearly out of its socket as he somersaulted and hit the ground. She fell facedown and tried to roll at the last moment, instinctively protecting the babies.

The air left her lungs in a rush, and she

drew up one leg as Luther lunged to pin her. She tried for his crotch, kicking out hard, but he turned enough to take the numbing blow in his thigh. He swore, doubling his fist and smashing it into her face. Briony saw stars, her left eye swelling so fast she lost vision immediately. Closing off all pain, she pushed up as he sat on her, rising to meet him, trying to get his weight off her stomach. Deliberately he shoved his knee into her hip, grinding down on the stitches she'd put there.

"Damn you, I told you not to try to get rough with me. You can't win. Do you have any idea how much I could hurt you if I used my full strength? That was just me teaching you a little lesson."

She shoved at his chest, his leg, doubling her fists and beating at him in an effort to get him off of her.

*Stay down! Stay down.*

Jack's voice moved through her head, nearly lost in the adrenaline and fear for her children. She hesitated and then dropped back to the ground. Warned by that small uncertainty, Luther threw himself off of her, rolling away as the bullet tore through his shoulder, where his head had been. He kept rolling away from her, into the mine entrance.

Briony scrambled on all fours toward the thicker cover of the woods. Her eye was swollen, keeping her from seeing properly. Hard hands caught at her and she fought, swinging wildly.

"Baby, it's me. You're safe. You're safe now." Jack enfolded her in his arms, tight against his chest. She could smell his scent, hear his heartbeat. He pulled back to look down at her. "Fuck! Son of a bitch!" He caught her close again and then pushed her toward Ken, turning his head toward the mine, his eyes glacier-cold.

"No!" Briony caught his arm and tried to pull him back to her. "He knows where she is. I have a sister. He knows where she is, Jack."

Jack didn't even turn his head to look back at her as he ran toward the mine.

"Jack! Please!"

*You jackass. You're not thinking.* Ken launched himself at his brother. *You don't track a wounded bear into his lair, no matter how much he needs killing.* He hit Jack low, at the knees, and brought him down as gunfire erupted from the mine.

*Get the fuck off me!*

*You have a foul mouth. Get your head out of your ass, Jack. Briony's been through enough, and she doesn't need to see you die because you're going off half-cocked. Let's get the hell out of here. We can track the bastard later.*

*Did you see what that son of a bitch did to her?*

*I saw. We'll get him — just not now. She needs you thinking, Jack.*

Jack took a breath — reached for calm. Anything to do with Briony seemed to shatter his composure, but the sight of her swelling face and blood soaking through her jeans and shirt on one side . . . He shoved Ken off of him and crawled through the brush back toward Briony.

Jack gathered her smaller body up against him. "It's okay, baby, I just lost my mind for a minute. You're getting a hell of a shiner there."

"I have a sister, Jack." It was humiliating, but she couldn't stop crying. "They have her. They're holding her somewhere, and Luther said she was being disciplined because she didn't want Brett touching her. He said it didn't matter if the woman was attracted — only the man. What kind of people are they?"

"Bastards, baby," Jack said, wiping her tears with the pads of his thumbs. Although he was infinitely gentle, she winced, and he dropped his hand. "What happened to your side?" He lifted her shirt to see the gauze pad soaked with blood. "What the hell, Briony! Baby, stop crying, you're killing me."

"He sat on me. You saw him sit on me. I don't know if he could have killed them just by sitting on my stomach, Jack. I don't know enough about babies."

The tears streaking down her face broke his heart. "I read that unborn babies were in a very protected environment, Briony. They're fine. They're safe."

"He said he was going to cut them out of me. He planned to take me to a clinic to abort them." A shudder ran through her body, and a fresh wave of tears began.

Jack wrapped his arms around her and dragged her into the protection of his body, looking a little helplessly at his brother. "Nothing is going to happen to them, Briony." He lifted her shirt again to reveal the wound on her hip.

"We've got to move or we'll be trapped, Jack," Ken cautioned, watching their back trail. "We aren't going to fool them for long. They'll know we left, and they'll come running. And Luther or one of the other enhanced soldiers is bound to be telepathic. He's pinned down in the mine, but the others will be running to cut us off."

Jack lowered her shirt with a slight frown and tucked her beneath his shoulder. The two men began to jog with her in between them, through the woods away from the house and away from the mine. Briony pressed her hand to her side to try to still the constant throbbing.

"What happened?" Jack repeated.

"The doctor planted a tracking device in my hip. I cut it out so they couldn't follow us."

Jack glared at her. "You did what?"

"Jack," Ken cautioned.

"What would you have done?" she demanded. He couldn't yell at her, or she was going to be sick all over him. Her eye throbbed with every step she took, shooting pain through her head, and her stomach kept lurching uncomfortably. She was worried about the babies with Luther sitting on them, in spite of the assurances Jack had given her. "Do we know where we're going?"

"We're heading for the pass. We'll take the canyon route. It looks like a dead end and we can draw them in," Ken explained. "They'll think we're trapped, but we have our own way through the pass."

"The sun's up and we'll need a good start on them," Jack added. "We should stop and fix your hip and eye. There's a grove just ahead that has a nice slope to it. We'll be a little safer there. You'll need to drink water. If you get tired and need to rest, don't be stupid — say so."

"They're going to hit us with everything they've got once we're in the canyon. You know they still have a helicopter, and they're going to be using it to track us as well. We have to stay in the trees as much as possible." Ken took the lead as the trail narrowed. "Watch the low branches, Briony."

"They'll be able to see where we go, Jack," Briony said fearfully.

"We always expected a helicopter," Jack assured Briony. "We can deal with it. The shrubbery is going to start getting dense. If you need to slow down, we can. The helicopter can't get in here."

"We're leaving tracks," Briony pointed out.

"We want them coming after us, baby," Jack said. "No worries. We have an escape route. Ken, did you call in reinforcements?"

Ken shook his head. "Thought about it, but we don't know, other than our team, who we can trust. If I contact our commander, the admiral, and he's in on this, we're screwed."

Jack glanced down at Briony, assessing the

strain on her face. She'd been through quite a bit, and they still had several miles up a steep mountainside to go. She flashed him a wan grin.

"I'm good, Jack. I want to put distance between them and us."

She didn't look good to him, and if he took her to a hospital — which he intended to do to check the babies — he was bound to be arrested for domestic violence. She looked as if she'd been in a war. He slowed the pace over several ground-eating strides. Ken glanced sharply at him then looked at Briony's bent head and kept his mouth shut, but he began to drop back where he could protect his brother and Briony should one of the enhanced soldiers come up on them from behind.

Briony ran for another mile, uphill, her lungs burning and her side cramping. Blood trickled down her hip in a steady stream, and she supported her stomach with one hand. Fear was uppermost in her mind, fear that she would slow Jack and Ken down and they wouldn't be able to escape the men following them. The helicopter had retreated for a little over an hour to get fuel she presumed, but was back, flying low along the trees in search of them.

Bile rose continually, and she tried desperately to suppress it, but eventually she had no choice. Tears blurring her vision, she halted and bent over, stomach heaving. "Morning sickness. I didn't eat anything. Sorry."

Jack's rifle went to his shoulder and he watched the surrounding trees. Ken kept his back to her, doing the same, their bodies still while their eyes were restless. The next hour passed with a similar pattern. Briony ran as long as she was able before vomiting, the twins running with her and both instantly protecting her while she was sick. She caught the glint of humor in Jack's mind and glanced suspiciously at his face and then at Ken. Both looked grim, but she wasn't buying it.

"You're laughing," she accused.

"It's either laugh or cry, baby." Jack glanced at her. "You have to admit, the situation is different from what we normally do. We should have thought to bring you some crackers."

"You probably would have thought of it too." Briony groused, stopping once again to bend over.

Jack knocked into her sideways, sending her flying. She hit the ground hard and lay still while bullets rained down around them. Ken calmly knelt down and sited in on the helicopter, taking his time to locate his target. Jack did the same. There was no wild shooting. It was obvious they believed in making every shot count. Ken fired first, and the man at the machine gun disappeared into the interior of the helicopter, knocked back by the bullet. The second soldier with an automatic crumbled straight to the floor, falling half-in and half-out of the copter.

The pilot veered off quickly, heading out over the canopy of trees to get away from the sharpshooters.

Jack helped Briony to her feet. "Are you all right?"

"I need to rest."

He glanced at his brother. Ken shook his head.

Jack handed her the canteen. "We can rest in a few minutes, in a place with more cover. Can you make it a few more miles, baby? We'll slow down and take a few minutes along the way, but we need to get into dense cover. If you don't think you can, we'll find a place to make a stand."

"I'm just worried." Briony rubbed her hand over her stomach. "I don't want to lose them."

Jack placed his hand over hers. "We're not losing the babies, Briony. They're tough, just like we are. They'll hang in there and trust us to get them to safety."

She touched his face, a light brush of her fingertips, but Jack felt it all the way to his toes. His stomach knotted and his heart did some sort of curious melting thing he didn't want to identify too closely. He glanced at his brother helplessly.

*Damn it, Ken. I'm so fucking in love with her. This isn't part of Whitney's experiment; he couldn't make me feel like this no matter what he planted between us.*

*I could have told you that. You've got it bad, bro. She's going to wrap you around her little finger, and you're going to make a bigger jackass of yourself than normal.*

Jack sent Ken a repressing glare, but it didn't stop the grin spreading across his twin's face. "Let's go. The helicopter is circling back."

Briony nodded and fell into step beside him. Jack still pushed their speed, but he'd slowed it enough that she could keep up, forcing one foot in front of the other, counting her steps to keep her mind away from the pain flashing through her side and head.

Sporadic shooting left them in no doubt they were being followed, but the twins' confidence never wavered. They moved through the forest as if it were their backyard, taking narrow animal trails, once walking behind a small waterfall. They climbed up boulders and sprinted over bare ground back into the protective canopy of the trees.

By late afternoon, Briony's legs felt rubbery. She didn't even try to think anymore, clinging only to the fact that they had to get away and their enemies seemed tenacious.

Jack slowed and came to a halt right on the edge of what appeared to be open meadow. Up ahead she could see a canyon, the sides steep, a ravine sloping down into thick brush, and the mountain rising with sheer walls on three sides.

"Jack, we can't cross in the open, and if we do go in there, how can we get out?"

He pulled off his pack and switched weapons. "This is the canyon I told you about. We'll make it out."

"Even if we could climb those walls, they have a helicopter," she protested.

"Have a little faith, baby," Jack said. "Rest for a few minutes. When we run across the meadow, you're going to be running full out, so be ready. Once we're in the canyon, no one's going to see us, the brush is too thick. We'll be able to stop and sleep for a while. We'll be climbing up to the pass at night."

Briony studied the sheer cliffs rising above

the canyon. They didn't look like anything she wanted to climb, but both Jack and Ken seemed certain. Her mouth went dry just looking at the distance. Even with enhanced speed, the helicopter could be on her in seconds.

Jack caught her face in his hand, forcing her to look at him. "You have any sight at all in that eye?"

"No. It's too swollen." She didn't want to do this. Jack was looking at her as if he had complete faith that she could sprint across the meadow in the face of the enemy, but she was tired, sick, and — truthfully — scared to death.

"I need you to do this, baby. Look at me. Look me in the eyes." When she complied, he traced her soft cheek with his thumb. "I would never let anything happen to you. You came to me believing I'd protect you, and I will."

The helicopter circled above them, a hovering menace she couldn't ignore. She wanted to scream that it was different, that this time he was asking her to bet her life — the lives of her children — but she knew she'd been doing that all along. She had to make a decision and put herself fully in his hands. Briony took a deep breath and nodded. "I can run. You tell me where, and one eye is all I need."

"That's my girl." He bent down to press a kiss to the corner of her mouth. "Tell me when, Briony."

He gave her confidence. And he made her feel safe. She rested her head against his chest, just leaned against him as if it was the most natural thing in the world to do to another human being — something she couldn't do with her own mother. There was no flash of pain, no distress at all, just a feeling of tranquility in the midst of chaos. The throbbing in her face lessened, as did the pain in her side.

Jack wrapped his arms around her, rifle and all, holding her close to him. He brushed several kisses into her hair. "We'll get out of this."

"I'm sure we will." Briony pressed close to him, absorbing his strength and confidence. "Tell me where I'm supposed to run."

"You go straight across the meadow to that log on the far side, the one close to the straggly tree surrounded by boulders. You see the log I'm talking about?"

She nodded. It looked a long way from them. The meadow was a wide expanse of grasses, flowers, and rocks, and seemed endless. With the helicopter circling overhead, she wasn't certain just how Jack thought they'd make it into the canyon.

"Slide under the log, you'll disappear from view into the scrub. We've got a trail there. You can start down the trail. We'll be right behind you." Jack caught her chin and tilted her head up to his. "Trust me, baby. I swear, I won't let anything happen to you."

"You just swear you both will be right behind me."

Jack kissed her mouth, gently. Tenderly. Wondering how the hell he'd managed to find her. "We'll be right behind you," he assured. He looked at his brother.

Jack and Ken stepped out of the trees, rifles to their shoulders, Ken's aimed at the helicopter, Jack's toward something in the meadow. They fired simultaneously. The helicopter lurched, and in the meadow a canister exploded, sending black smoke rising into the air. They fired a second time, and a second canister sent clouds of smoke billowing and spreading out. Ken's shot sent the helicopter into a spin.

"Go, Briony," Jack instructed. "Run, but don't breathe in. I'll be right with you."

She took off like a jackrabbit, bursting out of the trees into the safety of the smoke.

# CHAPTER 18

Briony heard another volley of shots and increased her speed, until she was in the very center of the smoke. Visibility went to zero, but she'd mapped out the steps in her mind, holding her course as straight as she could from memory. All the while she held her breath, but couldn't prevent her eyes from burning and tearing.

She heard Jack swear and another shot rang out. Red orange flames erupted to her left and black clouds swarmed around her. She winced each time Jack fired and the canisters leapt into the air, exploding into walls of flames and quickly turning to more smoke. It was everywhere now, thick and impenetrable, a great hiding place, but she couldn't breathe or see and was beginning to become disoriented.

Out of the gray swirling vapor a huge downed tree trunk loomed up, nearly hitting her in the stomach. At the last moment she managed to slip under it, landing hard on her bottom and sliding beneath the narrow archway of brambles forming a tunnel over her head. She crawled fast, moving quickly past the entrance to the canyon, staying close to the ground, where there was less of the dark smoke. She gulped fresh air, drawing it into her burning lungs, trying to wipe at her good eye in order to clear her vision.

Brambles caught in her hair, halting her forward progress, dragging her head back, and pulling at her scalp painfully. She reached back to free herself, and the stickers pricked her fingers and palm. The black smoke closed in around her like a wall, the brambles like the bars of a cage, until claustrophobia enveloped her.

*Jack!*

*I'm here, baby. Don't panic on me. We're almost clear. Keep moving. Follow the trail all the way in. You'll come to the camp. Ken and I need to cover the back trail and set a few surprises for anyone following us.*

Just hearing his voice stopped the rising fear. Briony kept crawling. The tunnel widened a bit, but still the thorns caught on her clothes, tearing at her skin like claws. Behind her, there were more shots, and she touched the weapon inside the waistband of her jeans to assure herself it was there.

"I'm right behind you," Ken said, his voice startling her. With the explosions and concentrating on racing through the brambles, she hadn't realized he was so close.

"Where's Jack?"

"Jack likes to play with explosives. He's enjoying himself at the moment. Keep moving. We're almost out of here."

"I can hear the helicopter. It sounds funny."

"I wounded it. Darn thing lurched to one side and spoiled my shot. I'll never hear the end of it from Jack."

"Could you tell if Luther was in the helicopter?" She asked anxiously.

"I didn't spot him, but then Jack shot him, so he's probably getting medical attention. Wait." Ken put a hand on her shoulder and fell silent.

Briony held her breath to keep from making noise while he listened intently. Small sounds penetrated the tunnel of brambles — the scampering of a lizard across the rock, the hum of bees nearby, the call of a bird, and the chattering of a squirrel in the distance.

"We just have to crawl for a couple of minutes and you'll come to a solid wall of bushes. It isn't easy to move the tangle of brush out of the way, because it's all stickers. If you can let me slide by you . . ."

"Are you nuts? There's no room for sliding by me. I can get it open."

"And then when Jack finds you all cut up to hell, he's going to get nasty with me. Have you noticed when it comes to you he has a protective streak a mile wide?"

Her laughter was muffled. "I noticed he has a protective streak for just about everyone. He just doesn't seem to realize it." She glanced at him over her shoulder, grateful they were away from the billowing clouds of smoke. "You're always watching out for him, aren't you?"

Ken shrugged. "I can handle certain things better than he can — and he's got my back on other stuff, so it all works out."

*And right at this moment, Ken, you're protecting what I hold most dear. I'll never be able to repay you for what you've done this day.*

*Shut the hell up, you're going to make me cry.* Ken sent it back with sarcasm, but the truth was, the naked emotion in Jack's mind was enough to make tears burn behind his eyes.

As Briony came up on what appeared to be a giant tangle of blackberry bushes, it suddenly occurred to her that Ken wasn't comfortable around others any more than Jack was, but for his brother's sake he pushed himself to deal with the everyday things in life.

She sent him a brief smile. "You drag him to the bar just to keep him civil, don't you?"

"He'd live in a cave if I didn't," Ken said. *And you would too,* including his brother in the conversation.

She studied his face. "So would you."

He flashed a faint grin, but it never reached his eyes, and faded immediately. "I'm not all that different from Jack. I've got my father in me too. I know Jack told you about him. We both have to live with what we might become given the right circumstances, and we both work hard at avoiding any situation that could bring him out in us."

"He isn't in you, Ken."

"Yes he is. I feel him there, crouched like a monster just waiting for me to let him out. Jack may have been the one to kill him, but I would have done it had I been able to. I attacked him with the bat when he was beating my mother's dead body. He took it away and broke my arms."

"It was self-defense. We all have a right to protect ourselves. I don't see how either of you can possibly equate who you are with that man. Both of you have been nothing but kind to me, protective of me."

"Jack is quite capable of violence, and so am I."

She shook her head. "That's not exactly a news flash, Ken. I am too. Most people are, given the right circumstances. Both of you have a much skewed view of who you really are. I'd take either of you over most people any day of the week."

"That's only because we're saving your butt right now, not bossing you around." He handed her a pair of gloves. "Put those on, they'll help."

"Thanks. You know, Ken, men can't boss women unless we let them. I let Jack take the lead because I want to learn from him. He knows how to survive, and he can teach me, and that will help me keep the children safe, but trust me, I've always been the type to do pretty much what I wanted to do and damn the consequences. My brothers were always lulled into a false sense of security because I went along with most of what they wanted. If something isn't that important to me one way or the other" — she shrugged — "if it's important to the other person, why not let them have their way?"

"Is that why you were performing in

public when it caused you pain?"

"No, silly, I did that because I love my family. Do you go to the grocery store and deal with the woodshops when you'd rather pull out your fingernails one by one?"

"Point taken."

Briony caught the edges of two strands of thick tangled vines looping toward her and dragged them to her right. "I've never been fond of berry bushes."

"Making an opening can be particularly uncomfortable if a bear happens to be having a little snack."

"Thanks for the warning."

"I did offer to be manly and go out first."

"Yes, you did. Thankfully I don't smell a bear close by, although I think your brother is coming up behind us fast."

*You must stink. Briony can smell you already,* Ken informed his brother.

*Pure aphrodisiac,* Jack sent back.

Jack slithered through the tunnel at top speed, wanting to get back to Briony. He'd felt such a burst of love — of pride and admiration — when she'd made the decision to trust him with her life. He'd felt humbled by her faith in him, by the love he saw in her eyes right before she turned and ran into an open field filled with smoke.

He needed to get to her to clean the

laceration in her side. The last thing she needed was an infection, and with the wound open she could easily get one. Mostly he wanted to find a place to take shelter and let her rest. He had told her the babies would be fine, but he wasn't so certain. He hadn't had a chance to read the entire book on pregnancy, and he was worried.

Briony parted the brambles and stepped out cautiously. Black smoke drifted by and curled around the tops of bushes and scrub trees. Ken moved up in front of her, his gun ready, eyes quartering the area around them with methodical patience. Behind them, Jack did the same thing.

"Follow Ken, baby. He'll lead you through the brush. Not too far from here we've got a small camp set up. You can rest there until nightfall."

"You don't think they'll come after us?"

"That's the idea. They'll think we're trapped here, and sooner or later they'll make their move."

"I need to find Luther, Jack. He can lead us back to Mari."

"You're absolutely certain you have a sister? Whitney might be just as capable of planting memories as taking them away."

Briony reached for him, mind to mind,

trying to make him feel what she felt — the emptiness, the joy of discovery, the sound of two voices mingling together. Jack and Ken had used telepathy — so had Briony and Mari.

"Try it. Try now," Jack suggested. He took her arm as they walked into a shallow stream. "The rocks are brutal, here, Briony. Watch your step."

Briony concentrated on remembering her sister — how it felt to be with her, to see her and interact with her, to be close to her. She felt the rocks sharp and slippery beneath her feet and the cold water seeping into her shoes, but her mind was already stretching, reaching for Mari. *Where are you? I can't find you. Do you know me — remember me? Mari. Answer me.*

Silence. Emptiness. Briony pressed a hand to her aching heart. "I can't reach her, Jack."

"Then we know she isn't somewhere close by," he answered.

His usual calm steadied her. "She's probably here in the States, though, right?"

"It won't be hard to trace Luther. If he flew in or out of the country at any point, we should be able to find a starting point. If he attacked you in Italy, he had to fly home and report to someone."

"I don't think Whitney is in the States. I

would get sick and Mom would call a number and Dr. Sparks would be there in a day. Sometimes within hours. Kadan told me Whitney has several private jets able to land at military bases around the world. If he has that kind of clout, he could easily smuggle someone out of one country and into another," Briony protested. "If these jets are used to bring prisoners from one place to another without the world knowing, Whitney could certainly get Luther in and out of the United States with no problem." She placed both hands protectively over her stomach. "He could take me out of the country."

"Not a chance, little darlin'," Ken said. "The United States was Whitney's stomping ground. He has friends in high places, and he certainly uses CIA tactics to run covert operations. He's embedded deep here, and yes, he may have places overseas, but he's going to want to stay right where he knows he has help — and that's the United States."

"How can we trust anyone?" Briony asked. "In the file Kadan gave me, there was an entire section on corporations that were fronts, and jets and military bases around the world, and hidden laboratories. You know he's got to have help. He isn't alone in this. He's creating an army of supersoldiers for someone."

Jack helped her over a particularly large set of rocks, up onto the embankment. "Don't sound so scared, Briony. He isn't going to get you."

"He has my sister."

"We'll find her. I've got a few friends I trust," Jack said, glancing at Ken over her head. *Is that true anymore? Who can we trust?*

*We trust each other and the members of our team — because that's all we have, Jack. They're in this with us. If we're expendable, they're expendable.*

Ken cleared his throat. "We're going on the assumption your sister — if she really exists — wants out. Whitney's managed to get quite a few men working for him and they appear fanatical. Is it possible she wants to be exactly where she is?"

"Luther said it wasn't necessary for the woman to agree. I think Whitney wants to see how far she'll go to fight him — and how far his supersoldier walking sperm banks will go to keep her." She touched her cheek. "Luther went from being gentle with me, talking reasonable, to flashes of jealousy and anger. No, I don't think she wants to be there, Ken. I think she's being held prisoner and they're hurting her to get her cooperation. I want to find her."

"We'll find her, Briony," Jack assured her.

They followed a faint deer path into a thick grove of trees. The branches overhead intertwined to form a thick canopy, providing shade and a refuge against the helicopter searching methodically above them. Jack went directly over to several thick ferns and pushed the leaves back, feeling along the ground until he found a rope.

The trapdoor opened to reveal a pit wide enough to accommodate supplies. He pulled out a heavy crate and set it to one side. Beneath it was a second one.

"Good grief. Are you planning on staying awhile?"

"We like comfort," Ken explained. "All the amenities of home. It's called being prepared, little sister. Better to stash a few supplies here and there than get caught with your pants down."

Jack spread out a groundsheet and tossed a sleeping bag on it, gesturing for Briony to sit down. "Everything but the baby book. Next time, we'll think to include things like that in all our caches, so if we lose one, we'll have another."

"You've got to be kidding."

"He's not," Ken said. "He's always got

books to read. I'm a music man myself."

She sat in the shade watching the two men set up a lethal field around the small camp. They seemed to have thought of everything. They had several small tabs to use should they need warmth, as well as supplies to eat. Mostly, she noticed, they had ammunition, guns, and explosives.

"Lay back, baby. Let me take care of that wound on your hip," Jack instructed. He heated up water using one of the field tabs. Crouching beside her, he pushed up her shirt and indicated she shove down her jeans enough to give him room to work.

"It doesn't hurt as bad now that we're not running," she told him.

"You're covered in blood."

"I was running. It was bound to bleed a lot. I didn't stick anything important," she said. "I was very careful."

He removed the blood-soaked gauze and peered closely at the small stitches. "Not a bad job, but a little uneven. You did better on me."

"Not a bad job?" She squeaked the words, glaring at him. "I sewed it up myself, thank you very much."

Ken burst out laughing. "He said the same thing to me once."

Briony winced as Jack cleaned the wound

again with the hot water and antiseptic. It burned and stung enough to bring tears to her eyes. "Where were you? How'd you get hurt?"

"Afghanistan," Ken said. "There's a ten-thousand-foot ridge known as the Whale's Back on the west side of a valley, and on the east the Shah-e-Kot mountains rise above, with the enemy sitting up around ten to twelve thousand feet, using everything from small arms, to mortar and heavy machine guns. The infantry was caught in the valley humping over bare ground with heavy gear and no cover. The enemy had all the advantages, sending heavy fire from very defensible positions, inflicting heavy casualities on the infantrymen."

"When you say infantry, aren't you talking a lot of troops?"

Ken shrugged. "I think a couple of battalions. They were chasing the resistance into the mountains in an attempt to mop up after the battle. We were sent in to provide additional defense for the troops."

"Ow!" Briony slapped at Jack's hand as he poured liquid over the wound. It burned even worse than the first brew he'd used.

"Stop being a baby," Jack murmured. "You sound just like Ken."

"I take it the situation got bad," Briony

prompted, gritting her teeth. Her side hurt worse than when she was running. The talk distracted her, and in any case, she liked catching glimpses into their world.

Jack pressed fresh gauze to the wound. "It went to hell very fast. The two battalions were taking heavy casualties and were pinned down. Six of us went in to try to clear out the enemy and get our men out of there. The enemy had them right where they wanted them."

"How did Ken get hurt?"

"I think he has ADD," Jack said. "He can't stay still."

Briony laughed, in spite of the fact that he was taping the gauze in place and the wound still burned from the double dose of disinfectant. She knew Ken could remain still for hours.

"You laugh," Jack said, "but it's the truth. We hooked up with the Airborne's brigade, and the enemy was throwing everything at us but the kitchen sink. We moved up to a better vantage point and began picking them off, but as soon as we got rid of one, another would take his place. The fighting went on so long we were running low on ammunition. We'd cached our gear below and Ken decided he'd just take a little run across the bare valley and up to a ridge about another one hundred meters and collect it for us. You, know, a little stroll through the park."

"And you sat up there and protected him while he did it," Briony guessed.

"Hell, someone had to. He's a maniac. He took a grenade launcher with him and made the run back and forth through heavy fire at over eleven thousand feet. The air's pretty thin, but not only did he drag our gear and ammo back, but he took out a nest of al-Qaeda hidden in a streambed firing mortars at us. Just as he came up over the ridge, I caught the edge of tree cancer just above us and knew a sniper had set up."

"What's tree cancer?"

"Snipers set up, and sometimes you catch the edge of their blind. It looks like a growth on the trunk, so we refer to it as cancer."

"Okay, I get it. So what happened after you spotted him?"

"I took out the shooter, but he got off a round and nailed Ken."

"He failed to mention the only reason I was able to make the run and live was because he took out anyone trying to cap my ass," Ken said.

"You do something like that again and I'll shoot you myself." Briony caught the rough affection and the fear for his brother swirling in Jack's mind, but as always his voice was calm and matter-of-fact.

"I picked up a pretty medal," Ken pointed out.

"You nearly picked it up after we buried you." Jack soaked a cloth in the warm water and pressed it gently to Briony's face. "Ken insisted on sewing up his wound, although he let me dig the bullet out of him."

"Precisely why you weren't sewing me up, you sadistic bastard. It hurt like hell."

Jack threw him a sleeping bag. "It's going to be a long night. I'll take first watch while you get some sleep."

Briony waited until Ken settled down a few yards from them before touching the tattoo on Jack's arm. "You, Ken, and Kadan all have the same tattoos. What are they?"

Jack studied the crest on his arm and the symbol. "Only GhostWalkers wear these tattoos. This is the GhostWalker crest. The globe represents the world, which basically is our hunting ground. We're responsible for protecting those who can't protect themselves. The keys signify our various missions, to walk unseen in enemy camps and collect the necessary information, and the knives are, of course, a silent kill. The Latin — *nox noctis est nostri* — means 'the night is ours,' which it is. The GhostWalkers own the night."

"And the other one?"

"The symbols put together have meaning. The triangle signifies shadow; this is the Greek letter for psi; this is protection against evil forces; and the last is the qualities of a knight. So basically the meaning is — shadow knights protect against evil forces using psychic powers, courage, and honor. We have a creed as well. It means something to us and we live by it."

"I like the tattoos, and I think it's especially cool that you use ink that requires special vision to even see them."

"You're a GhostWalker, Briony. You're more than entitled to wear them."

"Well, I might just get one — after I have the babies." She frowned. "Why did your team leave you behind in the enemy camp, Jack? You were wounded."

"I went in to get Ken out. I told them to leave and I knew they'd come back for me. The GhostWalker team mounted two strikes against Ekabela, but I was moved before they hit the camp, both times. They were planning another attack and would have kept doing so until they either found my body or got me out alive."

"You mean Ken would have."

"No, I mean all of them would have, orders or not." He grinned at her. "But Ken would have been leading the pack."

She flashed a small answering smile. "I really like your brother. He's a good man. He worries about it too, you know, about being like your father. He doesn't like being around people any more than you do."

"He's the best man I know, Briony, and he sure as hell isn't like our father."

"You look at me as if I'm your equal, Jack — your partner. Luther looked at me as if I was his possession. You're nothing like your father, Jack. Nothing at all — and neither is Ken. If we don't get out of this, I want you to know I'm not sorry for one minute I've been able to have with you."

He groaned softly. "That's a hell of thing for you to say with my brother only a few feet away."

She laid her head on his shoulder. "It wasn't meant to be sexual, you nut; I was being emotional."

"Just looking at you is sexual, let alone you saying something like that."

"Shut the hell up, Jack," Ken said without opening his eyes. "I feel like I'm at a porn movie. It's just wrong."

Briony laughed. "Are you both really going to go to sleep? Aren't we surrounded?"

"Ken is; he should be asleep already," Jack said. "We'll take turns. If the troops try to move into the canyon, we'll know. I'll just mosey on up to the top of that ridge and discourage them. They'll most likely wait until nightfall — just like we're waiting."

Briony stared up at the heavy canopy of branches and leaves. The air was cool and the last of the smoke had drifted away. They could have been out camping instead of hiding from a lethal military group. Neither man seemed stressed at all. Within a matter of minutes, she was certain Ken had actually gone to sleep.

Jack's hand found hers, tangling their fingers together. "You always want to conserve energy if possible, baby," he advised, bringing her hand to his mouth. His teeth nipped her finger. "You'll learn. If you can, go to sleep." He pulled a light blanket over her body to protect her from the colder temperatures.

"Talk to me. Tell me about you and Ken. How old were you when you lost your mother?" She didn't want to say *killed your father,* but somehow the words were there between them.

"Nine. We were nine years old."

"What happened to you?"

"They took us both to the hospital and

then tried various foster homes. Sometimes they split us up, but it was never a good idea. We'd break out and each track the other down. If either of us was mistreated, there was always retaliation. We spent a lot of time on the streets. Eventually, after earning a bad reputation, no one would take us, so for a while we were in a state-run home. That didn't work out very well either."

"I can imagine."

"Neither of us is very good following rules. Somewhere along the line we met Miss Judith."

"Miss Judith?" There was a wealth of affection in Jack's voice.

"She would come to the home as a volunteer and was the only person Ken and I would listen to. There was something about her, something very distinct and real. She genuinely wanted to help — she cared. Eventually she fostered us. We were nearly seventeen then, and twice her size, but she took us in against the advice of all the other workers. She had a ranch up in the hills and she gave us plenty of room to run free. In return, we excelled in schoolwork." He grinned at her. "Notice I didn't say anything about school. She took over our education and homeschooled us because no regular school wanted anything to do with us. We worked hard for her, and she gave us our first real taste of a home."

"Is she still alive?"

Jack hesitated. "Yes. But we don't let anyone know that. She could become . . ."

Briony lifted her head and narrowed her eyes at him. "A liability?"

Jack groaned. "I'm never going to live that down, am I? And no, Miss Judith needs protection so anyone coming after us won't be able to use our feelings for her against us. I don't want her vulnerable."

"Did you fake her death?" Briony asked curiously.

"Too easily disproved. No, we simply manufactured a very heated public argument and she disowned us. After several months she moved to another state and then, a year later, returned to her hometown, back to her family ranch. We're never seen near the place and she certainly doesn't come here. We never call her, so there is never a paper trail to follow. Most people have forgotten we were ever with her."

"I see." Briony frowned and turned her face up to the sky. "What about me, Jack — and the babies? What are we going to do after they're born?"

"You're going to marry me before they're born, and we're going to live together right here on this mountain. Ken will help me protect you and the kids, and we'll be fine. I think I can send a loud enough message to any enemy that if they dared mess with my family, I'd never stop until they were dead."

"I wouldn't want you to do that, Jack. Revenge isn't the way to live life," Briony said gently.

He tunneled his fingers in her hair. "You're not going to change who — or what — I am, baby. Ken and I tried that a long time ago. We know what we can and can't live with. No one is going to take you away from me."

She was silent for a long time, staring up at the clouds, her swollen eye watering and aching, but the fire in her side was slowly going away. She rubbed her hand over her stomach soothingly. "I've changed your life so much already, Jack."

"That's a good thing, Briony."

"And Ken said I can't marry you."

Jack felt his heart jump in his chest. He glanced at his sleeping brother. "Did he say why?"

"Yes." She kept her voice sober. "He said you have to ask me properly."

Relief made him weak. His pulse beat at his temples, throbbed in his neck. For one moment his fingers closed in her hair in a tight fist. "Properly? If I ask, you might say no, so I'm thinking we'll just start off right and I'll tell you and we'll get the thing done."

"Get the thing done?" Briony echoed.

Ken snorted aloud. "Jack, I'll take over watch and you get some sleep. I think you fried your brain up there on the roof."

"Pipe down over there," Jack said. "You're already stirring up trouble."

"Get the thing done?" Briony repeated slowly. "The thing being what exactly?"

"The ceremony. The paperwork. Whatever the hell it takes to make it legal."

Briony sat up and glared at him. "Take your 'it' and shove it, Jack."

"There's no need to be getting upset, Briony. We can't exactly go around with a bunch of kids and not do whatever the hell it is one does to make it legal."

"Whatever the hell it takes to make *what* legal?"

He shrugged. "How the hell would I know? I've never done this before. Sleeping together I guess."

"So you're going to marry me so it's legal to sleep with me?"

"This isn't coming out right."

"You think?"

"Don't get upset, baby. I don't understand why you're getting upset."

"Don't you 'baby' me, Jack," she said, narrowing her eyes in warning. "Marriage might not be anything but a ceremony to you, but to me it's something sacred. And you don't have to worry, I'm not about to insist on marriage. I told you from the beginning I'm quite capable of raising a child by myself."

"We're not having one child, Briony," he pointed out. "We're having two. I guess that means you need me whether you like it or not."

"I guess you're not getting it, Jack. I have no intention of marrying you." She half sat, glaring at him.

He raised an eyebrow. "Really? What are we going to tell all of our children? I don't think we'll be stopping at two, do you?"

Briony couldn't help the sudden urge to laugh. Jack was impossible — would always be impossible. She leaned over and kissed the corner of his mouth. "Two is already scaring the hell out of me. I don't think we'll be talking about having more for a long, long time. Do you have any idea how small a baby actually is, Jack? Have you ever held one?"

"Nope. But I'm sure we can manage.

There's bound to be a book on the subject somewhere. And don't think we're finished talking about the marriage thing."

"We're definitely finished."

She shivered beneath the thin blanket, and Jack reached out to pull her tight against the warmth of his body. "Come here. You're going to get chilled if you don't stay close to me," he said invitingly. His hands slid up and down her arms to rub heat into her.

Ken rose and caught up his rifle. "I'm going to do a little recon while you catch some shut-eye, Jack."

*Be careful bro. They'll have a sniper in the trees trying to catch a glimpse of one of us walking around.*

*Like I don't know that. I think it best to give you a chance to redeem yourself. You're such a jackass, and you can grovel better if I'm not around.* Ken flashed a grin at his brother and stalked off into heavier brush, back in the direction they'd come.

"Is he going to be all right?"

"He's giving us a little privacy." Jack turned onto his side, propping his head up with his hand to stare down at her face. "He thinks I'm making a jackass of myself."

"He's right."

"I know. I know it's too soon, Briony. There's no way you could fall in love with

562

me this fast, but I know how I feel about you. It has nothing to do with Whitney or pheromones or experiments. When I'm with you, I feel different — alive — happy — hell, even peaceful — even though you argue half the time."

"I don't argue."

He smiled at her, his free hand sliding down her throat in a gentle caress to trace the swell of her breasts. "You make me happy, Briony. It doesn't seem to matter where we are or what kind of hell we're walking into, when I'm with you, there's something inside of me that lights up. Tell me why you don't want to marry me."

Briony stared up at his face, so masculine — rough and weathered, with lines etched deep; his gray eyes that could ice up or go hot like the sun. He wasn't a man who smiled often, but he was a man who took care of his own. She traced those lines with her fingertips. Emotion swept over her, shaking her, setting her pulse racing and her stomach fluttering. "I didn't say I didn't want to marry you, Jack Norton, only that you hadn't asked me properly."

The look on her face — in her eyes — set his heart pounding. No one had ever looked at him like that before. He could wake up to that look every morning. He shifted his weight again so he could frame her face with his hands, wincing a little as his thigh connected with the groundsheet. "You ever heard of a book on this crap, because I'm going to need something."

Briony groaned and rolled onto her back, laughing helplessly. "You're hopeless, Jack. Hopeless."

"I love you, woman. What more is there to say?" Her laughter affected him more than he thought possible. To keep the overwhelming emotion at bay, he bent his head to hers and took possession of her mouth — a little desperately, a little wildly — mostly lovingly.

# CHAPTER 19

Briony circled Jack's neck with her arms and closed her eyes, opening her mouth to his, matching the fire in his kiss with her own. He had calluses on his hands and smelled of guns. She liked the roughness against her skin and knew that, no matter the danger, he would protect her and her children.

"You make me feel safe when you hold me, Jack," Briony confided. "I've always been so afraid, but even now, surrounded by our enemies, you make me feel safe." She murmured the words against the warmth of his mouth, kissed his chin and the small crow's feet around his eyes — not laugh lines, but from squinting in the sun. Grateful that Ken was on guard duty and had left them alone to sleep while waiting for nightfall, she was determined to take advantage of her opportunity alone with Jack.

Jack kissed the tip of her nose, the corners of her mouth, the small indentation in her chin. It seemed an impossibility to be lying there in the Montana grass, in the place he loved, and hold this one woman. And she kept looking at him with love in her eyes. Genuine love.

"You're a fucking miracle, Briony." He kissed her again, and slid his hands down to her stomach, pushing up the material of her blouse so he could cover bare skin with his palm. "I want to feel them move inside of you. A part of you and a part of me. I never imagined having kids or even having a woman of my own. Now that you're here with me, I can't imagine life without you."

She closed her eyes to savor the feel of his hands caressing her stomach. For one moment she thought she felt the flutter of a baby moving inside her, but the movement was so small and brief, she might have imagined it. "Don't say fucking, Jack." The truth was that, in spite of herself, she was becoming fond of that term when he said the things he said about her. "You have to clean up your language for the babies. But just in case you don't know it, I think you're a miracle too. I love you."

He went still — utterly and completely still. Even his breath ceased in his lungs. He waited until she opened her eyes and looked at him. "Don't say that unless you mean it, Briony. I don't want there to be any mistakes."

"There's no mistake. I love you more than anything. I'm happy I'm carrying your children. I love being with you."

"It's remote up here and the road is impassable some of the time. We get snow. You could get lonely."

"I love where you live and the house and all of it."

"Sometimes I'm as mean as a snake. I like my way, baby — maybe too much."

"Are you trying to talk me out of it? I know it snows. I don't get lonely and certainly won't with you, Ken, and two children running around, and if you're mean, I'll see what I can do to soothe you." Her hand slid over his chest, feather-light — suggestive. "And as for getting your way, you probably will most of the time, so when I really want something, of course you'll be more than happy to accommodate me."

"I will?" A slow grin curved his mouth, took a few moments to light his eyes. "I doubt you'll ever have much of a problem getting anything you want from me, but you already know that, don't you?"

"Yes, and you know what I want right this

minute?" She leaned up to brush her lips against his ear. "I want you inside me so bad I can't think straight." Because there was a part of her that feared she might lose him — that this might be the last opportunity they had to be together. "Do you think Ken will stay away long enough to give us time?" She whispered the invitation like a temptress.

*Ken, I need a little time alone with Briony.*

*You think? I'm sitting up here twiddling my thumbs, lover boy. You'd better win her over with your skills cuz you sorely lack in the romance department. You don't want to lose that woman.*

No, Jack definitely didn't want to lose her. He closed himself off to Ken, and kissed her gently. "I've got a hell of a great brother. He's watching our back trail for us."

"Go slow, Jack. I need you to go slow." She wanted to feel loved, wanted to be with him again just in case this was the last time — the only time she had left. It was wrong with poor Ken so close by and accommodating them — she should have felt embarrassed — but she only felt grateful. It wouldn't be long before they'd be fighting for their lives again, and she needed Jack now. "I'm sorry I look such a mess."

"Do you think that matters, Briony? No

one could be more beautiful to me. Swollen eye, bruises — it would never matter. You're a fighter, babe, and you make me proud of you."

He pushed her shirt further up her body, until the underside of her breasts were exposed, fingers stroking soft skin. "When I touch you, I swear, Briony, each time is like nothing I've ever experienced before. I feel like a fool trying to tell you what you mean to me, but I don't want you to ever think you weren't worth the effort for me to try to put the way I feel about you into words."

Jack feathered kisses over her gently rounded belly. Strands of his hair brushed against her breasts, sending shivers of awareness down her spine. Briony didn't know why she found it so erotic to be outside with him, danger surrounding them, and watching his eyes darken with desire and his body grow hard in anticipation. "You'll have to be on top so we don't take any chances hurting you or the babies." He lifted his head to look at her, his gray eyes nearly charcoal. "I'll be so gentle you won't even know it's me."

She couldn't believe how wet and hot she already was just looking at him. His hands cupped her breasts, kneading with exquisite care, rolling her nipple until she gasped, her vision hazing over. Briony's clothes felt too tight, the material scraping against her sensitive skin and impeding his roaming hands. She hastily opened her jeans and sat up to remove her clothes, glancing around to make certain they were concealed by the shrubbery and thick canopy. The angle of the canyon walls helped, and she could see why Jack had picked such a spot to hide while they waited for dark.

Jack had divested himself of clothing as well and reached up and tugged at her wrist until she was sitting on his lap, straddling him. He fisted his hands in her hair to drag her head back, wanting to devour her, his tongue sweeping into her mouth, teeth tugging at her lips, and all the while he deliberately pressed his hard cock against her wet channel. For a moment he sat still, absorbing the feel of her, the scent of her, the miracle of her being with him. He buried his face against her neck to hide the sudden overwhelming emotion he knew was naked on his face.

"Jack?"

He pulled her arms around his neck until her fingers dug into his muscle as he positioned her legs around his waist. She locked her ankles behind his back, opening her body even more to him, and he rocked her back, rubbing his cock deeper into her feminine heat. He could hear his name on her lips forever, that breathy little hesitation, the way love poured through her voice. He deliberately moved again to draw a little moan from her.

Briony gripped his shoulders hard and made a small keening sound, a soft wail of pleasure adding hot flames of excitement licking through his surging blood. Jack kissed her over and over, drowning in her taste, loving the way she responded, giving up her mouth the way she did her body — wholly — unconditionally. He kissed his way down her throat and shoulders, until he found the hot little points of her breasts, already stiff for him. She was so hot and wet already, rocking against him, letting him know how much she wanted him. That alone was an aphrodisiac.

Jack took her breast in his mouth, felt the unbelievable softness, tugged her nipple with his teeth, rolled it with his mouth, and when she cried out, went back to suckling. With each strong pull, he felt her grow hotter and wetter for him. He loved her body's reaction, and his hands began to stroke and caress her shoulders, down her back, to her buttocks, his mouth all the while lavishing attention on her breasts.

Briony flung back her head, arching into the heat of his mouth, nails digging into his shoulders. His slow hands and ravaging mouth sent her body pulsing with such aching need she tried to squirm onto him.

"Stop that," he said sharply and brought his hand down on her bottom, sending an unexpected flare of heat spiraling through her body. "We're taking this slow and easy, remember? Let it build." Because he wanted to stay inside her forever. Jack wanted to hold her to him any way that he could. He had no idea how she'd managed to invade his heart and soul — but she had — and he needed her as surely as he needed the sun to come up in the morning. He wanted forever — and he had only a short time — but every moment was going to count.

The terrible aching need was already built — already raging out of control. Briony felt the tension in her rising, the pressure tightening deep inside, until her body clenched and wept in need. "Jack. We don't have time."

"For this — for us — we have time." He kissed her neck, bit gently at her chin, found her breast again, and sent another shaft of desire curling through her with a strong pull of his hot mouth. Her body rubbing over him — pleading, demanding — hardened his cock into a thick instrument of flesh-and-blood steel.

Briony's hands gripped him harder as he lifted her up and positioned her over his lap. He lowered her until the broad head of his shaft began to force entry, invading her body inch by slow inch. She was soft — so soft it felt like a silken glove gripping him — and hot — so hot he groaned and let gravity help seat her, needing him to be as deep as possible. Her body wrapped him up in silk and velvet, squeezing and clenching so that he gasped with the sheer pleasure of it. He caught her hips and began to move her in a slow, sultry rhythm. "That's it, baby. Just take a nice easy ride."

Straddling her thighs, Jack buried himself deep in her body. Briony wiggled, a small movement, but it pushed him even deeper, pressing him tightly against her clit, so each stroke sent an electrical current racing through her body, straight up to her nipples. A hot streak of excitement filled her as she felt her building climax. She arched back further, lifting her hips to his slow, easy rhythm, but adding a circular motion, watching his eyes, his face, reveling in the mixture of lust and love she saw there.

Her breasts swayed erotically with every thrust of his hips; her nipples brushed Jack's chest to send hot sparks raining over her skin. She began to assert herself as her body wound tighter and tighter, lifting higher, grinding harder, riding him with a faster rhythm. His breath caught in his chest and she took him deeper, increasing the friction, deliberately contracting her muscles around him, drawing a harsh groan from him.

"Son of a bitch, Briony, you're going to kill me before we're through."

She wanted to drive him to swearing. With anyone else it wouldn't have seemed right — or sexy — but with Jack she knew she was pushing his limits and he was letting her. He didn't like giving up control — not even sexually — but he let her set the pace, do what she wanted — maybe needed — to do.

She looked him straight in the eye and smiled, a sultry, sexy smile of sheer bliss. "You know what, Jack? This is *me* — loving you."

His heart jumped in his chest. His cock thickened and jerked in answer.

Her fingertips slid over his face, traced every beloved line. When had he become so necessary to her? She felt love mingling with the terrible cravings of her body, and if it was possible, love for him increased her pleasure even more. She rocked forward and took his mouth, tongue sliding over his lips, teeth teasing and nibbling. His mouth opened, hot and hard and tasting so good. She moaned and wrapped her arms around his neck, all the while rocking and writhing and keeping a steady rhythm designed to drive him as crazy as she could manage.

And then his mouth moved against hers, and he was all at once dominant, hands tightening on her hips, forcing her body into a different, much harder and faster rhythm. She felt the instant flare of excitement — the heat rushing like a fireball through her body to tighten every muscle and heighten her pleasure even more. She tipped her head back in invitation as his mouth wandered down her throat to her breasts, teasing and nipping and driving her insane. She could feel her climax building and building, his mouth and hands and body pushing her closer and closer to the edge. He filled and stretched her, their combined bodies hotter than she'd imagined possible, as he picked up the pace and deliberately pressed into the bundle of sensitive nerves.

Briony bit back a scream and let herself go, muscles clamping down tightly, taking him with her, milking him dry, while her body rippled and quaked with a shocking orgasm. Jack gave a husky groan, as he emptied himself into her and dragged her against his chest to hold her in his arms, while they rocked together, clinging, his face buried in her hair, hers in his shoulder. They stayed that way a long time, just holding each other, while their hearts stopped racing, bodies still one — both feeling at peace.

"We have to get some rest," Jack prompted finally, reluctantly letting his arms slip away. "We have a long night in front of us." He poured water onto a small towel. "Lie back and I'll clean us up. You'll have to get dressed and sleep in your clothes. We'll need to be ready to move."

Briony should have felt embarrassed to have him gently wipe her thighs, but she felt loved and cared for. His eyes remained dark with emotion as they dressed and she lay down beside him, his arm tucking her close to his body, the cover pulled up over them. "Thank you, Jack. I needed to be with you."

His kiss was gentle. "We're going to get out of this. All of us will."

She closed her eyes and drifted off to sleep — reassured by the confidence in his voice and the warmth of his arms.

*Jack.* Ken resisted touching his brother's shoulder, knowing Jack would wake up brandishing a weapon and probably slit his throat. He stayed out of range, crouching low, as his twin sat up, already tracking with a gun. Ken waved the muzzle away from his body. *We're in trouble, bro. I climbed up the pass . . .*

"You did what?" Jack hissed. "Damn it, Ken. That was dangerous."

Immediately Briony stirred and sat up as well, looking from one brother to the other. "What's wrong?"

Ken sank down beside them, rifle cradled in his arms. "Sorry we woke you, Bri, but we're going to have company soon."

"What's going on, Ken?" Jack demanded.

"I got suspicious when the damned helicopter never made any sweeps. Why would they do that? I didn't put it out of commission. They may have wanted me to think I did, but I knew better. So while I was sitting up in the rocks, cooling my heels, I got this idea about Dr. Whitney and his files. Just suppose he managed to find a map of our property and he studied it and knew if we went for this canyon that we had a way up through the pass."

"Son of a bitch," Jack grated.

"So I took a little trip up, and sure enough, we've got company waiting." Ken flipped open his canteen and drank, wiping his mouth with the back of his hand.

"Can we take them?"

"They have the better position and a helicopter, Jack." Ken glanced at Briony, went to speak, and closed his mouth. *They'd kill us for certain.*

"Don't do that," Briony said sharply. "I'm not a child and I don't wilt because it gets rough. I want to know what's wrong." She captured Jack's hard gaze with her own. "Am I a part of this family or not?"

"You know damn well what you are to me," Jack snapped. "The only real way out of the canyon is the pass. We didn't think anyone knew there was a way up. The canyon is a box, and essentially we're trapped here. There wasn't a pass at all until we made one."

"So how did they know?" Ken asked. "No one's been here."

"He guessed. The bastard guessed," Jack said. "He's a fucking genius, and he looked at the map and figured out exactly how we think. The canyon's a natural trap. He knew we'd lead them here, and he put his men up above to sit and wait. We make the climb — it's steep and dangerous and will sap our strength, and they'll shoot us like ducks in a pond."

Briony took a deep breath, inhaling to try to catch the scent of danger. She smelled pine and fir and night air, but not soldiers. The temperature was falling rapidly, as it often did up high in the mountains. She shivered and reached for Jack's pack, pulling out a jacket to wrap around her.

"We'll be fine," Jack assured her.

"I know. I'm just cold." She wasn't certain how true what Jack said was, but she wanted it to be true. Fear was a constant companion, familiar to her and therefore easy to rise above. She shrugged it off and tangled her fingers with Jack's.

"We don't have a lot of choices," Jack said. "If we try the pass, it's tantamount to suicide. Maybe with both Ken and me giving you a lead, protecting you, you might make it, especially if they don't want to kill you."

She shook her head. "I'm staying with you."

"I could protect the two of you," Ken offered. "It makes sense, Jack. You know we have to get her out. It comes down to who's more important. Briony is carrying the babies. I'll lie up on the pass with the rifle . . ."

"The hell with that. We go together or not at all," Jack snapped. "If you think I'd run when they were gunning for you, Ken, you don't know me very well."

Briony shook her head violently. "I'm with Jack. Absolutely not."

"It was an idea."

"A stupid one."

"What about going back?" Briony interrupted, her fingers digging into Jack's palm. "We could go down the mountain — get some help."

Ken shook his head. "No way. They have us boxed in with heavy artillery."

"We stand a chance if we try to hold out right here and wait for reinforcements to arrive," Jack said. "We can radio the team and they'll move as quickly as possible."

"Twenty-four hours at the most. Twelve probably. If we're lucky they could be here by morning. We have the ammunition. We might do it," Ken agreed. "We've got enough C4 and you've already rigged some wires. It might be our best shot, Jack."

"What's wrong with the idea?" Briony asked. "Neither of you like it much."

"They can just as easily bring in reinforcements too," Jack replied. "Whitney has access to much more sophisticated equipment if we stay too long. We can't give him that kind of time — not unless we have no other choice."

There was a small silence. Ken sighed. "I'll climb up as high as possible and see if

I can get a clear enough signal to call for help."

"Wait." Briony held up her hand. "You have to climb the cliff anyway to get a signal? Isn't that dangerous?"

"We have no choice," Jack explained. "We're in a canyon, baby. We can't call a dog, let alone our team."

"If there's a way for Ken to climb the cliff and get high enough to call out, why can't we scale the cliffs and get out of here? We're all strong," Briony ventured.

Again there was a small silence, the men exchanging a long look.

"Maybe," Jack said thoughtfully. "With you pregnant, that's probably the last thing he'd expect."

Ken rubbed a scar on his left cheek as he frowned. "We tried the northern face that time, Jack. It has fingers and toeholds, some crevices we could maybe use, but most are a good fifteen feet apart. It would be tricky, especially in the dark."

Jack glanced up at the sky. "How much of a moon do we have?"

"Fairly decent. More than half. The night's clear." Ken turned his head to study the sheer, rising cliff. *She'll never make it, Jack. She's strong, but she's pregnant.*

Briony knew they were talking about her

in private. She pulled her hand away from Jack. "I'm a flyer, a high-wire performer and a darned good one at that. There isn't much I can't do."

"You don't like heights," Jack reminded her. "It's all right, Bri, we can hold out here."

"I don't like a lot of things, Jack, but it's never stopped me before. If I wasn't with you, what would you do?" she challenged.

"You are with us, so it doesn't matter."

"It matters to *me.* I don't want to sit here and wait for them if we have a chance to get out. I can handle heights as well or better than either one of you. Don't sell me short because I'm pregnant — or worse, because I'm a woman."

"We can't climb in the conventional manner, Briony," Jack explained. "We have to become a human ladder, one anchors while the other swings him like a pendulum and throws him up to the next hold. It's difficult and dangerous."

"So is staying here. Would you do it if I wasn't here? Tell the truth."

"We'd already be gone," Jack said.

"That's it then." Briony kicked aside the blanket and stood up. "Let's go."

Ken shook his head. "This is how it all starts, bro. She's getting bossy. I've heard women do that. They start out all soft and kittenish, leading a man on, and then the claws come out and they dig in and take over." He stood up, the rifle looking a natural part of him. "You're in for trouble, Jack."

"Probably," Jack agreed, pride and respect for her in his voice. "Let's get moving." He flashed her a small, approving grin.

Jack reached down to roll the sleeping bag, and an explosion rocked the night, shaking the ground, a huge red and orange ball churning with black smoke blasting upward and outward like a violent mushroom cloud. Birds screeched, taking to the skies, and the world seemed to be in chaos.

"They're coming for us," Jack said.

Both men calmly shouldered their gear and indicated to Briony to walk between them in single file, Ken leading the way. As the smoke and flash faded, the night once again turned eerily silent.

Jack handed Briony a gun and a knife, which she slipped into her belt as she walked behind Ken. The men made little noise, and she tried to do the same. There was enough moonlight to see their surroundings. There was no trail, not even a deer trail, but Ken seemed to know exactly where he was going.

Briony walked with them, trying to analyze why, when she was in the middle of an extremely dangerous situation, she wasn't nearly as afraid as normal. Oh, the adrenaline was running and her pulse was racing, but it wasn't debilitating like fear almost always was on the onset. She didn't have to force herself under control; she just walked between the brothers, trying to emulate their heightened awareness. It wasn't even the fact that the two men kept her from feeling the effects of the violence surrounding them, or from the battles they'd already fought.

Confidence. They exuded complete confidence. It was in the set of their shoulders, the way they moved with fluid, easy strides, the easy camaraderie between them, and the fact that they simply worked so well together. She glanced at Jack over her shoulder as she walked. He wasn't watching the ground, but all around them, up in the trees, the rising walls of the canyon, and their back trail. She tried to follow his actions, tried to see with her enhanced vision and hear what the night had to tell.

"Remember, baby," Jack whispered softly against her ear as they stopped just under an outcropping that grew a good twenty feet above their heads out of the steeply rising wall. "Sound carries in the night. We'll communicate with telepathy, and when we climb, try to make as little noise as possible. If this is going to work, we have to be ghosts just fading away."

She nodded to let him know she understood. *How do we do this?*

*We jump up to the outcropping and go from there. I'll take the lead and we'll have to use a swinging motion to get the person below up to the next hold. You'll see. It's much like you do on the trapeze. Jeb catches you — here, it will be either Ken or me.* He bent down to look in her eyes. *Are you okay with this? There can't be any hesitation once we start up.*

She took a breath. *You've climbed this before? Successfully?*

Jack pulled her into his arms. *Yes. I wouldn't risk this if we weren't in such a bind, baby, but I wouldn't try it if I didn't think you could handle it.*

That gave her more assurance than anything else he could have said. He had faith in her ability and respected her enough to try a hazardous gamble. She was more than a good flyer — she was a gifted one. She wouldn't let Jack down. Briony stroked her hand over her stomach in a small caress, her knuckles rubbing against Jack. He instantly placed his palm over hers and held her for a moment, his breath warm against her neck.

*This is going to work, Briony.*

*I hate leaving our home.*

*We'll be back someday. We'll have a cleanup crew out here by tomorrow night if Whitney doesn't pack his dead off with him, as I suspect he will. They did some damage to the house, but nothing we can't fix fairly quickly.*

Another explosion shook the earth, sending small rocks rolling down the slope of the ravine to bounce over branches and brush. Light flashed, and someone in the distance screamed hoarsely.

Ken cleared his throat softly to get their attention. *We have to move now, before they make it through all the trip wires. We've only slowed them down, not stopped them.*

*I'm ready,* Briony assured them, and tipped her head back to look at the outcropping.

Jack went first, crouching right below it and leaping. It was an extraordinary distance from a standing jump.

*You need help?* Ken asked.

Briony shook her head, but backed up a few feet to get a running start. She'd never been good at just standing and jumping like Jack had done. She cleared the distance easily and landed beside Jack, who instantly caught her by the arms and hauled her against the rock face. Ken followed them up.

*Get as close to the wall as you can to give me, room, baby.* Jack tied his pack firmly and strapped his rifle down. *Ken, use the radio as soon as we get high enough to make the call. Every minute will count. Make them aware of that. Call in both teams if you have to, but tell them we need an extraction like yesterday. Full combat conditions, tell them to come in hot.*

*Will do. I'll need to be up another thirty or forty feet before trying it.*

Briony watched with her heart in her throat as Jack looked up the sheer cliff face. Before he could react, she caught his hand and tugged, lifting her face to his. This was a life-and-death gamble — a struggle they might not survive — and she wanted him to know how important he was to her.

Jack framed her face and kissed her gently. *We'll get through this.*

*I know.* She poured her trust into her mind. If anyone could keep her safe — it was Jack. She felt his concern for her and smiled. *I can do this, Jack. I know I can.*

He nodded, kissed her a second time, and looked up at the sheer face rising above him, frowning a little. The crevice was to his right, and he had to leap up and jam his arm into the narrow opening. He'd done it once before successfully, but it had been full daylight. He crouched low and sprang, arm outstretched, fist closed tightly.

Beneath him, Ken waited to spot him. If Jack missed and came crashing down, he would only have a sliver of hope to keep him from hitting the ground below the outcropping.

The edges of the jagged rock face ripped and peeled back his skin as Jack slammed his fist hard into the tapered crack. Blood seeped down his arm, and his shoulder nearly snapped as it took the brunt of his full weight. He took a breath to still his rapidly beating heart, and slowly let it out, easing the pain away from his mind while he searched with the toes of his boots for the two-inch ledge he knew was there. It was a relief to find the tiny jutting rock to help take the weight of his body. Insuring his fist would hold tight in the crevice, he glanced down below him, free arm outstretched back toward his family.

*Ready Ken? Briony?*

Briony swallowed. Ready for what? They hadn't told her what they expected yet, but Ken tugged at her arm, drawing her away from the safety of the steep wall. She moistened her suddenly dry lips. *Tell me what to do.*

*Climb up onto Ken's shoulders and crouch to get extra spring. He'll help launch you. You have to hit my wrist, baby, just like your work. I'll catch you.*

One-handed. In the dark. Briony blew out her breath, rubbed one hand soothingly over her rounded tummy, and stepped onto Ken's bent thigh to get to his shoulders. Once in place, it was easy enough to keep her equilibrium. He was strong, his shoulders broad, and she was used to working with balance. She remained in a crouch, judging the distance, waiting for Jack's signal.

*Go.*

Briony burst into the sky, launched by her own powerful leg muscles as well as the extra push from Ken. She flew straight up, arm outstretched, gaze locked on her target. Her palm slapped Jack's wrist, fingers curling tight as he caught her in a viselike grip. *Feel for the ledge with your toes. It's only a couple of inches wide. Reach with your free hand and feel for the crack above your head.* With his enhanced strength, he pulled her up beside him.

Briony stretched her toes and ran her foot

along the wall as far down as she could, feeling along the rock face until she felt the tiny outcropping. She had to maintain her balance as she slid the fingers of her free hand up toward the crevice to find the edge. *I've got it, Jack. You can let go.*

Jack didn't want to let her go. They were thirty-five feet in the air, clinging to the side of a sheer cliff with rocks below. He wanted to shield her body with his, wrap her up in his strength, but it was impossible and Ken was waiting.

A blast sounded closer, and this time the crown of a tree exploded in the distance, shattering the night, the trunk cracking with loud groans before splitting with a grinding sound and falling to the ground.

Jack ignored the orange and red flames and leaned down toward his brother. *Go.*

Ken didn't hesitate, leaping with a smooth, practiced motion and gripping Jack's wrist hard. Instead of finding the ledge and planting his feet for safety, Jack began to swing him back and forth like a giant pendulum.

Briony watched in horror as Jack threw Ken up and over at least ten feet from where she clung to the cliff face. She couldn't tear her gaze away as Ken reached out with both hands, clawing at what appeared to be a smooth surface. His fingertips dug in and held. He hung there for a moment catching his breath, brow pressed against rock as he began to move his feet cautiously, looking for the widening crack where he could place his feet.

*Your turn, Briony.*

Jack's voice was a caress, but a shiver of protest skittered down her spine. *I think I'm going to be sick.*

*Wrong time, baby.* He held out his hand to her. *I'll let you know when you need to release. Ken will be waiting. You've done this kind of thing a million times.*

She glanced back at the tree burning in the distance far below them and squared her shoulders. Jack reached back for her and she told herself she had no choice. They had to get up the cliff if they wanted to survive. She leapt and caught his wrist, kicking out with her legs to help Jack swing her, just as Ken had done. Once in the air, instincts took over and she helped create the arc needed for the flight.

*Go.* The command came and she released, flying toward Ken and the huge expanse of rock. She did a graceful dive, arms outstretched, waiting for the familiar smack of flesh on flesh, the satisfying sting as they came together. Ken caught her wrist in a solid grip and held her for a moment while she caught her breath.

*That was great, Briony. The toehold is just to the left of your foot. Keep feeling for it. You're almost there.* Ken guided her to the safety of the small crevices.

The moment she was secure, she looked back down at Jack, her heart beating too fast. *How are you going to make it without help? It's too far on your own.*

*Ease over to the side to make room between you. I'm coming up.*

She reminded herself he'd done it before, but her mouth was dry and she felt close to panic as he slowly removed his fist from the crack and turned completely outward to face them. Even with the tiny ledge, he maintained his balance, but she could barely breathe with fear for him. She felt concentration in his mind, and in Ken's mind, and then Jack launched himself into the air, crouching precariously and using enhanced calf and thigh muscles to propel him into the air and over toward his brother.

Instinctively, Briony reached for him, using one arm to anchor her body while she stretched the other toward him. Ken was closer and bent back, the fingers of one hand digging into the ledge as the fingers of the other closed like a vise around Jack's wrist. Briony caught Jack's shirt, and they drew him up beside them so that all three pressed tightly against the cliff breathing heavily.

*You ready to do it again?* Jack asked.

Briony tilted her head to look up at the cliff face. It seemed miles away, an impossible task. They were enhanced, but their arms and legs ached with strain, and one tiny misstep would kill them all. Jack nuzzled her neck, leaned in close, and smiled at her, but the darkness hid any light that might have reached his eyes. *Makes you feel alive, doesn't it?*

*Jack. I love you. I do. But you're just a little bit crazy.* And that was the thing. He actually was enjoying himself. *You have ice water in your veins.*

*We have to make the top before dawn. We'll need a lead time before they come after us. I'll call in reinforcements at the next leg up,* Ken said. *But they won't be here for a few hours, and we're going to need a place to hole up and wait.*

Jack nodded and studied the wall rising above him. *The crevice runs through the rock about fifteen feet above our heads. It's too wide farther to the left to use for anything but a finger- or toehold, but it makes a good boost to the next level.*

Briony could barely concentrate on what he said — the need to wrap her arms around him and keep him safe was nearly overwhelming. She watched him spring up and over again, this time about a ten-foot jump, one easier than the last. She let herself breathe again when Jack hung above them waiting for her to join him.

The climb took hours, with a repeat over and over of their strange flying act. By the time they reached the top, all of them were exhausted, but exhilarated that they'd made it. They lay for a long time on the edge of the cliff, straining to breathe while they listened — and scented the wind for the enemy they knew would be waiting in the dark for them.

# CHAPTER 20

Jack touched Briony's shoulder and swept his hand up her arm to settle his fingers around the nape of her neck. Ken and he not only practiced such ascents, but had used them on occasion to escape enemies, but he'd never been so tense in a situation as he had in this one. Jack Norton didn't get clammy skin, sweaty palms, or a churning stomach in combat. He was infamous for the ice in his veins and his complete discipline over his emotions when he worked, but now — everything had changed. *Briony.* He massaged her neck and leaned against her, absorbing the warm satin of her skin.

*What is it?*

She turned her head to look at him, her dark chocolate eyes filled with such an intensity of love his stomach seemed to turn inside out.

*Damn, Ken, do men just make complete*

*idiots of themselves over women? I feel like a fool every time she looks at me like that.*

Jack felt more than a fool — he felt humble and undeserving, but most of all, there was a part of him that was afraid. If she left him, she'd rip out his heart and what was left of his soul. Sooner or later the rose-colored glasses were going to come off, leaving him naked and vulnerable to her scrutiny. She would see inside him, not just to the black violence always seething beneath the thin surface of ice he kept to cover it. No, she'd see the true monster — the one who *didn't* feel — couldn't feel.

Ken's sympathy moved in his mind. Ken knew — he felt the same rage, and the same detachment. The monster was a legacy from their father they would never be free of, and any woman in their lives would have to live, just as they did, with that unspeakable demon.

Ken dropped a hand on Jack's shoulder and looked toward the trees. *We can't stay in the open like this. It will be a good ten to twelve hours even with the teams scrambling to pick us up. We have to find cover and a defensible position.*

Jack nodded and helped Briony to her feet. They moved fast in single file, staying to the trees and brush, careful not to make a sound. In the night, any noise carried, and they couldn't afford to bring the enemy down on them. They needed as much distance as possible. As soon as they were a good mile from the cliffs, they began to pick up the pace, jogging now, using long, ground-eating strides.

Every muscle in Briony's body felt fatigued, but there was satisfaction in knowing she'd not only used her circus training to escape Whitney's men — but the very skills and abilities he'd provided. Even now, her enhanced muscles worked like a machine, carrying her fast over rugged terrain, and her vision enabled her to see in the dark when few others could have moved so quickly. And that was all due to Whitney's experiment and the education he'd insisted on providing for her.

They jogged for two hours, took a break, and ran again, this time slowed down by the thicker brush and trees as they started downhill. Obviously Jack and Ken had a particular place in mind. They took cover a few hundred yards from a clearing. They hunkered down in a spot that had plenty of cover, with boulders, trees, and brush, but more importantly, depressions in the ground provided an added element of protection.

"We'll rest here and wait," Jack said. "The

team is coming, and if we stay quiet, we might just get lucky."

The men set about building a blind, a cavern of twigs and leaves where they could lie and rest while they waited. As dawn streaked the sky, Briony found tension rising and tried to cover it. Jack lay beside her, his fingers curling around hers, and on her other side, Ken appeared to doze.

*How can you do that? Just go to sleep when we're being hunted like animals?*

Jack turned over to nuzzle her neck. *Conserve energy, baby. That's what it's always about. Grab sleep when you can. We're safe enough for a couple of hours. They have to figure out where we went before they can find us.* He pulled her closer, his hand pressing her head to his shoulder until she relaxed. Briony had no idea how, but she drifted to sleep.

She woke to find Jack and Ken gone. She sat up, looking around her, heart beating fast. In the distance she could see Ken lying in the open clearing, talking softly into a radio. Jack was harder to spot, but she was beginning to know their methods, and she searched above, in the trees and rocks, knowing he'd be protecting his brother. She thought she saw him in a tree, but blinked, and when she tried to look closer, he wasn't there. She nearly jumped out of her skin when he put a hand on her shoulder.

The familiar rifle was in his arms and his face looked grim. Ken returned, and there was a similar expression on his face. "Damn, Jack. I'm sorry. This is my mistake." Ken shook his head in disgust. "We take it for granted we're enhanced, and if they send anyone against us chances are the enhancement is only physical, but Whitney sent someone with psychic abilities too. I should have considered that possibility."

"There was no way to know." Jack shrugged as he crouched down beside his brother. "We had no choice; we had to use the radio to call our people in. Don't waste time trying to blame yourself. They were bound to find us, Ken, and you know it. We have to move, and fast." He held out a bottle of water to Briony.

"What happened?" Briony asked. She uncapped the bottle and swallowed quickly. The water was warm, but welcome all the same. She screwed the cap back on and offered the bottle to Ken.

"I had to use the radio and wanted to know how far out the extraction team was, but Whitney sent a radioman, a waver. They can sift through the frequencies at a rapid

— nearly computer fast — rate, and hear anything being transmitted. Whitney's people know exactly where the chopper is coming to get us, and they're on the way, and they'll get here first."

Jack swore softly. "How far out is our extraction team, Ken?"

Ken shook his head. "Thirty minutes — too long. We'll be dead by then."

Briony gripped Jack's hand. "What do we do?"

"We fight. We have no choice, baby; we have to fight. If we don't keep them off of us, they'll run us over in minutes — and it's going to be a gauntlet, baby, nothing less. Whitney's going to drop his team between us and the only extraction point and force us to fight our way through. He's coming at us with everything he has because he's running scared now. There's a possibility that you'll slip out of his hands. Once we reach Lily's, he won't be able to get near you." He closed his eyes briefly trying to tell her. He couldn't shield her from this one and he had to keep his mind open to her in order to convey commands.

Her hand brushed his face. She easily read his distress, but was uncertain why he was looking at her with such apprehension. "We've come this far, Jack; we're going to make it."

"I know. I wouldn't let anything happen to you — it's just that I have to do everything in my power to protect you — no matter the cost."

She stared into his gray eyes, reading a plea for understanding. Briony leaned close to kiss him. "The cost had better not include a scratch on your body. You've got enough scars. Be a little careful, Jack." She lifted her head to smile at Ken. "You too. Let's just get out of this and get to wherever we're going. Where are we going?"

The brothers exchanged another, almost despairing glance. She obviously hadn't understood what Jack had been trying to say. He could only hope she wouldn't turn away from him in horror when she discovered the real Jack — the one he kept hidden.

"We'll head to Lily Whitney's, the place Kadan told you about," he explained grimly. "She'll send a cleanup crew to the house; we'll make the necessary repairs and set up a better alarm system. We'll have to turn our home into a fortress if we go back."

"Tell me what you want me to do," Briony said.

There was so much trust in her eyes, Jack had to look away. This was battle, an all-out war, and it wasn't going to be pretty. There were the three of them against a helicopter filled with soldiers. Ken and Jack had limited ammunition and weapons, and every bullet was going to have to be a kill.

The sound of a helicopter grew louder as Whitney's men approached.

*Infantry taking up positions at nine and twelve o'clock,* Ken reported.

Jack handed Briony a gun and several clips of ammunition. *Don't waste this, baby. Shoot to kill.* He caught her chin, looked into her eyes. *You understand me? You shoot to kill. Ken and I will shield you from the repercussions.* Not the emotional ones, that was impossible, but they'd do what they could.

*Helicopter's coming in.* They could see it hovering over the thick grove of trees, whipping winds so that the leaves and branches swayed. Thick ropes dropped from the open doorway and several men began a fast descent toward the safety of the trees.

Briony stifled a cry of alarm when the first shot rang out, followed closely by a second and then a third. Jack reached up and yanked her down so that she lay prone on the ground between the two men. Three of the descending soldiers dropped instantly, crashing into the heavy branches. Ken calmly fired a fourth shot, and Jack took out a fifth soldier. It happened so fast she didn't do more than stare, gun in her hand.

The helicopter veered away in an effort to protect the remaining soldiers. Both Jack and Ken fired at the retreating mechanical bird, placing their shots with care and precision. Almost immediately black smoke billowed and the helicopter spun out of control.

*Go!* Jack yanked her back up, pushing her in the direction of the clearing. *Stay to cover but keep moving forward.*

They ran several feet and the ground soldiers suddenly swarmed around them. For a moment, Briony felt despair — it seemed impossible to break through their lines — but then Jack lobbed a grenade and took her to the ground, covering her body with his while the world blew up around them. That fast, he was on his feet, firing from the hip and running with her again.

Briony realized both brothers were shielding her body with theirs as they ran, and that they anticipated where the enemy would be and what they would do. Experience counted far more in actual battle than she'd realized when training. By the time she aimed, one of the brothers had already fired. They kept moving forward, lobbing grenades, firing at the soldiers, always in motion. Smoke swirled thickly around them, and men screamed in pain. For the first time in her life, she was in a real combat situation, and it was horrifying.

A man tackled her from behind, and Jack whirled around, knife in his fist, slicing fast across the soldier's throat as he fell with Briony. Blood sprayed over all of them, but neither man blinked; they simply hauled her to her feet and kept running. She was in Jack's mind and expected fear for her, horror of what he had to do, but there was only calm resolve, no emotion at all — as if he were the killing machine Luther had called him.

Briony locked her mind into Jack's in order to follow his lead. Her vision cleared, and she aimed and fired, bracing herself for the backlash of violence. When none came, she chose another target and fired again. The battle raged fast and furious, as they were pinned down.

*Getting low on ammo,* Ken reported.

*Fuck. Me too. We'll have to conserve and go hand-to-hand. Briony, stay out of the fighting if at all possible.* Jack signaled them forward, and they rushed in the direction of the clearing.

*To your left, to your left!* Ken flashed the warning just as a shot rang out. Beside her,

Ken faltered, stumbled, and went down.

Jack turned toward him, but whirled back to face the attack coming from his left side, a big man, moving fast, every bit as enhanced. *Luther.* He came out of the brush, his body blurred as he sped toward them.

*Run, Briony. Get to the edge of the clearing and stay under cover until the helicopter gets here.* It was Ken giving the order.

Jack and Luther crashed together hard, hands slapping away weapons as they tried to take each other down. They were like two huge bears, Luther roaring, Jack silent as they fought with fists and feet.

*Get Ken out of here.* Jack sounded calm, even as he delivered a round kick that drove Luther to the ground. Luther rolled away and came up onto his feet, wiping blood from his temple. He looked at it and smiled.

Briony spun around, reaching for Ken. *Screw running.* She snagged his shirt and crouched beside him, pushing the loaded gun into his hands. *I still have another clip. How bad, Ken?*

*I'm bleeding like a stuck pig.*

*We can't have that.* She found the entrance wound, up high on his thigh. It didn't look good to her. She took a belt and stick and made a quick field tourniquet, twisting tight to cut the flow of precious blood. *A few more minutes, Ken, and we'll have help.*

*Get me on my feet. I can make it. It'd be embarrassing if Jack had to carry me out of here.*

Briony felt a surge of strength — of adrenaline — as she helped him up, but his body crumpled, nearly dragging her to the ground. The gun bucked in his hand twice, the sound deafening. *It would be more embarrassing if I had to carry you. On your feet, Ken. We've got to go now.* She used her sternest voice, feeling him slipping away from her as he wavered toward unconsciousness. Jack was counting on her — trusting her with his beloved brother — and she wouldn't fail him. She wrapped her arm around him and heaved him to his feet.

Ken made a Herculean effort, leaning on her, gun firing as they half ran, half limped toward the clearing where the helicopter was setting down. Briony took him as far as the tree line, and when she saw the Ghost-Walker team leaping from the helicopter, she sat Ken down.

"He needs a medic right now. He's losing blood."

"Get in the helicopter, Briony," Kadan ordered.

It was the safest place on the mountain for her and the babies, but she didn't even consider it. Instead, she turned without hesitation and raced back to Jack.

The battle raged — two strong men well versed in hand-to-hand combat. The fight was the most brutal thing she'd ever witnessed — the two men punching and kicking, making every effort to literally smash each other into pieces.

She was in Jack's mind and she felt his deadly resolve. He was detached from the fight, but his implacable purpose wasn't. He was going to kill — there was no other thought in his head. He was going to smash his foot *through* Luther's chest — and he did. Briony heard the crunch of bones as Luther went down.

Her stomach lurched at the sound. *Don't kill him — my sister. He can lead us to my sister.*

Even wheezing and gasping for breath, Luther was lethal, drawing a long, razor-sharp knife from his boot and driving it up toward Jack's belly. Jack jumped back, circled, and went in for the kill. Briony closed her eyes, but she heard the punch as Jack drove his fist — with every bit of enhanced strength behind it — through Luther's skull, shattering it. The second punch smashed through Luther's face, reducing the nose and eye sockets to pulpy splinters. It was a methodical, brutal, and deliberate kill, and never once did Jack's mind shout for him to stop.

He knelt beside the body and looked up at her. *I'm not apologizing for who I am. You can either live with me or you can't.* But he was holding his breath. Terror robbed him of his ability to breathe. If she left him, his life was worthless.

A soldier ran toward them, leaping over a fallen log. His gun was gone and his shirt torn and bloody, but she suspected he was enhanced. Jack looked exhausted as he knelt beside Luther, looking up at her with a dark, unfathomable expression. Briony didn't hesitate, reaching past him to jerk the knife from Luther's fist. She turned and threw it in one smooth motion, using her strength as she never had. *I'm not apologizing for loving you. I can live with everything you are, Jack, and then some.*

He stared up at her face, there in the midst of blood and death, with his heart pounding and his mouth dry. *I absolutely love you, Briony, and I'm on my knees. So we're getting married — right? But say it fast before we get shot.*

Only Jack would ask — if you could call it asking — in the middle of a battlefield, with a man lying dead at his feet. *You idiot. Get up and let's get out of here. I love you too, and of course I'm marrying you. I'm not about to let you get away.*

He caught her to him and crushed her mouth beneath his. They turned and ran toward the helicopter and the tough-looking men, armed to the teeth, spreading out to cover them.

"He all right?" Jack asked the medic as he examined his brother lying on the floor, strapped to a board. "How bad is he hit?"

"He'll live; lost a lot of blood, but we've got some plasma going in," the medic assured him.

"Nice to see you in one piece, Jack," Kadan said to them. "Lily's going to be happy to see you, Briony. She considers you a sister."

Briony made a small sound of despair. Jack sank down, pulling Briony into his arms. She promptly burst into tears. He turned his body to shield her tears from the others. Once they were on board, the helicopter banked and made a wide turn, swinging out and away from the trees to climb a little higher. Smoke clouded the air, and far below them it looked like a battleground. Briony buried her face against his chest, silent sobs wracking her body. His fingers tangled in her hair as he held her to him, looking over her head at his brother.

"We're safe now, Briony. With all of us guarding you, he can't touch you," he murmured soothingly, stroking her hair.

"But *she's* not safe — my sister. With Luther dead, there's no way to find her. She's totally alone and I can't get to her." Briony covered her face with her hands. Marigold might at that very moment be praying for Briony to come — but it would be impossible. Her only hope to find Whitney's laboratory had been Luther. "I know it was necessary, Jack, don't get me wrong, you had to kill him — but I feel so lost."

"Listen to me, baby." He caught her chin and forced her to look into his eyes — eyes that were flat and as cold as ice — eyes that could warm her like the afternoon sun. "I never break my word — *never.* It's a matter of honor with me. We'll find your sister. We'll move heaven and earth if we have to, but we'll find her, and we'll take her away from him. You have my word on that."

Ken put his hand on her shoulder, ignoring the medic's scowl. "I'm in all the way, Briony. We're family. We stick together. We'll get her out."

Briony wiped at the streaming tears and looked from one man to the other. They were tough and scarred and could be difficult to live with — but she wouldn't trade them for anything. She nodded. "Okay. Okay then. We'll find her together." Because she believed them. "I love you, Jack. Very much."

"Hell of a time to tell me, babe." *We're in a helicopter surrounded by men and there's not much I can do about it now.*

Briony smiled in spite of the circumstances. *That was meant to be emotional, idiot, not sexual.*

*Don't say sexual — you'll give me a hard-on.*

Ken sighed. *Shut up, you two.*

Jack and Briony both looked at Ken, then at each other, and burst out laughing.

The employees of Thorndike Press hope you have enjoyed this Large Print book. All our Thorndike and Wheeler Large Print titles are designed for easy reading, and all our books are made to last. Other Thorndike Press Large Print books are available at your library, through selected bookstores, or directly from us.

For information about titles, please call:
    (800) 223-1244

or visit our Web site at:
    www.gale.com/thorndike
    www.gale.com/wheeler

To share your comments, please write:
    Publisher
    Thorndike Press
    295 Kennedy Memorial Drive
    Waterville, ME 04901